The Laughing Policeman

Brimstone Chorus

Elizabeth J. Brown

Kobold Books

Contents

Kobold Books Limited
71-75 Shelton Street, Covent Garden
London, WC2H 9JQ
koboldbooks.com

Paperback ISBN: 978-1-7398170-3-9
Hardcover ISBN: 978-1-7398170-5-3
E-book ISBN: 978-1-7398170-2-2

Cover design by Ben Baldwin: www.benbaldwin.co.uk
Editing by Kate Gallagher: nerdgirledits.com

To my parents, who answered all of my strange and disturbing questions without batting an eye, or reporting me to the authorities.

Prologue

'PRICK HAS RUN OFF again.' The woman's hand trembled as she raised the cigarette to her lips. 'I don't need you. Good riddance to you, you rancid little shite. Embarrassed to call you my son. I—' A hacking cough cut her off as the smoke hit the back of her throat.

She wheezed a breath and put the fag end back in her mouth.

'We need to move. It's not safe. Not safe. Where is that prick? Where is—'

Another coughing fit followed.

'Fuck.' The orange butt quivered between her fingers. A snarl escaped her lips as she jabbed it down into the glass ashtray, grinding it into the mound of ash and discarded stubs.

'Selfish little prick. Always has been. Where *is* he?' Her fist struck the table. The ashtray skipped across the wood-effect surface in a puff of grey that settled in grimy flecks. She snatched it up, pushed herself to her feet and tramped to the door.

Stupid boy. *Stupid*, stupid boy.

"Thick but harmless". That's what she'd heard them say. Never to her face though. Oh no, they wouldn't dare. But she'd heard it all the same.

'Harmless! Ha.'

The door clattered against its frame, hinges screaming, as she flung it open and hurled the ashtray outside. It shattered in a spray of crystal shards against an empty propane cylinder. She spotted movement in one of the neighbouring windows. A dark silhouette flittered behind the net curtains then disappeared. Nobody ever came to investigate the noise. They knew better.

She squinted up at the countless, white pinprick of stars against the inky canvas of the night sky, and absently fingered the leather drawstring pouch at her neck. It was late. The whir of insects rose above the distant hum of the motorway. Somewhere a fox shrieked; she'd always hated the noise—like someone being stabbed to death. Pressing a finger against her nostril, she snorted and spat a globule of mucus onto the ground. With a final glare at her surroundings, she slammed the door shut.

The floor groaned in protest as she stomped towards the table. She hesitated and turned back again. She eyed the symbols carved above the door and pursed her lips. Tracing a fingertip across the splintered plywood, she felt the thrum of energy skip across her skin and nodded to herself.

Yes. They would work. She moved back towards the table.

'We need to move. Been here too long.' She reached for the packet of Silk Cut with her nicotine-stained fingers and eased back into the seat. She selected a cigarette, thumbed the flint wheel on the lighter and sparked up. 'Too long.'

The door handle rattled. Narrowing her eyes, she squared her shoulders and turned to stare at it.

'Finally decided to show up, have you? You miserable little—' The insult died on her lips as the symbols blazed with white light.

The door burst inwards.

Cold, blue eyes locked her in place.

Her mouth dropped open. The fag fell into her lap and burnt her. She jumped up with a shriek and batted at her thigh, as the smouldering tip ruined the fabric of her trousers.

'You!' The word erupted from her throat.

The figure stood motionless, stooped down so that he could stare at her through the doorway. His face split into a broad grin, the dried blood caking the edges of his mouth flaking off. The flesh around his cheeks was ragged, like someone had hacked at him with a knife.

'Me.' The sound of his strident voice set her teeth on edge.

Her eyes darted to the glowing symbols above his head and she smirked. His brow furrowed at her reaction and he followed her gaze.

What? Had he expected her to scream? Well bollocks to that. She wasn't some frightened pup. He had no idea who she was.

He ducked his head to clear the doorframe and took a step forward.

The symbols flared bright. A wall of shimmering energy froze him in place. Her flesh pricked with the hum of power radiating off it.

She smirked. 'You're not welcome here, demon. Take that ruined body of yours and fuck off. It was never meant for you. It should've been left to rot. Just like you should've been left to rot inside that dagger.'

A burst of blinding white was the only warning before the light from the symbols guttered out in a shower of sparks. The demon stepped through the doorway, smoke curling in drifting wisps from the splintered wood behind him.

His hollow laughter filled the silence.

'Cute. The thing about this body, broken though it may be—' he rapped his knuckles lightly against his left leg, '—is that it affords me a degree of protection against basic warding spells. A layer of insulation if you like. Of course, you would have known that if you'd done your research. And we both know that you're capable of doing your research, don't we?' He tsked.

She staggered back until the tabletop stopped her; it bit into the back of her thighs. Her left hand stung where the sigil marked her flesh. She glanced at the three throbbing dots between her thumb and forefinger; the warding symbols should have been enough to stifle its call to the demon.

Her spellwork had been too weak.

The demon tracked her movements, its eyes lingering on her clenched fist. He gave her a knowing grin—the flesh around his disfigured mouth splitting apart—then let out a cackle.

His laughter ripped through her skull. Gouged at her brain. So loud.

Someone must have heard it.

Then it hit her. The blood on his tattered clothes was fresh. The shadow she'd seen in the window outside earlier...

'You!'

'Me.' He arched an eyebrow and ran a bloodied hand through his brown hair; it clumped where he touched it. 'I thought we'd already covered the introductions. Getting a bit of déjà vu here.'

She let out a breathless gasp. 'You killed them.'

He looked down at his hands, slick with gore. 'Yes. Obviously. Saving the best for last, as they say.'

Gone. They were all gone.

No. Not all. They would never *all* be gone. Never. Only the weak. And if those feckless pricks were too dim-witted to listen to her... to take precautions... well, that was on them.

She straightened, clenching her jaw. 'Mine are a strong and resourceful people. You can kill me, but we will find you. We will hunt you down and gut you. We will paint the walls of hell red with your blood.'

A chuckle burst from his ruined mouth. His laughter built until his body was shaking with each pitiless cackle.

She stared at him in silence. Her throat tight. Her mouth dry.

His laughter faded. He took a few deep breaths, wiped a tear from his cheek and fixed her with his intense, blue eyes.

He snorted. 'Sorry, that was rude.' The manic grin never left his face. 'No, really, I liked what you said. It was poetic. I think I might have to write it down.'

He lunged forward.

She grabbed the pouch at her neck and yanked at the leather cord, in a bid to open the bag fast. As her quivering fingers fumbled inside the contents clinked. With a gulp, she pulled out a fistful of bone tiles, each carved with its own unique rune.

She sneered. 'Fuck you. Cripple scum.'

He was in front of her in an instant. So close that she could smell the death upon him.

He smiled. 'Oh, no. That's not very hospitable is it?'

His hand closed around her extended wrist. With one sharp jerk, he wrenched it back at an impossible angle.

Bones cracked.

She howled with pain.

The runes scattered across the floor. And all the while he laughed.

He released her and bent to pluck something up from the ground. She staggered back. Her eyes watered and she clutched her wrist, her breath coming hard and fast, as the agony threatened to consume her.

When he rose, something white glinted between his fingers. She strained to focus on it through the tears. A rune. Broken.

He flicked his hand at her throat. 'Send my regards to M—'

His words fell on deaf ears as her knees buckled. She rasped, unable to catch a breath. She clutched at her throat. Blood gushed through her fingers. Her vision tunnelled.

The darkness grew darker.

Part I

Chapter 1

England, 1984

DETECTIVE CONSTABLE STEPHEN ANDERSON exhaled. Three years of compiling case files, taking witness statements and liaising with the Crown Prosecution Service had all culminated in this very moment, and damn it if he wasn't going to savour every last second.

He attempted to massage some of the discomfort from his left leg; sitting on the unforgiving wooden benches underneath the biting air conditioning always aggravated his old injury. He shifted position and looked past the prosecution barrister seated in front of him. His eyes wandered over the public gallery.

There they were.

The usual parasites from the press, overflowing from their allocated seating. They were even more conspicuous—peppered amongst the public—now that the spectator numbers had dwindled to family members, students and a handful of interested civilians.

Stephen's gaze came to rest on Aisling Boswell, mother of the offenders and matriarch of the notorious Boswell family. She sat between her two youngest sons, Mickey and Conner, dwarfed by their size. Well turned out in a cream dress suit, she could very nearly pass as respectable. The padding in her jacket gave her a strange, broad-shouldered silhouette that was incongruous against her diminutive frame. The notion of her being nothing more than a sugary, mild-mannered woman in her sixties was so ludicrous that Stephen had to stop himself from letting out a snort.

Aisling's grey eyes snapped to his, as if sensing his scrutiny. The corners of her mouth turned down.

If looks could kill.

It had been the same treatment throughout the trial. He'd become the sole focus of her anger and resentment. Never mind anyone else's involvement in the case, or the minor detail that he'd only been there because her sons had broken the law. Apparently, it was his fault that her precious little darlings were about to be sentenced.

She was lucky that Mickey and Conner hadn't been stupid enough to join their brothers in the dock. Not that Mickey had the mental capacity to mastermind any sort of complex criminal activity. Dressing in a nice suit didn't conceal the simplicity behind his brown eyes—eyes that mirrored his younger brother's in colour alone.

Conner was a different story entirely. Where Aisling's rage boiled on the surface for all to see, Conner's was a cold and calculated thing. Calculated anger made a person dangerous. Sons to be proud of for sure.

Aisling continued to stare. Stephen looked away before she burst a blood vessel. Her silent promises of payback had become so extreme that he hadn't driven his car to the court today. Well, that and he planned to celebrate the end of the case with his colleagues at the station bar, after his shift tonight. One of the perks of sentence hearings? No paperwork.

The judge, a pinch-faced man whose sallow complexion was worsened by the pure-white bench wig upon his head, cleared his throat and directed his attention towards the Boswell brothers. 'Dermot and Niall Boswell, these are serious, violent offences where you both displayed a complete lack of regard for people's property and had no compunction in using violence against innocent members of the public.' He paused, weighing their response, then with a passing frown, continued. 'You have been justifiably convicted by the jury. Your culpability is quite clear. I detect no remorse from you and, given your prior convictions and habitual pattern of reoffending, see no scope for improvement. I hereby sentence you both to fourteen years. Gaoler, take them to the cells.'

Stephen turned his attention back to the public gallery and the sound of shuffling. It wasn't prohibited for anyone to leave the court before being dismissed by the judge, but it was unusual. Aisling Boswell stood in silence, flanked by Mickey and Conner. The unadulterated loathing written across her face made the hairs on his arms stand on end.

Definitely a good idea to leave the car at home.

He met her unwavering glare, keeping his expression neutral, despite the uneasy sensation that was crawling up his spine.

The staring contest hadn't gone unnoticed by members of the public, who whispered and shifted in their seats.

The judge coughed meaningfully, in an attempt to regain control over his courtroom.

Aisling set her jaw, turned and walked out. Mickey and Conner followed dutifully.

A couple of the reporters twitched, as if prepared to follow, then sat back down. Clearly, they thought better of that pursuit.

Stephen watched the gallery door swing to a close behind Aisling Boswell and her delinquent sons, and let out a breath.

God, let that be the last I have to see of that appalling family.

It was time to start the next chapter of his life.

Mickey Boswell stood outside the Crown Court, under the crushing heat of the midday sun. He removed his navy suit jacket and draped it over his forearm. The relief as he loosened his tie and unfastened his collar felt so good, it should have come with an R18 movie warning. He'd never been comfortable in fancy clothes; how those pencil pushers working in offices day-in day-out managed it he'd never know.

He watched his mammy blow a plume of blue smoke through her thin, wrinkled lips and pass the cigarette to his younger brother, Conner. Conner nodded, took a drag, then handed it back.

'Did you see that prick? Smiling, he was. May demons take his soul.' Mammy took another pull, her hand shaking. 'Fourteen years. Can you believe it? My poor babies. Fourteen fucking years for taking back what was rightfully ours. That dagger has been in our family for generations. If he knew what it truly was...' She shuddered. 'He should be thanking us, not locking us away. Filthy gavver scum.'

'Don't worry, Mammy,' said Mickey. 'He won't be smiling after we're done with him.' He held out his hand for the cigarette.

'Shut up, Mickey, you eejit.' She flicked the cigarette onto the concrete in a shower of sparks, before crushing it under the sole of her cream, Bally court shoe. 'Don't be talking about that here. Come on, let's get back to the car.'

Mickey gave his brother a sidelong glance as they followed Mammy towards her two-door, white Ford Escort. Sure enough, there was Conner's oily smirk.

Mickey cursed under his breath and pulled out a crumpled packet of Silk Cut from his trouser pocket. Placing one of the least mangled cigarettes between his lips, he poked inside the box for his lighter. Gone. *Shite*.

People often said that Conner could be his twin. On the surface, maybe. They shared the same deep-brown eyes, sharp cheekbones and chiselled jaw. But inside, they couldn't be more different. Little brother or not, Conner had a screw loose.

Mickey patted himself down and cursed again. Not a chance he was asking Conner for a light. The little shite would only start up again about how useless he was. *Fecking Conner.* With a sigh, he put the fag behind his ear for later.

Mammy stopped at the car and rooted through her handbag, still muttering about the holy show of a sentencing. She pulled out her keychain-crammed keys. Gold-plated horseshoes; neon rabbits' feet—it looked as if she'd attached every single piece of tat ever given to her by her children or grandchildren. She tossed them to Conner, who caught them with one hand, walked over to open the driver's door and got in.

'Well?' Mammy raised an eyebrow at Mickey. 'Are you getting in or are you just going to stand there all day?'

Mickey scowled at the car. 'Why have I got to get in the back? I was in the back on the way here. I'm always in the back.'

'Conner is driving and there's no fecking way I'm getting in the back, is there?'

Mickey lifted his chin. 'I'll drive then, Mammy. Conner can sit in the back.' His hope wilted when her frown became a glare, adding more creases to the leathery skin around her grey eyes. How could such a tiny woman be so intimidating? Standing straight, her head barely reached his shoulders.

With a huff, he opened the back door, yanked up the handle on the side of the seat and wrenched it forward. It clattered in protest, stopping with a jolt that shot up his arm.

The car bobbed under his weight as he clambered unceremoniously into the back. Conner turned and threw him a smug look. *Fecking Conner.*

'Be careful would you, you're scratching my seats,' his mammy reprimanded, as she slid the seat back into position and lowered herself inside. She placed her handbag in the footwell and pulled the door shut with a soft thud.

Mickey snorted in response, dragged a hand through his hair in discomfort, and turned to stare out the side window.

'Right.' Aisling angled herself so she could look at each of her sons in turn. 'Our boyo Colin followed that prick to his house and got his address and the reg of his car. He wrote it down for you.' She twisted back round, rifled in her bag for a few seconds, then pulled out a crumpled scrap of paper and handed it to Conner.

Mickey craned forward, trying to read the scrawled handwriting over his brother's shoulder. He just about made out the house number and the road name before Conner folded it in half and tucked it into the breast pocket of his shirt.

'I want you to teach that fucker he messed with the wrong family,' she said. 'I want you to beat him so badly that he won't remember his own name. Nobody does that to my babies and gets away with it.' She paused to snatch a few wheezing breaths.

Conner fingered the leather bracelet on his wrist—the one engraved with odd little symbols that Mammy had made for him. 'When do you want us to do it?' he asked, knowing not to comment on her agitated state. At least he had the decency to show a little compassion to their mammy; it almost made him seem like less of a prick.

Almost.

'Tonight. I want you both to go there tonight. Make sure he's definitely there mind you. Are you listening, Mickey?'

'Yes, Mammy. I heard you. Make sure he's home,' Mickey replied sharply. Did she always have to talk to him like he was a complete moron? He was two years older than Conner, for God's sake. He was the head of the family now that his older brothers were out of the picture. Wasn't he entitled to a little respect? After all, *he* hadn't been stupid enough to get locked up stealing back some dusty, old family heirloom. He'd never understood Mammy's obsession with that dagger, why she was so desperate to get it back. If it was as cursed as she said it was, he'd have thought she'd want rid of the thing.

'I don't want you making a bags of this. The two of you are all I've got now your brothers have been put away.' A touch of sadness entered her voice, and her hard mask momentarily slipped to reveal a vulnerability and desperation that Mickey had never seen before. His anger and resentment towards her dissolved in a wave of guilt. Shifting uncomfortably he glanced at Conner, surprised to see the same look of astonishment mirrored back at him.

'We'll do you proud, Mammy, I promise,' Mickey said. 'We'll make him pay. You'll see.'

Chapter 2

STEPHEN STEADIED HIMSELF AGAINST the railings before limping down the stairs outside the Crown Court. The August warmth seeped back into his cold muscles.

'Detective Anderson?'

A man in an ill-fitting, grey, tweed suit approached him. Young. Eager. He licked his lips. His pale eyes darted nervously behind a pair of milk-bottle lenses.

Stephen suppressed a sigh. 'Yes?'

The man pulled a notebook from his pocket and flicked it open, pen at the ready. 'Richard Head, *Kent Messenger*. As the investigating officer in this case, how do you feel about the sentencing?'

'It was fair, considering the gravity of the crimes committed.'

'The Boswells were responsible for a string of violent burglaries over a period of decades, targeting the rich and elderly in particular. Would you say that their actions have placed a strain on the already tense relations between Gypsies and the wider community?'

Stephen gave him a flat look. 'As I said, it was a fair sentence.'

The reporter flipped back through his notes. The pages whispered beneath his fingers. 'Archibald Morgan. One of the Boswells' victims. He was in his eighties. They shattered his jaw, fractured his eye socket. All for some jewellery, a few antiques and a bit of cash.'

Stephen shuddered. It wasn't the vivid bruising on the old boy's face, or even the swelling that had imprinted itself forever in his mind. It was the haunted look in the eyes of a man who would never again feel safe in his own home. Who would live out the remainder of his years in inescapable fear.

The reporter continued. 'Don't you think their kind should be given life for that level of brutality?'

Stephen frowned. 'Their *kind*? You mean criminals?'

'Gypsies.'

'I think we're done here.'

'Yes, but—'

'Dick, was it?'

'Richard.'

'Richard, that's all I'm prepared to say on the matter.'

The reporter blinked at him. He snapped the notebook shut. 'Thanks for your time,' he muttered, stuffing it in his pocket before striding away.

Stephen watched him leave, shook his head, and made his way towards DC Chris Greene, who was propping up the wall.

Chris pulled the cigarette from his mouth and exhaled a steady stream of smoke. 'Local rag?'

'Yeah. Charming bloke.'

'Thought I recognised him. Rich something?'

'Head.'

Chris' eyes widened. 'You're joking?'

'Nope. Dick Head.'

The two men looked at each other. Stephen crumbled first, his face creasing as he guffawed. After a few moments he composed himself. *Christ*, he'd needed a good laugh.

'How did it go?' Chris nodded towards the court entrance.

'Fourteen years a piece.' Stephen waved away Chris' offer of a Marlboro.

'Not bad.'

It wasn't bad as far as sentences went, but it was way less than they deserved. Always was.

Stephen rolled his shoulders, stretching out some of the tension in his chest. 'What about yours? Thought I'd be out long before you.'

'Acquitted. Prosecution ballsed up the case.' Chris rolled his eyes and took another drag. There was a faint crackle of burning tobacco. He exhaled. Smoke hung in the air between them.

Stephen frowned and stroked his jaw; his thumb trailed along the end of the smooth line of scar tissue on his right cheek.

Christ.

What was there to say? It happened. Sometimes mistakes got made and guilty people went free.

Stephen sighed. 'It's not hopscotch.'

'Hmm?'

'Just something my old man used to say. He used to get his words muddled. Sometimes I think he did it on purpose, just to wind my mum up.'

Chris tilted his head, clearly not sure what to make of that. 'That's twice this month a suspect's gotten off. I swear these prosecutors are on the take.'

That was a sobering thought. If there was one thing Stephen couldn't stomach it was offenders going unpunished.

He never could. Not even as a child. The first tooth he'd lost had been in the playground when Jimmy Barnes sucker punched him in the mouth after Stephen had told him to pick on someone his own size. The tooth had been loose anyway, but that hadn't been the point.

Chris crushed the butt of his cigarette under his heel. 'Ready?'

'As I'll ever be. Thanks for giving me a lift to the station. I owe you a pint.'

The sound of hurried footsteps and the inquisitive look on his colleague's face made Stephen turn.

Christ, not another one.

A man in an expensive looking, off-white suit, gold tie and matching pocket-square came to a stop in front of him. He had dirty-blond, slicked back hair and an air about him that was just as greasy. Nope. Definitely not the press. Was this what was considered trendy nowadays? If so, he wasn't keen. Not that he could really pass judgement; Linda picked out his outfits most days. Apparently she didn't want a 'knock on the door from the fashion police'.

Stephen arched an eyebrow as he considered the man with an envelope clutched in his hand. He looked familiar. The smile plastered across the stranger's face faltered as soon as he met Stephen's eyes.

Stephen was used to this reaction. It was his eye colour—a blue so intense it looked unnatural. Still, British social awkwardness had provided him with much entertainment over the years. Always good for a giggle, that. Strangers and new acquaintances frequently came close to whiplash while doing a double take. Usually the novelty wore off after a few minutes, but twice Stephen had been refused entry into properties because the occupants had accused him of 'having the evil eye'.

The man recovered and extended a hand. 'Detective Constable Anderson, my name is William Morgan. I just wanted to offer my thanks. You wouldn't believe what a relief it is to know those men will be behind bars. My grandfather might finally be able to get a little peace.'

Morgan—*that* explained it. The grandson of Archibald Morgan. Now that he could put a name to the face, the resemblance was uncanny. William had been in the public gallery throughout the trial.

Stephen smiled and shook William's hand. 'You're more than welcome.'

'I was wondering whether any of the stolen property had been recovered. My grandfather had quite a few antiques taken. Been in the family for generations. Quite irreplaceable, you understand. I've got a few photographs of the items, if it would help?'

'I understand,' Stephen said. This wasn't the first time he'd been accosted by a family member outside of court; it certainly wasn't going to be the last. Although, being spoken to rather than screamed at was a refreshing change of pace. 'Your grandfather will be notified in due course if any of his property has been recovered—'

William interrupted. '*If?*'

'If,' Stephen repeated evenly. 'If any of his property has been recovered, he will be given details of when and where to collect it.'

A slight twitch of his lips was the only sign of William's frustration. 'Of course. Of course.' He opened the envelope and started to flick through the contents.

Stephen exchanged a glance with Chris. Call it intuition, but there was something about this meeting that felt off.

'Would you mind if I left this with you?' William held out one of the photographs. 'Just in case. My grandfather would be *extremely* grateful if this item found its way back to him.'

Ignoring the thinly veiled attempt at a bribe, Stephen took the photo, even though it was pointless. They already had a list of stolen property from each burglary, for identification purposes. They probably had a copy of this exact picture on file. If it had been recovered it *would* be returned. It wasn't like Kent Police was running an elaborate side hustle selling stolen goods.

Stephen felt William's eyes on him as he looked at the image. It was of a decorative dagger that looked old. Symbols of some kind were etched into the mottled blade, and what looked like a ruby was set into the black, marbled hilt. For all he knew it could be some priceless, historical artefact or a stage prop. He had no real experience or interest in antiques.

He was seized by a sudden chill.

'I—' Words failed him. Pain lanced through his skull. He squeezed his eyes shut and exhaled. When he prised them open, the mist of his icy breath dissipated in front of him. The sensation passed. *What the fuck?*

'Are you feeling quite alright, detective?' William tilted his head in apparent concern.

Stephen looked over at Chris, who arched an eyebrow in response. Seriously, had neither one of them just seen his breath fog, in the height of summer? *Great.* Now he was delusional. He took a breath and collected himself. Christ, he really *had* spent too long working this case.

William nodded at the picture of the dagger. 'I don't need it back.'

'Right, no problem.' Stephen tucked the photo in his suit-jacket pocket. 'As I said, your grandfather will be notified if any of the stolen items have been found.'

Whatever this exchange had really been about, William seemed satisfied with his answer. 'Once again, you have my thanks. Goodbye, gentlemen. Keep up the good work.'

Stephen and Chris watched in mutual confusion as William Morgan palmed a hand over his hair and went on his way.

Chris' eyebrows knitted together. 'What was that about?

'Buggered if I know.'

Chapter 3

STEPHEN CHUCKLED, TOOK A breath, snorted and chuckled again.

'I can't believe you just said that to me, Marie.'

The lines around the barmaid's eyes deepened as she gave him a wicked grin. She winked, then turned to take the order of the officer next to him.

Stephen picked up the four pints of Castlemaine, and with two in each hand, made his way through the press of bodies back to his colleagues. He thought about Marie's remark and sniggered. Cool liquid sloshed over his fingers. *No.* He needed to concentrate. His limp wasn't helping matters; neither was the fact that the floor seemed to be uneven.

He planted the glasses on the table and looked up at Charlie with a triumphant grin. 'See, I told you I could do it.' He dried his fingers on the sides of his trousers before taking a seat.

'You did.' Charlie agreed, shuffling to the side to make room for Stephen in the booth. 'Never doubted you, mate.'

Without the luxury of air conditioning, the pressing summer heat made a sauna of the station bar. At least the alcohol had numbed the discomfort in his leg, and—unlike being inside a sauna—they got to keep their clothes on. Stephen glanced at the men around him and laughed. There wasn't enough alcohol in the station bar for that scenario to play out. Just as well, it would probably end up in a disciplinary anyway. The higher-ups frowned upon that sort of thing.

'Right. I'm afraid, lads, that I am going to have to call it a night. My taxi will be here in a second.' Sergeant Gerald Booker stifled a belch. 'Steve, well done. We couldn't have hoped for a better outcome.' The stocky giant of a man rose to his feet with the help of the table, which wobbled in complaint, causing lager to splatter across the dark mahogany surface.

'Thanks, Gerry.'

'I mean it, really. Well done.' He thrust a meaty hand towards Stephen, who shook it gratefully. 'It's just a shame we didn't get the other two. Still, I'm sure it won't be long before they do something stupid to get our attention.'

With a brief look of confusion at the lager dripping off the table, the sergeant nodded to the four remaining men and wandered towards the exit. He paused to exchange pleasantries with a couple of officers waiting for their turn at the snooker table. He clapped one on the shoulder, then let out a booming belly-laugh.

There was movement around Stephen as the booth's occupants spread out.

'Oi, Earth to Steve?' A nasal voice cut through his reverie. 'Has Linda got something to worry about here?

I mean, yeah, I can see how some might consider the Sarge to be a bit of a silver fox. Ears are a bit big for my liking, but then I guess it's something to hold on to.'

Stephen rolled his eyes at the chinless detective. Brian Waite—more commonly known as "Rabbit" because he never stopped talking—was aggravating enough when he was sober. Seven pints in and he had become a grating little shit.

Brian continued. 'He's right you know, Steve. Good outcome. Although, a better one would be burning down their caravans in the middle of the night. Fucking pikeys.'

Stephen blinked. 'Christ, Brian.'

'What? It's not like you weren't all thinking it. They turn up, steal everything that isn't bolted down, then disappear, leaving nothing but shit behind. And I'm talking literal shit.'

'Jesus.' Charlie shook his head. He tapped his lighter on the table three times and lit a cigarette, levelling a look at Brian as he exhaled.

'What?' Brian shrugged, and turned to look at DC Adeola Rousseau.

Adeola winced.

Brian laughed. 'Oh come on, it was just a joke.'

'Hilarious.' Charlie flicked the ash from his cigarette into the glass ashtray. He let the silence build by taking another drag; Brian fidgeted.

Stephen sniggered. One of the things he loved about Charles Haynes was his deadpan sense of humour. After the accident, when it was clear that uniform duty was no longer going to be an option—not with his mangled leg—the two of them had trained to be detectives together and had hit it off immediately. It wasn't the career path he would have chosen, but a lot of good had come from it—above all his friendship with Charlie.

Sure, Charlie was a bit of an oddball, but he was also loyal, steadfast and honest. Admittedly, he could be a bit *too* honest at times, but it was part of his charm. It was just one of the many reasons that Charlie had been best man at his and Linda's wedding and why he was godfather to their daughter, Bethany.

'No sense of humour, you lot.' Brian huffed, dragging his finger through a spill of lager on the table.

'Congratulations.' A soft voice broke the tension. Stephen hadn't noticed a woman walk over.

Maybe I've had too much to drink.

He recognised her as one of the uniformed officers but couldn't place her name. She blinked at him with large, coquettish brown eyes. Her thick, dark auburn hair fell around her face as she leant in towards him. 'I just wanted to come over and tell you what a great job you did.'

Brian gawped. His gaze flicked between the two of them, as if he were watching some outlandish tennis game. 'Unbelievable.' He took a mouthful of his pint.

The silence stretched out. Stephen knew he should probably say something. Her cloying perfume mingled with the smell of smoke and stale beer. He could almost taste it. 'Uh, thank you.'

Smooth.

'You know,' she said, pausing to bite her lower lip, 'I could do with a few pointers. Maybe I could give you my number and you could tell me all about it?'

Stephen blinked. He looked at Charlie, pleading for him to intervene, but Charlie just raised an eyebrow in amusement.

'I'm married.' Stephen gestured clumsily to his wedding ring, as if its presence alone could ward her off. Given the amount of alcohol he'd consumed, it wasn't too bad as far as drunk responses went.

'Shame.' She turned her attention to Charlie, who also pointed to his wedding ring, but with effortless composure.

Bastard.

'Bloody hell, Charlie. I thought you enjoyed shooting your load at unsuspecting birds.' Brian grinned as Charlie's shocked reaction quickly morphed into embarrassment.

'Clays.' Charlie clarified for the woman, a deeper touch of crimson staining his already flushed cheeks. 'He means that I like clay shooting.'

The four men waited for her reaction. She appraised Charlie for a few seconds, then gave him a wink before walking away.

Stephen chuckled at Charlie's startled expression. Some women liked their men strong and silent, some athletic, others outdoorsy. Charlie ticked all those boxes. He even had a natural curl to his dusty-blond hair that seemed to make the women go wild, no matter their age. Not that they stood a chance; Charlie had been besotted with Debbie since the day they met. They were the benchmark couple; a constant in an ever-changing world. It was strangely comforting.

Yes, Charlie was definitely a catch, but Stephen was taller. Six feet to Charlie's five feet ten. Inches mattered. He chuckled again at the thought, getting an eye-roll from his friend in return.

Brian shook his head, watching her make her way to another table. 'I tell you what, lads, if none of you are willing to share a cab with me, I'd be happy to ride the station bike home.'

'Jesus,' Charlie snapped, checking with a wary glance to see if she'd heard.

'So, Steve,' Brian continued, oblivious to Charlie's scowl, 'are you leaving your car at the station tonight?'

'It's at home. Linda brought me in today.'

'Right, right. The lovely Linda.' He nodded, the obnoxious grin never leaving his face. 'Very kind of her. Is she picking you up? Because if she is, do you think she'd mind giving me and Adeola a lift home?'

Stephen glanced at Adeola, who gave him an apologetic shrug, as if embarrassed to be dragged into the conversation. 'I'm getting a cab.'

'Right, sure. Okay. How about you, Charlie? Is Debbie coming to get you?'

'Nope,' Charlie said, stubbing out his cigarette with a little too much force.

'Okay then.' Brian took a sip of his pint and placed it back on the table. 'It's not right, you know. I'm the only single one at this table. You've got women throwing themselves at you—' he gestured in the direction of the uniformed policewoman, '—and wives waiting for you when you get home. If I had a woman like Linda or Debbie warming my bed I wouldn't be slumming it in the station bar with the likes of you. That's all I'm saying.'

'Give it a rest would you?' Charlie bristled. He wiped the sweat off his brow with the back of his hand, then tugged irritably at the cuffs of his sleeves.

'Come on, Charlie. Debbie's a stunner. But one day she's going to realise that she's missing out on all of this—' he thumbed at himself, '—and I'll be ready and waiting.'

'Fuck off. I mean it, Rabbit.'

Brian's mouth puckered at the name. He leant forward, but before he could respond, Adeola grasped his shoulder and shook his head in warning.

Stephen frowned. Charlie might be prickly, but he could take a joke as well as the rest of them. Maybe it was the heat.

'*What?* It was a compliment. What's wrong with you lot?' Brian downed the dregs of his pint and slammed the glass down on the table. 'Whatever. I'm going home.'

He stood, rummaged in his trouser pockets, and produced a set of car keys, which he promptly dropped on the floor amid a torrent of creative curses. Bending down, one hand clutching the table for support, he reached out to pick them up.

'Are you fucking serious?' Stephen stamped down with his good leg so hard that Brian nearly lost his balance; he snatched his hand back from the keys. 'There's no way you're getting behind the wheel!'

A wave of emotions distorted Brian's features as he glared up at Stephen. Anger. Realisation. Shame.

'Shit, Stephen. I forgot. Sorry, mate.'

Stephen winced. Was it too much to ask that his private life was kept just that—private? He flexed the muscles in his damaged leg, wishing he didn't have the constant reminder of what he'd lived through.

In one swift movement he plucked up the keys and handed them to Charlie. 'Keep these until tomorrow.'

Charlie slipped them into his pocket, fixed Brian with a smirk, and nodded towards the door. 'Looks like you're out of luck.'

Brian twisted round. The promiscuous, auburn-haired officer from earlier was making an exit, unsuccessful in her night's hunt. Muttering about the injustice of being single, he sidled back into his seat.

'You know,' Adeola offered, 'instead of just bitching about it, you could grow a pair and go after her.'

Charlie snorted.

Brian glowered at him, opened his mouth, closed it again, and shrank back. 'My house key is on there,' he said to Charlie, his bluster gone.

'Sounds like a *you* problem.' Charlie finished his drink.

Brian's shoulders slumped; he turned to Adeola and gave him an imploring look.

'Fine.' Adeola sighed, smoothing a hand over his cropped black hair. 'But you're sleeping on the sofa. My wife is not going to be happy about it. She never is.'

Chapter 4

Mickey pulled the car up outside Anderson's gaff, grimacing at the sound of the hubcaps grinding against concrete. A blanket of darkness stretched across the semi-detached houses lining the sleepy cul-de-sac, not a light on among them.

Conner scoffed.

He ignored him and killed the engine. It was his first real opportunity to prove to Mammy that he wasn't the blundering idiot that everyone seemed to think he was. He wasn't about to screw it up.

'Took long enough to get here didn't it?' Conner said. 'Mammy drives faster than you do.'

'Piss off, Conner. I wasn't about to risk us getting caught before we even got here, was I? I told you, I have everything under control.'

He shifted in his seat, took the tattered piece of paper out of his pocket and angled it under the phosphorous glow of the street lighting. Not that he needed to read it; he'd read it countless times after eventually managing to get it off Conner. *The little gobshite*. After tonight Mickey would get the respect he deserved.

'Well, don't let me interrupt you,' Conner said. 'Crack on.'

Mickey glared at his younger brother, who was idly fiddling with the leather strap around his wrist. *Conner and that fecking bracelet.* The prick had always indulged Mammy's superstitious practices—not that he was jealous of their connection. Why should he care that she hadn't made one for him as well? He wasn't a girl after all. He gave the thing one last scowl, then turned his attention back to the paper. He squinted, checking the details against the house and the red Vauxhall Astra parked on the driveway. Right house. Right car. He looked again, just to be sure.

Can't give Mammy any reason to complain.

'That's it.' Mickey nodded at the house. 'Right. Stick to the plan. We get inside. Smash up the gaff a little. Lure the scum out, then beat the shite out of him. Then we leave. Got it?' He looked at Conner, who sighed in apparent boredom. 'Got it?'

'Got it.'

Mickey pointed at the glove box. 'Balaclavas and gloves.'

Conner squeezed the panel open, pulled out the two black balaclavas and pairs of gloves then shut it again with a soft click. He tossed one set to Mickey, then turned the other over in his hand, rubbing his thumb across the coarse material.

'Do you not think,' Conner said, as he pulled on the gloves and dangled the balaclava in the air, 'it would be better to put these on once we're inside? I mean,

I'm no expert, but we wouldn't want the old, curtain twitchers calling up the gavvers about two masked men roaming the neighbourhood, would we? But then what do I know? You've got everything under control.'

'I didn't mean put them on now, did I? Eejit.' He sucked his teeth in response to Conner's knowing smile. *Prick.* 'Come on. Let's do this.'

Conner leant forward suddenly, causing Mickey to flinch. He inhaled the air around Mickey and a smile touched his lips. 'You smell like a tart's handbag. Are you wearing perfume?'

Mickey sat in dumb silence as the words hit home.

'It's not perfume.' He eventually said, to mask the injury from Conner's insult. 'The woman in the shop said the ladies go mad for it.'

'I'm sure they do,' Conner drawled. 'It must be very popular among the *ladies.*'

Mickey scowled and climbed out of the car. He stuffed the balaclava into his jeans pocket, before tugging on his own pair of gloves. *Fecking Conner.* He regretted his decision to grab the first thing he could find; wool always chafed his skin. Something to think about for the next job.

He closed the car door as quietly as possible, leaving the key in the ignition—it would make for a faster get away.

Conner grabbed a rucksack from the footwell, a smirk still plastered across his face, and followed suit. The dull clunk of his door echoed softly in the night.

They walked towards the house, their footsteps, resounding in the stillness of the cul-de-sac, impossibly loud. Mickey's heart pounded inside his chest. He scanned the upper windows of the neighbouring houses, running his tongue over his dry lips. *Come on, Mickey, you can do this*. He sucked in a deep breath and glanced at Conner. Not a bother on him. How could that prick look so calm? Was that even normal?

Mickey gestured towards the wooden side gate. Conner nodded and quickened his pace, as Mickey took a last furtive glance at the windows.

Satisfied they were not being watched, he joined his brother; who had one arm stretched over the gate, jerking the bolt open on the other side. The door juddered open a few inches and then stopped. Conner pressed his weight into it, slowly pushing it forward with a scraping noise that made Mickey's arse pucker. He hissed at Conner who shrugged, and then squeezed himself through the gap and disappeared out of sight.

Mickey shook his head and followed.

Conner placed the rucksack next to the back door and unzipped it. The contents clanked as he rummaged inside, before grinning and pulling out a short crowbar. He spread his feet wide, wedged the crowbar between the door and the frame—as close to the lock as he could manage—and applied a small amount of pressure.

Mickey watched as the lock buckled, nodding in approval at Conner's speed. He had to give his brother his dues; the man was fierce handy with his tools.

With a grunt, Conner drove his full weight down onto the crowbar before pushing it away. There was a sharp crack, followed by a growled curse from Conner. A stray piece of debris had nicked his cheek. He stepped back and checked his face for blood. Connor's eyes narrowed, challenging Mickey to say something.

He knew when to keep his mouth shut.

Mickey kept his expression neutral. 'Is it open?'

'It's open,' Conner snapped.

As soon as his brother turned back to the door and began wrenching it towards him, Mickey allowed a quick grin.

Conner put the crowbar back inside the rucksack and slung the bag over his shoulder. With a final sneer at Mickey, he took the balaclava out of his pocket and pulled it down over his head before stepping inside the house.

Well, that's an improvement to be sure. Mickey tugged his own balaclava on. Jesus, it was hot. He could already feel the sweat pricking his forehead. *You can do this.* He followed his brother inside.

It took a few seconds to get his bearings.

They were in the kitchen; a nice looking kitchen from what he could make out. It was nearly the size of his caravan. That didn't seem fair. As the light from Conner's torch flitted around the room, he examined the white tiles, ivory worktops and white, wood-lined, no-handle cabinets. He stepped forward and prodded one of the cabinet doors with his finger. *How the feck do you open that?*

'Would you stop pissing about?' Conner whispered. 'This is supposed to look like a burglary. Nothing worth stealing from a kitchen.'

'Just go cut the phone line, would you?' he hissed back. There was no way he was losing control over this. No way that Conner would be the one taking all the credit.

Conner sucked his teeth and disappeared from sight.

Mickey gave the cabinet one last bemused poke and strode from the kitchen into the living room.

He waited for Conner to come back from wherever Anderson kept the landline phone. His eyes readjusted to the darkness and he listened to the faint ticking of a clock he couldn't see.

'Right then.' Conner strode in and flashed the torchlight into Mickey's eyes. 'Let's have a little fun.'

Blinking against the flash blindness Mickey swore, recovering just in time to see a pickaxe handle hurtle towards him. He raised his arms and sucked in a sharp breath as it cracked him in the elbow, then clattered to the floor. *Fecking Conner.*

'Nice catch,' Conner said, whistling through his teeth, as he pulled a second pickaxe handle out of his rucksack.

'You're a fecking prick. What the fu—'

'Daddy?' a soft voice said.

New light exploded in the room.

Mickey watched in paralysed disbelief as a snarling Conner swung round and struck out.

A child screamed. The blunt thump of wood against flesh cut the screams of sheer terror dead. A burst of shattering glass followed as the child crashed through the coffee table.

His stomach lurched. *Oh, Jesus.*

It took a few seconds for his frozen body to catch up with his brain. He let out a hiss and raced forward.

'No! Conner, what the fuck?'

Anderson's little girl—it had to be her—lay crumpled within the warped table frame. Her body was partially suspended, limbs contorted at sickening angles. A few crystalline shards dropped to join the glass fragments spread out around her. She twitched, whimpering breathlessly. Her long brown hair, the same colour as her da's, was a tangled mess across her face, dusted with translucent splinters and spotted with beads of red.

'Fuck. Fuck. Fuck.' Mickey stood over the girl. His blood turned to ice.

She stared up at him, bright-blue eyes wide with shock. If he'd needed more confirmation that she was Anderson's, those eyes gave it. A blue like you wouldn't believe. Tears rolled down her cheeks. She spluttered. Crimson droplets, mingled with her last breath, sprayed over her chin.

Her body sagged.

Mickey watched in horror as her stare turned glassy. Bile burnt the back of his throat. Her blood soaked into the carpet; he snatched his foot back away from it. *Fuck*.

A heart-stopping cry ripped through the silence.

Oh, Jesus. Oh, Jesus.

Mickey spun around. A woman—the girl's mammy—snatched a vase from the side table just inside the doorway and launched it at Conner's head with a shriek. It shattered. Fragments of glass glanced off him. The symbols on his bracelet glowed white; smoke drifted up from the leather band and it disintegrated.

What the fuck? Mickey gaped when the woman jostled past Conner, knocking him sideways, and sprinted towards her daughter. Her baby.

'No!' Recovering his senses, Mickey lunged for her, driving her back. She crashed into him. He winced at the force of the impact and sucked in a painful breath, as he pinned her arms to her sides. 'No. Don't look. Don't look.'

She was strong. Stronger than he'd expected her to be. Mickey grunted, barely able to restrain her. The screaming next to his ears was unbearable. It throbbed in his brain, tore at his heart. He wasn't going to be able to hold her. *Please, don't look.* He squeezed his eyes shut, fighting against the sting of tears.

She fought him. Struggled with all her might. Her shrieks had become hysterical. She writhed and twisted in his arms, like a feral beast. He broke out into a cold sweat, despite the heat of the night and warmth of his disguise.

Just as he thought she was about to break free, she was yanked backwards. Mickey stumbled, falling to his knees. It took a moment for him to realise what had just happened.

But he knew.

Conner stood over her, a boot planted firmly on her chest and her thrashing on the floor. Clumps of her long, dark hair—torn from her scalp—hung limply from his clenched fist. His other hand held the pickaxe handle.

'Conner? What are you doing?' Mickey yelled, realisation dawning too late as Conner raised his weapon.

'What do you think?'

There was nothing he could do except watch Connor crack her skull wide open, again and again. The sharp blows quietened into wet squelches as bone became tissue. What remained of her face was a yawning mess of flesh and gore.

Mickey stared. His lungs burnt as his breath came faster and faster. *Jesus.* He turned away and gagged. Covering his mouth with a gloved hand, he swallowed the vomit back down. He wasn't going down for this. This was Conner's mess.

'Jesus.' He staggered to his feet. 'Conner, what have you done?'

'What have *I* done? Are you having a laugh? Her screaming probably woke up half the fecking street. We need to get out of here. Mammy's not going to be happy about this.'

'Mammy? *Mammy?* Jesus, Conner, you've just *killed* them. She was just a baby girl. We were only supposed to teach Anderson a lesson. We weren't meant to kill anyone.'

'So what? Are you forgetting that prick just put *your* family away for fourteen years? I'd say we've taught him a lesson, alright.'

'Oh Jesus. Oh Jesus.' Mickey squeezed his eyes shut, trying to push the scene away. His head became so heavy he couldn't think. His body trembled as he stumbled towards the fireplace, legs dead weight. *Jesus.* He propped himself up against the mantle, swallowed the spit filling his mouth, and fought to keep his food down.

Jesus, could things get any worse?

The faint sound of a key scratching against the lock came from the hallway.

Shite.

Chapter 5

STEPHEN SNORTED WHEN HE missed the lock and scraped the key down the door. It was nice to be out of the taxi, away from the reek of cigarettes and alcohol—although he couldn't be a hundred percent sure that hadn't been him.

He could still hear the low, pulsing beat of Bowie's *Ashes to Ashes* from the taxi as it rounded the corner. The music drifted away until all that remained was the ringing in his ears. Well, he *had* asked the cabbie to crank up the volume.

'I'm so happy, hope you're really happy too,' he belted out, in a rough approximation of the tune. He winced at his volume and peered up at Mrs Johnson's window. Seeing no obvious curtain movement, he shushed himself with a chuckle. She wouldn't have heard him anyway—deaf as a post without her hearing aid.

It had been a good night; it was nice to let loose. He hadn't realised quite how much the case had been playing on his mind. The fact that he could finally put it to bed had lifted a weight off him.

The Boswells had been brought to justice—well two of them anyway. Time to focus on his own family. His antisocial shifts made it hard to spend quality time with them; it wasn't fair. He owed it to Linda and Bethany to be around more.

An unfamiliar car parked outside the house caught his attention. He peered at it, nearly losing his balance. The more he tried to concentrate, the more his head swam. He waved a hand at it dismissively and turned back to the front door. The neighbours were always having relatives over to stay. Why they couldn't park outside their house was beyond him.

At least Linda had left the living room light on for him; not that it was helping with getting the door unlocked.

God, he loved her. She had the most beautiful smile. He was worried for a while, after the accident, that he might never see it again. But she was strong, so much stronger than him. If it hadn't been for her he wouldn't have pieced himself back together again. The physio had been hard, retraining even harder, but it was the emotional scars that affected him the most. How she'd managed to cope he had no idea, but day after day that smile slowly returned.

Just when he didn't think he could love her any more, Bethany arrived. His family was all he needed. *Hell, I wouldn't be me without them.*

Closing one eye, he aimed the key at the lock. With a determined thrust he managed to hit the target. He twisted the key and pulled down the handle with a barely restrained *whoop*.

The door clattered into the wooden telephone table and knocked the handset from its cradle. Stephen cringed. On the third attempt, he picked up the receiver and put it back in its rightful place. Satisfied, he hobbled towards the living room. No sense in keeping the light on now that he was home.

Stephen froze.

A strangled gasp escaped his throat. His legs threatened to buckle.

The blood, it was everywhere. Sprayed up the walls. Saturating the carpet.

So much blood. He'd never seen so much.

Linda lay in a heap on the floor. Her matted, dark hair covered her face, sodden with thick, red lumps.

Something white glinted on the floor, near her hand. *Is that... a tooth?*

Throat tight, Stephen looked past her and howled. *'Bethany!'*

He hadn't noticed the two men standing there. Or maybe he had, but couldn't process anything beyond the sight of his little girl's lifeless body, twisted and broken among a sea of warped metal, shattered glass and blood.

White-hot pain erupted in his head as something struck him. His neck snapped to the side. His vision went black. The ground rose to meet him.

'Don't just fucking stand there,' one of the men said. 'I thought you wanted to teach this prick a lesson.'

The thick brogue scarcely registered in Stephen's mind as he covered his head and curled in on himself.

A sharp crack to the chest forced the air from his lungs. He rasped out a breath. Another clout to the head came. Then another to the torso.

Kick after kick, blow after blow, the beating continued. His body went into shock, numbing itself against the crippling torture. He spat out blood and forced his eyes open, to get one final look at his wife and daughter. Before it was too late.

It's okay baby, Daddy's going to be with you soon. Mummy and Daddy will be with you, always.

'For fuck's sake, Mickey. Are you just going to stand there? Right, you finish this fucker off, and I'm going to grab his watch and her jewellery. Useless eejit.'

Stephen felt consciousness slip away as the voice became distant.

Breathing got harder.

The light in the room became dimmer.

'Nobody was supposed to die,' the other man said. 'Jesus, that poor little girl. We'll be damned for this. Our souls will be marked. It's not right. Jesus, she was just a child...'

The anxious words became mutterings, then died away, as Stephen's world descended into darkness.

Chapter 6

CHARLIE THUMBED THROUGH THE paperwork on his desk and sighed. It was no good; he could feel the promise of a migraine throbbing behind his eyes. The conversations of his colleagues and general activity in the office had melded into a relentless droning that set his teeth on edge. He placed the papers down gently and squeezed the bridge of his nose.

To make a crappy morning worse, someone had moved the pens on his desk. *Again*. He'd tried not to let it bother him, but knowing they were in the wrong place nagged him. God knows when his OCD had worsened? Maybe it was after his dad hurled abuse and empty bottles at the TV, and Charlie had spent countless hours arranging his Dinky die-cast cars into neat little lines, ordering them by model, make and size to distract himself. How could he have possibly known that it would have him seething now over which arsehole had moved his pens?

He suspected Brian; he seemed to get a kick out of it. No doubt the gangly twat had been watching from the other side of the office, knowing that he'd have to arrange them all again before he could do anything else. Whoever it was had stopped for a few weeks after the murders. Maybe they thought they were helping to phase him back into the normal routine of office banter. Maybe they were just being a knob.

I need a coffee.

He reached for his mug and paused. Stephen said that coffee only made a migraine worse. He pulled his hand back and pressed his lips together. His shoulders sagged. Not being able to sleep wasn't making his ability to cope any better.

It had been five weeks since Linda and Bethany were murdered and Stephen was attacked, but that morning kept replaying in his mind as if it were yesterday. It didn't matter what he did. Didn't matter how busy he kept himself. The memories always crept back in, like ivy burrowing inside the walls of his resolve until it all but crumbled, leaving only an aching pain.

They were worse at night.

An incessant, shrill beeping had woken him up that fateful morning. He'd been so hung over, it had taken him a few minutes to figure out it was his pager going off. There was a message to call the office. His first reaction was panic. Was he in trouble? Had he said something inappropriate? His sense of humour was dry and could be quite dark at times.

Debbie had come down to find him drenched in tears and snot. They'd cried together for what seemed like hours. Then, somehow, he'd managed to get himself cleaned up and dressed and they'd driven down to the hospital.

He'd left his contact details with the doctors, with instructions to phone him when Stephen woke up.

Days turned into weeks. When turned into if.

Charlie startled when the phone on his desk rang, jolting him out of his memories, like a slap to the face. He winced against the throb in his head and answered.

'Mr Haynes?' It was a woman calling.

'Yes?' His heart rate increased. She had referred to him as 'Mr' not 'Detective'. This call was not work related. His mind began to race with the possibilities. He swallowed, realising that she was speaking and he wasn't listening. She paused.

'We have some news. It's about Mr Anderson.'

Charlie's heart sank. *Oh, God.*

The dull beeping became sharper, opening the floodgates for a cacophony of sounds. Stephen blinked, eyelids heavy. He attempted to sit, gave up and let his head sink back into the pillow.

'Just take it easy, Steve.'

The familiar scent of rich, woody aftershave cut through the smell of disinfectant. He breathed it in, let it ground him. His eyes strained against the harsh, artificial lighting.

'Charlie?' he croaked. His mouth was so dry. Forming the word felt clumsy, unnatural.

It took a few moments to remember that he was in the intensive care unit. According to the doctors, he'd been slipping in and out of consciousness for the past few days. Knowing this had not numbed the shock of seeing tubes and medical equipment every time he opened his eyes.

'I've got some water,' Charlie said. 'Here, take a sip.'

Stephen closed his lips around the straw and sucked. The cold hit his throat; he spluttered a cough. Intense pain blazed through his chest and he gasped. His fists clenched around his bed sheets.

As the agony eased, he became aware of Charlie's panicked apologies and curses. Stephen took a shaky breath and relaxed his hands.

Charlie stared at him with unbridled concern. He looked tired, ill even. It was strange seeing him look so drained. There were dark shadows under his hazel eyes and he had stubble—which was unusual for him, that gave him a rugged look. It was a look that one of the nurses noticed, and she gave him an appreciative glance when she thought no one was watching.

'They tell me,' Stephen said breathlessly, 'that you've been visiting me. Every day.'

Charlie smiled sadly. 'Of course. The doctors said that hearing a familiar voice might help to bring you out of the coma. It wasn't just me; quite a few of us have come to see you. Booker, Adeola, Brian, Debbie, Linda's parents...'

An uncomfortable silence filled the space between them. Tears welled in Stephen's eyes. He would never see his wife or daughter again. He choked out a sob.

Charlie fidgeted, glancing at the ward sister, before perching on the end of his bed. Charlie had never been good in intimate social situations, but he always tried. His friend opened his mouth to speak, closed it again and looked down at the floor.

'What am I going to do, Charlie? They were my life. They were my *whole* life. I'm nothing without them.' He began to weep.

The bed creaked when Charlie leant forward and gripped his hand, careful not to disturb the inserted cannula. Stephen composed himself and looked up. Charlie's eyes were red-rimmed, his cheeks glistening with tears of his own. The grief that was mirrored back at him set Stephen off again. Each sob sent a spasm of pain through his broken body until he thought he might pass out.

After a few minutes the tears subsided a little.

He inhaled and exhaled. 'Did I miss the funeral?' He braced himself for the answer. Charlie's sullen face gave it to him.

'Linda's parents—' His voice waivered; he cleared his throat. 'They didn't know if you would make it. You were in a really bad way, Steve. You were in a coma for five weeks. You're lucky to be alive.' He winced as the words left his mouth. He glanced at Stephen nervously before continuing. 'It was a beautiful service. Really beautiful.'

Stephen squeezed his eyes shut. He'd missed the funeral. Missed the chance to say goodbye to his wife and daughter. His heart ached, like it was being crushed under the weight of his anguish.

Stephen's breathing became faster. 'It was the Boswells.'

'*What?*' Charlie straightened.

'It was the fucking Boswells!'

'Are you sure? You saw them?'

'They were wearing balaclavas. The accent though, it was definitely them. Christ... one of them even called the other Mickey. It was them, Charlie. It *was* them.'

Charlie stood and shot a concerned glance at the ward sister, who was now frowning at them. 'Alright, alright, Steve. Try not to get worked up.'

'*Worked up?* The Boswells killed my fucking family, Charlie.' His thoughts were getting foggy, his words coming out slurred.

Charlie came closer and placed a hand gently on Stephen's shoulder.

The sister approached them. 'Excuse me, sir. I think perhaps it would be best if you came back later and give Stephen a chance to get some rest.' Her tone brooked no argument.

'I know it was them...' Stephen's words were now mutters. 'You didn't see the way... the way she was looking at me... in court.'

Before he lost consciousness, he caught the worried tone in Charlie's voice as he spoke hurriedly with the ward sister.

'I need to use a phone, now.'

Chapter 7

MICKEY NURSED A PINT of Guinness in the local pub, watching beneath heavy eyelids as condensation ran down the side of the glass and pooled onto the tattered beer mat. The landlord shot him another angry glance as he wiped down the bar. He was starting to get on his last nerve.

Mickey knew why and he didn't care. Given the disgruntled murmurs from some patrons, he was sitting on a favourite stool belonging to one of the pub's barflies. Not that he gave a shite; he'd sit wherever he wanted. Anyone with a problem could take it up with him. He almost wished they would. He could do with a good brawl. Let off a little steam.

'Can't even enjoy the black stuff in peace without being gawked at.' He helped himself to a handful of salted peanuts from a bowl. Several missed his mouth and scattered across the floor.

The landlord tutted.

Mickey glowered at him, narrowing his eyes, until exhaustion caught him and nodded his head forward. The child's bright-blue eyes stared back at him, vacant and cold. He jolted out of his reverie, knocking his pint off the bar. It smashed on the floor behind the taps, splashing Guinness over the landlord's shoes and trousers. The man jumped back with a curse.

'Right. You've had enough. It's time for you to leave.' The gruff voice held no patience. Mutters of agreement made it clear that he'd outstayed his welcome.

Lofty pricks.

Mickey lurched to his feet and squared his shoulders. He gave the landlord a long, measuring look. The man looked in his fifties, his five o'clock shadow liberally peppered with white, and he was stocky. He had the build of someone who had worked out in a past life, but had allowed that muscle to go in recent years. There was still enough brawn for Mickey to reassess his interest in fighting. He ground his teeth and gave the man one last scowl, before staggering towards the exit.

The door swung shut behind him, cutting off the noise from inside.

'Arsehole.' Mickey spat on the ground. His bravado had returned with a few yards and solid wood between them.

He rocked on his feet then steadied himself, checking which direction to take. Where was the nearest pub he hadn't been barred from? Just a few more drinks and he could pass out. Just a few more drinks and he wouldn't have to see the kid's face whenever he closed his eyes. What he wouldn't give for a decent night's kip.

Just a few more drinks.

It would be a long slog back to the caravan site. What if, by the time he got there, the numbing comfort of the alcohol had worn away? The thought made him shudder. He couldn't face Mammy sober.

She'd gone out of her mind when he and Conner had returned from the job and Mickey had filled her in on what had happened. Of course it had all been *his* fault; her precious Conner could never put a foot wrong.

How could he have known that Anderson wouldn't be there? His car had been parked on the driveway; he'd checked the licence plate. It wasn't *him* who'd messed everything up. Wasn't him who'd killed that little girl. There had been no need for her to die, or her mammy. No need.

I bet Conner doesn't have any problems sleeping at night. The fecking psycho.

Mickey took a cigarette out of his pocket and sparked up. Smoke filled his lungs. He held it there until it burnt. When he couldn't hold it any longer, he blew it out into the close, night air and yawned.

Jesus, he was tired. If only he could sleep.

Conner had ruined everything. Everything had been under control, but Conner had gone and screwed it all up. Mickey's chance to prove he was capable of leading the family had been stolen from him that night. *Fecking Conner.* Now Mammy barely said a word to him, except to tell him how thick he was, while his little brother walked around with that smug look on his face. And what had poor old Mickey got to show for it? Nightmares and a drinking problem, that's what.

'I'd love to punch that smirk right off his face, the piss stain. Speaking of piss...' Mickey flicked the cigarette away, unzipped his fly and pulled out his cock. With a sigh, he relieved himself onto the path, urine splattering back over his trainers.

The door swung open. A burst of music caught him by surprise. He turned in the direction of the noise; warmth spread down his leg. 'Shite.'

'Mate, that's disgusting.' Someone sniggered as a group of men spilled out of the pub and pressed past him. Their conversation faded the farther they got down the road.

The last thing he heard before the voices trailed off was: 'Was he wearing perfume?'

He sniffed himself and frowned. Why did people keep saying that? He'd asked the woman in the shop to give him something that was popular with the ladies. It was clearly aftershave. She wouldn't have sold it to him otherwise. Would she?

With a mutter, Mickey shook himself dry and zipped up. It was time to call it a night and head home. He might find a bottle of something stashed away when he got back.

Several dogs barked in the distance when Mickey stumbled into the site, moaning to himself about the landlord at the pub. The warm buzz from a solid day's drinking still numbed him and he was grateful for it.

Alcohol was the only thing that softened the memories of that little girl's piercing blue eyes, pleading and afraid. That and the drugs. Though they were few and far between, now that he'd been cut off. Used to be the name Mickey Boswell was currency enough, but ever since the Anderson job, it was mud—Conner had seen to that. He was good for the money, he told them. He just needed time. But apparently his word wasn't enough anymore.

I bet Conner doesn't have the same problem.

He stopped to catch his breath and noticed, with a sinking feeling, that the lights were on inside his caravan. That could only mean one thing. Someone was waiting up for him. The thought of kipping on a park bench became more appealing by the second, but his feet ached, and he knew from experience that delaying the inevitable only made it worse. Especially after the hangover had set in.

He braced himself, then climbed the three short steps leading to the caravan door and pulled it open.

'Well, Conner, would you look who finally decided to come back home?' Mammy was perched on the end of his bed. Conner stood next to her, arms folded. She looked Mickey up and down. Her face was wrinkled with disgust.

Conner's lips twisted sardonically. 'Fecking hell, Mickey, I can smell the booze on you from here.' His gaze stopped on Mickey's thighs and he barked a laugh. 'Mickey, you've pissed yourself. Again.'

'Feck off.' Mickey staggered back a little. He grasped for the doorframe. Mammy hissed her disapproval and Conner chuckled softly, clearly delighted with the evening's entertainment so far.

'Look at him, Mammy, he's sozzled.'

'What do you want, Conner?' Mickey demanded, attempting to sound less drunk than he was. He could tell by Conner's amused expression that he'd failed. Miserably.

'Are you even aware, Mickey,' Mammy said in a clipped voice, 'that while you were off making a fool of yourself, embarrassing your family, the place was being turned upside down?'

Everything he'd done was for the good of the family. He wouldn't have even been out drinking if it weren't for Conner blundering the Anderson job. If he hadn't knocked that little girl flying through that glass table, they'd be having a different conversation.

He shook his head, to push the memory away.

Her words finally sunk in. Mickey folded his arms across his chest. 'What do you mean?'

'What do you think I mean, you eejit?' Mammy said. 'The gavvers were here, asking questions. Looking for you, for Christ's sake. They arrested me. *Me*. I was stuck in a cell for near on two days. Because of you. Not only did you make a bags of teaching Anderson a lesson, you didn't even finish him off knowing he could finger you for it.' The veins on her temples bulged; she paused to catch her breath.

Mickey frowned. Two days? Had he really been gone that long?

The shock of his mammy's arrest faded fast when he remembered Conner kicking the shite out of Anderson until he'd stopped groaning, stopped moving. There was no way Anderson could have survived the beating that Conner had given him. He hadn't even been breathing when they'd left. Had he?

Mammy continued. 'You're lucky that you and your brother weren't here when the filthy scum tore the place apart. Our home.' She fought a cough, her chest heaving. 'I've got you an alibi, not that *you* bleedin' deserve it, you useless little shite. So, if they come back—*when* they come back—you and your brother were staying at the Fox and Hound Guest House working on a job out of town. I paid extra to get receipts and your names in the check-in book.'

She stopped speaking and glared at Mickey. Her raspy breath rattled in her throat. Conner, who had been standing dutifully by her side the whole time, placed a hand on her shoulder.

'Aren't you going to thank Mammy?' Conner asked. There was just enough inflection in his voice to make it sound like Mickey was being ungrateful. Especially since Mammy had clearly gone out of her way to do something so selfless for her wayward son. The scene made him sick.

Mammy squeezed Conner's hand—the picture of a proud, doting mother.

Mickey gritted his teeth. The more he focused on his brother's taunting smirk the more he wanted to punch his face in. He clenched his fists by his sides. 'Thank her? None of this would have happened if it weren't for *you*. This is all *your* fault. But no, it's me who gets the blame, isn't it? Because you can't put a foot wrong. *You* get the special treatment. *You* get the magical, fecking bracelet, or whatever the feck it was I saw that day.' He thrust a finger at Conner's wrist where a new, almost identical, band of leather was tied. '*You*—'

'Michael Daniel Boswell, how dare you speak to your brother like that! You should be ashamed.' Each word hit Mickey like a physical blow. 'It wasn't Conner dragging you down the pub every night, tipping booze down your throat. You were in charge of the Anderson job. You messed it up. Now, you're trying to blame your little brother. And you call yourself a man? You're an embarrassment. I'm glad Dermot and Niall aren't here to see what a disgrace you've become. Glad your da isn't alive to see you now. He must be turning in his grave.'

Mickey cringed, his rage waning fast under his mammy's disapproval.

Mammy stood and strode forward, forcing Mickey to move out of her way. She marched out the door and down the steps. Conner followed.

'When the scum come back, and they will,' she shouted over her shoulder, 'you'd better hope you're not here. Because they can take you for all I care. I'm not bailing you out this time. I'm done with you.'

Mickey stared into the darkness, bathed in the glow of light from his home. He sagged against the doorframe and sniffed, blinking away tears. The worst part of it was he knew his night wasn't going to get any better; that the memory of piercing-blue eyes would haunt him well into the early hours.

It just wasn't fair.

Chapter 8

CHARLIE SHAVED OVER THE avocado-green sink in his bathroom. After a quick check of his handiwork in the mirror, he squinted at his reflection.

The bags under his hazel eyes were so dark, it looked like he'd lost a bar fight. His gaze dropped to his scar-ridden chest and arms. Charlie flinched and turned away.

No matter what he did, he couldn't escape his childhood. The scars were his permanent reminder. He couldn't wish away the cigarette burns, or the marks left by repeated hits with a belt buckle.

What really pissed him off was the summer, and having to wear long-sleeved shirts because of his deadbeat, alcoholic shit of a father. Most of his co-workers were used to his unusual choice of summer wardrobe. Some even knew the reasons behind it.

The new people were the problem and the same overworked comments.

'Aren't you hot wearing that shirt?'

'Why don't you just roll your sleeves up?'

He had once, but the stares and discomfort it triggered had put paid to the idea pretty quickly.

The sound of movement from the bedroom broke his train of thought. 'Debs, is that you?' Silence followed. 'Debs?'

His wife appeared briefly at the door. Loose, blonde curls brushed against the threadlike straps of her sheer, white-satin night gown. 'Of course it's me. Who the hell else would it be? Hurry up. You're going to make me late for work.'

'I'll just be a second.'

'Hurry up.' There was a crashing sound as Debbie slammed a drawer shut.

Brilliant. The day hadn't even begun and she was already pissed at him.

He hadn't noticed the cracks start to appear, but now it seemed like their whole marriage was about to crumble.

And I don't have the faintest idea what I need to do to fix it.

She'd been so full of life when they'd met. An intoxicating mix of energy and exuberance. He'd fallen for her instantly; she was beautiful, fun and had a razor-sharp wit.

Of course her parents hadn't approved of their relationship. They'd taken every opportunity to whisper poison in her ear. A policeman wasn't who they wanted for their daughter. Didn't earn enough. Job was too dangerous. Notoriously unfaithful.

Granted, some of those things were true. The money wasn't as good as banking and of course it could be dangerous, but he would never cheat on her. Never.

He'd seen colleagues throw away relationships, even their homes and families, because they were flattered by a bit of attention—but not him. It wasn't in his nature, or Stephen's, or Adeola's come to think of it. Brian... well, he'd have to find someone who could stomach him in the first place...

He was as infatuated with her now as he was then, but something had changed between them. She was pulling away from him. Whatever he tried to make things right only made her balk more. He was completely lost.

Why can't I be more like Stephen?

With his easy laugh and cheerful nature, Stephen could walk into a room full of strangers and leave with a room full of friends.

I hope I get to hear him laugh again. One day.

Charlie stepped into the bedroom and put on a smile for Debbie. 'Are you going to visit Steve today?'

He didn't need to ask. Debbie and Linda had been like sisters; she'd do anything for Stephen. The loss had been devastating for both of them.

'Yes. I'll try and pop in and see him on my lunch break.' As she went to walk past him, her floral perfume surrounded him in an intoxicating haze.

He drank in the sight of her. Her nightgown clung to the curves of her body, stopping midway up her thighs and leaving little to the imagination. It was enough to make any man's pulse race.

Charlie's body responded to her. He wanted to grab her, pull her close and kiss her the way they used to kiss.

He missed the way she felt, pressed against him. Missed her touch. Her smell.

God, he was lonely.

He touched her shoulder lightly and got an icy scowl for his efforts. 'Thank you.'

She huffed in response.

He kissed her on the cheek. She drew away in horror and shrugged his hand off her shoulder.

They stared at each other. The look of incredulity she gave him felt like a slap to the face.

All he could do was watch her walk out of the room.

When had everything gone so wrong between them?

Chapter 9

CHARLIE WEDGED THE PHONE receiver against his shoulder, to free up his hands. He scribbled down notes and flicked through the neatly organised statements on his desk, while listening to the voice on the other end.

He jotted down another address. His wrist clipped the edge of one of his biros, moving it out of place. He frowned and positioned it back to point north. Charlie exhaled as the sense of unease ebbed.

Sweat already dampened his lower back. The long sleeves weren't helping either. He arched his spine and peeled the damp fabric away. The fan on his desk was doing little more than moving hot air around; he couldn't turn it up for fear of scattering his ordered paperwork across the floor. It made him yearn for another court date—at least the building had air con.

The sound of angry voices coming from the other end of the office alarmed him.

'Sorry, could you hang on just a second?' He interrupted the caller and stood up slightly.

The commotion hadn't gone unnoticed by the rest of the office. One by one heads turned. A couple of people stood and walked over to the source of the noise, as if they might be required to step in if needed. These sorts of arguments you'd expect down at the front desk or the cells, not in the detectives' office.

Adeola hurried over to Charlie, his brow furrowed. He kept his voice low. 'It's Stephen. He's in Booker's office.'

'I'm going to have to call you back.' Charlie hung up the phone and nodded his thanks to Adeola.

He jogged across the room. A thousand thoughts raced through his mind. Why was Stephen out of hospital? For Christ's sake, he'd only been out of the coma for two weeks. What was he doing here? Why hadn't the hospital called him? He'd explicitly told them to contact him when Stephen was ready to be discharged.

Bloody hospitals.

He'd never liked the places. "White coat syndrome" they called it. As a child, his dad had only ever taken him to the hospital once. A drunken rage and a poorly aimed beer bottle had left Charlie with a broken toe. If it had been anywhere else they'd have seen the scars, and he'd have been placed on the Child Protection Register and removed to a place of safety. But it hadn't been. From that point on, his dad had been careful not to break any more bones—it was amazing how much pain could be inflicted before that happened.

The two DCs who'd got up to investigate offered Charlie a sympathetic look as they made their way back to their desks.

That can't be good.

Charlie burst through the door of Booker's office. Neither of the men acknowledged his sudden entrance.

Stephen was agitated, but clearly still under the influence of the pain medication. He was swaying on his feet and his words were indistinct and clumsy.

What the hell were they thinking releasing him? He was going to have a few stern words with someone.

'It's just not hopscotch, Gerry,' Stephen protested with a slur.

Christ.

'I told you, Steve. It's not my decision. The DCI decides when you're fit to come back to work, not me. Even if it was my decision, it's quite clear you still need to recover. You can barely stand. Go back... to the hospital.' The pique in Booker's tone softened as he spoke.

Charlie winced, anxious that the sergeant was about to order Stephen to go home. Booker glanced at him, all but imploring Charlie to diffuse the situation. Under any other circumstances Booker would have shut this down immediately, but before him was a broken man. A man who had nothing.

'Steve?' Charlie ventured, keeping his voice low and calm.

Stephen turned, as though he had only just noticed Charlie standing in the doorway.

'Charlie, why are the Boswells still out there?' The desperation in his voice was unnerving. 'It was them. I swear to God, Charlie.'

Charlie held up his hands in a placating gesture. 'I know Steve. I know. I'm sorry that I didn't keep you updated. I didn't want to get your hopes up before I had anything concrete to tell you.' He stepped towards his friend, his movements controlled. In his state he had no idea what Steve would do, or how he would react.

'Get my hopes up?'

'After you woke up and told me what you saw I filled Gerry in. Officers went to the site, en masse. Arrests were made, but Mickey and Conner weren't there. We even applied for an extension to hold Aisling in the hopes that she'd crack, but we had to release her on bail.' He paused, watching Stephen's body language closely, trying to think how best to phrase what he was going to say next.

It was no good. He was going to have to rip the plaster off and hope for the best. 'They have an alibi and evidence linking them to a guest house out of town the night you were attacked. There are even a couple of witnesses who claimed to be drinking with them in the bar that evening.'

What little colour Stephen had left in his cheeks drained away. He stood in stunned silence, his face contorted in disbelief.

Charlie and the sergeant exchanged a wary glance.

'No. *No*, Charlie. It was them.' The anger rose in Stephen's voice. 'One of them was called Mickey, are you just telling me that's a coincidence?'

'We're still looking into it, Steve. I'm just giving you the facts.'

'This is unbelievable. The Boswells killed my fucking family. My family, Charlie. Linda. Bethany...' His voice cracked with the mention of his daughter's name. 'And they're walking around because they've managed to buy off some twat for a dodgy alibi?' He scrunched up his face, as if he were trying to remember something. Then his eyes widened. 'They took my watch. Did you find it? It's engraved. It will prove they were there.'

'I'm sorry, Steve,' Booker said, his voice gentle. 'We haven't found anything incriminating. Are you certain it was them? You said they were wearing balaclavas. Plus you'd been drinking—'

Stephen thrust a finger at Booker. 'Are you saying that I was too pissed to know what was going on?'

Charlie tensed, ready to put himself between his friend and the sergeant if he needed to. He'd never seen Steve out of control.

I can't believe they let him out in this state.

'Mr Anderson,' Booker said, reminding Stephen with two words that he was currently a civilian and could stay that way, 'I think you need to go and collect yourself. I'm happy to discuss this further, at a later date. For now I just want you to recover. We will continue with the investigation and update you at such a time when we feel it necessary. Please, Steve.'

Stephen recoiled as if Booker had physically struck him. His body sagged and his gaze dropped to the ground. 'I have nothing, Gerry. Nothing. This job is the only family I have left.'

Charlie felt a lump rise in his throat. He looked across at Booker, who wore an expression caught halfway between shock and guilt. Charlie needed to get Steve out of here. *Now*.

'Steve, come on. Let's go grab a coffee in the break room. I'll call you a taxi to take you back to mine; you can wait for it there. The guest room has been made up for you for a while now.' He placed a hand on Stephen's back. With a final glance at Booker, who nodded before turning his attention to the files on his desk, Charlie ushered Steve out of the office.

As the taxi pulled away, Charlie wiped a trickle of sweat from his temple. Seeing his friend like that had left a knot in his stomach. How Stephen had managed to discharge himself in that state was anyone's guess.

He pulled the lighter and packet of Embassy out of his suit pocket and selected a cigarette. Still focused on the taxi, he tapped the lighter on his palm three times, lit up and took a long drag. As the smoke filled his lungs, it took the edge off his nerves. Exhaling, he walked back inside the police station.

The fishing looks from his colleagues failed to bait him on his way back to his desk. He sat down hard in his chair and ground out the rest of his cigarette in the metal ashtray. The attention quickly dissipated.

He checked his watch: four o'clock in the afternoon. Debbie should be at the house by now. If not, Steve had his front door key. Still, he should probably ring to let her know Steve was on his way.

A deliberate cough close to him jarred him from his thoughts. Brian stood next to his desk.

'It's a good job you're such a bloody good detective, because you're not going to win any friends with that face on you.'

'What do you want?' Charlie barked, in no mood for any of Brian's bullshit. He eyed Brian's hand nervously. *I swear to God, if he touches another one of my pens...*

Brian held up his hands. 'Just here to pass on a message. The hospital rang for you. They want you to call them back.'

Charlie huffed out a breath. His eyes flicked to Brian's left hand as it inched closer to his desk.

His heart pounded. 'Don't touch anything. Or, I swear to God, I'll stab you with a pen.'

Brian smirked, but stopped his hand. 'Nah, you wouldn't do that. I know how you feel about mess and stuff. There's no way you'd want the pen back after they removed it from me.'

Charlie met the man's eyes. 'What makes you think they'd be able to remove it?'

Brian pulled his hand back and left without another word.

He remembered Brian's message.

Bloody hospital.

If they wanted to tell him that Stephen had discharged himself, it was a bit late.

His pager beeped. He yanked it off his belt and read the text as it scrolled across the screen. It was an instruction to phone the hospital. 'Unbelievable.' Oh, he was going to phone them back alright.

As he slammed the pager down on his desk, provoking a few startled glances, he had the vague sense that there was another call he was supposed to make.

Chapter 10

THE TAXI LURCHED OVER another speed bump. Stephen grunted and scowled at the back of the cabbie's head.

The man had tried to make conversation with Stephen at first, but nothing he said had sunk in. Stephen was still replaying the conversation he'd had with Booker over in his mind. Trying to analyse the details from his medication-addled memory was like trying to hunt for shadows in the pitch dark.

The cabbie had eventually given up, instead flicking the occasional cautious glance at Stephen in the rear-view mirror. The journey since then had been silent.

Stephen rubbed at the stubble on his jaw, then trailed a finger down the new scar on his cheek. It didn't make any sense. He was certain the Boswells had murdered his family. It was definitely Mickey and he was confident that the other man had been Mickey's younger brother, Conner. How could they have gotten away with it, just like that?

If only they'd found my damned watch...

His heart pounded inside his chest. Blood pulsed loudly in his ears. He squeezed the key Charlie had given him until it pinched.

Another speed bump.

Stephen hissed. That one had hurt. His pain relief was wearing off, making it more difficult to concentrate.

'Take it easy, mate. I just got out of hospital.'

The cabbie gawked at him in the rear-view mirror and muttered an apology.

He'd limped out of the hospital without pills to help with his injuries. They'd warned him that if he discharged himself, the on-site pharmacy wouldn't have enough notice to supply him with the proper course of medication. But he couldn't stay there any longer. When he was lucid, thoughts of his wife and daughter's final moments consumed him, until he became riddled with grief and rage. When he wasn't, he had nightmares so vivid, he woke screaming and drenched in sweat. He needed to know the Boswells were being brought to justice for what they had done.

Charlie and Debbie's semi-detached house came into view and the taxi slowed to a halt.

The cabbie threw him another anxious glance, before hurriedly getting out of the vehicle and opening the rear passenger door for him.

'Far be it from me to pry, but are you sure you wouldn't be better off back in hospital? You look like you're in a lot of pain.' He offered Stephen his hand.

Stephen scowled up at him.

Pain? He had no idea. 'I'm good, thanks.'

The cabbie pulled his hand back, watching him like he might attack.

Amid a mix of gasps and curses, Stephen heaved himself out of the taxi.

Without another word, the cabbie got back in the car and drove off.

Stephen shambled to the front door, his bad leg even more of a dead weight than usual. Stopping under the porch to catch his breath, he uncurled his fist and peeled the key off his sweaty palm. It had left a deep indentation on his skin. He couldn't remember squeezing the key. His short-term recall was out of whack since waking up from the coma. That was to be expected though, surely?

He stared at the obscured, glass-door panels and hesitated. This was a safe place, he'd been here hundreds of times, but everything felt different now. Everything felt wrong. He swallowed. Where else could he go? He wasn't ready to go home. The thought of it made him feel physically sick.

No. Charlie and Debbie were all he had left. The last vestige of stability in his otherwise shattered life. It was what he needed right now. *They* were what he needed right now.

He opened the door. The scent of Debbie's flowery perfume hit him. He called out her name softly, in case she was resting.

Not hearing a response, he stepped inside. Something crunched underneath his shoe. He lifted his foot. A few shards of blue glass skittered across the beech laminate. A handful of yellow roses lay amongst the debris in a pool of water, clustered against the feet of the wooden telephone table.

Stephen's chest tightened. His mind began to slowly process the scenes of a struggle.

A high-pitched squeal came from upstairs.

He lunged for the stairs, hauling himself up as fast as his damaged leg would allow, adrenaline suppressing the pain of his injuries.

A male grunt urged him faster. He wasn't about to let the Boswells hurt Debbie. They had taken enough people he loved away from him.

How had they found out about Charlie? He'd had no involvement in the case. Maybe if his brain wasn't so foggy he could puzzle it out. It didn't matter. Debbie needed his help; he could work out the details later.

He burst through the door, his cry feral. The sight before him made him freeze. What was left of his world came crashing down.

Chapter 11

'JESUS! STEPHEN.' DEBBIE CLAMBERED off the man she'd been straddling. In a blur of naked flesh she scrambled from the bed and snatched up a white-satin robe in a crumpled heap on the floor. She wrapped herself in it, yanking the belt into a firm knot.

The stranger sat up on the creased sheets and blinked at Stephen, as he attempted to process the situation. After a few seconds, the blood appeared to return to his head. He cursed and yanked the duvet over his wilting manhood.

'Fuck, Debbie! How could you do this to Charlie?' Stephen roared.

The robe did little to cover her. He could see her nipples through the sheer material. He looked away.

She followed his gaze and blushed, folding her arms firmly over her chest. 'Steve... I—'

'Spare me, Debbie. What the fuck are you thinking? You'll break his heart.'

The colour drained from her face. She dropped her gaze to the floor, tousled, blonde curls touching her shoulders.

The sound of rustling caught Stephen's attention. He looked over to see the lanky stranger pull on a pair of jeans. His dark hair was cut in a mullet style and had enough product to be a fire risk. And, of course, he had to have a goatee.

Seriously? This guy?

Under Stephen's unwavering glare, the man stood next to Debbie and casually draped his arm across her shoulders. She shrugged it off violently and took a step to the side, which only added to the confusion on his gormless face.

He cleared his throat and extended a hand towards Stephen. 'I'm Russell.'

Stephen glowered at the outstretched hand, then at Debbie. She made herself smaller, looking sick to her stomach.

'Or Russ, whichever you prefer—'

Stephen lashed out and struck Russell's nose. Cartilage crunched beneath his knuckles.

Christ, that felt good.

Russell staggered back, clamping his hands over his face. Blood seeped through his fingers and down his wrists. Tears streamed from his eyes.

'Jesus, Steve.' Debbie gasped at the spray of red on her robe.

'Where are your keys?' Stephen demanded. 'I'm taking your car.'

Debbie flinched. 'In the kitchen. The bowl on the side.' Her eyes shone with unshed tears. 'Please, Steve. Don't tell Charlie.'

'That man would go through hell and back for you, Debbie. I'd give anything to have my family back and you're throwing yours away.'

Stephen turned and limped away. He couldn't look at her anymore. How could she? Charlie was devoted to her. It would destroy him if he found out.

He tried to block out their arguing voices as he made his way down the stairs.

'Debs, I think he broke my nose.'

'Shut up, Russell.'

Stephen scanned the worktops and snatched Debbie's keys from a wooden bowl with loose change and assorted odds and ends.

A thought struck him.

He flicked through the bowl's contents until he found it; a small silver key. Turning it over in his fingers, he eyed it with a predatory hunger.

What was Debbie thinking? Screwing around with that gangly, greasy twat upstairs?

Stephen shook his head and focused. Glass he'd dragged upstairs crunched beneath his shoes as he made his way back into the hallway. He stopped beside the stairs and eased himself into a crouch. He pulled on the cupboard door. It opened with a soft pop.

He brushed away a few fragments of blue crystal and crawled inside. Nestled among the shadows was a dented, green, metal cabinet. He pushed the key into the lock and opened the lid.

The shotgun was stunning; he could appreciate now why Charlie raved about it so much. He'd never really paid it much attention the few times the two of them had gone clay shooting together.

He lifted the weapon out and pulled himself back up to standing. Blood rushed to his brain and he swayed. After a few deep breaths the sensation passed.

Now to find the cartridges.

Stephen had always appreciated Charlie's attention to detail and methodical approach; it was one of the things that made him such a great detective. He was a creature of habit, everything had to be just so. If you knew him well enough you could just about predict the way his mind worked.

And I know him very well.

Stephen held up the shotgun and tapped the intricate engraving of a gundog flushing out a grouse on the embellished, metal plate. A smile tugged at the corners of his mouth—Charlie always did like things to match.

Water sloshed beneath his shoes as he swapped the hallway for the living room. He paid no attention to the damp footprints that trailed behind him as he hobbled across the cream shag carpet.

After a quick scan of the room, he spotted a Famous Grouse whisky box standing proudly on the top shelf of a teak display cabinet. He'd always wondered why it was on show; Charlie was a Lagavulin drinker. His suspicions were aroused again. It was neatly positioned next to a photo of Charlie and Debbie on their wedding day, both staring affectionately at one another, and a handful of shooting trophies. The scene upstairs replayed in his head. His stomach twisted. Ignoring the photo, he reached up and pulled the box down. Inside were the cartridges that proved his theory.

Floorboards creaked above him.

He grabbed a fistful of yellow 20-gauge cartridges and stuffed them in his pocket, then staggered out of the house. There was no way he was sticking around for when Debbie and her conquest felt brave enough to come downstairs.

Stephen opened the driver's side door of the burnt-orange Vauxhall Cavalier and tossed the unloaded shotgun onto the passenger seat. The twisting motion as he climbed into the car made his chest burn.

They'd really done a number on him; fractured ribs, a fractured eye socket. The doctors said that the severity of his head injuries had caused him to slip into the coma. The lacerations on his face, black eyes and split lip were not too dissimilar to the injuries the old man had suffered—the one who the older Boswell boys had beaten up and robbed. *What was his name again?*

Morgan... Archibald Morgan... yes, that was it.

Fucking Boswells. The world would be a better place without the likes of them.

He put the key in the ignition. The engine roared into life. Stephen put the car in gear and floored it. Wheels spun on the spot with a high-pitched screech before the car lurched down the driveway, forcing him back into the chair with a sharp hiss. Setting his jaw, he gripped the steering wheel until his knuckles turned white.

The Boswell's were going to pay for what they'd done. *Even if it's the last thing I do.*

Chapter 12

SPIT FILLED MICKEY'S MOUTH. He bent over and retched. Vomit splashed on the pavement. After a few dry heaves, he straightened with a stagger. A young woman pushing a pram gave him a judgemental look and crossed the road.

What was her problem? *Slag.*

Mickey wiped his mouth with the back of his hand and carried on down the road. He checked his watch, squinting at the scuffed face, trying to make out the numbers through the web of cracks. This was a new low, even for him. It was barely 6pm and he'd already been barred. He paused and counted on his fingers. Add in walking for an hour and a half... *Jesus...* this *really* was a new low.

Mickey spotted a taxi and flagged it down. The cab slowed and pulled up next to him. All four windows were rolled down.

The driver nodded to him. 'Where to, mate?'

Mickey leant in towards the window. Before he'd even uttered a word the driver's smile dropped. His eyes fixed on Mickey's t-shirt, then his face. He sniffed a few times and shook his head, lips pressed together.

'Nah. Sorry, mate. Don't think so. Not in your state.'

'What? You fecking prick.' Mickey kicked out at the taxi as it drove away. His foot connected with the moving door, making him stumble. What was *his* problem? He frowned down at his top, stained with patches of vomit. 'Fecking fantastic.' With a sigh, he flicked away a couple of loose chunks of something he couldn't remember eating.

He rubbed his face; stubble scratched his hand. He was knackered. Even the alcohol wasn't enough to dull the experience of dragging his dead-weight body back to the caravan site. It was taking more drink each time to numb himself to the world. He was running out of things to pawn, now that Mammy refused to let him work on any more jobs. Apparently he wasn't "reliable".

When was the last time he'd had a proper kip? Not since the Anderson cockup. Seven weeks ago? *Jesus.* If he did fall asleep he'd only wake up in a cold sweat, screaming. The image of that little girl's face seared into his mind. Her bright-blue eyes blaming him for her death. *Him.* Yet, it was Conner who'd killed her. Not Mickey. But Conner slept like a babe. Conner didn't see her face at night. Conner didn't need to drink just to get through the days, didn't get the shakes if he didn't. Conner was golden. *Fecking Conner.*

Mickey blundered forward, grinding his teeth. The people he passed moved out of his way like he was some sort of pariah. So he was a little sozzled, so what? It's not like any of them had never overindulged. Judgemental pricks. The closer he got to home the less people he saw. Nobody ever came too near to the halting site, not if they didn't belong. He wasn't even sure that he belonged there anymore.

Where else would I go?

Mickey climbed over the remnants of an old tyre and stumbled through the entrance to the site. He stumbled again and cursed when a small tan-and-white Jack Russell Terrier darted between his feet, yapping enthusiastically while it chased its playmates.

A small girl watched a couple of grubby-faced boys play shirtless in the heat of the evening, swatting each other with sticks. Shona's girl, Cici. She twiddled with her fiery-red hair that was falling loose from its ponytail, and ignored the impatient calls of her mammy from inside a nearby caravan.

The girl had her mammy's red hair and light dusting of freckles, but not her eyes. Her eyes were brown, like his. He'd always had a soft spot for Shona; she was a fine looking woman. When they'd been younger, he'd spent an age lost in her deep-green eyes, stealing kisses when her daddy was around. More when he wasn't. He'd been sure they'd end up together, get married, have babies.

Except she wasn't his wife and Cici wasn't his kid. Although she could have been—except for the hair, she bore an uncanny resemblance to him.

'Look it's Mickey,' said one of the boys. 'He's pissed again. Ha. Look, he can't even walk straight.'

Mickey stopped and growled. Brady and Devin—little feckers. He headed in their direction. It was about time they learnt a little respect.

'Get on with you now, Cici,' Mickey slurred.

The girl gave Brady a questioning look, tucked a strand of red hair behind her ear and stayed put.

He turned his scowl on the little gobshites.

Shona stepped out into the light, fists planted on her shapely hips. She pursed her lips at Mickey, stopping him with a look. His anger wilted under the heat of her glare. How was it that every mammy knew the right look?

'On your way home now boys,' she said. 'Cici, inside.'

Cici giggled when Brady dropped his stick and gave Mickey the finger. She brushed past her mammy and ducked inside the caravan. The two boys sprinted away, laughing.

Shona stood there for what felt like an eternity, holding him captive. Her eyes, like emeralds flecked with gold, were just as lovely as he remembered them. There was a rosy bloom to her cheeks; a few strands of her copper hair clung to her glistening skin. She had a little more meat to her bones now, and it only made her all the more attractive.

'Shona...' His mind went blank.

The wrinkles between her eyes smoothed and her scowl softened into a look he couldn't quite place. Sadness maybe? She looked him up and down. For a moment he thought she was going to say something. Instead, she set her jaw, turned back inside, and closed the door firmly behind her. He knew she'd soon have to open it again in this heat, but the message was clear. She'd no time for a dosser like him.

Mickey stared at the door. Those odd symbols he'd seen around the site but had never paid mind to—like the ones on Conner's bracelet—had been carved into it. With a heavy sigh, he carried on walking. What had happened between him and Shona? It'd been so long he couldn't remember. All he knew was that she'd had a blazing row with Niall's wife, Róisín, and then gone cold on him. It made no sense.

Mickey had always had a way with the ladies; they'd loved his roguish grin and deep-brown eyes. He knew he was a good looking lad—they'd certainly always told him so.

'It's a good job you're a fine thing, because there's not much else to you,' they'd joke. Not that he'd liked being called thick, mind, but he'd appreciated the compliment about his looks all the same.

That was before Conner banjaxed the Anderson job. Now the ladies wouldn't touch him with a barge pole. He couldn't even get a smile, let alone a kiss or a cuddle. All the more reason to drink. A bottle had no hang-ups about the company it kept.

He rounded the corner, his thoughts still heady with the memories of Shona in a past life. It took him a few beats to notice a figure hobbling towards his mammy's caravan.

Transfixed, he watched as the man closed the distance. By the looks of his awkward movements, he'd either been out on the lash or had been banged up pretty badly.

Mickey squinted. There was something familiar about him. He definitely knew him from somewhere...

Oh fuck.

Chapter 13

STEPHEN SHUDDERED AS WHITE-HOT rage enveloped him. A scream ripped from his throat, so raw and hate-filled, that he didn't recognise it as his own. 'Mickey! Mickey Boswell, I've come for you!'

A flicker of movement through the window of an adjacent caravan caught his attention. Judging by the outline, it was definitely male. He could hear a woman's voice punctuated with a hacking cough.

Aisling. Where Aisling went Mickey followed, like the dutiful, simple-minded lapdog he was.

The figure moved towards the door.

Stephen lifted the shotgun and nestled the butt into his shoulder. He squeezed the trigger. There was an explosion of sound. The door to the caravan disintegrated in a cloud of debris. Pain tore through his chest and arm as the recoil jolted him back. He went sprawling backwards and dropped the gun.

His vision swam.

His ears rang.

He watched as someone staggered forward, clutching their mangled chest. Strange little symbols on their bracelet glowed white, then guttered out in a curl of smoke. The person tumbled down the three steps outside the caravan and collapsed in a heap at the bottom. Blood pooled from the corpse, soaking into the dry, cracked earth.

Even through the ringing in his ears, Stephen heard a woman's frenzied screams. Shouts of confusion quickly followed.

He was struck from behind. His face smashed into the dirt. He strained to push himself back up. His arms buckled from the effort.

A sharp crack to the back of his head was the last thing that registered before he lost consciousness.

Stephen peeled his eyes open and squinted against the harsh light, trying to focus on his surroundings. He was face down on vinyl flooring.

His head hurt like hell. The stabbing pain in his skull made him feel nauseous; the keening in his ears didn't help either. The rest of his body hadn't fared much better. Everything either ached or throbbed.

Raised voices cut through the fog of his thoughts. Mickey was shouting over his mother's anguished wails.

Mickey? Wait... then who did I shoot?

'Mammy, stop. Stop! Would you stop hitting me?'

'He's dead! I can't believe my baby is dead. Why? Why did this happen? Oh Conner. Oh my poor baby boy.' Aisling took a few laboured breaths and choked out another sob. 'Why did it have to be my baby?'

'Well, if it makes you feel any better, I don't think it was Conner he was after.' Mickey's tone was clipped, lacking compassion. That surprised Stephen.

'What did you bring him inside for? I don't want that filthy scum inside my home.'

Inside. He was inside the caravan. The caravan he'd just blown the door off.

Stephen exhaled, stirring up a cloud of dust that scattered grit into his eyes. He blinked against the sharp scratching, tears trailing down his cheeks.

'This never would've happened if you'd killed the prick. If you'd done your fucking job instead of acting the maggot.' Aisling bawled.

'*Me?*' Mickey's voice raised an octave or two. 'It was Conner who fucked the whole thing up. He killed the girl, not me. He beat her mammy to a pulp, not me. *You* said not to kill anyone. *You* said just to teach Anderson a lesson.' The caravan floor creaked as Mickey paced. 'But somehow it's all my fault, is it? It couldn't possibly ever be Conner, could it? Your perfect, precious little Conner.'

'Don't you *dare* say his name. How dare you. What did I ever do to deserve such a dimwit for a son?' She broke into a coughing fit and, after a few rasping breaths, said in an iron voice. 'It should be you out there, lying dead in a pool of your own blood and shit on the ground. Not Conner.'

Mickey made a sucking noise with his teeth.

'You'd better deal with this prick, Mickey,' Aisling hissed. 'The place will be swarming with his scum soon—they're like cockroaches. Just kill the fucker and be done with it. I need to get Conner fixed up. See to his caravan. It's not right him being out there like that.' Another breathless sob followed.

Fighting against his brain's sluggish resistance, Stephen struggled to piece together their conversation. It was Conner he'd killed. Conner who had murdered his family.

If nothing else, at least he'd rid the world of one evil bastard.

Chapter 14

MICKEY CLENCHED HIS JAW so tightly his teeth hurt. He didn't know whether he wanted to punch something or cry.

Punch something. Definitely punch something.

How could she say that to him? His own Mammy?

Anderson let out a groan.

Mickey's breathing became faster. If it hadn't been for Anderson, his life wouldn't be a shit show right now. If Anderson had been at home, like he was supposed to be, nobody would've died. They could have stuck to his plan and he'd have had the recognition he deserved. It was Anderson's fault that he couldn't sleep at night, that he was either bawling his eyes out or off his face on booze. That he couldn't get that little girl's terrified expression out of his head. It was Anderson's fault that his mammy didn't give him the respect he deserved.

The caravan rocked as Mickey tramped over to Anderson. He booted him in the chest, then hauled the gavver onto his back. The choked sound of pain that bubbled from Anderson's bloodied mouth dredged a vindictive smile from the bowels of Mickey's resentment.

This fecker is going to pay.

Mickey ran his tongue over his dry lips, and pressed his right knee into Anderson's chest. Using his other leg to steady himself, just in case Anderson fought back, he leant in close until their faces were just inches apart. The cry of agony from the man was delicious. It was enough to make him forget his mammy's howling sobs.

The occupants of the site were keeping their distance out of respect for her. It wouldn't be long before they wanted their revenge, to beat the shite out of the only gavver thick enough to kill one of their own with no backup. Mickey wasn't about to let them ruin his fun. Not after what he'd been through, night after night, day after day. Anderson had near ruined his life.

Sweat dripped from his forehead. His hands shook. He curled his fists around the neckline of Anderson's t-shirt, squeezed until his knuckles turned white, and yanked him up, so that he could stare him right in his freakish, blue eyes.

'Why don't you just kill me?' Anderson wheezed. 'Or is it just women and children you murder?'

Mickey snarled in response. Saliva speckled his chin. 'I didn't kill them. You did. You should've been home. You were supposed to be home.'

Anderson's head lolled back. Mickey adjusted his grip to compensate for his weight. Strained to fend off the trembling in his arms. Jesus, he needed a drink.

A blur of motion was all he saw, before Anderson's forehead connected with his nose. He reeled back and his vision flashed white.

'Fuck!' Mickey touched his face. Blood gushed through his fingers. Tears streamed down his cheeks. *That fucking gavver just broke my nose.*

His mother's shrieks echoed in his ears. If she didn't stop yelling, half the site would try piling into the caravan any minute now. He had to finish this quickly.

Squeezing his eyes shut against the blazing pain, he scrambled to his feet awkwardly. He flailed his arms to grab hold of anything, before he lost his balance. His clumsy fingers, slick with blood, caught the edges of something smooth on the shelf. A flash of white had him opening his eyes. An electric jolt ripped through his arm. His hand spasmed. Mickey yelped and stumbled sideways before righting himself. The item clattered to the floor. *Fuck.* Blinking through tears, he stamped down on Anderson's gut. He was rewarded with a winded groan as the gavver tried to curl in on himself.

'I'm going to kill you!' Mickey adjusted himself to land another blow. His ankle twisted when he stepped on something hard and jagged. He cursed and moved his foot to see what it was.

The box he'd knocked off the shelf had shattered, spilling its contents across the dust-coated floor. Coins and jewellery shone brightly among the splintered chunks of wood—wood that had been carved with more of those fecking symbols. There was something else poking out from under the wreckage. He nudged it with the toe of his trainer until he dislodged it.

An ornate dagger. The one Niall had stolen, pawned, then gotten himself locked up over. It was a fine looking thing. Its blade was mottled steel with his mammy's symbols etched into it, flowery silver patterns decorating the guard. The handle was smooth, veined, black marble, with a red gemstone set into the pommel—which shared the same fancy design. Probably worth a few quid.

No wonder Mammy wanted the thing back.

As he stared, he became aware of a low throbbing sensation emanating from it. It quivered through his body, beckoning to him.

Mickey snatched up the dagger and tested its weight. It fit perfectly in his hand, like it had been made specifically for him. Just holding it made him feel stronger somehow. With a frown, he rubbed his thumb over the jewel, to wipe away the smears of blood. *His* blood. The crimson stone gleamed, feeling oddly warm. Light danced across its facets, causing a strange, pulsating illusion.

A strangled cackle pulled his attention away from the dagger. Anderson was clutching something in his hand, laughing like a madman. The fecker had just murdered his brother, broken his nose, and now he was laughing?

Mickey stood on Anderson's wrist, increasing the pressure, until the scum's fingers uncurled to reveal a gold watch. He grabbed it by the strap and straightened to inspect it. He could barely make out the inscription engraved on the back of the case.

His lip curled in glee as he read it aloud. 'To Stephen. I love you more with each passing second. Yours forever, Linda.'

Anderson grinned up at him in defiance. There was something strangely triumphant and infuriating about that look. Mickey scowled down at him, then thrust the watch at his face. It struck the gavver's forehead and skipped across the floor.

The laughter started up again, this time hollow, chilling, and devoid of any humour.

'You think this is funny?' Mickey screamed. 'I'll give you something to laugh about.' He crouched, and in a single, shaky swipe, slashed the dagger down Anderson's cheek. The skin split open like a ripe peach. The blade sliced cleanly through the edge of his lip. Blood poured from the skin flap and into Anderson's mouth, until he started to choke. He turned his head and gobbed blood onto the floor.

'No! What are you doing you moron? Stop, Mickey. Stop!' Aisling lurched forward and grabbed hold of Mickey's arm. She scratched him as she tried to pull him back.

What was her problem? First she wanted Anderson dead, now she didn't want him getting stabbed? Did she have a screw loose?

Mickey wrenched his arm from her grasp. Aisling toppled, screaming bloody murder as she fell. Her shoulder rammed into his back, jolting him forward.

I've really had enough of this shite.

'Moron, am I? I tell you what, Mammy. You want this prick dead? Fine.' Ignoring her hysterical protests, he plunged the dagger into Anderson's chest. The blade juddered slightly as it scored a rib, then came to a jarring halt at the dagger's quillons.

A slow smile spread across Mickey's face as blood blossomed through Anderson's top. He was vaguely aware of his mammy screeching behind him. The gavver writhed and gasped, spluttering blood as he struggled for air. He was done for. This was it. The colour had drained from his sweat and blood-drenched face. His blue eyes darted around wildly before going still. The dagger stood proud, still embedded, the crimson jewel sparkling.

'Well, are you happy now, Mammy?' Mickey turned to her, ready to accept the praise he deserved for finally ridding their family of the prick that had ruined all their lives. It had been a long time coming.

What he saw wiped the grin off his face.

Knelt on all fours, Mammy gaped at Anderson's corpse. Her grey eyes were fixed on the dagger. Other than the shaky rasps of her breathing, she wasn't making a sound. There was no gratitude. No admiration. Not even a smile. If anything she looked petrified.

Mickey frowned. What the feck was going on?

'You've doomed us all.' Her voice was little more than a whisper.

Shouts came from outside. Murmured protests and a few curses followed Shona through the wrecked doorway into the caravan.

Shit was about to hit the fan.

'Aisling? Mickey? What's all the fuss?' Shona gasped and rushed to help Aisling to her feet. Funny thing, that. Until Cici was born Mammy and Shona couldn't stand each other, but after... it was like they were bosom buddies. 'Mickey what in the hell...?' Her gaze fixed on Anderson's lifeless body. Her rosebud lips twisted into a smirk, but dropped away when she saw the dagger.

'What's the matter with you two? I thought you'd be pleased.' Mickey pushed himself up. His muscles quivered. Jesus, but he needed a drink.

Shona started suddenly, as if she'd only just realised he was there. She gawked at his bloodied face. Her gaze moved down his chest, his arms, his hands and then back to the dagger again. She released her grip on Aisling and pointed shakily at the hilt.

'Mickey... is that your blood on the dagger?' She exchanged a concerned look with Mammy.

'I don't know? Probably. The fucker broke my nose, if you hadn't noticed.' He gestured to his face.

Shona gasped, looking like she might faint. Mickey thought he heard her whisper something about Cici, but the pounding in his head made it difficult to work out if it was just his imagination.

What was going on? What was *wrong* with everyone?

'We need to leave,' Mammy barked, her voice filling the caravan. 'Everyone needs to leave. Right now.' She tried to usher Shona out, but Shona wouldn't budge. With a huff, Aisling turned to look at Mickey. 'You leave that blade alone. I'm warning you, just leave it and get your things. We're packing up and moving on.'

'Packing up? We've lived on this site almost my entire life.'

'And now you've gone and fucked it all up.' She shook her head with a sneer. 'You always were a dope.'

'A dope? Everything I've ever done has been for you, you fucking bitch.' The words were out of his mouth before Mickey could stop them.

Time stood still, as if the world was holding its breath. Or maybe that was just him.

Mammy's lips quivered. Her face turned a deep shade of crimson. 'May you die alone, Michael Boswell. You're no son of mine. Not anymore.'

Mickey watched in silence as his mammy barged past Shona, grabbed a small leather pouch from the counter, and disappeared. Her frenzied shouts tore through the site like wildfire. He pressed his nose gently and hissed.

'Don't you realise what you've done?' Shona whispered. 'How could you, Mickey? How could you?'

'How could *I*?' Mickey balled his fists by his side, staring at her in disbelief. 'What about you, Shona? You roll around with me in the sheets. Wait for me to fall in love with you, then take my heart and stamp all over it. Ignore me every day since. With no explanation. Not even a Dear John. Don't I deserve a reason? This is the first time you've said more than two words to me in almost nine years. I thought we had something. Something real.' His body trembled. Warm tears rolled down his cheeks. He waited for her to say something. Anything.

Those emerald eyes smouldered. The fire beneath them rose closer to the surface with every passing second. 'Cici is my baby and I love her. I love her, Mickey. Do you understand?'

Mickey shook his head. He really didn't, not a word. What had Cici got to do with anything?

Her mouth twisted. 'Don't you think my heart was broken too? I made a mistake. I was trying to protect you. I knew Róisín would use it against me.'

'Róisín? What has Niall's wife got to do with anything?'

She continued as if she hadn't heard him. 'Then Cici came along and I had no choice but to find a husband.'

'And you chose Callum—over me?' Mickey slammed his fist into the wall. He'd never liked Shona's husband. Not because he'd been jealous. Okay, maybe a bit. But because Callum Delaney had been a weak-jawed, long-legged dosser. Mickey had lost no sleep the day they'd put him in the dirt.

She scoffed. 'I couldn't. Not after... Do you truly not understand?' Her expression softened, just for a second, then her eyes narrowed. She jabbed a finger at Anderson's body. 'Don't you know what that dagger's about, Mickey? Why your mammy wanted it back so badly after Niall pawned it?' Her voiced hitched on his brother's name.

'No, I just—'

'That's *your* blood, Mickey. My girl is in danger because of *you*. Because she shares your blood.'

My blood? He frowned, doing the maths in his head. There was no way Cici could be his. Was there? Maybe... It *would* explain the resemblance. 'Shona, are you saying that Cici is my daughter?'

'*What?* Are you a complete moron? No, she's not yours.' She threw up her arms. 'For your sake you better hope that the stories about that dagger are just fairy tales. Because if anything happens to my girl, I'll hunt you down myself.'

'Stories? What stories?' Granted, Mammy had rambled on about the thing being cursed, but that was just cock-and-bull. Wasn't it?

Shona gave him a look that could have melted the flesh from his bones, and stormed out of the caravan.

'What the fuck?' He kicked Anderson in the leg hard enough to shake the corpse. 'At least you won't be bothering me anymore. Won't be bothering anyone now.'

As he glanced outside, watching his follow Travellers disperse, he became aware of a rising ache in the flesh between the curve of his left finger and thumb. With a scowl he stared down at the inflamed scratches—three dots on either side of a curved line—on his hand, then at the dead gavver. 'Lucky git.'

Chapter 15

CHARLIE HEAVED OUT A sigh as he entered his house. He glanced back at the driveway. His brow furrowed. Debbie's car was gone. It was unlike her to be out this late. She must have gone out to get something for Steve. Where else could she be?

He shook his head and stepped into the hallway. It'd been a long day. The incident with Steve and Booker had left him rattled, and the probing comments from his colleagues had put him in a foul mood.

He threw his car keys into the dish on the telephone table and frowned at the empty space where the vase had been. The roses he'd bought for Debbie were only a couple of days old. Maybe she'd moved them somewhere else. She'd been acting so strange for the last few months, he honestly wouldn't be surprised if she had thrown them out.

'Charlie?' Debbie called from upstairs.

'Debs? Where's your car?' He peered into the living room. 'Is Steve up there?'

His questions were met with silence.

Muttering, he took off his shoes, placed them neatly in their usual spot in the corner by the front door, and walked into the kitchen. Only the sounds of the washing machine greeted him. He could feel his frustration building. Why wasn't anyone answering him? Exhaling slowly, he headed up the stairs, hearing the familiar creaks that even the thick, shag carpet wasn't able to dampen.

Why do I have a feeling my evening isn't going to get any better?

Debbie waited on the landing, arms folded, chewing her bottom lip.

'Debbie, where's your car?' he asked again, his tone more abrupt than intended. *Brilliant.* That wouldn't go down well. Debbie didn't need much excuse for a blazing row these days, and he could really do without disturbing Steve. Or spending another night on the sofa.

Where *was* Steve anyway?

He glanced at the open door to the guest bedroom and back to his wife. Debbie stared at the floor.

Oh shit.

'You didn't! Debbie, what were you thinking letting him drive? He's up to his eyeballs on pain meds. Where did he go?' All the frustration of the day exploded from him.

'I don't know... he didn't say. I'm sorry, Charlie. I'm sorry.' Her body shook as she sobbed.

In any other situation her reaction would have given him pause, but the worry knot in his stomach was all he could focus on.

He bolted back down the stairs, skidded across the laminate floor and wrenched open the cupboard door.

His heart skipped a beat. His shotgun cabinet was empty.

'Christ, Steve, what are you thinking?' He prayed silently as he sprinted into the living room.

His breath caught in his throat. The whisky box where he kept the cartridges had been moved. He reached up, grabbed it, and fumbled inside. His heart sank. Several of the shells were missing. If Charlie's habits weren't so damn predictable maybe Steve wouldn't have found them. How would he forgive himself if something happened to him?

He put the box down and squeezed his eyes shut. *Think, Charlie. Think.*

He darted back to the hallway, snatched up the phone receiver and punched in the number for Booker's direct line. The wait was excruciating. Each ring added more sweat to his palms.

There was a soft click. 'Sergeant Gerald Booker.'

'Gerry, it's Charlie. Steve's gone. He's taken Debbie's car and my shotgun. I think he's on his way to the Boswell's caravan site. I think he's about to do something really stupid.'

'Shit.' A pause followed. 'Charlie, stay where you are. I'll send as many officers as I can spare. I mean it, Charlie, stay at home.'

'With all due respect, Gerry, there's not a chance in hell I'm staying put if Steve's in danger.'

Booker sighed. 'Just stay safe. I don't need another officer getting injured.' The line went dead.

Debbie lingered at the top of the stairs while Charlie stuffed his feet into his shoes and grabbed his keys. In all the years they'd been married, he couldn't think of a time he'd been as angry with her as he was right now. What was she thinking letting Steve take her car in his state?

Without so much as a goodbye, he slammed the door shut.

Please don't let me be too late.

❦

Charlie jammed his foot on the brake. A cloud of dust spewed into the air outside the halting site.

A few marked police cars were already on the scene; a blockade had been erected between flashing blue lights to deter curious civilians. Uniformed officers bustled around, talking into their handheld radios and jotting down observations in their notebooks. A couple of officers glanced up at Charlie, offered a nod of recognition, and resumed what they were doing. There was something in their expressions that made him uneasy, but the thought vanished as he took in the carnage.

'Jesus Christ.' A wide-eyed Charlie killed the engine and stepped out of his car.

The Traveller site had been completely abandoned, save for the blackened shell of one burnt out caravan. Bare patches of earth marked the spot of the missing vehicles, the ground gored and churned up by tyres and trailers, in their haste to leave. Anything that wasn't essential had been dumped in amongst the litter and debris. The smell of smoke and oil lingered in the evening heat. They couldn't have been gone more than a few hours.

'Uh, Detective?' A young, male officer with flushed cheeks approached Charlie, tugging at his collar. He waited for Charlie to nod before continuing. 'The body is just over there. We've called the pathologist. He's on the way.'

The words sounded distant as Charlie followed the PC's gesture. A fist of ice slammed into his chest. He staggered back. Stephen was on the ground, his body coated in blood, a dagger protruding from his chest. Charlie sprinted towards his friend. The young officer hurried after him.

'Steve?' Charlie dropped to his knees, next to him. He listened out for signs of breathing.

Nothing.

His heart threatened to explode as he straightened up, eyes fixed on Stephen's chest. He checked for a pulse just beneath his jaw. 'No... No, this can't be happening... Steve?' The strangled noise Charlie made sounded alien.

He stared at Stephen's face. His left cheek was split open, from cheekbone to lip. A yawning gash to add to the scars already inflicted by Conner and Mickey. And the blood. Stephen was covered in it. The sight of it flipped his stomach. Time stood still. Officers around him continued to secure the scene, occasionally shouting to one another. They carried on doing their jobs as if it were just another day, just another body, while their friend and colleague lay dead on the ground. This was the way things were, how it needed to be. But he couldn't help but take it personally.

This was Steve—how could they be so detached?

Grief and anger roiled through him, creating an intensity of emotion desperate for an outlet. He drove it down before he erupted at an undeserving co-worker. He would deal with it later. His hands squeezed into fists. Charlie released them and forced his attention back to his friend.

Squeeze, release. Squeeze, release. Squeeze, release.

The action gave him control.

He seared every detail of Steve into his memory. This would be the last time he'd see him. His mangled face would haunt him forever, but he needed to take it all in.

Stephen's bright-blue eyes stared up at nothing. It was an unsettling moment—intimate almost. Charlie closed his friend's eyelids for what would be the final time.

He became aware of the young uniformed officer beside him, stammering on about protocol and evidence.

A glint caught his eye.

Something metallic lodged in the dirt next to Steve's body was reflecting back the pulsating blue light of the police vehicles. He dug his fingers into the dried soil, and prised the item out. A gold watch?

Charlie wiped the dust off with his thumb and turned it over in his hand. He read the message engraved on the back and smiled, despite his grief. Steve had been right about his assumptions. He usually was. His dogged determination to see something through to the end, to ensure justice was served, made him—*had* made him—one of the best detectives on the force.

At least you got the vindication you were looking for.

Still, it was a terrible way to go. To die alone in a field, without a friendly face in his final moments? It tore Charlie up inside.

He looked closer at the dagger. It was familiar. Where had he seen it before?

Then it came to him. Steve had shown him a photo of it weeks ago. A relative of one of the Boswell's victims had given it to him in the hopes it might be found.

Charlie swiped at his wet eyes and swallowed the lump in his throat. 'Oh, Steve.'

But something troubled him about this murder. Why had the Boswells left the weapon at the scene? Especially one that was so distinctive? It was clearly a decorative piece, and judging by the red gemstone set into the intricately decorated pommel of the black, marbled handle, it was probably worth a fair amount. The guard even looked like the floral scroll filigree was inlaid with silver on the ricasso and quillon.

Something about it called to him; like a sonorous, rhythmic throb—felt rather than heard. Charlie reached out for it.

A firm hand squeezed his shoulder before he touched the handle. He jerked his hand back and looked up to see Adeola. A strange expression flickered across the man's face before settling into a look of empathy.

'I'm sorry, Charlie. He was dead when we got here.' Adeola offered his hand to Charlie—who accepted it silently—and pulled him to his feet.

⁂

The next few hours passed in a blur.

Charlie wasn't sure when Sergeant Booker had arrived at the scene and insisted he go home. He'd refused to leave until Steve's body had left for the morgue. Steve was his friend and he was going to make damn sure to be with him until the very last moment.

Charlie had watched in a state of immobile shock as the pathologist, shadowed by his assistant, examined Steve's body. It was as if he'd observed the whole thing through someone else's eyes, so numb and broken that he struggled to process the reality of it.

Eventually, Stephen was taken away.

Adeola drove Charlie home and arranged for one of the uniformed officers to drive Charlie's car back. It was a good thing too; he was in no fit state to drive. Even if he wasn't so physically exhausted, his mind was so wrecked that he probably wouldn't have made it back in one piece.

He stepped through the front door, in the early hours of the morning. The lights were off and there wasn't a sound. Debbie was probably in bed. He sat on the sofa in the darkness, staring at nothing in particular.

His mind tied itself up in knots trying to work out what happened. Nothing felt real. It couldn't be real.

First Linda, then little Bethany. How would he cope now that Stephen had been ripped out of his life? It wasn't fair, damn it. Thieves, rapists and murderers walked the streets, without a care in the world, and good people got their lives stolen from them. It was fucked up.

Dawn broke and Charlie still sat in silence, his cheeks damp, his heart shattered. Exhaustion finally overwhelmed him and his eyes drooped shut—his thoughts still on Stephen, lying dead in the dirt with that dagger in his chest.

Chapter 16

CHARLIE LOOKED AROUND AT the faces of the gathered mourners. The turnout was impressive; a testament to Steve's popularity. Some stood huddled under umbrellas, while others held their own against the persistent drizzle. There was just enough moisture to make everyone sticky and uncomfortable in the close, unpredictable British weather. None more so than the uniformed officers chosen as pallbearers, who stood in respectful silence among Stephen's closest friends.

In truth, he was glad for the rain. It concealed his tears. He'd never been comfortable with his own emotions. Standing here in front of all these people, feeling so raw and exposed, was horrific.

I owe it to Steve. Suck it up.

Linda's parents stood at Steve's graveside. Her father comforted her mother as she dabbed her eyes with a tissue. Her shoulders shook as she wept. She looked so much like Linda it hurt. A little shorter maybe, her hair grey where Linda's had still been dark, but the resemblance was uncanny.

What must it be like to lose your child, grandchild and then son-in-law, all in the space of a couple of months?

He couldn't begin to imagine. It was a wonder they were still functioning. It was a huge relief that Debbie was by their side to offer whispers of support and sympathetic reassurance.

She'd really come through for him since the night of Steve's death. Her recent indifference towards him had been replaced with a warmth and compassion that he desperately needed.

Charlie cleared his throat and unfolded the now damp sheet of paper in his hands. 'There's a quote by Lucy Maud Montgomery that always springs to mind whenever I think of Stephen... Steve: "Life is worth living as long as there's a laugh in it". Before I met Steve I'd never known anyone who could laugh so easily. He was someone who made friends effortlessly. There are some who radiate warmth and energy, and Steve was definitely one of those people. It speaks volumes that there are so many of you here today to celebrate his life.' Hushed sobs and sniffles filled the silence. Charlie drew in a shaky breath. His notes quivered. People either nodded in agreement or smiled sadly.

'Steve was an amazing husband, father and friend. Dedicated, loyal and loving. Everybody on the force, and I see many of you here today, as well as those closest to him, knew how important family was to him. You couldn't have a conversation without him gushing about Linda and Bethany, whether you brought them up or not.' Soft laughter rippled through the sea of black-clad bodies. 'Today, Steve is reunited with his family. The three of them together, forever.' Charlie's voice broke. He paused and pinched the bridge of his nose, refusing to look at Linda's parents or Debbie, in case their heartache reduced him to a bawling mess.

After a deep breath, he continued. 'Steve was an exceptional detective. He worked many high-profile cases, finding patterns that were often missed. Patterns that led to the inevitable arrest of many, now infamous, criminals. Yet, for all his gifts, Linda always used to joke that she could never understand why he had such problems matching an outfit.' Warm laughter ensued.

'She often told me that one of the main reasons he joined the police force was so he didn't have to choose his clothes. The real reason, though, was because he had a very clear sense of right and wrong. Some of you will know that Steve and Linda were involved in an RTA... uh, sorry, road traffic accident, involving a drunk driver. The doctors told him that the damage to his leg was so severe, that his career in the police was effectively over. But Steve being Steve wouldn't let a little thing like that get in his way. After his recovery he retrained as a detective, which is where I met him for the first time. He wanted to make the world a safer place. To see victims get the justice they deserved, come hell or high water. And he did. The world was better for having him in it, despite some of the odd suit and tie combinations.' Charlie took another breath and blinked away tears.

'Steve wasn't one for fuss, so I'll try to keep the rest of this short. He certainly wouldn't want our final thoughts of him to be sad ones. He'd want us to remember the happier times. The times of laughter and fun. The times that really mattered.' Charlie folded the sodden piece of paper and tucked it into his trouser pocket, next to the order of service taken from the church.

'And now, I'll hand you over to Sergeant Gerald Booker. Thank you.' Charlie exhaled, looked over at Booker and gave him a nod.

His legs shook as he made his way back to Debbie. All his energy had leeched out of him, until nothing remained but a hollow shell.

Goodbye, Steve. I'll miss you.

Charlie shrugged out of his suit jacket and hung it up in the wardrobe, mechanically. His muscles ached; every movement felt like an exertion. He just wanted to sleep. Sleep until it didn't hurt anymore.

Debbie stepped into the bedroom and behind him. 'Would you like a drink?'

He turned to face her, his fingers fumbling with his cufflinks as he tried to remove them. 'No thanks, Debs. Not right now.' He attempted a reassuring smile. Her floral perfume wafted around him, filling his senses. God, she was beautiful. Even with her brown eyes, red-rimmed and blood-shot, and her loose, blonde curls frizzled from the rain.

She stepped in to help him, swatting his hand away from his shirt cuff. She removed the cufflinks and dropped them into his palm. 'How are you holding up?'

He fought the urge to give her the usual reflex response.

'Not great. I miss him. I miss all of them.' It wasn't Shakespeare, but it was a start. He dropped his gaze to her hands. She closed his fist around his cufflinks.

'I know. I do, too.' Her fingers lingered on his for a second, then she pulled away and loosened the knot in his tie.

He dropped his arms as his eyes wandered back to her face. She tugged at his collar—letting the tie fall to the floor—until the button popped open. Her fingers worked the rest of the shirt open, exposing his bare chest.

She trailed one finger over the raised, silver scars on his abdomen. He tensed. Her touch whispered across his skin as she traced the curve of his muscles. He caught her hand gently and stepped in closer. A soft gasp escaped her lips. Her pupils dilated as she looked up at him.

He brushed his lips against hers, his pulse racing. Why was he so nervous? He felt like a schoolboy again, half expecting her to pull away. But then she pressed her body against his and slid her hands up his chest and around his neck, as she hungrily returned the kiss.

Chapter 17

NOTHING BUT DARKNESS.

Suffocating darkness.

But different somehow. Not the infinite void that had surrounded him for nearly a century. Something more. Something tangible.

Finally.

He shifted against some form of enclosure.

Peculiar. He hadn't expected this.

This wasn't what the memories that echoed across the perpetual void of his prison had prepared him for. He pressed his fingers against a smooth, crisp material as he probed, trying to get a sense of the space around him.

He was trapped. *Again.*

With a low growl, he dug his nails into the fabric above him, pulling and tearing at it, until it surrendered to a new surface. Solid. Rigid. Wood. The damp odour of wet earth mingled with a chemical smell he didn't recognise.

Where was he? In all the decades he'd been forced to endure the chattering recollections of the dead, never had there been mention he might emerge into a dark box. Not once. Had they been deceiving him? No. That couldn't be right. They weren't sentient enough for games; they were ripples caught in time, driving him insane with their incessant noise.

He snorted out a breath. An odd lethargy edged its way into his body. Nausea too. Something was wrong.

He twisted as much as the space would allow, braced one hand against the tattered fabric above him and punched up with the other.

Skin split. Bone crunched. Wood cracked.

He punched again; warm blood speckled his face upon impact and a white-hot pain tore through his fist. The mangled hand he would worry about later. Right now, he needed oxygen. One more solid strike and the surface above him fractured. Pieces of it pierced the tender flesh of his upper body. Dense earth piled through the opening, the weight of it crushing his chest until his lungs screamed. He wrenched out the fragments of wood, while dirt filled his mouth and nostrils.

Muscles tense, he re-orientatcd so that he could drive himself upward. He clawed at the shifting soil as it continued to fill the space around him, impeding his efforts. His oxygen-deprived lungs were on fire.

Diverting all remaining strength he dug faster, scooping and kicking his way out of the squeezing earth. With one final heave, he broke through the surface and gulped in a breath of pain and ecstasy.

He dragged the rest of him out into the cool night air, hacked up dirt, and collapsed in a heap, gasping.

This wasn't the way it was supposed to happen. He'd seen the process through their eyes, time and time again.

Studied it until he knew it so well, the memories might as well have been his own. It wasn't like there was anything else for him to do, while imprisoned in that infernal darkness.

The vessel was supposed to have been prepared for him. A prime specimen, honed since childhood, at the peak of its physical condition. But this body... *his* body, had been an inch away from death. Battered, bruised, broken. Worse, it hadn't even been plied with the proper toxins and opiates, to make its mind malleable enough to accept the transition.

The loose, damp dirt shifted under his weight as he curled into a foetal position. He blinked the grit from his eyes. With each biting breath he could smell the dank earth, the trees, the mouldering of lichen, the delicate perfume of flowers—and in the distance, meat. His stomach growled.

He was so hungry. So weak. There wasn't anything left in his reserves. What little energy remained was keeping his body alive. Until his synthesis with the body was complete, he couldn't afford to let it die. There was nothing left to do but wait for its mind to regain consciousness and hope it didn't break under the weight of his presence.

This was his only choice. There was no way he was going back to that dagger. No way would he lose himself again to the madness, until his essence was so faded, he became just another voice in the clamour of vacant memories.

Chapter 18

STEPHEN SAT BOLT UPRIGHT with a strangled gasp. The sensation of his lungs as they filled with air was immediately satisfying, like he'd pulled himself back from the brink of drowning. But he choked on his next breath. Why was his mouth so dry and full of... dirt?

What the hell?

He spat out what he could on the grass and blinked. Grit scratched at his eyes, blurring his vision. He rubbed at them and yowled in pain, jerking his hands back. The knuckles on his right hand were a bloodied mess; bone jutted through tattered flesh. They were also caked in... mud? He examined his cracked nails and the shredded skin on his fingertips. What the hell had happened?

Stephen took a deep breath and allowed his eyes to adjust to the darkness. The last thing he remembered was someone stabbing him. He clawed at his shirt buttons, instantly regretting it when his broken fingers flared with pain.

Wait, shirt buttons? *I wasn't wearing a shirt.*

Someone had dressed him in a suit. *Seriously, what the hell?* No, not a suit. His police uniform. Except it was torn and smeared in wet earth, as if it had been dragged across the ground. Repeatedly.

His head swam as he tried to piece together what had happened. No matter how hard he tried, he couldn't get past the glaring gap in his memory. How much time had he lost? The last place he'd been was inside the caravan. Mickey had plunged a dagger into his chest. Now he was outside. Somewhere.

A quick scan of his surroundings confirmed that he was in a cemetery. Maybe the Boswells had dumped him here, left him for dead.

He worked his fingers under his tie, between his shirt buttons, and felt for the dagger wound. Moonlight spilled over the headstones and monuments in regimented lines around him, casting them as shadows across the glistening silver grass. The skin on his chest was unbroken. Nothing. No gaping hole. No blood. No pain.

Stephen pulled his hand away. He frowned and touched his left cheek where Mickey had slashed his face open. Again, no wound. It was as if it'd never happened. Had he imagined the whole thing? Could the pain medication have caused him to hallucinate his altercation? Was he hallucinating right now?

He prodded at more skin on his face. The scar from the car accident was still there.

Hallucination *would* explain the lack of wounds and the fact that he was sitting alone. In the dark. In a cemetery. On what felt like a soft pile of soggy soil.

Even the ache of his broken fingers and torn nails was subsiding.

He held his hands up and inspected his knuckles under the pale beams of light. The broken flesh was knitting itself back together right before his eyes.

'Holy shit!' Stephen scrambled back, sending out sprays of dirt. He fell on his back and cracked his head against something hard. With a groan, he clutched his throbbing scalp, and turned to see what he had hit. A headstone. He was on someone's freshly laid grave.

He cringed back, realising he had crushed several of the flower arrangements that had been left by friends and relatives of the person just buried. There were mounds of earth everywhere, scattered across the grass, half burying the few flowers he hadn't trampled. Surely this wasn't his doing. All he'd done was stumble and fall. Disrespecting the dead was bad luck.

There was an inscription on the smooth, flecked, blue-pearl granite:

Stephen Richard Anderson
12.04.1946 - 22.09.1984
Much loved Husband and Father.
Your laughter will live forever in our hearts.

'What the...'

Stephen jerked back and shook his head. Then curiosity got the better of him. He pushed onto his knees and crawled up to the headstone, fingers sinking in the soft earth. His hand shook as he reached out and traced the lettering. It was almost a surprise when his skin met the cold, smooth stone. It made it real somehow, like just seeing it wasn't enough. This was *his* grave.

Out of the corner of his eye, he caught sight of a double memorial, just feet from his own. Guilt and grief hit his gut like a physical blow. He struggled to catch his breath. The tributes for his wife and daughter. It suddenly hit him that this was the first time he'd seen their graves. All that was left of them was a plain, granite headstone with their family name etched above the inscriptions. Why hadn't he visited them as soon as he'd left the hospital? Paid his respects? Said a proper goodbye?

His chest tightened. It hadn't been their time to die.

I CAN HELP YOU GET THE JUSTICE THEY DESERVE.

Stephen yelled with fright. He clutched his throbbing head, as he looked around to find the source of the voice.

He hissed a breath through his teeth. 'Who said that?'

Silence.

The voice, high and grating, had sounded so close, but he couldn't see anyone nearby. Yet, he felt like someone was watching him.

Probably just paranoia.

'Is anyone there?' he ventured, just to be sure.

The pain in his head intensified, causing him to retch and vomit what looked to be a mixture of bile and congealed blood onto the soft grave soil.

Curiosity rose up from within him. Sentiments that were not his own battled against his thoughts and feelings.

Fragments of memories flashed through his mind. Skirmishes with Jimmy Barnes in the playground. Joining the police force. Learning that the drunk driver who'd killed his unborn son received nothing more than a fine. Coming home to find his family slaughtered. Mickey Boswell.

Each memory flickered through his brain like a kaleidoscope explosion. He could feel his every experience being analysed, prodded, pulled apart and dismissed. Some lingered for a fraction longer than others, as if they held particular interest, before being discarded for the next.

A scream ripped from Stephen's throat. The weight of the mental onslaught was too much to bear; his body crumpled to the ground.

And then, just as quickly as the probing had begun, it stopped.

A panting Stephen pushed up to his knees and massaged his temples, as the pain ebbed away. The memory of the night he'd found Linda and Bethany remained, as if it had been dredged up from the depths of his nightmares and given pride of place in his grief-riddled consciousness. But grief was not all he felt. Something else fanned the flames of his anger, stoked his desire for revenge. Whatever it was, it was offering him the chance for retribution. For justice.

I CAN HELP YOU.

That voice again. Stephen dropped his arms to his sides as he realised something.

'Wait... you're inside my head?' His mind still reeled from being wrenched apart, then mashed back together again.

SORRY. I'VE HEARD THAT THE FIRST TIME CAN BE UNCOMFORTABLE FOR HUMANS.

Was that supposed to be a joke? Wait... humans?

A chuckle resounded through his skull. NOT LAUGHING? IT'S BEEN A WHILE SINCE I'VE HAD ANYONE TO TALK TO. I MIGHT BE A BIT RUSTY.

'Who are you? *What* are you?'

A... FRIEND.

'Friend?' His thoughts were wispy. It felt like his brain had been scrambled. 'How are you in my head?'

The presence's consciousness shifted, deep within the recesses of his mind. FUNNY STORY. IT SEEMS THAT THE MAN WHO TRIED TO MURDER YOU PUT ME HERE.

'That's funny?' Stephen glanced around, still not convinced there wasn't someone else in the cemetery with him. Just someone's sick idea of a joke. Seeing nothing but the sway of branches as the wind whispered its secrets to the dead, he shuddered and flexed his right hand. The pain from the broken bones was gone.

YES. WHEN HE STABBED YOU, I WAS ABLE TO ENTER YOUR BODY AND SAVE YOUR LIFE.

Stephen frowned, struggling to process the information.

YOU'RE WELCOME BY THE WAY.

'You were... inside the dagger?'

YES. AM I NOT BEING CLEAR? IT HAS BEEN A WHILE, AS I SAID. NINETY-SIX YEARS IN YOUR TIME. IN MY DEFENCE, I LEARNT HOW TO COMMUNICATE FROM YOUR MEMORIES, SO IF YOU DON'T UNDERSTAND ME, IT'S REALLY YOUR FAULT.

'Ninety-six... what are you? Some kind of ghost?'

Amusement that was not Stephen's rolled through him.

Maybe he really *had* died and this was his eternal damnation. Or maybe his mind had snapped and he was caught in some twisted delusion.

A GHOST? VERY NEARLY. BUT NO, I AM NOT A GHOST. I AM... SOMETHING ELSE.

Well, that narrowed things down.

'Okay, not a ghost. So you entered my body—my mind—through the dagger?' Stephen swallowed. Each breath came faster than the last. 'Great, but can you leave now?'

The voice hesitated. NO.

'What do you mean "no"?'

I MEAN *NO*. THAT IS THE RIGHT WORD, IS IT NOT? NO. NOPE. NEGATIVE.

'Why not?' Hysteria tinged his words.

...THINK OF IT AS A ONE-WAY TICKET. A SYMBIOSIS BETWEEN MY ESSENCE AND YOUR BODY.

'You've possessed me?'

I SAVED YOU.

'Like something from the Exorcist? A demon? I've been possessed by a fucking demon?'

EXORCIST? The fronds of its presence probed the edges of his mind. Creeping. Exploring. I SEE. AMUSING. THAT IS MERELY FICTION. I WAS PULLED THROUGH THE FABRIC OF YOUR REALM AND IMPRISONED IN THAT DAGGER. IT WAS NOT MY CHOICE TO END UP INSIDE YOU.

Stephen cringed. The last thing he wanted to think about right now was anyone being "inside" him. 'Do you have to say it like that?'

LIKE WHAT?

'Like... never mind.'

IF IT HELPS FOR YOU TO REFER TO ME AS A DEMON, SO BE IT.

Stephen opened his mouth to ask another question, but doubled over with a grunt, clutching his stomach.

NEED TO EAT, the voice said simply. IF WE DO NOT REPLENISH THE ENERGY I USED TO REPAIR YOUR BODY AND DIG YOU OUT OF THAT HOLE, YOU WILL NOT SURVIVE.

'And what if I don't want to survive?' Stephen panted through the pain in his gut. His eyes flicked back to the memorial of his wife and little girl.

HOW CAN THE DEAD DEMAND JUSTICE WITH NO VOICE? YOUR FAMILY WAS SLAUGHTERED, THEIR KILLERS WALK FREE. IF YOU DO NOTHING THEY WILL GO UNPUNISHED. YOU HAVE EXPERIENCE OF THIS, DO YOU NOT? YOUR UNBORN SON WAS TAKEN FROM

YOU, MURDERED IN THE WOMB. AND WHAT SENTENCE FOR THE MAN RESPONSIBLE FOR HIS DEATH? NOTHING, BUT A TOKEN WERGILD. YOUR JUDICIAL SYSTEM HAS FAILED YOU TIME AND AGAIN. I CAN HELP YOU, BUT YOU NEED TO LET ME.

The demon's last words caught Stephen's attention. The smouldering in his chest ignited. He let out a snarl. 'You can help me find Mickey Boswell?'

I CAN HELP YOU HUNT HIM TO THE ENDS OF THE EARTH. HELP YOU DESTROY HIM. DESTROY ALL OF THEM.

Images of his wife and daughter played before his eyes, bodies broken and bloodied. He nodded.

'Yes. Help me.'

A pressure deep in his skull released so abruptly, his whole body trembled. It made him suck in a breath and drop to all fours. His skin tingled, prickling from his scalp to his toes, like his nerve endings were electrified.

With eyes squeezed shut, he gulped down air until the sensation passed.

Whatever the voice inside his head was, demon or not, it was a part of him now, woven into the very fabric of his being. He couldn't explain the insanity of it, but he was sure.

A sense of calm washed over him. A sense of purpose.

The demon flooded his muscles, seizing control of his body. It rose and eased the weight off his lame leg. A smile split his face. Awareness, like déjà vu, pulsed throughout Stephen's body. With a laugh, that was not entirely his own, he realised he knew exactly where he could find Mickey Boswell. It was as if the fucker was calling out to him, like a beacon in the night.

This was a game-changer.

Chapter 19

MICKEY GRABBED A BARSTOOL and scraped it back with a screech. He sat down on it and glowered at the arrangement of bottles behind the counter.

He hated it here. Hated this sleepy town and sprawling countryside. Hated that everyone knew each other and could, in a heartbeat, single him out as not belonging. Hated that he couldn't understand a word the locals said to him. He'd pointed it out once and they'd laughed at him. Laughed at *him*. Like it was the funniest thing they'd heard all year. They were definitely not the full shilling round these parts.

He'd be glad when his family left this shitehole. It wouldn't be long now before Mammy started up again about how they needed to move. How it wasn't safe.

Mickey sighed heavily.

The bartender, a heavy-set man who waddled as he walked, approached and gave him a friendly nod. 'Be reight, lad,' he said in an uplifting tone.

Mickey squinted at him and shook his head. Was the fella an eejit? What was wrong with these people?

Undeterred, the man pressed on, and a smile tugged at his jowls. 'What can I get ye?'

'I'll have a Fosters.'

The man's face twisted, like he'd smelt something rotten. They were all the fecking same round these parts. As soon as they heard the accent that was it.

Racist.

It was the same everywhere he went. He'd much preferred Kent to Yorkshire. Although, if he was being honest, it'd been the same there too. All he'd needed to do was open his mouth and the atmosphere in the room would change. Instantly.

He couldn't put his finger on why, in this new town, it bothered him now. Maybe it was because there were fewer pubs in the rolling hills than in the bustling towns he was used to. Or maybe it was that after all was said and done, he'd been able to go home and rest his head on his pillow, surrounded by his kin.

But that had been before. Before Anderson. Before his mammy had lost her mind and forced the halting site to up sticks and leg it, abandoning their home in the dead of night, near on a month ago. All because he'd used *that* dagger to stab the prick of a gavver to death with. He'd only been defending Conner's honour.

What *was* it about the jewel encrusted dagger that she loved so much?

When Mammy had found out Niall had pawned it all those months ago, she'd completely lost the plot. It had been brutal, hearing her screech about how it had been in the family for generations, handed down from her mammy, and her mammy before her. How she'd been planning on giving it to her granddaughter when she came of age. That right there told Mickey she was losing it: all her grandbabies were boys.

Niall had near enough caved the filthy-rich, old bloke's head in getting it back after they'd tracked him down. Always did have a bit of a temper, Niall.

Mickey couldn't make sense of it. He'd used Mammy's precious dagger once and she'd blown a fuse. It cut as well as any other knife though. And after all that, she'd told him just to leave the thing stuck in Anderson's chest.

He should've been hailed as a hero for finally ridding them of the scum, but here Mickey was. Alone. A pariah, stuck with what was left of their community that would have him—and even they weren't happy about it. Where in the country the rest of the Boswells had scurried off to Jesus only knew, but good riddance to the lot of them. Ungrateful, superstitious pricks.

He did miss some of his nephews, truth be told. Not all of them, mind; some of them were right little shites. When Mammy had found out that Cici was gone, she'd howled like a cat being skinned. You'd have thought the two of them were related the way she was carrying on.

Superstition. It was a load of bullshit anyway. A cursed dagger? Only a complete moron would buy into that bollocks. Even so, it didn't change the fact that he was in a kip of a pub being gawked at by the locals, while they babbled to one another incoherently.

What had hurt him the most had been the way things had been left with Shona.

The scent of her lavender perfume still lingered in his mind, rousing images of her soft, ivory flesh pressed against his. He still recalled, like it were yesterday, the way her freckled cheeks flushed pink whenever they were together under the sheets.

But the way she looked at him that night in the caravan... like he'd destroyed her world. What was that about?

The last memory he had of her was her clutching Cici and hauling her away from him as if he meant to do her some sort of harm. As if he would; it was a fecking insult.

Now all he had left was Mammy giving him earache about how he'd cursed the lot of them. Doomed them all. Brought Death to their door. He was sure that she'd finally lost her mind, but why the others were going along with it he had no idea.

Mickey scowled up at the bartender, who was still eyeing him distastefully, and pushed a crumpled, blue five-pound note across the bar. The man took one glimpse at the dour-looking Duke of Wellington, snatched it up, and shuffled off to get a pint glass, muttering.

Cold hard cash. Universally spoken, universally understood.

Mickey watched his drink get pulled, albeit begrudgingly, and rubbed at the raised scar on his left hand, between his thumb and index finger. He caught himself, stopped, and peered down at it.

It was a strange thing, shaped like a thin crescent moon, flanked on either side by three uniformly spaced dots. He'd only noticed it a few weeks ago, but couldn't for the life of him remember where he'd got it. Maybe when he'd stuck Anderson with that dagger? He must have cut himself and not noticed. What was weird was that the scar looked like it'd been there for years.

The bartender slammed his pint down in front of him. Cool liquid sloshed over his hand. He brushed away the splatters of lager and bit back an insult. Glaring at the man, he took a long sip.

Just for that, he was going to stay here until his money ran dry; all night if it came to it. He'd have to if he wanted to get sozzled. Alcohol didn't seem to affect him the way it used to. Just a few weeks ago he'd have staggered about, puking his guts up after a night's drinking. But now it might as well be water. The shakes, sweats and permanent sick feeling had gone too—not that he'd missed those. He felt good. Healthy. It was nice.

Yet, he longed for the numbing warmth that a few pints used to give him. The way it made him forget. Forget his mammy's disappointment. Forget his rivalry with Conner. Forget that little girl with her bright-blue eyes. Forget who he was.

He scratched the wooden countertop as he drank, pausing every now and then to flick away the varnish and grime that had accumulated under his fingernail. Fragments of conversation drifted from the people at the back of the pub and caught his attention—well the bits he could make out anyway.

'... some sort of serial killer. Apparently, he takes the eyes from his victims,' one of the men said, in a conspiratorial tone.

Someone choked on their drink. 'Eh? Why would you want someone's eyes? What's he doing with 'em?'

'I dunno. Eating 'em?'

'Give over. I don't buy that for one second.'

'I'm telling you it's true. Working his way up the country for weeks, by the sounds of it. Might not be too long getting here and ye won't be needing 'em glasses,' the first voice insisted, with a touch of indignation.

Mickey shook his head and clucked his tongue. He downed the rest of his pint and gestured to the bartender for a refill, getting a dark look for his efforts.

He *really* hated it here.

Chapter 20

MICKEY SWALLOWED THE LAST dregs of his Fosters and put his glass down on the counter next to the bar towel; something that'd become a bit of a game throughout the evening. The bartender had made a point of pushing one of those cardboard beer mats towards him every now and again. Which he, of course, had ignored.

He shifted to the right, and pulled the last bit of change out of his pocket. Not enough for a packet of crisps let alone a pint. He stood with an exhale, and pocketed the coins. As he turned to leave, he felt the heat of the bartender's glare burning a hole in his back.

A smirk spread across his face as he decided he would make this his regular watering hole. Well, until Mammy moved them on again. It'd be rude not to, wouldn't it? Especially after the bartender had given him such dedicated service all night.

'Night, fellas,' he called over his shoulder, before the door swung shut and cut off the unhappy mutters of the locals. Yes, he'd definitely be coming back here again.

Still grinning to himself, he took the packet of Silk Cut from his pocket and probed inside. Empty. *Typical.*

The smile slid from his face; he crumpled the pack and tossed it on the ground.

Time to call it a night.

Another night ahead of Mammy bending his ear about that fecking dagger. What he wouldn't give to be drunk or high right now. Or even just to be able to enjoy a fag in peace. Was that too much to ask?

His heavy footsteps echoed as he walked. He was so absorbed in his own thoughts that he nearly missed another sound. A second set of footsteps. Had the bartender sent someone after him to rough him up a bit? What were those bumpkins saying about a serial killer?

Calm down, Mickey. You're getting spooked over nothing. Still...

Mickey ducked down the next alley and backed up against the rough, stone wall, concealing himself in the shadows. If someone was following him, he wasn't about to lose his advantage.

Come on then, you fecker.

The footsteps grew louder. Mickey tensed.

Seconds later a man, bathed in the orange glow of the street lights, walked past the entrance to the alley. He appeared oblivious to the fact that Mickey was even there.

Mickey chuckled. He'd listened to his mammy blather on about that ridiculous curse for far too long. It was enough to make anyone paranoid. He'd just got caught up in the heat of the moment, that's all. What with it being dark, in a place he didn't know, and the yokels carrying on about a murderer on the loose. It'd play tricks on anyone's mind, wouldn't it? Anyway, it wasn't like he was hiding. He had to go down this alleyway regardless; it was the quickest route back to the caravans. No, definitely not hiding.

Mickey shook his head and turned into the darkness. He was just being a moron, jumping at shadows.

A man blocked his way. A high-pitched squeal escaped Mickey. He stumbled backwards, managing to right himself with a clumsy hand on the wall.

'Shite.' He cleared his throat and lowered his voice an octave. 'I didn't see you standing there.'

The figure, his features lost to Mickey in the darkness, stood motionless before him. The man's rasping breath penetrated the space between them. A strong earthy smell filled the air, tinged with something decaying and eyewatering.

'Er...' Mickey took another few steps back. His bravado gave way to the knot twisting his stomach. Something deep within screamed at him to run. The only thing grounding him was the burning sensation in his left hand, right where his strange scar was. He must've grazed it when he grabbed the wall.

'Look fella, you may think this is funny, but it ain't.' He tried to keep his voice steady, as he slipped his hand into his jeans pocket where he kept his switchblade.

'Funny?' The man's voice was high and jarring, yet oddly familiar. He mouthed the word, like he was tasting it. 'Funny...'

And then the man laughed. A coarse, grating sound that set Mickey's teeth on edge and turned his bowels to water.

Manic laughter aside, this felt wrong, Mickey pulled the blade out of his pocket. It was probably a good thing that he wasn't sozzled, otherwise he would definitely be on the arse-end of a beating tonight.

The man's laughter died away. He cocked his head to the side, not moving. Light glinted off something on his chest. Several somethings. Metal buttons?

The stranger noticed the attention and made an amused sound, before taking a step to the side. There was enough ambient glow from the streetlights for Mickey to make out his face.

Mickey choked on a gasp. *No. No, it can't be.*

'Anderson?' It looked just like him, but it couldn't be. Anderson was dead. What was happening?

Whoever it was wore one of those gavver uniforms. Except it was a mess. Sections of the fabric hung open, revealing a stained and tattered shirt underneath. And the stench... It made him want to gag.

Maybe it wasn't Anderson. He'd never seen him in a uniform before—only a suit. In any case, he'd stuck Anderson good. There was no way he could have survived.

Mickey shuddered. It definitely looked like the prick who'd ruined his life...

The man laughed again, a shrill and soulless sound.

Without missing a beat, Mickey thumbed the button on the knife and lunged forward, as the blade sprang open. The force of the impact reverberated up his arm when the blade sunk into the scum's chest and came to an abrupt halt. Mickey took a step back and stared. The gavver just stood there, still cackling at the top of his lungs.

This close, it definitely looked like Anderson. He had those same freakishly blue eyes. Mickey would recognise those eyes anywhere. They haunted him every night.

Shite.

'I'll give you something to laugh about,' Anderson drawled. The familiar words tickled Mickey's mind. Where had he heard them before?

Anderson pulled the knife from his chest. The frenzied grin never left his face.

Mickey recoiled. Rather than attack, the psycho just stood there studying the blade in his hand. Brittle seconds passed, then the gavver looked up and lifted the weapon to his own face.

What the feck is he up to?

In one swift movement, he slashed the blade down his cheek, until it had cut cleanly through the edge of his lip, recreating a sick parody of the night in the caravan. He repeated the process on the other side. Blood gushed from his grotesquely exaggerated grin. He dropped the knife; it clattered to the ground.

Jesus! He's mutilated himself.

The manic laughter started again, bubbling and wet.

Mickey retched, spraying bile and Fosters across the ground. He turned to run but was tackled from behind.

He hit the ground. Hard.

White-hot pain flared in his chcst. Had he cracked a rib? He must have torn the skin on his hand too, because the burning where the scar marred his flesh was near enough as painful as his ribcage.

Mickey wanted to scream, wanted to fight, but Anderson's weight pressed him into the concrete, squeezed the air from his lungs. His heart hammered so hard he thought it might explode. He could barely breathe.

Something warm trickled down the back of his neck when Anderson's breath brushed his skin. Realising it was the gavver's blood, Mickey dry heaved.

Fuck. I'm going to die. I'm going to die.

He closed his eyes. This was it.

Chapter 21

AH.

Stephen felt the demon within him become impotent. His own confusion overrode its heady mix of bloodlust and loathing, allowing Stephen to regain control of his body. He pushed himself up slightly as he straddled Mickey, keeping his weight firm on his back.

"*Ah*"? The rush of exhilaration he'd felt tackling Mickey to the ground had been snuffed out; the pain and noise in his brain erupted with a rising howl. *What do you mean "ah"?* It was all Stephen could manage beneath the incessant pulsating sound in his head.

According to the demon the pulse was the lure of the sigils—symbols imbued by the power of the dagger that marked the Boswells for the murdering delinquents they were. Everyone in Mickey's bloodline had one now, apparently, ever since Stephen had allowed the demon to bond with his consciousness. Handy for him. They could run but not hide. And he was going to find them. *All* of them.

He'd heard the call that night in the cemetery, felt it guiding him towards the Boswells, giving him an overwhelming compulsion to hunt. Imparting an insatiable need that wrenched at his core and threatened to tear him apart from the inside out. It was like they were crying out to him. Their heartbeats were jeering insults drumming against the edges of his sanity, pounding in time with the force that was driving him to find them. Fighting the call was like fighting the urge to breathe—painful, maddening and entirely pointless. Only when their last gasp had choked from their lungs, only when the light in their eyes had gone out would his need be satiated. Only then would the clamour to hunt settle. For a while at least.

Once or twice it had become so all-consuming he'd lost himself to it completely, no longer able to recognise where he ended and the demon began. He'd come into the moment, drenched in blood and surrounded by bodies, only to find that he had no memory of what had just occurred.

But they deserved it. They'd taken his family from him; it would be only fair to return the favour.

Mickey though, Mickey was special. Even the demon had an interest in hunting him down; Stephen had felt its mounting excitement each day they drew closer to the fucker.

The demon finally answered him. I MEAN, AH, WE APPEAR TO HAVE A PROBLEM.

'No shit.' The words dribbled from the jagged edges of Stephen's ruined mouth. He switched to inner thought. *Why did you do this to my face?* He shifted position, ignoring Mickey's grunt of protest, and brought a hand to his cheek. Blood seeped through his mangled flesh to coat his fingers.

IT'S POETIC, YOU SEE. HE CUT YOU IN THE SAME WAY—I JUST EVENED IT OUT A LITTLE... BUT YOU'RE OWNING THE LOOK. SENDS A MESSAGE.

Owning it? Stephen shook his head at the depraved rationale and took a few more seconds to adjust to being back in the driver's seat. His damp and sticky uniform was becoming more uncomfortable, but at least his injuries weren't bothering him. As if in response to his thoughts, the bleeding slowed to a stop.

Had *he* done that? He still wasn't used to the new capabilities of his body.

He snatched at Mickey's hand, wrenched it up, and peered down at the strange scar on it—the sigil. The bastard's loud, strangled whimpers hardly registered above the hammering inside his skull as he focused on the pale, raised skin. Six dots bisected by a convex line. It looked like it'd been there for years; other than the unusual pattern, it didn't appear to be special. But Stephen knew better.

He'd noticed similar sigils on some of the other Boswells. Always on the left hand, between the thumb and index finger. But none like this. 'What does it mean?'

THIS SIGIL IS DIFFERENT. I'M NOT SURE.

He adjusted position when Mickey tried to wriggle free. A suffocated groan was his reply when Stephen applied more pressure to the man's back. The squirming stopped.

'Not sure?' he replied, using his voice. His injuries no longer impeded his speech. 'Aren't you the expert? Didn't your voices mention anything about another sigil?'

The demon's frustration flooded through their mental connection. It had no first-hand experience of inhabiting a host body. Its understanding of the 'human realm', as it put it, had been based entirely upon the residual memories of the dagger's previous occupants—long dead.

NO. THEY DID NOT. CLEARLY. LET ME CONCENTRATE.

Without warning, the scar on Mickey's hand flared with an orange glow. Stephen blinked. He could feel a raw power emanating from it. It pulsed like the beating of a heart. No, *exactly* like the beating of a heart. Mickey's. It called out like a siren's song promising gratification, but there was something else there, too. An invisible force that drove him back—stopping him before he could act. The chaos of it made his head swim, but one thing was clear. Whatever it was, it was preventing the pair from killing Mickey Boswell.

The glow faded.

IT WOULD APPEAR THAT HE'S UNDER THE DAGGER'S PROTECTION.

'*What?*' The question exploded from Stephen's mouth. He'd travelled the length of the country to hunt down the man who'd stood by and watched Linda and Bethany be slaughtered. And now there was nothing he could do about it?

He wanted justice, damn it. Justice for his wife and daughter. 'How can he be under its protection? He's got a sigil. It led us here.'

I DON'T KNOW. THE MEMORIES HAVE NEVER EXPOSED ME TO THIS PARTICULAR SIGIL. AS FAR AS I CAN TELL, THIS HASN'T HAPPENED BEFORE. I CAN'T KILL HIM.

A low growl escaped Stephen's lips. Mickey flinched underneath his weight, still unable to move.

In the weeks since the demon had taken up residence inside his mind, it had not failed in its promise to him. Boswell after Boswell had been slaughtered. Age or gender didn't matter. It had wreaked bloody retribution on them all. So what in the hell was happening now? Why couldn't they kill this one?

The demon bristled. Its aggravation seeped into Stephen's mind.

'You said you'd help me. You said you could give me what I wanted. You lied to me.' Stephen snarled through the mess of his ruined mouth.

He was answered with a wave of outrage.

Mickey gasped. 'I don't know what you're talking about.' He had an edge to his voice that said he was close to breaking point. He made another weak attempt to squirm free.

A gut-wrenching howl tore from Stephen's throat. He grabbed a fistful of Mickey's hair, pulled his head back, and then smashed it against the pavement with a loud crack. 'Shut up. I'm not talking to you.'

I CAN'T KILL HIM.

A sudden thought, too obscure for Stephen to comprehend, flashed through his mind. But the emotion behind it was unmistakable. Excitement. Genuine excitement.

BUT *YOU* CAN. IT'S ONLY RIGHT THAT HE DIES BY YOUR HAND. YOU WILL NOT HAVE LONG.

Not have long? What did that mean?

The demon relinquished the bond and withdrew into the depths of Stephen's mind. Stephen quivered when it lingered in his consciousness, but only as a spectator. It was like finally being able to breathe again. The pulsing lure of the sigil had stilled, releasing the pressure inside his skull.

Mickey writhed beneath him, threatening to throw him off balance. The Traveller babbled something in his thick accent, the words too fast to comprehend. A prayer maybe? Stephen could barely process the sound. His limbs were leaden, like the energy had been sucked out of every fibre of his being.

It was as if his senses had been dampened. The night's darkness was oppressive, swallowing details that had been obvious just seconds ago. He widened his eyes and blinked in an effort to see more, but it made no difference. Everything he saw was a watered-down version of before.

The dull ache in his leg returned with a vengeance. Stephen's chest was on fire. He clamped one hand on the back of Mickey's neck—as hard as his waning strength would allow—and pressed the other against his own bloody shirt, where his flesh stung. It came away wet.

I TOLD YOU. YOU DON'T HAVE LONG.

Mickey thrashed in earnest, as if he'd sensed the sudden dip in energy—his one chance at escape.

If Stephen wasn't careful, this would turn into a full-blown punch-up. *And I feel like I'm about to drop dead at any moment.*

YOU ARE. HURRY UP AND KILL HIM.

Stephen's eyes darted as he struggled to keep Mickey pinned beneath him. He caught sight of the switchblade that the demon had dropped and grimaced. If he had any chance of getting to it, he'd have to let go of Mickey.

With a grunt, he drove Mickey's face into the ground, lunged back and off the Traveller, and grappled for the weapon.

Mickey scrambled to his feet. An errant foot caught Stephen's ankle. He hit the ground with an *oof* as the air left his lungs.

Stephen grappled for the blade, his face set in a rictus snarl. He pushed himself up, ignoring the dirt and shards of broken glass digging into his palms.

Mickey bolted away down the alley.

HE'S GETTING AWAY. HURRY!

Stephen clenched his jaw, biting back a heated reply. He mustered his remaining strength and sprinted after Mickey as fast as his gammy leg would allow. The sound of his own footsteps hammered in his ears. Sweat dripped from his forehead.

Mickey stopped dead at the entrance to the alleyway. He staggered back, as if met by an invisible force. Something on the ground had caught his attention. He shook his head and looked away from whatever it was.

Stephen closed the distance between them. He twisted at the last second and rammed his shoulder into Mickey's side. The two men collided, falling over each other out of the alley and under the wash of the streetlights. Stephen recovered first, rolled to his knees, and raised the switchblade into the air. He stuck it into Mickey's chest.

Droplets of blood sprayed off the knife in a parabola when Stephen wrenched it free and brought it down again. And again. And again. His clenched fist slipped down the handle, made slick with the force of each blow. His palm juddered over the diminutive guard and down the exposed blade, which sliced it open.

Panting hard, Stephen lowered his arm. His muscles quivered as the adrenaline ebbed away. He was covered in blood. There was no way of telling which was his and which was Mickey's. Did it even matter?

Mickey lay motionless, his mouth hung open in a silent scream. Under the artificial lighting, his gore-soaked T-shirt looked black.

Justice was done. He'd finally avenged Linda and Bethany, and yet he felt... empty. And tired. So tired.

His eyes flickered shut as his body swayed. The switchblade slipped from his grasp.

YOU'RE DYING. LET ME HELP YOU.

Maybe he should just slip into oblivion. Let the pain carry him away.

A sudden rising anxiety radiated through him.

AISLING BOSWELL SENT HER SONS TO KILL YOU. TO KILL YOUR FAMILY. SHE TOLD THEM WHERE TO FIND YOU. SENT THEM TO YOUR HOME. ARE YOU GOING TO JUST LET HER GET AWAY WITH IT?

A spark of anger flashed through the fog of his dying mind. He wasn't ready to go. 'Help me.'

His strength gave out and he collapsed sideways. The pavement gave his face a cold, hard smack. He blinked through the pain. The faintest glint of steel caught his eye amid the spots in his vision. How did the switchblade get over there?

No. Not the switchblade. The dagger. That's what Mickey had been staring at.

A roar burst from his ruined mouth as the demon surged forward. Its tendrils gouged into his consciousness to re-establish their bond. Stephen's body convulsed with the same surge of power he'd felt that night in the cemetery. The energy danced across his skin. His muscles trembled, leaving him gasping for air.

WE SURVIVED. WELL DONE. THOUGHT YOU WEREN'T GOING TO MAKE IT FOR A SECOND THERE.

Stephen untangled himself from Mickey's corpse and climbed to his feet. Through a gaping hole in his shirt, he pressed his fingers to his chest. Although his skin was still damp with blood, the wound was already healing. Even the slashed skin on his palm, where the switchblade had split his flesh, was weaving itself back together.

With a roll of his shoulders, he glanced around to see if the fight had attracted any unwanted attention. Satisfied it hadn't, he refocused on Mickey.

'What happened?' he asked the demon.

THE DAGGER WAS PROTECTING HIM. HE INVOKED THE BLOOD DEBT THE NIGHT HE STABBED YOU, CLAIMING DOMINION OVER IT.

'Why is it here?' Stephen nudged the dagger with the tip of his boot. The second he did intense pain flared inside his head. He clutched it. A groan clawed up his throat; he tried not to vomit over his shoes.

DON'T TOUCH IT! The demon coursed into his muscles and forced him to take a step backwards. The moment his contact with the dagger broke the agony receded. The demon withdrew its hold on his body.

Shit.

THE DAGGER IS HERE BECAUSE IT ALWAYS RETURNS TO ITS MASTER WHEN SUMMONED.

Summoned? Mickey didn't summon it.

THE CONNECTION BETWEEN THE DAGGER AND ITS MASTER TRANSCENDS THE NEED FOR MERE WORDS. THE BOND IS PHYSICAL, EMOTIONAL. It paused, before adding with a touch of amusement, MAGICAL.

Stephen eyed it and sunk back into the shadows. 'What happened to me? I nearly died.'

BUT YOU DIDN'T.

'That's not...' Stephen took a breath. 'Why did I nearly die?'

I HAD TO DISRUPT OUR CONNECTION SO THAT YOU COULD SLAY THE BOSWELL MALE, BUT THAT MEANT RETURNING YOU TO THE STATE YOU WERE IN THE NIGHT YOU WERE STABBED. I AM PHYSICALLY UNABLE TO HARM ANY UNDER THE DAGGER'S PROTECTION, PREVENTED FROM BREAKING THE OBLIGATIONS OF MY SERVICE BY THE MAGIC THAT BINDS MY ESSENCE TO IT. IT HAD TO BE YOU THAT KILLED HIM. YOU ALONE. IT WAS THE ONLY WAY.

'You didn't think to warn me?'

I DID WARN YOU. I TOLD YOU THAT YOU DIDN'T HAVE LONG.

'I didn't think you were being literal.'

A cramp in Stephen's gut stole the air from his lungs. HUNGRY.

Oh God. He hated this part. The nausea he felt was met with glee; the demon poured itself into his body. There was that excitement again.

Saliva filled Stephen's mouth. His tongue, under the demon's control, traced the soft and ragged edges of his maimed cheeks. His mangled face broke into a grin.

An unbidden chuckle bubbled from his lips as he hunkered down next to Mickey's corpse. It raked Stephen's hand over the dead man's chest and over his face, leaving little tracks of blood wherever his fingertips landed. His palm thumped against the dead Traveller's forehead.

The wind eddied around them with a rasping shriek, whipping up dust, grit, glass—anything it could claw free—into a lashing cyclone that could scour the flesh from bone. The demon threw back Stephen's head, eyes rolling up in the ecstasy of the moment, and trembled. Raw energy flooded through Stephen, filling him with an intoxicating rush of euphoria. Energising, regenerating, invigorating.

The demon released his grip on the corpse and gasped. The rattling squall scattered its haul across the ground in a billowing flurry.

Stephen didn't mind the rush of exhilaration that came from consuming a life force. In fact, he enjoyed it just as much as the demon. It was what came next that he despised. There was no point trying to fight it. Yes, the demon needed to eat, but the essence of its—of *their* still-warm victims should have been sufficient to meet that appetite.

The demon never stopped there.

A high squeal of delight left his lips as it plunged his thumb and two fingers into Mickey's eye socket. Tissue ripped. There was a soft splat when it wrenched the eyeball and optic nerve out.

In one quick movement, it clamped the eyeball between Stephen's teeth. A warm spurt of pulp followed. Ooze dribbled out of the lacerations in his cheek and down his jaw as it chewed. The squelching was broken only by a slight crunching sound when it bit through the cornea. The congealed lump slid down Stephen's throat.

The demon looked at the second eyeball. Bile churned in Stephen's stomach.

Do you have to?

There was another wet tearing sound as it used Stephen's hand to rip the second eyeball from Mickey's skull, and devoured it. Stephen was forced to swallow the last mucoid mouthful as the demon braced itself for what came next. Memories from the last few days played across the backdrop of his mind. Whether it was something to do with the dagger's magic or the demon itself, Stephen didn't know, but it happened every time he ate the eyes of their victims.

Half a dozen caravans were hauled up in a back road, hitched to vehicles that varied in colour as much as condition. Discarded butane and propane cylinders were abandoned among wood piles and debris.

Aisling Boswell looked older and frailer than she had just weeks ago, the skin beneath her eyes sunken and paper-thin. She was ranting. Raving. Jabbing a finger in accusation and chain-smoking when she wasn't hacking up her guts.

Mickey propping up the bar while nursing a pint of Fosters and getting the stink eye from a stout bartender.

And underpinning it all, rooted deeper than Mickey's self-pity, confusion and frustration, was an uncompromising guilt. Guilt over the death of a little girl with shocking blue eyes who never had the chance to grow up.

Stephen's anger erupted.

Guilt didn't change the fact that Mickey had done nothing while Stephen's wife and daughter bled out, terrified and alone.

The demon straightened and slammed his fist into the wall. Brick exploded and fragments scattered across the ground. It spat out a strange assortment of sounds that Stephen didn't recognise as a language.

But there was something else buried beneath the echoed fury, something the demon was attempting to conceal. Disappointment? That didn't make sense. It had been just as eager to find Mickey as he was.

I don't understand?

I... NOTHING. IT DOESN'T MATTER. The demon inhaled. WHY DOES MICKEY SMELL LIKE FLOWERS?

The demon was keeping something from him. Stephen let it go for now. *I think he's wearing perfume?*

YOU ARE AN ODD SPECIES.

A familiar scent rose above the stench of Mickey's blood and bile: the scent of another Boswell. A grin tugged at the devastated flesh on Stephen's cheeks. The demon let out a shrill cackle that echoed deep into the night, and homed in on the pulsing call of the sigils that resonated through his body.

Without a second glance it stepped over Mickey's corpse—giving the dagger a wide berth—and headed in the direction of the caravans they'd seen in the dead man's memories.

Towards Aisling Boswell.

Chapter 22

CHARLIE TOOK ONE LAST drag on his cigarette, flicked the butt to the ground and crushed it under his heel. He unlocked his front door. Debbie had been a bit prickly about him smoking inside the house since she'd quit; apparently the smell turned her stomach. He exhaled the last of the smoke out the side of his mouth and shook his head.

While he admired her commitment, he hadn't enjoyed the mood swings that came with her nicotine cravings. It was like living with Jekyll and Hyde, but infinitely more passive-aggressive.

There had been more than a few passing comments about Charlie giving up too, but he needed a way to unwind, what with the recent cases that he'd been involved in.

He picked up the trampled butt and entered the house, closing the front door softly behind him. At least with Debbie having kicked the habit, he'd have fewer to clean up.

He loosened his tie, unbuttoned his shirt collar and sighed.

I need a nightcap.

A lot of disturbing shit had been happening in the month since they'd buried Stephen. Someone—or potentially more than one someone—had been murdering Travellers, and by all accounts, were enjoying themselves in the process. Numerous bodies had been mutilated, their eyeballs removed. Whether it was a feud gone wrong or just some sicko was still to be determined. They'd even gone after the children. It made him nauseous to think about it. And it had all started on his watch.

He shuddered, placed his keys in the dish on the telephone table, and headed towards the kitchen.

Granted, throughout his career, he'd seen things that would haunt him until the day he died, humanity at its lowest, but this case was going for gold. A true contender in the fucked up Olympics.

To make matters worse an external agency had become involved, stepping on everyone's toes. He'd heard some of the detectives on the murder squad fuming about it in passing. Questioning Booker about it hadn't shed light on their involvement either. Turned out the sergeant was also in the dark. Apparently, it was above his pay grade.

Charlie walked into the kitchen, flicked on the lights, and disposed of the cigarette butt.

It was at times like these that he missed Steve more than ever. If he'd still been alive, they'd have bounced theories off one another. This wasn't a case he wanted to discuss with Debbie; he didn't want to share the grim details. They didn't both need to lose sleep over it.

His shoulders sagged.

I should really go and visit Linda and Bethany's graves again soon. It's been a while.

He grabbed a crystal glass from the cupboard, opened a bottle of Lagavulin single malt scotch and poured himself a generous two fingers. He inhaled; the deep, smoky scent hit him. He swallowed it in one mouthful. The full-bodied, spiced-oak flavour lingered on his palate, while the familiar warmth worked its way down his throat.

God man, you're becoming a walking cliché.

A floorboard creaked above him. It was unlike Debbie to be up this late; probably the nicotine withdrawal. He'd heard it could cause insomnia.

Cold turkey—the gift that keeps on giving.

He washed the glass, dried it with a tea towel and put it back in the exact spot it had been in the cupboard. Flipping the kitchen lights back off, he made his way upstairs.

He stepped into the bedroom. Debbie, wearing a black-satin nightgown, stood with her back to him in the doorway of their en suite.

Steeling himself against her anger about the smell of booze and cigarettes, he cleared his throat. 'Everything okay, Debs?'

Her shoulders shook. 'Erm... Debs? Are you alright?'

She turned to him, her face ashen. Her brown eyes shimmered with tears. She hugged herself and sobbed.

God, please let this just be another mood swing. I'm not sure I can take any more bad news.

He rushed over and took her in his arms. She melted against him; her body trembled as she wept. Not sure what else he could do, he rubbed her back, in what he hoped was a comforting gesture.

'Be a man'. That's what his father had always told him as a boy, and if words couldn't get the point across then his belt certainly clarified things. Charlie had quickly learnt to bury his feelings deep down, if only to protect himself from his father's drunken rages. The physical scars he could cope with, but the fact he now lacked the emotional sensitivity to comfort his wife was more than he could bear.

That bastard really did a number on me.

He nuzzled his face in Debbie's hair and pulled himself back into the present. Wallowing in his memories wouldn't do either of them any good. His brow furrowed when something on the bathroom vanity unit caught his attention. He straightened and tilted his head to get a better look.

'Debbie? What's that?'

She stiffened in his arms. 'It's a home pregnancy test,' she said, her muffled voice catching. She pulled back and looked him in the eyes. 'I'm pregnant. I'll need to go to the doctor to be sure, but it's positive.'

The words sunk in. A grin spread across Charlie's face. They were having a baby? They were having a baby! He beamed down at Debbie, who sobbed even harder and nestled into his chest again.

No wonder she'd been having so many mood swings. How could he have missed it? Some detective he was, he couldn't even see what was right under his nose.

He pulled her tight against him as her body shook, tears soaking his shirt.

He'd heard that pregnancy could play havoc with a woman's hormones. *So the inconsolable crying is a perfectly normal reaction, right?*

Chapter 23

SOMEONE SCREAMED ON A landing above Stephen. Just another noise that was swallowed by the prison alarm bell blaring through the speaker system.

He watched the chaos playing out in every wing of the lower floor. His vantage point gave him a perfect view of the pandemonium. Each block branched from the prison's centre where he stood. A towering walkway rose up and around him, its bare, metal skeleton ascending floor by floor, encircling its core, like the ribs of a long-dead gargantuan beast.

Stephen looked up, to watch a handful of inmates wrestle a prison officer through a rupture in the wire mesh barrier and over the top of the metal railings. The man's shriek of terror was cut short when his head struck the floor. His navy, peaked cap landed a few feet from his motionless body.

The coppery tang of blood hung heavy in the air around them, mingling with the stench of sweat, shit and, somewhere from the depths of C wing, smoke. The fire would spread soon, choking the dated, Victorian corridors, the corpses of the men still locked in their cells adding to its fuel.

It hadn't taken long for the prison to descend into anarchy. Any prison officers who weren't unlucky enough to be swept up in the surge of rioting convicts had fled. Stephen couldn't blame them; severe overcrowding had stacked the odds against them—they didn't stand a fighting chance. Keys had been stolen, cells opened, inmates set free.

But not in C wing. Not where the worst of the sex offenders and child abusers were held.

The thought of the flesh bubbling on their bones made Stephen smile; the action tore at the threads holding his mangled cheeks together. As a detective, the cases involving children had haunted him the most.

Stephen lowered his gaze back to the man, writhing beneath his grip.

'Niall Boswell,' he said. 'You certainly put up more of a fight than your brother, Dermot. And Mickey come to think of it. But listen to me jabbering... I could go on and on.' He waved his free hand at nothing in particular, as if they were just having a friendly catch-up.

Niall blinked up at him. Blood trickled from a gash on his forehead that had turned his brown fringe into dark clumps. He looked unable to support himself—it might have had something to do with the ruptured kidney or broken ankle, but who could say? Stephen bore the brunt of his weight. It had been a long day for everyone. Niall really *had* put up a good fight, even managed to land a few half-decent blows. How was Niall supposed to know that Stephen's body could regenerate faster than he could throw a punch?

Stephen felt the hammering of the man's heart through the blue-pinstripe shirt bunched in his fist. It was the same pounding rhythm that throbbed inside his head, jarring at the remnants of his sanity.

'There's nothing you can do to me that the screws ain't already tried,' Niall spat out.

Was it the hitch in his voice that betrayed his fear? Or the way he stared wide-eyed at the jagged wounds around Stephen's ruined mouth? His chestnut-coloured eyes held a grim acceptance; his time was up.

Stephen laughed. The discordant sound clashed with the piercing wail of the alarm. 'Ah, thank you. I needed that. It's been a few days since I've had a good giggle.'

Another inmate jogged past, paused to gawk at them, and darted up one of the curving metal staircases to the next landing.

With one last chuckle, Stephen dropped Niall to the ground. He let out a huff of pain. Before the man could flinch, Stephen drove his foot down onto Niall's skull. Bone crunched, flesh burst, brain matter squelched out from under his heel.

The pulsing in his head settled into a dull, distant throb. The demon squirmed into his muscles, took a breath, and shuddered. It squatted next to the corpse, slid his fingers through Niall's pulp-spattered hair and yanked his head back.

URGH. DISGUSTING.

What?

THERE'S DIRT ON HIS EYE.

Are you serious? You're about to eat his eyeballs and you're worried about a little dirt?

IT'S NOT HYGIENIC. THIS FLOOR IS FILTHY.

You eat *eyeballs.*

DO I COMMENT WHEN YOU EAT BURGERS FROM THOSE VANS?

That's different.

HARDLY. AT LEAST I KNOW WHAT I'M EATING.

So do I. Beef.

THAT'S FUNNY. Genuine amusement rolled through their bond.

...What? No, really. What's in those burgers?

The demon ignored his growing sense of unease and smirked. It pressed his fingers into the soft tissue surrounding Niall's left eye and jerked it free with a wet snap. Grimacing, it cleaned the organ on his sleeve, gave it one last inspection and dropped it into Stephen's mouth.

Stephen's jaw chewed while the demon popped the right eye out.

Niall's memories came to him. Walking in slow circles around the exercise yard in the segregation block. Supervised by a bored prison officer, who was more interested in smoothing down the lapels of his fitted, navy jacket than he was in actually watching them.

Lying awake at night in a cell thinking about Cici, wondering if he'd get to see her again.

Remembering the expression on the face of the old man he'd beaten near to death, trying to get back the dagger Niall had pawned. How the prick's outrage, not fear, had sent a chill down his spine, and Niall hitting the man all the harder for it.

A swell of anger rose in Stephen's gut as Niall's recollections faded. Seeing Archibald Morgan's assault first-hand, experiencing it as if he had delivered the jaw-breaking blows, made his blood boil.

Dust whirled in the air around him when the demon pressed his hand against what remained of Niall's pulverised head. The energy hit him as the demon drew it in, like a jolt of lightning, making his muscles tense and quiver simultaneously. The pure rapture of vitality, life force, spirit... whatever it was called, was exhilarating. A taste of the power of creation.

And then it was over. The demon receded into the back of his mind, allowing Stephen to take control of his body once more.

Stephen released his hold and stood, wiping the bloody chunks from his hand.

The air stilled, and the smoke became more obvious. It crept its way towards the heart of the prison, like a dark, stalking shadow. The stench of it made him cough—a sulphurous mix of methane, copper and meat, thick enough to taste.

TIME TO LEAVE?

Wait. Stephen gritted his teeth against the persistent wail of the alarm and turned to study the dead prison officer lying a few feet away. Part of him hated himself for even thinking it, but he was still wearing the same clothes he'd been buried in—what remained of them anyway.

IT'S NOT LIKE HE NEEDS THEM ANYMORE.

That much was true.

He walked towards the body and shrugged out of the tattered shreds of his filth-encrusted police uniform. The fire would take it soon enough. That part of his life was over.

While he dressed, three more inmates scurried past. If they thought finding a half-naked man with a slashed-up face, surrounded by bodies and outfitting himself in a dead screw's uniform was odd, they didn't stop to point it out.

Stephen rolled his shoulders, testing the give on the jacket, and nodded to himself. It wasn't the best fit, but it was better than his old clothes. He flicked dirt from one of the epaulets and turned towards the heavy, white, barred iron door to his right.

THIS PLACE IS FULL OF CRIMINALS.

It's a prison. That's generally the idea.

HUNDREDS OF MEN, POSSIBLY OVER A THOUSAND, ALL A DRAIN ON SOCIETY. FED, DRESSED, HOUSED AT THE EXPENSE OF THE LAW-ABIDING PUBLIC.

What's your point?

WHY DON'T WE DO SOMETHING TO ADDRESS THAT?

We're not killing everyone here.

WHY NOT?

Stephen yanked on the door, ignoring the demon inside his head.

Locked.

The demon had a point though. Murderers, rapists, terrorists, kidnappers, drug dealers and worse, all threats to the public and all under one roof. Would it be so bad if they didn't make it?

He gripped the iron bars and gave them a shake. *They've been given their sentences.*

LIKE THE DRUNK WHO CRIPPLED YOU AND KILLED YOUR SON?

Stephen growled, deep in the back of his throat. It wasn't until he felt the warm trickle of blood that he realised he'd crushed the bars, twisting the metal into a contorted diamond shape.

With a new breath, he ripped the door from its hinges and launched it through the air. It smashed against the tiled concrete with a clatter, a sound that rose above the alarm.

TEMPER, TEMPER.

We're leaving.

SO... THAT'S A NO TO THE KILLING?

That's a no to the killing. The demon's disappointment seeped into him. Was it the hunt or the kill that gave it the most pleasure? Either way, it was like an addict, always itching for one more taste.

SHAME. STILL, THERE ARE MORE BOSWELLS TO FIND.

The steady throb in the back of his mind was intensifying. In days, hours, maybe even minutes, it would launch a full-scale assault on his ability to reason. Pummel away at his rationality, until he had no choice but to follow its call or be driven senseless.

The lighting dimmed to a wan orange as Stephen retraced his steps back through F wing. The broken remains of furniture had been piled into its centre by inmates. Bed frames, mattresses, chairs and anything else that could be moved had been added to the mound. Here and there the wreckage served as blockades, to prevent doors from being opened or locked. He skirted around it all and pressed forward until he reached the exercise yard.

The crisp, night air filled his lungs. He looked up at the outer prison walls, at least twenty feet tall, lined along the top with mesh fencing that angled inward sharply. If that wasn't deterrent enough, it was finished with some serious rolls of barbed wire.

'Thank God,' a voice wheezed. It belonged to a grey-haired prison officer who was slumped on the ground, clutching his abdomen. 'One of the cons got me good.'

Stephen limped forward.

KILL HIM.

No. He's not even an inmate.

HE'S DYING. CAN'T YOU SMELL IT? IT WOULD BE KINDER JUST TO PUT HIM OUT OF HIS MISERY.

He *could* smell it. The perforated bowel. The blood. All of it.

He'll be fine.

NO ONE IS COMING. KILL HIM.

The emergency services will be here soon. He turned to look at the flames erupting out of the prison's roof, vomiting smoke into the night sky. *They'll patch him up.*

The force from the demon worming its way into his limbs made Stephen stagger. He clenched his jaw and willed the entity back, fighting for control of his body with a grunt. Reluctantly, the demon withdrew. If it hadn't already fed off Dermot, Niall and the handful of other convicts who'd chanced their arm with him, things might have played out differently.

The officer squinted up at him, trying to get a look at his face, hidden by the shadows. The lack of terror told him that all he could see was the silhouette of a fellow prison officer.

'Help me.' Pain took the energy from his words until they were nothing but a broken whisper.

Stephen turned and limped to the wall, away from the officer.

'No! Please, help me. Don't leave me here with them. Please!'

YOU SHOULD KILL HIM. HE COULD IDENTIFY YOU.

To whom? I'm dead, remember? Anyway, who's going to believe him? I think you need to work on your priorities.

Silence with the slightest hint of disapproval followed.

Stephen pressed his fingers against the mesh enclosing the yard, pushing it away until it touched the coarse brick behind. With a sharp yank, he wrenched the mesh apart. The wire screamed with the voice of a thousand rusty springs as it split open, its edges fraying into jagged points. Stunned silence replaced the pleas of desperation from the felled prison officer.

Stephen squeezed through into the gap between the fence and the wall. He braced his back against the mesh and began his ascent.

WHY ARE YOU USING THE WIRE FENCE TO SUPPORT US? WE DON'T NEED A SAFETY NET.

I know, but it's reassuring. And this way avoids the barbed wire. A chunk of brick fractured beneath his grip, exploding in a spray of dust. Even the most resilient of structures couldn't compete with over a century's worth of weather exposure. Demon-enhanced strength probably hadn't been factored into the architecture either.

WE DIDN'T NEED A SAFETY NET ON THE WAY IN.

It wasn't an option on the way in.

YOU WON'T FALL. I WON'T LET YOU. EVEN IF YOU DID, I WOULD REPAIR YOUR BODY.

Wait, are you offended?

DON'T BE RIDICULOUS. YOU ARE JUST SLOWING US DOWN, THAT'S ALL.

You are. You're offended.

A chuckling Stephen hauled himself up the last few feet of the wall face, smirked at the lack of response, and pulled himself onto the coping.

He twisted around, tearing his jacket on a rough corner of concrete. 'Shit. I've only been wearing this five minutes.'

IT'S AN OUTFIT, the demon responded with creeping satisfaction. I THINK YOU NEED TO WORK ON *YOUR* PRIORITIES.

You're a monster, you know that, right? He pulled the jacket around and assessed the damage with a frown.

MONSTER? COUNT YOURSELF LUCKY. THERE ARE SOME SPECIES IN MY REALM THAT CONSUME THEIR OWN MOTHERS.

Stephen paused. *You ate your mother?* His stomach churned.

DON'T BE ABSURD. MY KIND DON'T EAT OUR PARENTS.

That was a relief. Although, he wouldn't have put it past the demon for a second.

WE EAT OUR YOUNG.

What?

The demon chuckled. I'M JOKING. OBVIOUSLY.

Stephen shook his head, shimmied over the top of the wall and began the descent.

THAT RARELY EVER HAPPENS.

Part II

Chapter 24
Thirty-Four Years Later

CIARA USHERED HER DAUGHTER, Addison, out onto the boarding bridge with a nudge and smiled at the flight attendant. Her stomach churned; being bounced around like a ragdoll when they landed had been bad enough, but it was the rising tension that really knotted in her gut; the 'what if'. She glanced over her shoulder at the people disembarking behind her and exhaled. *No*. Everything was fine. No need to be so paranoid.

Wincing at the artificial light reflecting off the bridge windows, she peered past it to the runway. It felt strange getting off the plane at night, like she'd lost a part of herself over the North Atlantic ocean. Which part, she couldn't say, but a weight had lifted. Anxiety still raged inside her, fighting to extinguish the spark of hope she'd allowed herself to nurture, but every step she took was one away from the life she'd left behind. Still, if it meant that she could crawl into a warm bed in the next few hours and sleep off the apprehension, then she could stick it out for the time being.

Jesus, how many years had it been since she was last on a plane? Thirty-three? Thirty-four? Her life had come around full circle. Her mother had forced her to flee to the US when she was just a child, and now she was scurrying back to the UK with Addison.

It's hardly the same thing. If I'd stayed there he would have killed me. And who knows what he would've done to Addy without me there to protect her? Sometimes the bravest thing you can do is run.

Hardly the same thing at all. She'd never got a valid reason for why they'd left in the first place. Her mother remained tight-lipped about the whole situation—even in her final days, when her mind had begun to fail.

Her reflection stared back at her, fiery-red hair a dishevelled mess, shadows under her chestnut-brown eyes. She sighed.

A blow to the shoulder made her stagger with a grunt. A man hurried past, his rucksack slung over his arm, oblivious to her existence, as he stared down at his phone screen. She glared after him and tucked a loose strand of hair behind her ear. 'Rude.'

'Who's rude, Mom?' Addison glanced up at her, then looked around.

'Never mind, honey.' Ciara ruffled her daughter's tawny-brown hair. 'Are you looking forward to seeing where I was born?'

'Yeah, this is going to be so cool.'

'What are you looking forward to the most?'

Addison pursed her lips and raised an eyebrow. 'I think I'd like to try some proper fish and chips.' She nodded to herself.

Ciara chuckled and shook her head. She should have known; the girl's world revolved around her stomach.

With one last scowl at the back of the man's head, Ciara tightened her grip on the handle of her carry-on and increased her pace. 'Come on, Addy, let's get moving.'

Ciara chewed on her lower lip and reminded herself to breathe as they worked their way through the arrivals hall. The tension in her shoulders had spread to her neck and she knew it wouldn't be long before she had a pounding headache.

It was a good thing they'd only brought carry-on with them—not that they'd had much of a choice. They'd had to leave everything behind; only the clothes on their backs and a few treasured possessions had made the seven-hour flight with them. Still, she was grateful that they didn't have to wait for baggage. She just wanted to meet her contact and get out of Heathrow as quickly as possible. Call it paranoia, but everywhere she looked she thought someone was watching her.

She dried her palms on her jeans and scanned the cluster of people milling around. It was a colourful mix of what she assumed was expectant relatives and friends, and a few men in tired-looking suits that strained at the buttons. Some held signs, their expressions ranging from unrestrained excitement to familiar indifference.

After what felt like a lifetime, Ciara spotted a petite, dark-haired woman with plump cheeks and thin lips clutching an A4 sheet of paper with 'Olivia Smith' written in thick, looping letters. That was the name they'd agreed upon during one of their many phone calls, to conceal her identity.

Ciara gave her a nod and walked towards her, with Addison in tow. She kept her pace steady. Paranoia pulled at the threads of her composure, unravelling it, until all that remained were the frayed edges of her nerves. Her husband was as ruthless as he was determined. If he'd caught even the faintest whiff of her plan, his thugs would be planted around the airport, ready to drag them both back to the US kicking and screaming, and there would be nothing she could do about it.

Her mother had warned her about falling for a settled man.

Thank God for her sister-in-law, Audrey. Without her they might never have escaped his clutches. They hadn't always seen eye to eye, but the moment Addison was born, Audrey had fallen in love with her. Brother or not, there wasn't a chance in hell Audrey was going to let her niece grow up thinking getting slapped about by a man was okay.

It was Audrey who'd put her in touch with Fiona from the domestic abuse charity and paid for their flights back to the UK. In truth, she'd probably saved their lives.

'Fiona?' Ciara swallowed the lump in her throat. It was all she could do not to break down in tears. She couldn't let Addy see her become a wreck. It was one thing to cry alone at night when nobody was around, but in front of her daughter, she had to stay strong. The poor girl had been through enough.

The woman's features softened into a smile, the crinkles at the corners of her eyes suggesting that she was older than she'd first appeared. 'We have a taxi waiting for us in the pickup zone. The drive to your new accommodation should only take around an hour and a half, then you can both have a nice rest. How was the flight?'

Ciara exchanged small talk with Fiona while they proceeded to the idling cab. It wasn't until the car pulled out of the airport and onto the M3 that she finally allowed herself to relax.

'I understand that you were born in England?' Fiona tilted her head as she brushed her hands over her skirt and smoothed out the wrinkles.

It was clearly just a tactic to help put her at ease—Fiona knew the answer already—but Ciara appreciated the effort all the same. 'Yes, that's right. We left here when I was around Addy's age. My mother and I.'

'Oh, right.' Fiona nodded with genuine interest. 'Your father?'

'No, he... he died when I was six. Well... the man I *thought* was my father died when I was six. My real father was in prison at the time. I think he died in an attempted riot or something, shortly after we arrived in the US.' Oh God, why had she just told Fiona that? Her cheeks flushed.

'That's awful. I'm sorry.'

'No, it's okay. I can't really remember him... either of them. Memories are funny things, aren't they? You can't trust them.' She exhaled. 'I've seen photos of the man I called my father growing up, but there's nothing of him about me—obviously. It's like looking at pictures of a stranger. I only found out the truth after my mother died. When I was clearing out her things, I found one of her old diaries. I thought it might give me a glimpse into her life, so I read it. It was really quite sad. She was in love, but she was young. Her head got turned by his brother. He was older, more experienced. He was also married. My mother called things off with her boyfriend. She knew if she stayed with him and he ever found out, it would break his heart. Shortly after, she married the man in the photos.' She pressed her lips together and glanced at Fiona.

'Do you think that had anything to do with the reason you and your mother left the UK?'

Ciara shrugged.

There was something about Fiona that made Ciara feel safe, something motherly. It'd been a long time since she'd let her guard down and the emotions threatened to overwhelm her. She cleared her throat, blinked back tears and stared intently at her clasped hands on her lap. Now was not the time to open the floodgates.

'I can't remember why we left, not exactly. We went in the middle of the night. There was a lot of shouting. You know what your imagination is like when you're small.' The words tumbled from her mouth.

Why was she saying all of this? She must sound like an idiot. She lifted her gaze to the woman sat opposite her, expecting the same judgemental look her husband got whenever she spoke about her past. Whenever she spoke about most things, actually. But Fiona was all patience and attention. It very nearly made her well up again.

She cast a sideward glance at Addison, whose head was dropping, and lowered her voice. 'There was some sort of fight and someone got hurt. I think I remember hearing talk about someone getting shot... or it might have been stabbed. It was so long ago.'

'What a terrible experience for a child,' Fiona said softly. 'Well, you'll have plenty of opportunities to make good memories now. We've arranged a flat for you both to stay in. It's not huge, but it should be more than suitable for the two of you. It's fully furnished, so you should have everything you need, and there's a little bit of food in the fridge for you both. Enough to last you a couple of days, until you find the time to do a proper shop.'

'That's wonderful. Thank you so much, you don't know how much this means to me.' Ciara's cheeks flushed; she shifted in her seat. Had she just made a fool of herself? She would never normally share anything about her past, let alone with a complete stranger. It must be the jetlag, or that returning back to England after all these years had stirred up some repressed emotional issues.

Whatever it was, there was something about Fiona that made her want to open up, and that frightened her.

Chapter 25

A DRUNKEN BELCH FOLLOWED by raucous laughter wrenched Stephen from a fitful sleep. He rubbed a rough hand over his face and peeled his eyelids open, hissing sharply when he noticed the sun was setting.

He hunkered down farther into his threadbare blankets while the echoing voices grew louder, and turned his face away. The last thing he needed was another group of local lads attacking him, getting it into their heads that it was their civic duty to rid the streets of all the down-and-outs. It wouldn't end well. For *them* anyway. Especially not now that the setting sun had stained the skies red with its dying light.

If he didn't move a muscle, they might not notice him. Just another heap of rags marring the entrance to one of the many whitewashed, abandoned shops along the once-popular high street. Easier said than done. The solid concrete paving was cutting off the circulation to his legs.

Sometimes not moving worked, sometimes it didn't. He'd been yelled at, sworn at, spat at, punched, kicked and pissed on. Someone had even tried to set him alight once, but as vile as those things were, he could handle it all. As long as it happened during the day when he had control. Mostly.

The slurred conversation of the local lads tailed off as they stumbled down the road and out of sight. Stephen waited a few more seconds just to be sure they were gone, before sitting up. He rolled the stiffness out of his shoulders. The blankets fell from his torso as he cracked his neck. He was just beginning to enjoy the sensation of the vertebrae clicking and popping, when he caught sight of his reflection in one of the glass door panels. No matter how many times he saw it, it always made him cringe.

The mutilated flesh around his mouth, giving him a permanent monstrous grin, was a constant physical reminder of the control the demonic presence had over him.

As if I could ever forget.

Over the years he'd learnt how to manipulate the foreign energy that coursed through his veins; exerted enough control to knit the ruined skin and muscle back together without the demon's assistance. Exertion didn't begin to cover it. It required an immeasurable amount of willpower. The effort usually left him physically and mentally drained. Then when night fell, the demon would rip it open again, as easily as tearing a sheet of paper. In the end it wasn't worth it. So he left the wound.

All because the demon was sulking.

Holding a grudge for more than two decades was a little disproportionate. But, anything that could tolerate a century of imprisonment inside a magical dagger had probably learnt to bide its time.

Stephen's features were like a stamp of supremacy, ensuring that his gruesome appearance kept him isolated. Not being able to form meaningful relationships had castrated Stephen's dissidence and made him the good little meat puppet he was today. Although, the demon probably did him a favour. Emotional attachments were a weakness.

Attachments were what had caused the entity's little tantrum in the first place.

Twenty-three years. That's how long it'd been. Almost to the day. Stephen had been sleeping rough, avoiding hostels, avoiding the other homeless—especially if they had dogs. Dogs always sensed there was something not right about him; his presence would always set them off. He was an apex predator and they knew it.

Then she'd found him. An unassuming, petite blonde in her early thirties, with eyes that were such a light shade of brown, they looked like liquid gold.

He'd been holed up in a secluded patch of woodland on the outskirts of town, under the curving arch of an old granite bridge that crossed a slow-moving stretch of river. Despite the odd patch of graffiti appearing now and again, the place was generally deserted, especially at night. That's why he'd chosen it. That and there was something about being near the water that took the edge off the endless pulsing inside his head. As long as he didn't venture too far into the water he was okay—that jolted the demon into a raging fit. Never a good idea.

So, he'd been stunned when she'd suddenly appeared in the mottled daylight and approached him, without an ounce of fear or disgust.

First visit, she'd told him that she was part of an outreach programme, offered him some food and went on her way. She came back the next day, and the next. It'd been good to talk to someone who wasn't actively encouraging him to murder people and eat their eyeballs. She was a distraction from the throbbing need to hunt, ticking like a metronome in his brain. A never-ending beat that stole his concentration by day and his sleep by night.

Try as they might, Stephen and the demon had not been able to track down the last of the Boswells. They were still out there somewhere. The rhythm of their hearts pulsed through the magic sigils that bonded their victims to the demon within him, and he heard it day and night.

He felt them. Felt them when they were born. Felt them when they died. It was all maddening, but it was just a fraction of what he had experienced when he'd first emerged from his grave. Wherever they were, it wasn't anywhere in Great Britain. They'd worked out that much at least, after searching the island from coast to coast. Once they'd even tried to steal onto a boat, but something about the water had sent the demon into a frenzy.

People had died that night.

On the woman's fifth visit, she'd sat down next to him and offered him a polystyrene cup filled with tea, sugar and a splash of milk. Just the way he liked it.

'I'm Dee.' She extended her hand to him, not the slightest bit bothered that his fingers were covered in grime, or that he must have stunk to high heaven.

After a few seconds of stunned silence, he accepted the handshake. 'Steve.' His cheeks flushed, realising he hadn't bothered to ask her name. So much for manners.

DON'T EVEN THINK ABOUT IT.

He took a sip of tea, ignored the voice and let the heat from the cup warm his hands.

'Steve,' she repeated, smiling at him as if he were just another normal human being.

It was nice.

SERIOUSLY, DON'T EVEN THINK ABOUT IT.

Okay, I'll bite. Think about what?

MATING WITH THAT PUNY HUMAN.

He almost spat out his tea. *What?*

I CAN FEEL THE WAY YOUR PULSE RISES WHEN YOU LOOK AT HER. IT'S DISGUSTING.

Disgusting?

THE THOUGHT OF YOUR PINK, SQUISHY BODIES MASHING TOGETHER. IT'S NAUSEATING.

Nauseating? Seriously? I've watched you crack open a man's skull and feast on his brain.

THAT IS DIFFERENT. THAT WAS FOOD. THIS IS PERVERSE. I DON'T WANT TO WATCH YOUR SICK, BREEDING RITUAL. I'M A DEMON, NOT A DEVIANT.

Stephen shook his head and sighed.

ANYWAY, HER HIPS ARE FAR TOO SMALL TO BEAR YOU A SUFFICIENT AMOUNT OF YOUNG. YOU NEED A MUCH LARGER MATE. ONE WITH STRONG BONES AND SOLID HORNS.

Wait, what? Horns?

'Too hot?' Dee asked. She pointed to the cup.

'Oh, no. Sorry, I was just... thinking.'

'Don't let me interrupt.' She grinned and placed her hand on his.

Her fingers were soft against his skin; the warmth of them radiated through his hand. His brow furrowed. Why did he smell burning matches?

His body spasmed suddenly.

He lurched to his feet and crushed the polystyrene cup in his fist. Hot liquid scolded his bare flesh and he hissed.

'What the hell?' he said.

He rounded on Dee. She watched him, expression curious. His hand continued to ache. Distracted, he flicked his gaze down to the reddened flesh, astonished that the burn hadn't already healed.

What just happened?

Silence.

That was odd. In fact, now that he focused on it, even the pulsing rhythm in the depths of his consciousness had calmed to a soft murmur.

'It's still in there,' Dee said conversationally, 'just sleeping, if you like.'

'What did you do to me?' Stephen demanded. He dried his tender hand down his trousers.

'She tranquilised it. With magic,' said a voice, with the subtle traces of a German accent. A man in his mid to late thirties emerged from the trees. He had wavy shoulder-length brown hair and designer stubble. He carried himself with assurance, hands resting in the pockets of his denim jeans, as if he was trying to show that he wasn't a threat.

Stephen took a step back. His eyes darted from Dee to the newcomer. *Tranquilised.* That would explain why the tissue on his hand hadn't regenerated yet.

He gasped and clutched at his chest.

'It's okay.' Dee got to her feet. 'The symbiosis that binds you to the demon is still intact. You're not about to drop dead; its abilities have just been temporarily neutralised. But we don't have long.'

'You know about the demon?' Stephen said. 'Wait, what do you mean "we don't have long"?'

The man came closer, removed his hands from his pockets and held them up in a placating gesture. 'Yes we know about the demon. We've been watching you for a while now. We are part of an organisation that specialises in locating individuals, such as yourself, and helping them.'

They'd been *watching* him? 'Such as myself?'

'Those afflicted with demonic energies, manipulated by dark magics, possessed. That sort of thing.'

'I see.' Stephen adjusted his stance. If things were about to turn to shit, he wanted the advantage.

The man stopped and lowered his hands slowly to his sides. 'My name is Jonas. We really *do* want to help you. At the very least, we can show you ways to shield yourself from its influence. Mitigate its control over you. But as Dee said, we don't have long. The spellwork she used is temporary. If you want our help, we need to work quickly.' It was more a question than a statement.

Stephen regarded them both. 'Can you get rid of it?'

Jonas and Dee exchanged a glance. Finally, Jonas gave him a troubled look. 'Honestly, I don't know. We don't know what we're up against yet—the type of possession, the species of demon, the rituals involved. But, if we can figure it out, then it's possible. Theoretically.'

Theoretically. Great.

Stephen took a breath. The near silence in his head rejuvenated him. Without a way of locating the remaining Boswells, he'd be forced to endure the torturous call of the sigils forever. Impotent against the pain and frustration that roiled in his head, with no release. Driven to kill in order to satiate the demon and make sure it held his body together.

What did he have to lose?

'Okay.' He relaxed. 'What do you need to know?'

From that point onwards, Dee and Jonas met with him on an almost daily basis. Taught him methods to build a wall of protection around his mind, then strengthen it brick by brick. They'd listened intently to everything he told them about the night he'd been stabbed. The dagger. The demon. All so they could take the information back to O.O.T.I.S, the organisation for which they worked, and research his condition. Dee had eventually told him it stood for the Order of the Iron Seal. It was probably a good thing that they'd been so evasive on details. If they'd told him before he'd become invested in what sounded like a religious cult, he'd have walked. Hell, he'd have run.

He'd left out some of the details, of course. Like the night he'd found Linda and Bethany. Alone and helpless in their home. The home he'd failed to protect. There would always be a gaping hole in his heart where his family lived. Prodding at the past would do nothing but hurt.

At the end of each session they would manipulate the threads of his memories; a light touch that spun a false story in the tapestry of his mind, something that could be followed without arousing suspicion.

Until the day it all went wrong.

Chapter 26

'GOOD.' DEE REMOVED HER fingers from Stephen's forehead.

He smiled at her then looked over at Jonas, who watched them with approval. It hadn't taken him long to figure out the two were a couple. It had never come up, but he'd noticed the wedding rings, the shared glances and the way they moved around each other with a coordination that only came from spending a significant amount of time together. He couldn't deny the pang of jealousy he sometimes felt, but that was a dark path to tread—following it would only lead back to the toxic rage corroding his soul day by day.

Jonas helped Dee back to her feet from her cross-legged position in front of Stephen. 'Okay. We're going to try something a little different today.'

Stephen shrugged and went to get up.

'No, no. You can stay there, Steve.' Jonas gestured for him to sit.

'Oh. Sure.' Stephen settled back down and shifted uncomfortably. The muscles in his lame left leg throbbed. He glanced at Dee as he stretched, who brushed the dust from her trousers. He spotted the pensive look she gave Jonas.

'Right.' Jonas nodded and turned his attention to Stephen. 'I'm going to draw a circle on the ground around you.'

'Okay.' This was new, but they hadn't steered him wrong so far. He folded his legs and waited, while Jonas cleared the area of dry leaves, twigs and stones and drew a wide circle around him with chalk. 'Do I need to do anything?'

Jonas gave him a tight smile. 'No, stay where you are. I'm just setting up.'

Stephen frowned but nodded, getting an uneasy feeling deep in his gut.

He watched Jonas a little closer as the man sketched strange symbols around the circle's perimeter, each contained within its own smaller circle. Jonas shuffled so as not to scuff any of the chalk lines, and connected them together. Finally, he drew one last sweeping circle around the whole thing.

Christ. At least Stephen wasn't sat in the centre of a pentacle. That would've really set the alarm bells ringing.

Jonas nodded to himself and placed the chalk on the ground, then walked over to a backpack he'd left unzipped on the crumbled remains of a nearby wall. He rummaged inside for a few moments and then returned to Stephen, clutching a random assortment of objects. A pen knife, a vial containing a viscous red liquid, the skull of a small bird, what looked like a hooked claw or talon, and an ornate, antique-looking bronze box no larger than the palm of his hand.

'Is that blood?' Stephen nodded at the vial.

Jonas looked at the collection in his hands and took a step forward. 'Yes. Don't worry, it's mine.'

That didn't make him feel any better. Stephen choked out a laugh.

Jonas met his eyes. 'Blood is a potent part of the spellwork. It acts as an anchor, bonding my energies to the circle. The circle itself acts as a sort of barrier, preventing the demon's essence from penetrating through to our side.'

'Oh.' Stephen frowned. 'I don't have to drink it or anything, do I?'

'No. It will remain in the vial. It, along with these other objects, will act as a layer of protection. Their use is not strictly necessary—a circle of blood alone would suffice—but it would leave you more exposed. This way is safer.'

Jonas carefully placed one item in each of the five smaller circles. He straightened, dusted off his hands, and scrutinised his handiwork. Wiping a bead of sweat from his forehead, he turned and nodded at Dee, who hadn't moved an inch.

'Is this dangerous?' Stephen asked. Something unsaid passed between him and Jonas. Dee took a breath, her body tense.

She turned towards him. 'We're going to attempt to remove the demon.' Her fingers worried at the fabric on her top.

'Well, that's good. Isn't it?' said Stephen.

'Yes.' Her gaze dropped to her feet as she said it, then flicked back up to him. 'You're going to have to remain very still.'

Shit. As a detective, he'd interviewed enough people to recognise when he was being lied to.

'Dee—' the hairs on the back of his neck stood on end, '—what's going on?'

She looked at Jonas, a question in her golden eyes. He simply nodded and set his jaw.

Double shit. 'You know what? I'm not feeling great about this.' Stephen made to stand.

Before he could, Jonas and Dee lifted their arms. They mouthed words too silent for him to hear. A wall of energy rushed up around him, with an accompanying sound like a blade being dragged across a whetstone. An invisible force drove him down to the ground. With his body dead weight, Stephen squeezed his eyes shut against the blast of dust and grit caused by their magic. Unable to lift his hands to protect his face, he bellowed.

IDIOT. THEY ARE GOING TO KILL YOU.

'Dee?' He ignored the demon's sudden reappearance. 'Dee? What's going on?'

Her body was no more than a vague shape behind the translucent magic wall encircling him. Only Jonas was visible; everything else was a blur. He strained against his unseen bonds, as the dust settled back on the ground between him and the boundaries of his prison. His heart hammered inside his chest. He couldn't move.

'No. No they wouldn't,' he replied to the demon.

I KNEW YOU WERE UP TO SOMETHING. YOU PUT YOUR TRUST IN WITCHES. WHAT DID YOU EXPECT?

'They're helping me.'

SO I SEE. HOW'S THAT WORKING OUT FOR YOU?

Stephen had no answer. He stared wide-eyed at the blue glow emanating from the symbols that Jonas had drawn.

What is that?

BINDING RITUAL. THEY'RE GOING TO INCAPACITATE US, KILL YOU AND IMPRISON ME BACK IN THAT CURSED DAGGER.

Shit. He'd contemplated death, even begged for it, knowing that the demon was slowly eating away at his morality, twisting him into a dark and deranged version of himself. But faced with it right here, right now, knowing that someone was trying to kill him, he couldn't suppress his desire to survive.

I CAN'T BELIEVE YOU. AFTER ALL I'VE DONE FOR YOU. THIS IS HOW YOU REPAY ME? IDIOT.

Okay. I'm an idiot. How do we get out of this?

While the demon contemplated the question, Stephen's eyes darted between the glowing blue symbols.

YOU NEED TO BREAK THE CIRCLE.

How? I can't move.

A feeling, like a mental sigh of exasperation, washed over him. The familiar disdain was strangely comforting.

I'LL JUST DO EVERYTHING, SHALL I? JUST REMEMBER, BREAK THE CIRCLE. I'LL DO THE REST. AGREED?

Okay.

SAY YOU AGREE.

Yes! Yes, I agree.

Stephen's body toppled as the demon withdrew its hold on him, negating the magic that bound him in place. Pain flared in his chest as his flesh tore open once more around the fatal stab wound. Blood flowed freely. He lay motionless and wheezed in a breath.

BREAK THE CIRCLE!

His fingers twitched as his body tried to revolt against his mind's orders. He inched his hand towards the line of chalk in front of him. His weak and trembling muscles threatened to crush his feeble attempts. He jerked his hand onto the chalk, and let out a strangled whimper, as he scrubbed it from the dry earth. His strength gave out and he lay there, panting. Darkness crept along the edges of his vision.

The wall of energy collapsed around him. A familiar agony ripped through his brain. His body convulsed as fire blazed through his every synapse. The presence within him took control.

He was upright in an instant. He hurtled towards Jonas, who'd only just realised that the circle had been breached. Their bodies collided with such force that it drove the air from Stephen's lungs. They crashed to the floor. By the time Dee let out a howl, the demon was already on his feet again, his fists clutching Jonas' warm, dripping intestines.

The demon fixed Dee with a glare. 'That was uncalled for.' It spoke in a flat tone, voice coarse.

Dee whimpered. 'It's you.' Her eyes flicked from the bloody mass in Stephen's hands to Jonas, squirming on the ground. She turned as white as a sheet and let out a tortured wail.

'Dee... run,' Jonas croaked. Sweat rolled down his face, sickly grey in colour, and matted his hair to his forehead. His eyes were wild, but somehow he managed to remain focused on her.

The demon laughed. It was a penetrating cackle filled with malice. With a casual flick of his wrists, he dumped Jonas' innards and turned towards Dee.

'Such a shame,' the presence drawled, gesturing vaguely at Stephen's body. 'I think he really liked you. You made him smile. But *I* can make him smile too.'

With a humourless chuckle, the demon spread Stephen's arms wide and tilted his head, magic tearing the skin around his mouth.

Dee recoiled. Tears streamed down her cheeks as she watched the lacerations yawn open, only stopping when they reached his cheekbones. But she didn't run. Whether it was some misguided act of defiance, or that her body had frozen in shock was unknown. Either way she was dead.

The stench of blood and a tinge of sulphur filled the air between them. Jonas squirmed in the mess of his own gore. 'Run!' he howled.

This time Dee listened. She ran as fast as her legs would allow.

The demon grinned. If there was one thing it loved, it was a good chase.

An explosion—loud enough to shake the mortar from the bricks above him and propel a flock of screeching birds into the sky—hurled Stephen through the air in a wave of raw heat. He landed face down in the dirt, several feet from where he'd been. The demon receded back into the depths of his mind with a malicious chuckle, forcing him to feel the full extent of his injuries.

Stephen hissed and pushed up to his feet. His ears rang. The bubbling blisters of melted flesh on his calves and back, where the heat had scorched through his clothes, were already knitting back together. He raised an eyebrow and turned to see the remains of Jonas' burning corpse inside a wide circle of charred earth. Blackened flesh crumbled in clumps from the man's desiccated face and body, tongues of flame and belching black smoke parting to expose skull and bone.

HE WON'T BE WALKING THAT OFF ANYTIME SOON.

What happened?

HE EXPLODED.

Yes, I can see that. But why?

MAGIC. CLEARLY.

Stephen dropped the subject and cast a look around at the trees. Dee was gone. Part of him was glad she'd escaped. Her husband was dead because of him. The hypocrisy of the situation was a kick to the gut. But another part, much larger and darker, felt the sharp stab of betrayal. He'd trusted them, trusted *her*, and they'd tried to kill him.

Lesson learnt. Never trust anyone.

Stephen collected the objects that Jonas had placed around the perimeter of the chalk circle, and then snatched up the rucksack still open on the wall.

YOU HAVE POOR TASTE IN FRIENDS.

Ignoring the demon, he dumped everything in the fire that was consuming what was left of Jonas, and watched it burn.

He'd just learnt two very important lessons. One, he'd made himself a person of interest to an organisation that specialised in finding all the things that go bump in the night. Two, friendships were a weakness.

To this day he lived by those lessons.

Stephen shook the memory away and averted his gaze from the shop window. He readjusted the striped scarf to cover his jaw. He liked the scarf, with an assortment of muted mustards, toffees, beiges and the occasional splash of burgundy in varying thicknesses. It reminded him of the one Tom Baker wore in Doctor Who. It also paired quite nicely with the shabby olive-green parka jacket that he'd recently acquired. *Just because I'm a horribly disfigured prisoner in my own body doesn't mean I can't accessorise.*

NO. HAVING NO TASTE IN CLOTHING MEANS YOU CAN'T ACCESSORISE.

He fingered through the contents of the bashed paper cup to his side. A few coppers and a pound coin. Not

197

enough for a coffee, let alone something to eat. Maybe he'd have better luck tomorrow. His stomach growled. When was the last time he'd eaten? Two days ago? Three? He'd have to find something soon or suffer the consequences.

If he let his body starve, the demon would take matters into its own hands, figuratively speaking. It's not like it actually had hands of its own.

Heh.

DON'T GLOAT. IT'S UNBECOMING.

Unlike him, the demon had no misgivings about eating human flesh. In fact, it enjoyed it. Eyeballs were a particular delicacy. But it was the raw energy infusing every living soul that the demon craved most.

No, that wasn't quite right... it was more than just a craving, it was a *need*.

Without it the demon's strength would wane, his body would unravel, and the magic that bound them together would drive its essence back into the dagger upon Stephen's death. It would be a cold day in hell before the entity let that happen. Its reservations about being imprisoned again went way beyond apprehension. There was more to that story than it was letting on, but the demon had kept obstinately tight-lipped about it for thirty-four years, so Stephen wasn't holding his breath.

Stephen got to his feet, pocketed the change and collected up his blankets. Time wasn't on his side. He needed to find somewhere less populated, quickly.

They'd come to an agreement after the Dee and Jonas incident: they'd only dredge from the worst of society's sordid backwaters. Nobody that would be missed. Nobody that would draw the attention of the police or O.O.T.I.S. For the most part it had worked out, but every now and again the demon just couldn't help itself. Especially if it was hungry.

Stephen doubled over with a grunt as the demon vied for control of his body. 'Christ, calm down. What's the matter with you?'

CAN'T YOU FEEL IT?

He could. It was so obvious now. The pulsing rhythm that lingered in the backdrop of his existence had intensified. How had he missed it?

After all these years, the hunt was back on.

BUT FIRST, I THINK IT'S TIME FOR A SNACK.

The demon seeped into his muscles and discarded the blankets with a sneer. There was no use fighting it. Whether it was something to do with the dagger's magic or just some perverse law of nature, the demon was always at its strongest after the sun buried itself beneath the horizon.

Great. Decent blankets were hard to come by when your primary income was loose change.

A smirk spread across Stephen's face in response.

Vindictive bastard.

At least he still had his scarf.

Chapter 27

Wilcott Road cemetery was eerily quiet under the crushed-velvet night sky. Home to the ghosts of faded memories. Or was that ghosts *and* faded memories? If the last few decades had taught Stephen anything, it was that his knowledge of the supernatural was severely lacking.

The demon forced him to listen, staring absently at the moonlit façade of the weathered stone chapel. A soft breeze teased at the leaves of a few ancient elms, bringing with it a crisp, autumnal chill and the earthy, herbal scent of marijuana.

Stephen should have known where the local kids had been headed. From time to time the demon liked to bring him back here. Maybe Stephen's memories and emotional trauma had seeped into the entity over the decades, as much a part of it as they were of him. Or maybe the presence just liked getting him riled up. Making him more amenable to the impending bloodshed.

Pointless really. His anger was a volatile thing. It simmered just beneath the fragile surface of his broken mind. A lifetime of having a demon whisper its dark poison in your ear would do that. The incessant pounding in his skull, compelling him to hunt, didn't help either. And the call was getting stronger by the minute.

The presence turned his head towards the distant sound of voices and the low, throaty growl of unintelligible lyrics screaming from tinny sounding speakers. Most likely from a mobile. Phones, heavy metal and weed usually added up to teenagers. Not good.

NAUGHTY, NAUGHTY. NARCOTICS ON A SCHOOL NIGHT.

A grin tugged at the raw edges of his cheeks as the demon cracked his knuckles and followed the noise.

Four adolescents, wearing black hoodies and skinny jeans, sat in a loose circle around a glowing phone screen. Each took a turn to take a drag from a joint before passing it on. Discarded on the grass around them were several empty Smirnoff Ice bottles and crumpled Fosters cans. It looked like they were having a good time. Their night was about to go downhill. Fast.

One of them, a female, leant forward and scrolled her finger across the phone screen. Although her upper body was buried under a hoodie, Stephen could see she had a slight build. What she lacked in size she compensated for with intimidating, black eye makeup and bright-red lipstick. Strands of loosely curled, silver-white hair fell from her hood and about her face as she nodded at the device and squinted. 'Nine Inch Nails.

Old school.' She grinned, sat back and waved a hand to decline the proffered joint.

'Nice, Jack. I haven't heard this in ages,' said one of the males to the girl with the heavy makeup. A hint of a Polish accent played at the edges of his words.

He leant across her to take the spliff, his other arm around her shoulders. He was taller than she was, in that lanky way teenage boys often were. His hair was dyed black, in stark contrast to Jack's silver-white hair, and hung straight around his face, partially obscuring his eyes. He placed the joint between his lips and inhaled. A brief flash of orange glinted off the two piercings protruding from his lower lip. He exhaled a thin stream of smoke and ground the remains against a weathered granite headstone.

A headstone that sat feet from Stephen's. A headstone that belonged to his wife and daughter.

Stephen's jaw clenched when the demon responded to his surge of emotion. A snarl rumbled through his chest.

'Not cool, Alek. That's someone's relative,' a soft, feminine voice chided.

From his vantage point, there was nothing discerning about the speaker that Stephen could see other than her vibrant red hair—the kind that comes from a bottle. Nor anything about the male hunkered down by her side. Just two shapes drowned in black fabric and cheap body spray.

'No. The relative is buried six feet under.' Alek smirked and pointed at the ground.

That little shit. An eruption of fury pushed Stephen back to the fore. All worry about being tracked down by O.O.T.I.S evaporated.

'Urgh. Have a word with him, Jack,' the redhead said. 'He might listen to you.'

Jack chuckled and shrugged in a way that said, "I'm not getting involved".

Alek stuck out his tongue at her, then kissed Jack on the cheek. His lips lingered. Taking Jack's chin between his thumb and forefinger, he tilted her face up, brushed his lips against hers, and kissed her deeply.

'And on that note, I need a piss,' a second male voice grunted.

'What?' The girl said. 'Jacob, don't leave me alone with the lovebirds.'

'You'll be alright for a couple of minutes, Liv. If they start dry-humping just chuck a beer over them or something. You know Alek wouldn't let a good beer go to waste.' Jacob pushed himself to his feet, gave Liv a consolatory pat on the shoulder, and walked off into the shadows with a light stagger.

Stephen curled his mouth into a sneer that tore at the strands of taught flesh around his jaw. He moved to tail Jacob through the cemetery, muscles tense.

The boy was by far the largest of the four, with thick thighs that suggested he was into some form of athletics. Not that it would help him.

The farther they got from the chapel the less impressive the monuments became. Towering displays of wealth and social standing gave way to the simple and unadorned markers of workhouse employees, dead over a hundred years ago. Abandoned and forgotten, the granite had weathered until the lettering was either too worn or reclaimed by moss and lichen to be legible.

Jacob stopped in front of the substantial trunk of an ancient elm and unzipped his fly; the metal chain, from his belt loop to something in his pocket, clinked softly with the jerky motion. He let out a sigh and a steady stream of steaming urine splattered against the thickly scaled bark.

Stephen came to a stop behind the teenager.

'Jacob, Jacob, Jacob,' Stephen taunted. 'I'd definitely class this as offensive behaviour in a public place.'

Jacob jolted mid-stream. 'What the fuck?' He tried to look back while maintaining his dignity. It would have been comical in any other situation. 'Who—' The word had barely left his mouth before Stephen was squeezing his throat with one hand and slamming him back against the tree.

The force of the impact drove the air from the boy's lungs. His eyes bulged as Stephen's unnaturally strong grip crushed his larynx.

'Tsk, tsk. Indecent exposure is hardly appropriate in our current setting now is it, Jacob?' Stephen nodded towards the boy's exposed penis with a look of mock offence. He lifted him off the ground in a measured motion.

Jacob dangled in place, his face turning purple. He kicked out and clawed at Stephen's hand. Poor kid, asphyxiation was a terrible way to go.

It would have been kinder to snap the boy's neck and be done with it, but he was pissed off about them using his wife and daughter's memorial as an ashtray. And as far as the demon cared, this was all part of the fun.

Jacob's kicks petered out.

With one last exertion, the boy reached out a hand. It froze in the air, a hair's breadth from Stephen's face, then dropped. As his body went limp, his fingers caught the scarf concealing Stephen's disfigured mouth. It was a blessing that he was dead, before he had to see the rictus grin of mutilated flesh.

Stephen considered the dead teenager, his anger faltering. The demon exploited his hesitation and surged forward. The entity shook the corpse from side to side, like a rag doll. Stephen knew what was about to happen. The greedy excitement rolled through him in waves. His stomach growled.

I don't think this is a good idea.

With a discordant giggle that would have given the most unhinged psychopath a run for their money, the demon forced Stephen's thumb and index finger into Jacob's eye socket and ripped the eyeball out.

WE WILL BE LONG GONE BEFORE ANYONE FROM THE ORDER CAN TRACK US DOWN.

Blood and viscous gore coated his palm as the demon rolled the eyeball around, enjoying the feel of it. It tossed the bloody organ up into the air and caught it in his mouth. It burst between his teeth before he swallowed and repeated the process with the other eye.

I meant because he was as high as a kite.

OH.

Great. Just what we need. The munchies.

Jacob's memories flooded through Stephen's head.

Playing the bass guitar with his band mates in a grotty little back room of a dingy pub, used mainly to store chairs and racks of glasses.

Going all-out during sprint training until his thighs and lungs burnt, sweat dripping down his body. The feeling of elation at beating his personal best.

Exchanging awkward glances with Liv, wondering if she felt the same for him as he did for her. Trying to find the words to ask her out, losing his nerve at the last second, and making a complete tit of himself as he tried to cover up the attempt by pointing out her hair colour to her.

URGH, DULL. THIS IS WHAT PASSES FOR HUMAN ENTERTAINMENT? Unearthing nothing of interest, the demon dismissed all the memories. IN MY REALM WE HUNT, FIGHT, BATHE IN THE BLOOD OF OUR VANQUISHED FOES. IF YOU'RE NOT COVERED IN THE ENTRAILS OF YOUR ENEMIES, YOU'RE NOT HAVING FUN.

Sounds like a Friday night in the Medway towns.

The demon shifted his weight and tittered; Stephen's muscles trembled with hungry anticipation. The entity focused on the gossamer threads of vitality still woven into Jacob's warm, lifeless corpse, and pulled them out, drawing them into itself.

The wind churned more violently around them, harrying the leaves on the branches of the towering elms. Energy exploded through him. The presence inhaled sharply.

The gale settled and the demon exhaled with a shuddering sigh.

NOW *THAT*... THAT WAS A HIGH.

'Jacob? What's taking you so long? I really don't want to waste a beer on these two.' Liv called out in the darkness.

The demon dumped Jacob's body on the ground and turned towards the remaining adolescents. Three distinct scents mingled with the aroma of alcohol, weed and... pheromones.

Well, that's a whole new level of unpleasant.

Of all the romantic settings, surrounded by countless decomposing corpses, buried or otherwise, was definitely not in Stephen's top three. What was wrong with a nice meal followed by the cinema? He used to love the cinema. Linda had chosen their last film together, *Splash*. Despite all odds he'd actually enjoyed it; as far as romantic comedies went, it wasn't half bad. Daryl Hannah had been easy on the eyes too.

Liv, Alek and the girl named Jack hadn't moved. Liv was hunched over the mobile, most likely trying to distract herself from the face sucking in front of her.

LOOKS LIKE THEY'RE ABOUT SIXTY SECONDS AWAY FROM REALLY DEFILING THE GRAVES OF YOUR WIFE AND DAUGHTER.

If Stephen had needed more fuel to feed the fires of his fury, then the demon's voice, echoing in the depths of his mind, was a veritable gas can.

SOME STAINS YOU CAN NEVER GET OUT.

Enough!

The presence turned its attention to Liv. The angle as she bent forward revealed white writing on the back of her hoodie.

RAMMSTEIN?

Stephen gave a mental shrug. His knowledge of bands had fallen by the wayside after the whole untimely murder thing in 1984. The typeface suggested it was metal; he'd always been more of a rock guy. Charlie might have known; he was into heavier music.

CHARLIE, CHARLIE, CHARLIE, the presence scoffed.

Where had that come from? *Are you jealous?*

DON'T BE RIDICULOUS. WHY WOULD I BE JEALOUS OF A MEAT BAG? I SAVED YOUR LIFE. DID CHARLIE SAVE YOUR LIFE? COULD CHARLIE DO THIS?

Whatever superhuman feat the demon was about to demonstrate got cut short when it forced Stephen onto his lame leg. They both pitched into the dirt. Pain radiated through his crippled limb. The entity sucked air through his teeth.

STUPID, SUBSTANDARD BODY. The demon pushed them up with a growl.

You're high, aren't you?

NO. *YOU'RE* HIGH.

Great. Just great.

'Jacob?' Liv turned towards the commotion, her nose crinkled as she squinted. The piercing scream she gave echoed through the graveyard, causing Alek and Jack to jerk away from each other.

'Shhh—' The demon raised a finger to Stephen's lips, '—you'll wake the dead.' It threw back his head and laughed, exposing the true extent of his mangled face.

'O kurwa!' Alek scrambled backwards. His Converse tore up chunks of earth as he struggled to his feet and grabbed at Jack's arm.

'Jacob!' Liv shrieked. She backed away to join her friends. Her heel cracked the phone screen.

'I'm afraid Jacob won't be joining us. He's a little worse for wear.' The presence cupped a hand to Stephen's mouth and darted his eyes from left to right. It whispered, 'Too much alcohol. You might say that he's dead to the world.' The entity advanced towards them, giggling at its own joke.

Liv shook her head and backed up to the headstone Alek had used as a makeshift ashtray. Her ankle glanced off its foundation, throwing her off balance. She fell and hit the ground with a yelp.

'Jack, run!' Alek rushed to help Liv to her feet.

The demon stopped laughing. Stephen's eyes slid from Liv to the gravestone. The silence was nothing but a brittle dam against a rising swell of tension. A smudge of grey ash clung to the granite face where the boy had ground out his joint, marring the inscription of Bethany's name. A guttural growl reverberated through Stephen's chest.

Jack shrieked. Her ice-blue eyes darted from Liv to Stephen. Liv rolled into a crouch with a whimper just as Alek reached her side.

Why wasn't Jack running?

Her face contorted in fear when he got closer. To them he was a disfigured, homeless man, full of cold, calculated ill-intent. If he were Jack, he'd have been long gone by now.

The strands of tissue connecting the jagged edges of his cheeks began to strain and snap with a new grin. Disregarding Jack, the demon stooped down and dragged Liv up to her feet.

Liv screeched and lashed out, raining blows wherever she could land them. Her grunts of frenzied exertion turned into screams when the presence picked her up by her left arm.

'Let her go,' Alek yelled, pulling and trying to free Liv.

Stephen cringed as the demon's invisible tendrils slithered through his memories. It didn't matter how often it happened, he couldn't get used to the sensation. It was intimate, violating.

You really don't understand the concept of boundaries do you?

IMMATERIAL DON'T YOU THINK? I AM A PART OF YOU. INSIDE OF YOU. DEEP, DEEP INSIDE OF YOU.

You do that on purpose, don't you?

NO IDEA WHAT YOU MEAN.

Amusement rolled off the demon as it clamped the boy's face with one hand and shoved him to the ground, cutting his efforts short. 'Now, now. Your friend Jacob was in breach of section five of the Public Order Act, and things didn't work out too well for him. Don't any of you realise you're guilty of an offence? It's not hopscotch.' More of Stephen's face tore apart when the presence cackled.

Seriously?

WHAT? THEY ARE.

You just ate part of their friend. A friend that you murdered.

YOU MURDERED... ANYWAY, I'M A DEMON, WHAT DO YOU EXPECT?

And don't do that.

DO WHAT?

"It's not hopscotch". Don't quote my dead father.

An indignant huff replaced the laughter in Stephen's skull. The demon took a step forward.

To his credit, Alek rolled away and got to his feet, and continued to wrestle Liv away from her attacker. Sweat pricked at his forehead.

The scent of adrenaline and cortisol, as it flooded the boy's body, filled the air between them. The odour sparked a deep-seated, primal reaction within the demon; a predatory instinct. As the stale musk filled Stephen's nostrils, he sensed the mounting excitement undulate across their bond.

That was all it took to lose interest in Liv.

At the demon's bidding, Stephen flung her through the air. She landed a few feet away, cracking her head against a lichen-stained gravestone. Sprawled motionless on the flattened grass, blood flowed freely from the yawning wound on her scalp, casting a dark stain through her bright-red hair. She wouldn't be getting back up again.

Alek had no time to respond before the demon got a hand around his throat. Lifting. Crushing.

Jack screamed.

Why hadn't she run?

The demon shifted its gaze towards her. The hint of something familiar hit his nostrils—burnt matches. A low hiss escaped his lips.

Shit.

BRIMSTONE.

She's like Dee and Jonas.

SHE'S A WITCH... OH...

What? Stephen mentally braced for an attack. The last time they'd come up against witches things hadn't gone all that well. Just thinking about Dee and Jonas made his skin crawl. If the demon had to break their bond again, he wasn't sure he'd have the strength to survive it this time.

I JUST SAW A FOX.

Stephen projected his irritation towards the presence as they eyed the animal. *Christ. You* are *high.*

The demon looked away from the fox in time to see Jack blink, and limped forward a step. She shook her head as if stirring from a stupor, then sprinted from the graveyard.

DID YOU SEE IT? DID YOU SEE THE FOX?

Unbelievable.

The demon snapped its attention back to Alek, still in his clutches. The boy rasped and his head lolled to the side, his grip on consciousness slipping. The presence eased off and let the teenager rattle out a breath.

We don't have time for this. We need to leave before that girl, Jack, calls this in.

The sound of grinding teeth filled his head.

FINE.

Stephen's wrist twisted involuntarily. The boy's neck snapped with a sickening crunch.

The demon ran his tongue across the rough lacerations inside Stephen's cheek and dropped Alek's limp corpse to the ground.

YOU'RE NO FUN.

With a scowl, the demon wiped the gore on Stephen's scarf and tossed it away. Without so much as a second glance, it stepped over Alek's prone corpse.

As if Stephen's night hadn't been bad enough. *I liked that scarf.*

WHY? IT'S UGLY.

It's not ugly. It made me look like Doctor Who.

THAT PROGRAMME WITH THE LITTLE ROBOTS THAT CAN'T WORK STAIRS?

Daleks.

CAN'T SAY I SEE THE APPEAL.

You really are a monster.

Chapter 28

THE LOW THRUM OF Charlie's mobile vibrating on the bedside cabinet roused him from a deep sleep. With a zombie-like groan, he fumbled for it, contemplating whether or not to answer.

He peeled his eyelids open and squinted at the screen. It was no good; without his reading glasses the caller name was just a blur. He stabbed at the green button.

'Charles Haynes,' he said, sleepily.

'Sorry to disturb you so early, Charlie,' said Nick. He sounded apologetic.

'Not a problem, Nick. What's up?'

'Three kids got murdered last night. The sole survivor, Jacqueline Fletcher, saw the whole thing. We were wondering if you could help with asking her a few questions?'

Charlie frowned. 'Of course I can help out, but isn't that the murder investigation team's job? What's really going on here, Nick?'

A few seconds of silence followed. Nick sighed. 'One of the victims had their eyes removed. It has the same M.O. as the case you were working in the eighties with all those Traveller murders.'

Charlie sat bolt upright in his bed, phone clutched so tightly it bit into his palm.

Nick continued. 'It could be that we have a copycat on our hands, or it could just be a sick coincidence, but with your experience, you may know what to look out for.'

Charlie relaxed his grip and took a breath. 'Sure. Text me the address and time, and I'll meet you there.'

'Thanks, Charlie.' Nick exhaled before ending the call.

Thirty-four years. That's how long it had been since the first gruesome murder had taken place. The killings had spanned over a few years, with no real leads and little in the way of traceable evidence. It had taken an embarrassingly long time to even find the connection, which the press jumped on.

"The Caravan Cannibal" they'd dubbed the killer. Not that there was any concrete proof that the victims eyes had been eaten, but when had facts ever stood in the way of a good headline?

Still, it wasn't like today where everyone was so hyper-connected, you couldn't break wind without your aunt twice-removed hearing about it on social media. The tabloids had their uses and back then it had been one of the best methods of getting assistance from the public.

It had all led back to the Boswells.

Steve had been murdered on their site. Charlie had arrived that night to find the site cleared and the Boswells scattered across the country and beyond. From that point onwards someone—though based on the meticulous level of planning that would have been required, probably more than one someone—had hunted them down, leaving no survivors and a lot of collateral damage. Occasionally corpses would turn up that didn't fit the killer's pattern, possibly done to throw them off the scent. But in the main, every cluster of murders included at least one member of the Boswell family, immediate or extended.

Theories were banded about the media, and the station for that matter, as to who the killers were. A rival Traveller community? A cult? A handful of likeminded sickos? His money had been on rival Travellers. Still was. They would have needed intimate knowledge of the Boswell lineage and their probable hideouts to pursue them so obstinately. Nothing else made sense.

Then, just like that, the trail had gone cold. Every now and again another eyeless cadaver would be unearthed, but there would be nothing to tie it to the previous murders.

Charlie had spent a lifetime obsessing over it. It had cost him pretty much everything. Worst of all, he'd lost years of quality time with his daughter. And the case still remained unsolved.

The only thing he had left now was his job—a civilian working in the unsolved crimes unit.

After only two weeks of retirement there had been a knock at his door, and someone asking him to take the position. He didn't know what had been more embarrassing: that they didn't have anyone else with the experience or skill needed for the role, or that he had no reason to turn them down. The unit had grown since then, with people coming and going, but he'd stayed on. It wasn't like there was anything else for him to do.

Realising that he was still holding the phone to his head, Charlie sighed and lowered his hand. It was no good letting himself get carried away, he'd been down that rabbit hole before and it didn't lead anywhere good. The likelihood of these new murders was that it was simply a coincidence, just like Nick said.

He swung his legs over the edge of the bed and got up slowly. A shower would help clear away the cobwebs and ease some of the pain in his back. When had he gotten so old?

He rubbed his eyes, padded across the hallway into the marbled greys and pristine whites of his bathroom, and flicked on the lights. He'd need to make a quick stop at police headquarters before meeting up with Nick. There were a few files that he wanted to look over, to refresh his memory. It always paid to be prepared. That and get a coffee from the neighbouring Costa. At this stage, he wasn't sure which of the two was the most important.

Probably the coffee.

Hazel eyes, surrounded by frown lines, crow's feet and a sprinkle of liver spots, contemplated a way forward in the mirror. He waved a hand under it to turn on the inbuilt demister and strip lighting.

He pressed the control for the shower, allowing his thoughts to wander while waiting for it to reach the right temperature.

Thirty-four years and still investigating gruesome murders. Some things never change.

He glanced down at the single toothbrush in its holder on the sink. An abrupt reminder that some things did.

Chapter 29

CHARLIE ENTERED THE WHITE, rendered semi with a coffee in each hand. The detective who opened the door for him—Sam something... Bennett?—nodded to the hallway door on the left. Bennett's eyes lingered hopefully on one of the cups, as he shut the front door. Charlie shrugged a sorry and the detective sulked.

The house was painted a uniform magnolia; lazy decorating that screamed rented accommodation. There was little in the way of décor, except for a photo of a young woman and possibly her mother, and a few pieces of furniture that were best described as "functional". This family was either big on minimalism or they hadn't been here that long.

Charlie paused at the doorway and observed the living room Bennett had indicated to.

Nick stood on the far side in front of a small bay window, rubbing the back of his neck. His pale-blue eyes flicked between the two women from the photo, who were sitting in silence on a deep-set, off-white corduroy sofa. The younger of the two, presumably Jacqueline, frowned at the laminate flooring, her arms

ELIZABETH J. BROWN

folded across her chest. Her mother, he assumed, was making a show of checking her watch.

Tough crowd.

Nick looked up at him, excused himself and walked over, gesturing out into the hallway. He led Charlie into the kitchen where Bennett was jotting something down in his notebook.

As soon as he closed the kitchen door behind them, Nick's shoulders relaxed. He accepted the offered coffee with a half-smile.

From his hunched position over the white, farmhouse-style kitchen island, Bennett glanced up, then continued writing. But not before he gave his glass of water a sullen look.

'Soya milk latte?' Nick peeled back the lid and inhaled, with a look of near ecstasy, before replacing it firmly.

Charlie rolled his eyes. 'Yes. We all know you're lactose intolerant.'

Nick frowned. 'I'm not lactose intolerant. I'm vegan.'

'*Really?* You've never mentioned it.'

'Dick.'

Charlie smirked. He'd worked with Nick Stacey, in one form or another, for a few years now. He was a decent guy and an excellent detective, but that didn't mean he was above having his buttons pushed every once in a while.

'Going well?' Charlie asked, quirking an eyebrow. He already knew the answer based on Nick's body language alone.

Nick's mouth twitched as he shook his head. His frown lines deepened.

He took a long sip and exhaled, meeting Charlie's eyes. 'Jacqueline Fletcher, or Jack as she prefers to be called, witnessed two of the three murders. She's the one who called it in. Apparently they were all partaking in a little underage drinking and cannabis at Wilcott Road cemetery when they were attacked. Her account ties in with what's been found at the scene so far. I think she knows more than she's letting on—' his brow creased, '—but her mother is guarding her like a Rottweiler.'

Charlie nodded, set his coffee down on the worktop, and poked at a clementine balanced precariously on top of a brimming fruit bowl. It rolled forward. He grabbed it before it hit the counter, and gave it a thoughtful look. It wasn't unusual for parents to be overprotective under these circumstances. Hell, all any parent wanted was for their children to be safe. The world was terrifying enough without the thought of murderers roaming the streets.

Charlie tossed the piece of fruit in the air and caught it. 'And you think she'll talk to me?'

Nick shrugged and ran a hand through his auburn hair. He looked tired. Someone in their early forties without kids had no right to look so exhausted. Was this how Charlie had looked at his age?

'Your daughter was a teenager once. Albeit a *long* time ago.' Nick smirked. 'You've got the edge on this one. Maybe you can coax something out of her, even with her mother there. Anyway, since when has the renowned Charlie Haynes ever balked at a challenge?'

Charlie snorted in response and gave Nick a good-natured scowl. Bennett looked up from his notebook at the mention of Charlie's full name and regarded him with renewed interest.

'If my experience has taught me anything,' said Charlie, 'it's that if a teenage girl doesn't want to talk in front of her mum, she's not going to.'

Nick cursed and took another sip of his drink. A little air whistled through the tiny hole in the lid.

Charlie scanned the kitchen, rubbing at the base of his ring finger distractedly. The place was understated and meticulously tidy, in keeping with what he'd seen so far. If they took much longer, it was likely that Jack's mother would ask them all to leave.

'Think fast.' He threw the clementine to Bennett.

The man's eyebrows rose as he made a clumsy attempt to catch the fruit. His hand clipped the glass of water. It toppled and shattered on the floor. His eyes widened and he looked from the floor to Charlie.

Charlie gave him an apologetic shrug, opened the kitchen door, and made his way back to Jack and her mother. He made a mental note to buy the detective a coffee the next time he saw him; after all, the poor bloke was probably about to get a new one torn.

He knocked three times to announce his presence, and looked down at Jack's glowering mother. 'I'm terribly sorry. One of my colleagues dropped one of your glasses. We will, of course, pay for the damage.'

The hint of a smirk played at Jack's mouth as she looked from her mother to Charlie. She brushed a strand of silver-white hair behind her ear, and scrutinised him through heavy layers of smudged black makeup. Light glistened off a small, silver hoop in her nose.

Everything about her reeked of teenage rebellion. Piercings. Check. Dyed hair. Check. Boys, drugs and alcohol. Check. Controlling mother? Check.

'Fantastic. Just what I need,' the woman spat. Her lips curled back in a snarl that was all bite and no bark. She gave her daughter a sidelong glance, probably trying to decide whether or not to leave her alone with him. Then, with a loud huff, she pushed up from the sofa and stormed out towards the kitchen.

Okay, maybe he owed Bennett two coffees.

Jack watched her mother leave through narrowed eyes. Once she was gone, Jack leant in towards Charlie and gave him a measuring look.

'How many detectives does it take to interview a witness?' she asked, as if it were the set-up to a bad joke.

'I'm not a detective. I work in unsolved crimes. My name is Charles Haynes, but you can call me Charlie if you like.' He extended a hand towards her.

After a few seconds of contemplation she accepted the handshake. 'Jack.'

'Nice to meet you, Jack. Mind if I sit?'

She shrugged. 'It's a free country.'

Charlie lowered himself into the armchair directly opposite and sank into the deep, plush cushions. It was going to be a bitch to get back out of again.

A range of emotions flickered across the girl's face. 'Unsolved crimes? How long has this psycho been running around slaughtering people?' Her voice caught on the last two words, exposing the edges of her grief.

Charlie gave her a few seconds to collect herself before answering. Poor kid, she couldn't have been older than seventeen. What she'd seen would stay with her for the rest of her life.

'It's unlikely to be the same person, but there are definite similarities between this and other cases. I'm here to establish whether those similarities are just that, or if the cases are connected. Any information you can give me, anything you can think of that you haven't already mentioned would be a big help, Jack.'

He heard the sound of muttering, Nick's placating voice and a door being shut a little too firmly. Jack simply hugged herself tighter and tapped her foot on the flooring. She met his eyes, her face set in a mask of defiance.

The walls we build.

She eased back into the sofa. 'Aren't you a bit old to be working for the police?'

Charlie smiled. He'd had a lifetime to thicken his skin, and getting called old didn't bother him. 'Probably,' he admitted, 'but it pays the bills.'

'Your clothes are new, your watch is expensive. You're not doing it for the money.' Jack tongued her cheek and looked him up and down. She dropped her defences a little, her ice-blue eyes alive with the thrill of the puzzle before her. She'd probably make a good detective.

Her gaze lingered on his left hand. She looked him square in the eye and crinkled her nose. 'Oh. You're doing it to keep busy. Since the divorce. That sucks.'

Damn, smart kid. He rubbed where his ring used to be and shrugged. 'It happens.'

'Why'd she leave? I mean, I assume it was a she?'

Blunt and to the point. He liked her. 'A little on the nose.' He maintained eye contact and allowed the silence to build. She shifted ever so slightly, and he quirked a smile, letting her know that he was just teasing her. 'How can you be so sure that she left me?'

'I can't, not really. But you do that without realising it—' she gestured vaguely in the direction of his hand, '—like you miss the ring being there, which you wouldn't if you'd left her. Also you flinched, just a little, when I asked. It still hurts, even though it was probably a while ago. There's no indentation or tan line on your finger.'

He nodded, impressed. Clearly, Jack was not one to sugarcoat the truth. She obviously valued honesty. He could relate to that.

'She said that I put the job before her. That I wasn't the man she'd married and that she needed more. Then she took our daughter and left.'

'That's shitty. What a bitch.'

Charlie barked out a laugh.

Jack's face softened into a smile. She rolled her shoulders, some of the tension lifting from her body, and glanced furtively at the doorway.

'Look—' she said in a hushed tone, as she scooted forward on the seat cushion, '—mum doesn't want me to say anything. She thinks that I'll either get charged for wasting police time or get locked up in a nut house somewhere. There was something not right about the man who killed my friends. Besides the being a murdering psycho part.' She snorted. 'His face, it was messed up. Slashed from ear to ear. It looked like a fresh wound, but there was no blood. And he was strong, like stronger than human strong. He lifted Alek... Aleksander... off the floor with just one hand around his throat.' She paused, took a breath, and looked up at Charlie with uncertainty. There was the hint of a challenge in the set of her jaw, as if she was waiting for him to dismiss her claims as teenage bullshit.

He nodded at her to continue.

'I know it sounds crazy and I should've just got out of there, but something made me stop and look back. I shouldn't have, but I did. And I wish I hadn't. He snapped Alek's neck like it was nothing. And God, that laugh.' She shuddered at the memory and shook her head. 'It wasn't human. Whatever it was. It looked human, but it wasn't.'

'Do you have any idea why he let you go?'

'Not a clue.' She lifted her hands and dropped them. 'He saw me and just stared, like he'd spaced out. I don't know, maybe he was just some schizo. But Charlie—' she wet her lips, took another look at the doorway and lowered her voice to a whisper, '—I think he—'

The soft creak of laminate announced her mother's arrival seconds before she entered the room. Her lips were drawn into a thin line that exaggerated the sharp contours of her face. Under normal circumstances she could be an attractive woman, but her scowl was about as inviting as being asked to run naked into a swarm of angry wasps. She made no attempt to hide her unhappiness about them being there, muttering about 'police incompetence' and a few other choice words.

Jack stiffened and shuffled back. Her face became an emotionless mask. She gave her mother a fleeting glance, folded her arms across her chest and turned her head to look out of the window.

Christ, did the room just get colder? What was it about teenage girls and their mothers?

That was that then.

'Thank you for your time, Jack.' Charlie pushed up out of the armchair. His joints creaked in protest. Any chance he had of getting more answers from his only witness was gone, crushed under the mounting tension in the room.

'If you remember anything else, anything at all—' he pulled a small card out of his pocket and extended it out towards Jack, '—feel free to drop by the office or give me a call.'

Before she could react, her mother plucked it from Charlie's fingers.

'Thank you, detective.' She turned it over at arm's length, as if it might bite, and squinted down at the printed text. Her lip curled into a sneer as she read, 'Hmm. No, not detective. *Mr* Haynes. I'm sure if *Jacqueline* has anything else to add, you'll be the first to know.'

227

Charlie smiled at her. 'Right, I think that's everything. Thank you again for your time and hospitality.' He added just the right level of sincerity to mask the sarcasm. All the 'up yours' he could muster without an official complaint. A technique he'd picked up over the years.

It was the little wins that made life worth living after all.

Chapter 30

CIARA STIFLED A SIGH when Addison opened the fridge, took a quick look inside and closed it again. She'd lost count of the number of times that door had opened in the last ten minutes. What the girl expected to see in there that she hadn't seen before was beyond her. But apparently the fridge was where all the excitement was.

They'd already had cereal, but if there was one thing Addy did well, it was eat. Where she put it all God only knew; there was barely any meat on her. Her father was the same. Ciara shuddered and buried the thought. That man had no place in their future.

With a sulk, Addison rooted through one of the drawers and pulled out a green silicone cup. 'Mom, what's this for?'

'That's for poaching eggs, Addy.' Ciara raised an eyebrow and smiled. She couldn't blame her for being curious about their new home. By the time the cab had pulled up outside, and Fiona had given them a lightning-fast tour and handed over the keys, they'd both been so exhausted. They'd crawled into bed and slept like the dead.

In the light of day, the flat was actually a lot better than she'd expected. The open-plan kitchen and living area was modest, but finished to a good standard. Everything had been painted white to create a sense of space. Accents of grey in the tiling was carried through to the property's furnishings. The worktops and some of the fittings looked oak, or at least oak effect, adding enough warmth to soften the overall clinical look.

It was nice. Homely. A far cry from the contemporary, five-bedroom, bay-front home they'd left behind in Long Beach, but it was safe and it was theirs.

'Oh.' Addy's face dropped. 'There's some weird stuff in here.' She gave a gap-toothed grin and pulled out an elaborate decorative knife. She waved it about. 'Look, Mom.'

The ruby set in the black marbled handle refracted the light, casting flecks of red across Addison's hand. Ciara frowned. Something about it strove for her attention. She could almost feel it—a low droning noise that made the air quiver around her. She dismissed the sensation and smiled at Addy. 'That's a letter opener, I think. Be careful, it might be sharp. You know how clumsy you can be.'

'Who even gets letters anymore?' Addy put the letter opener back with a world-weary sigh that only an eight-year-old could muster. The contents of the drawer clattered as she slammed it shut.

'Come on, let's go and explore. Fiona said the high street was only a short bus journey away.'

There was only so much banging and crashing she could take at 10am. Still, at least she'd avoided any jet lag.

✧

Ciara thanked the driver and hopped off the bus a few steps behind Addison. The shadow of a building, all sweeping archways and decorative columns, loomed over them. A giant NatWest sign protruded from the pale, weathered stone, incongruous against it and the ancient looking, heavy-duty wooden doors below. At a guess she'd have placed the building as renaissance, or possibly baroque, she'd never really grasped the difference. That had been Dean's world, not hers. She shook her head and pushed the thought from her mind.

Buildings vied for attention along the bustling high street. It was a confused blend of architecture; structures that looked as if they'd been plucked straight out of a Dickens novel versus sharp-edged, glass-fronted monstrosities with cavernous insides, and everything in between. Somehow, the mix worked. It looked like a commentary of styles through the ages, giving the place a unique character.

The town had an energy to it, clean and vibrant. On the surface anyway. This place was nothing like the cramped and dingy shops she vaguely remembered from her youth; indistinguishable from one another, except for the colours of their awnings and obnoxious signage. This place even had litter wardens. Actual litter wardens.

She recalled something Fiona had said in the taxi about the town having been part of a regeneration project a few years ago, but Ciara had been too tired and stressed to give the conversation her full attention.

But like any town, wealth often drew beggars and con artists with its siren song. She'd read an article somewhere once that said some "beggars" earned as much in a year as a fully qualified teacher. How was that right?

Ciara pressed her lips together and glanced over at a man, sat huddled under a stained blanket in the doorway of an unoccupied shop. His face was mostly obscured; the lower half was covered by a dull-grey scarf, the upper half was cast in shadow by the hood he wore. Fallen on hard times, or just out to fleece a few kindhearted saps?

She couldn't tell.

The man looked down on his luck, dozing among his mouldering heap. That didn't mean he wasn't some junkie though. She winced at her presumption.

That's not fair. I don't know anything about him. Most people are just one pay cheque away from being homeless.

It's not like she had any money to her name. Not anymore. Only what the charity and Audrey had given her. She would need Fiona to find her a job, otherwise a doorway could be her and Addison's future. Living here was going to be an adjustment. She'd never needed to work before. Dean had always provided for her.

Generously at first, but over the years, it had become just another method of control.

No, finding a job and paying her own way would be a good thing. She needed to stand on her own two feet.

Ciara sighed and coaxed Addison along, trying not to focus too much on the pile of rags as they headed in that direction. The chill autumn breeze toyed with a few dry leaves, sending them skittering along the concrete paving. Ciara pulled her jacket tighter around herself.

'Right, Addy, we're going to get you a phone—'

Addison's squeal cut her off. 'Seriously?'

'Don't get too excited. It's not going to be anything fancy. Just something for emergencies.'

'Awesome. Thanks, Mom.'

Ciara's stomach tensed as they neared the homeless man. It wasn't until Addy slowed down to an obvious dawdle that she realised his eyes were open. He watched them, unblinking.

To say that his eyes were blue would be like describing the moon as a huge ball of rock. It might be true, but it lacked the artistry needed to paint a proper picture. They were *blue*, with a capital B.

She lowered her gaze to the pavement. Fingers of ice crept down the back of her neck. Jesus, what was wrong with her? She'd spent a lifetime being judged because of her accent alone. Sneered at, screamed at, even spat at as a child, and now she was judging someone else? Hypocrisy was a hard pill to swallow.

Despite the revelation, she moved Addy to her other side, putting herself closer to the dispossessed, potentially dangerous man.

He shrank back into the doorway as they walked past.

Did she feel shitty? Yes. But hypocrite or not, she would protect her daughter from any threat, imagined or otherwise. It didn't help that she was still paranoid about her ex finding out where they were.

The man was muttering to himself under his scarf. He probably hadn't even noticed them pass.

Still, she increased her pace and guided Addy away, down the high street, towards the glass-fronted phone shop.

⁂

The enthusiasm dropped from the lanky, adolescent shop-assistant's face when he realised that there would be little, if any, commission attached to the sale. He'd tried his hardest to up sell a better phone, his squeaky voice methodically listing available add-ons and accessories.

Ciara felt a little sorry for him as they left without the better phone and extras. Money was tight, and it wasn't like an eight-year-old needed unlimited bandwidth, or the ability to stream endless YouTube videos. It was for emergencies. Anyway, the less accessibility to social media, the less likely it would be that Addy's dad tracked them down.

'Look Mom, money.' Addison bent down and plucked up the coin. She straightened, held it up and turned it over. Her eyes widened. 'What is it?'

Ciara's eyebrows drew together. 'It's a pound. They didn't look like that when I was younger though. They used to be round and all gold. You're rich.' She mussed up her daughter's hair with a smile.

Her handbag tucked under her arm vibrated. She took a few steps to the side, motioned for Addy to stop and pulled out her phone.

An explosion of butterflies danced in her stomach when she saw the caller ID. She hit the green button.

'Hi, Audrey.' She shook off her paranoia. Audrey was likely just checking in.

'Ciara—' Audrey exhaled. 'Um, are you both okay? I mean, um, was the flight good? You got there alright?'

Audrey sounded nervous. Ciara had known her long enough to recognise it.

'Audrey, tell me what's wrong.' She surprised herself with how calm she sounded.

'Oh, um, right. It's Dean... He knows, Ciara. He knows about you and Addy. He knows you're in England.'

Ciara swallowed out of fear. She couldn't find the words to answer. Part of her was sure she'd lose her breakfast if she tried. She flicked her eyes to Addy and made a strangled sound in the back of her throat.

'I don't know how,' Audrey continued. 'I think he must've suspected something. I overheard him talking to someone, um, I think... I think he might have someone looking for you.'

'But, we were so careful,' Ciara whispered, trying to keep her breathing even, before she had a full-blown panic attack in the middle of the street.

'I know.'

'Is he here?'

'No. No, thank God. He's still in the US. I think he's called in a few favours. Arranged for a couple of hired goons to track you down. I can't be certain. I only caught part of his conversation. Look, I have to go. Just be careful. Get in touch with Fiona, let her know. Stay safe, Ciara. Look after my beautiful little niece.'

The phone chirped and Audrey was gone.

Ciara imagined Dean's reaction to the news: his brown eyes, so dark they might as well have been black, taking on their usual dangerous glint, while his face held no emotion.

Then the violence would start.

Not the heated passion of rage that made some men see red, but calculated and cold. She'd seen both kinds in her lifetime—there had been quite a few brawls when she'd been growing up—but Dean's detached cruelty was by far the worst. The memory made her chest tighten.

She sucked in a long, slow breath. Exhale. Inhale. Repeat. She couldn't panic. She needed a clear head. It wouldn't do any good to scare Addy.

She looked down to her side. Where *was* Addy? Her stomach dropped. Her world stood still.

Then she saw her. Addy stood a couple of feet away from the homeless man with the eerily blue eyes.

Ciara raced over to her before her brain had a chance to catch up.

'Addison!' The word ripped from her throat in a near-scream, as she fumbled her phone back into her bag. Adrenaline had a way of doing that. And she would know; she'd been fiery in her youth. Before the fire got snuffed out of her.

Addy and the man snapped their eyes to her, forcing her into a slower, less panicked pace. Ciara schooled her expression and took a breath.

Addison didn't need to know that they were in danger.

Chapter 31

STEPHEN STRAINED AGAINST THE raging firestorm inside his head. He wanted to cry, to scream, to rip open his own skull. Anything to stop the incessant pounding in his brain. It was consuming him, gorging on his remaining sanity.

Breathe. Just breathe.

THIS IS NO TIME TO TAKE UP YOGA. YOU KNOW THERE'S ONLY ONE WAY TO MAKE IT STOP.

Stephen hissed through his teeth, clenched and unclenched his fists. He felt like he was constantly being watched, like his sixth sense had crawled through his body and taken root in his gut. He gasped a breath and scanned his surroundings.

A girl—she couldn't have been more than eight years old—stared at him with a mixture of sadness and concern. Her pale cheeks, nipped by the chill autumn breeze, were ruddy, with a generous scatter of freckles. Tawny-brown hair caught by the breeze danced around the shoulders of her padded black jacket.

She brushed a few loose strands out of her face. Her expression didn't change, even when her mother attempted to steer her around him, trying not to be obvious and failing miserably.

IT'S THEM! KILL THEM. KILL THEM NOW!

Stephen shrank back from the girl's interest and clenched his jaw.

She's just a child.

SO? THE BLOOD DEBT MUST BE FULFILLED. KILL HER.

'She's only a couple of years older than Bethany is... was,' Stephen murmured. He tucked his chin in to his chest.

JUST KILL THEM. OR I WILL.

Pain seared through his head. His body became rigid. From deep within him a rage and desperation, so primal it stole the air from his lungs, flooded his body. The adrenaline made his nerves tingle and his skin burn. If he could have caught his breath he'd be screaming right now. Sweat trickled down his spine, despite the chill in the air, as he fought to keep the demon from writhing into his muscles.

What are you doing? We're in broad daylight.

KILL THEM.

The demon had never been this agitated before. Not even on the night they'd found Mickey. There was more to this than just fulfilling the blood debt.

KILL THEM.

Stephen's grasp on reality slipped further. It wouldn't be long before he lost himself to the raging bloodlust that screamed in response to the call of the sigils. How much time before that little girl and her mother would get torn to bloody shreds in front of everyone?

The lines of his ethical boundaries had become so blurred. Over the years he'd felt his rage blacken his personality and fracture his morality, like a coal-seam fire, crumbling it until nothing but molten fury drove him at times. Whether it was the demon's influence, or what he'd allowed himself to become, he wasn't sure. But a strong part of him revelled in the wanton carnage, in the bestial act of inflicting unrestrained violence on those who deserved it—and it scared him shitless.

But this wasn't a lowlife criminal before him who'd weaselled their way past some gap in the justice system. This was a child. A child who deserved the chance to live, just like Bethany had.

KILL THEM.

No.

He screwed his eyes shut and exerted all his will to drive the demon back. His body strained with the effort, muscles quivering, as exhaustion began to set in. Giving up wasn't an option.

He visualised a glowing white ball, just like Dee had taught him, before she'd betrayed him. One by one, he added a brick to the image, gradually building around it, fortifying it one layer at a time. There was no way to tell how much time had passed while he strengthened the walls of his resolve. It could have been hours, it could have been minutes. The demon's ire became distant, but it was still there. It launched itself at the perimeter of his defences, trying to find a gap to breach.

Cold fingers grasped his hand and pressed something into his palm. He made a strangled noise and yanked his arm back. Energy lanced through him, raw and unseen. It fixed him in place with invisible wires, wrapping around him so tight he thought he might black out. Just like when he'd been trapped in Jonas' magic circle.

The demon's presence recoiled from it, slamming back with such force, it made Stephen gasp.

'Don't be scared.' A reedy, American accent cut through the thudding of his pounding heart. 'I know it's not much, but it's all I have. You need it more than I do.'

He turned towards the voice, blinking dumbly. His jaw dropped open as he gawked at the little girl he'd been trying to keep alive. He flinched back from her and buried his chin into his chest, concealing more of his ruined face in his scarf. Just looking at her hurt too much. The pain from his head was now throbbing behind his eyes.

She gave him a nervous grin, showing off a gap in her teeth. 'It's okay, I—'

'Addison!' Her mother all but screamed her name.

The girl jumped and stepped back. Her forehead creased.

The woman shot Stephen an anxious look as she reached her daughter. She mumbled something, ignored the curious glances from the handful of onlookers, placed a hand on her daughter's arm and guided her away. The tension visibly melted from her shoulders with the distance.

Neither of them looked back at him.

Stephen uncurled his fingers, little by little. His stomach churned. Whatever was in his hand had shattered the demon's grasp on his will, incapacitating it—at least for the time being. He'd felt the object's intensity all but rip him apart. Something that powerful was almost certainly dangerous and he was *touching* it.

The dull, two-toned surface of a twelve-sided coin sat in his palm. *A pound?* A one-pound coin had fended off a full-scale mental assault from the demon?

Seriously?

He stroked the raised face of Queen Elizabeth II, turned it over and did the same to the coronet encircled rose, leek, thistle and shamrock on the other side. Nothing. There was *nothing* unusual about it. No residual thrum of energy, no mild tingling sensation, not even a temperature discrepancy. It was just a coin.

I don't understand. His attempts to think only increased the pain in his head, making him feel nauseous. Nothing about it made sense.

He pushed the coin firmly into his pocket. Whatever it had done, he might be able to use it again. For the first time in decades he felt a glimmer of hope.

The sound of his own laughter burst from his lips.

He hadn't heard it in so long.

Chapter 32

CHARLIE RACED TO BEAT the flashing green man, careful not to crush the box tucked neatly under his arm. It would have been faster to drive to the shops, but he wasn't about to risk losing his coveted parking space at the station. Besides, the exercise was good for him.

That was the problem with these privately built, multi-million pound police stations. They may have had all the state-of-the-art facilities, but they never had enough damn parking.

He glanced up at the behemoth of a building. It was hard not to be impressed by the sharp lines of red brick flanking a tiered, curved wall of leaded blue-green glass that tapered with each storey.

As he slowed to a trot, a few familiar faces nodded to him. He punched his code into the panel and stepped inside.

Clean, modern and utterly corporate.

'Hey, Charlie,' someone called to him, a voice as smooth as silk.

'Jasmin.' He turned, a broad smile splitting his face.

She flashed him a grin. Her blue eyes sparkled. Jasmin Khatri had always been a pretty girl; as a woman she was stunning. Her rich, brown hair was tied back in a tight ponytail emphasising her strong, square jaw. Rather than being masculine, it added to her looks, giving her an air of strength.

Jasmin and his daughter had been joined at the hip ever since secondary school. During her mid-teens, Meghan had butted heads with Debbie almost daily. She would stay with Charlie until they'd both had a chance to cool down, and more often than not, Jasmin would come with her.

It was no secret that Jasmin had family issues of her own. The police force, much like it had been for him, had become a surrogate family, and she'd blossomed into a capable and confident adult. He found it comforting having her nearby. She reminded him of those few years he'd spent quality time with his daughter. As a newbie on probation, a few of the lads had given Jasmin a hard time, but her commitment and ambition had proved she was no pushover. That and the fact that she had a mean right-hook. Charlie had sparred with her a few times at the gym and she could definitely hold her own. She was a detective now, and a formidable one at that. He couldn't be prouder of the person she'd become.

'Who's the lucky lady?' She nodded at the chocolates under his arm.

He barked a laugh and held up the box, as if showing it explained everything. 'I think I'm too long in the tooth to have to worry about any of that.'

'I dunno, Charlie—' she purred, nudging him with her elbow, '—you're easy on the eye, you work out. If I was so inclined, I'd give you a run for your money.'

Charlie's cheeks grew warm. He cleared his throat and concentrated on the box in his hand. 'They're for my granddaughter. I was thinking of dropping in to see her and Meghan on my way home tonight. It's been a while since I've seen Evelyn. I wouldn't want her to forget what I look like.'

'Oh.'

'What?' That wasn't the reaction he'd expected. He studied her expression. 'Jasmin? What is it?'

'They've gone away for the week. Half-term. Meghan said she was going to tell you.'

He shrugged with a smile that didn't reach his eyes. 'Maybe it slipped her mind.'

'They wouldn't have eaten them anyway. Evie has decided that she's a vegan now.' She made a face. 'And you know how Meghan will do anything to encourage free thought and individuality, because y'know, stifling mother and all that?'

'You don't have to tell me. I lived it. Vegan you say? Seems to be a lot of that going around lately.'

She held up her hands. 'Don't get me wrong, I can absolutely see the moral reasoning behind it. I'm just not there yet. I've compromised by only buying ethically farmed meat. Costs more, but then that's the price you pay for... your friends.'

Charlie suppressed a sigh. When had he become so out of touch? This was his daughter and his granddaughter for Christ's sake. He should know what was going on in their lives, what was important to them.

He held out the box to her. 'In that case, would you like them? Of course, if you take them into the office, you'll have to fight the gannets for them.'

She held her hand out for the box for the briefest moment, then pulled it back with a grimace. 'I probably shouldn't. But thanks.'

'No problem. You're a good friend to Meghan, she's lucky to have you.' It was his turn to watch her blush.

Then her eyes widened. 'Shit. I completely forgot to tell you, there's a young woman waiting for you in your office. She says her name's Jack?'

'Ah, good. I was hoping she'd get in touch. Right, I'd better go and see what she has to say. See you later, Jasmin.' Charlie nodded his goodbye and turned away.

His office wasn't so much an office as it was just another clinical open-plan space. It also wasn't his alone. He shared it with three other civilians under the supervision of DI Clarke, who incidentally *did* have his own office.

Like everywhere else in the building, the walls were white and sterile. The only injection of warmth came from the orange glow of the LED strip lights, embedded in the ceiling panels above.

Jack sat hunched in a black swivel chair in front of his desk. She was tapping her scuffed, black-and-white-chequered trainers on the leg. The hoodie she wore enveloped her like a blanket and made her look even younger than her seventeen years.

Maybe it belonged to Aleksander?

The office's only other occupant ignored them, muttering lightly, her acrylic nails a frantic burst of taps on the keyboard.

'Jack, I wasn't sure if I'd see you again.' Charlie placed the box of chocolates on the desk and sat down across from her. He positioned himself past the monitors. 'You want a chocolate?'

'Erm, no. Thank you.' She shook her head, and frowned briefly at the woman at the adjacent desk. 'These chairs are really uncomfortable. How do you manage to sit in them all day, especially at your age?'

Charlie snorted. His colleague had stopped typing and was stifling a laugh. He gave her a halfhearted glare. 'Thank you, Rosie. Isn't it your turn to make the coffee?'

'Fine, but only because we have company and she doesn't need to see what you're like without your post-lunch caffeine fix.' Rosie pushed back from the desk and stood, giving Jack a wink. She shuffled out of the room.

Charlie rolled his eyes and gave Jack a knowing look. 'So, what can I do for you, Jack?'

Jack fiddled with stray bits of fabric on the rips in her black skinny jeans. She chewed on her lower lip. 'We're leaving. Mum is making us move. Again. I just wanted to come and talk to you before we go. She'd blow a fuse if she knew I was here.'

'That must be frustrating for you.'

She grunted and swiped the back of her hand across her eyes that were covered in dark makeup. 'You have no idea. I'm sick of it. Sick of never being in the same place for more than a year.' She sucked in a breath and blinked away the tears.

Poor kid, first her friends get killed right in front of her, then she has to leave her home.

'Those things you said,' she continued, 'about the serial killer. You really think you can catch him?'

'I do. But I need help. Anything you can tell me, anything you remember could make all the difference.'

She nodded, as if he had convinced her it was true. 'I want you to get him, Charlie. I want you to get the bastard that murdered Alek, murdered my friends,' Her voice shook. Tears rolled down her cheeks.

'I will, Jack. I promise.' What was he doing giving her false hope like that? He'd had thirty-four years to solve this case and hadn't managed it. What was different now? He was only assuming there was a connection.

She glanced back at the door then leant in towards him. 'I think he might be one of your lot, Charlie. The things he said, the things he knew. He was reciting all this stuff about a Public Order Act. It sounded, I don't know, kind of police-y.'

Well, shit. That was just what he needed. A rogue officer.

'Is there anything else, *anything* that might help me identify him?'

'Aside from the great big Joker smile across his face?' She sighed. 'He had a limp. Like he'd hurt his left leg or something.'

Charlie frowned. 'A limp?'

'It... it was dark... and I was too busy watching my boyfriend getting his neck snapped in two.' She slammed her white-knuckled fists down on his desk. She looked down at them, her eyes wide. 'Sorry, I'm sorry...'

'It's okay, Jack. It's fine, take your time.'

She tucked a loose curl of silver-white hair behind her ear, and flicked her eyes back to the door again. Her body sagged. 'His eyes were blue, not like mine, I mean *really* blue. Like one of those White Walkers from *Game of Thrones*. Other than that... I don't know. I'm sorry.'

Charlie considered her without expression. A chill crept down his spine.

She shook her head and rubbed at her hands. Her body began to tremble. 'It's not hopscotch,' she murmured, choking back a sob.

Charlie's eyes widened. 'What did you just say?'

Jack looked up at him, mascara leaving dark tracks down her cheeks. 'It's what he said. Just before he murdered Liv.'

He wasn't sure what struck him first: the feel of his stomach hitting the floor or the realisation that he might vomit. He tapped on the desk three times, to stop the shaking in his fingers, then took a steadying breath and reached for his wallet. He plucked out a creased photo and showed it to her.

'Jack, I want you to look carefully at this picture.'

This was a ridiculous idea. What was he doing?

Making a fool of himself, that's what.

With a strangled gasp, Jack jumped up and knocked the chair over. It drew a few enquiring looks from outside.

Her reaction shocked him.

'Why do you have that?' Her voice quavered as she backed away from him. Her pained expression wrenched at his heart.

Charlie set the photo down and held his hands up. 'It's okay, Jack.' He kept his voice even. The nausea returned, creeping its way up the back of his throat. He swallowed. His palms grew clammy.

It was definitely *not* okay.

'No! It's not,' she screamed. 'Why do you have a photo of *him* in your wallet, Charlie? I trusted you.'

Rosie entered the room. 'Right your lordship, one coffee. Oh—'

Jack ran out the door in a blur, knocking into Rosie. Hot coffee splattered against the floor tiles.

Charlie watched Jack disappear from view with a sinking feeling. *Could it really be? No, impossible.*

He rapped a steady rhythm on the desk as he looked down at the photo. *Tap, tap, tap.* Pause. *Tap, tap, tap.* Pause. The photo was so old that parts of the image had worn away, but Jack was convinced she had *seen* the man in it.

'Charming the ladies again I see, Charlie,' Rosie huffed. She slammed his coffee down on his desk, then waddled to the other side of the office to grab the kitchen roll.

He ignored the coffee and, without answering, placed the photo back inside his wallet. He shook his head, struggling to process what he'd just learnt.

This wasn't the way he'd expected his afternoon to go.

Chapter 33

CIARA SIPPED HER TEA. The warmth of the mug seeped into her palms. It gave her something to focus on, something other than the gnawing sense of despair that had grown steadily throughout the day.

Her conversation with Audrey had left her shaken. She could say with absolute certainty that if it wasn't for Addy, she'd have shut down completely. Children gave mothers a strength that they never thought they could possess. A primal urge to protect and nurture. She needed her little girl every bit as much as Addy needed her and she'd do anything to keep her safe. *Anything.*

With an exhale, she shifted position in the deep-cushioned grey armchair and stretched out her legs. The joints in her ankles popped as she rotated her feet, loosening her muscles. Sitting for over an hour, wallowing in her thoughts hadn't helped.

She had thought Fiona would dismiss her concerns about Dean sending goons after her as paranoia. It must be par for the course that people in her position found themselves jumping at shadows, seeing their abusers in the faces of strangers. Yet, Fiona had listened, offered reassurances and a level-headed perspective on the situation.

'Mom.' Addy blinked up at her. She'd been sat cross-legged on the carpet for a while now, mesmerised by the screen on her new phone. The fact that she'd managed to drag her eyes away from it was an achievement all in itself. 'I'm getting hungry. Can we have fish and chips?'

Ah. *That* explained it.

Ciara glanced down at her watch. 7pm. Already? How had that happened? There was still some food in the fridge, but she didn't feel like cooking. She'd never really been good in the kitchen; it'd never been one of her interests. Her mother had always made the meals, and then, when she moved in with Dean, they'd had hired help to do it all.

She should probably save the money, but she was frazzled and Addy had been looking forward to trying fish and chips. It was mostly all she'd talked about on the flight from New York.

It wasn't until her own stomach growled that she realised just how hungry she was. 'Sure.' Ciara smiled. 'Let me get my coat and I'll nip out and get some.'

'I'll get my coat too.'

'No, honey.' Ciara blinked at the new edge in her voice, and softened her tone. No need to let the paranoia take more control. 'It's already dark out and cold. You stay here. It's just down the road, I won't be long. You've got my number in your phone now, so you can always call me if you need to.'

Addison knitted her brow, and then in a theatrical voice, she said, 'If you insist, I guess I can stay inside and play with my phone.' She grinned.

'I thought that might be the case.' Ciara got up and walked into the kitchen, dropping her mug by the sink. She grabbed her keys and shrugged herself into her coat. 'Don't open the door for anyone.'

'Not even you?' Addy smirked and raised an eyebrow.

'I have my keys, smarty-pants.' She looked at her daughter for a few seconds more, then let herself out of the flat, locked the door and walked briskly down two flights of stairs.

Frigid night air enveloped her the second she exited the main entrance. The door swung to a close behind her. She inhaled deeply and let the chill fill her lungs and clear her head.

Traffic hummed in the distance, blending with the sound of her footsteps, as she walked across the car park and through a gate.

It didn't take long to reach the parade of shops she'd seen on the bus journey that morning. Wafts of chip fat hung in the air. Her stomach rumbled. At least she knew she was in the right place. She smiled up at the signage and pushed open the door to *The Cod Father*.

Ciara stepped inside and joined the queue.

'Yes, love?' The man behind the counter glanced up at her, then turned his attention back to the fryer, and dropped in a generous portion of freshly coated fish. It spluttered and spat enthusiastically, as it plunged into the oil.

'Uh, hi. Medium cod, small cod and a large chips, please.' She fixed a smile in place as he eyed her again. It was the accent. It always was. This side of the pond, she probably sounded like just another brash American from a seventies gangster film.

'It'll be about ten minutes, that alright?'

'Sure, no problem.' Ciara took a step back and paid at the till.

The chippy was clean and modern, fronted with huge, glass windows set into rustic wooden panels. White vinyl sans-serif lettering listing its food covered roughly half of one of the panes. The other boasted an enlarged version of *The Cod Father* logo.

The small shop had a steady queue of patrons who stood in silence, either passing the time with their phones or staring at nothing in particular, until their order was called. Which made it all the more apparent when the door opened, bringing with it an arctic blast that sent a shudder down the back of her neck.

Two men that looked like bouncers walked in. Thick necked and muscled, they looked like they spent far too much time in the gym and ate far too much chicken and rice. There was more stubble on their faces than on their heads, and she would have bet money that their arms, obscured by their jackets, were covered in sleeves of tattoos. When one of them caught her staring, she looked away and focused on the menu mounted on the wall behind the counter.

Did one item really say "battered Mars Bar"? Gross.

She cast another quick glance in their direction when one of them grunted his order in a gravelly voice, and handed over his money. The other glared at her. She dropped her eyes to her feet.

Odd that they both came in together, isn't it? It's pretty cramped already. You'd have thought one of them would have waited outside, wouldn't you? Does it need two of them just to order a portion of chips? I'm just being paranoid, again.

Was it her imagination or were they both staring at her now?

She flicked her gaze at them again. *Yeah, definitely staring.*

Her breath quickened. Should she walk out? She didn't like her odds against two behemoths that looked to be one link too low on the evolutionary chain. But it would confirm if they'd been sent to follow her. Give her a chance to run. To lead them away from Addy and get help.

Her thumb traced the raised buttons on the phone inside her pocket. Should she stay? She could hole up inside, call Fiona. Call the police if she had to. But if her ex-husband's men had found her, maybe they'd found Addy too, all alone in the flat.

'Large chips,' the man behind the counter announced, holding out a neatly wrapped white-paper parcel.

One of the men grabbed it and they both left.

Ciara let out a breath. She really needed to get a handle on her emotions; no wonder her hair had started to turn grey. Maybe she should try yoga, anything to relieve the pent up tension.

Yes, Dean might have turned out to be a high-ranking figure in a criminal enterprise that had territories in at least two boroughs of the metropolis, but that didn't mean he had the resources to chase her half way around the world, despite what Audrey said. Did it? Or that he'd have connections in the UK.

That would be insane, wouldn't it? Sure. Sure it would. Just a little paranoia, that's all. Anyway, Audrey even said that she'd only caught part of the conversation. Who knew what that call was really about?

'Love?'

Ciara jumped. Heat rose in her cheeks when she realised her order was ready.

'Uh. Oh, sorry. Sorry.' She reached out and grabbed the bag, mumbled thanks and turned to leave.

She felt eyes on her as the door swung shut behind her, closing her off from the warmth and safety.

Chapter 34

A LIGHT SPATTER OF drizzle hit Ciara's cheeks as she left the parade of shops behind. She blinked the droplets from her eyes and sighed. Her breath fogged into a great white plume. *I should have just cooked at home.* She hugged the hot bag of food; warmth seeped into her chest. She increased her speed until her walk became a jog.

Ciara froze when she saw someone standing outside the communal door to her flats. A dark-skinned woman was jabbing randomly at the intercom system mounted on the wall. Her black hair was tied in a messy bun; a few wisps were plastered to her face. Judging by the flimsy, low-cut T-shirt, ripped jeans and silver slingback shoes, she clearly hadn't prepared to be outside.

Ciara repositioned the bag as she approached, hunting in her pocket for her keys. She cast a wary glance at the stranger.

The woman stepped aside to allow Ciara access. She tapped the fob against the reader; the door unlocked.

The woman pushed the door open with a huff of effort, and gestured at her top. Ciara stepped in beside her.

'Bloody typical, isn't it?' the woman said. 'I only went to put something in my car.'

Ciara smiled politely. 'Forget your key?'

'Yeah. I must have left it inside. Hey, are you American?'

'I am. Was it the accent that gave me away?' It was easier to pretend than give her life story.

The woman let out a belly laugh. 'I like you. A little advice, if you ever forget your key, just mash all the buttons. One of the flats will usually buzz you in. I'm Anna by the way. Anyway, this floor is me. See you around.'

'Ciara. Good to know, thank you.' She watched as the woman flashed a smile and rounded the corner, still murmuring complaints about the weather.

Ciara's calves were on fire by the time she reached the second floor. When had she become so out of shape? She unlocked the door; it shouldn't have surprised her to find Addy in exactly the same place as she'd left her. Still staring at her phone.

'Really, Addy? Have you even moved since I left?'

'Yeah, Mom. I got a drink, see?' Addison grinned up at her and pointed to the glass of water sitting on the set of nested oak tables.

Maybe Ciara was biased, but the missing tooth made her daughter just so adorable. No wonder she got away with so much.

'Hmm. Go wash your hands and get ready to eat.'

In the time it took Addy to get back from the bathroom, Ciara had already piled two plates high with food and placed them on the table. Addison sat down with a squeal and shuffled her chair closer, with a few scrapes.

'That smells yummy.' She picked up a chip and rammed it into her mouth, giving a murmur of pure delight.

'Do you know what I saw while I was in the fish and chip shop?' Ciara said.

'No?' Addy looked up mid-chew, and shrugged.

'They sell battered Mars Bars.'

Addy's eyes widened. '*What?* Did you buy one? Tell me you bought one.'

'No. Because I love you and I don't want your heart to explode.'

Addison rolled her eyes and made an exasperated sound, then tucked into her food.

A buzzing noise made them both look up from their meals. It took a beat for Ciara to figure out that it was coming from their intercom system. Someone was buzzing up from outside.

'What is that, Mom?'

Ciara thought of Anna. She relaxed her shoulders. 'People do that when they forget their key. They're trying to get someone to open the door.'

'Are you going to open it for them?'

'No. We're having our dinner. Anyway, someone else will probably buzz them in. But it's not something I want you to start doing. The whole point of having a security system is to keep people out.'

They chatted and giggled in between mouthfuls, until a knock at the door made them both jump, stopping the conversation dead. Ciara schooled her expression in response to Addison's frown. She stood and padded over to the door.

Pressing her eye up against the peephole revealed nobody there. Her skin bristled and the hairs on her arms stood on end. Something didn't feel right. But she'd been on edge all evening and nothing had happened. Maybe they just had the wrong flat? She gave Addy a shrug.

Ciara went to turn, then a second knock stopped her dead.

'Who is it?' She put more confidence into the question than she felt. There was no reason to worry Addy. She slipped the security chain into the lock.

'Package. Needs to be signed for.' The voice was deep. Definitely male.

'I haven't ordered anything. I think you've got the wrong flat.'

'Says eighty-four. That's you. If you want I can give you a card and you can pick the parcel up from your local depot after twenty-four hours? Or not. Up to you.' There was no threat to his tone, just indifference.

She wondered if Fiona had sent her something.

'Uh, slide the card under the door, please.'

After a few seconds, there was a muffled sigh followed by a weary 'fine.' The man pushed a red card part way under the door, enough for her to see the word "sorry" and the top corner of a white logo. It bunched up against the floor.

The man tried again, making it worse.

Ciara opened the door, leaving a little slack in the chain.

The door exploded inward. The chain ripped from its fixtures and tore from the frame.

'Addy. Room. Lock the door!' Ciara screamed as she stumbled backwards from the force of the door.

Addison's face blanched; she did as she was told. Her food scattered when she scrambled off her chair, ran to her room and slammed the door shut.

'Ciara, isn't it?' The man stepped through the doorway, holding out a thick, calloused palm to catch the door on the rebound. He was shadowed by a second hulking slab of muscle.

The pair from the fish and chip shop stood just inside her flat, taking in their surroundings with the composure of two predators. The first man quirked a wolfish smile at her and then flicked the crumpled, red card to the floor. She cursed herself for not trusting her instincts.

'Get out.' The strength in her voice wavered. She placed herself between the men and the way to Addy's room. 'I said get out!'

'Now, now. We're just here to make sure you both get home safely, Ciara. Isn't that right, Price?' The slightly taller of the two, obviously the brains of the operation, lifted his palms in peace, but his apathy didn't fool her for a moment.

'Yeah. Yeah, that's right, Davis. That's right,' Price agreed. A cruel smile danced on his lips. His body was coiled for violence.

'We're not going anywhere with you. Tell Dean to go fuck himself.'

'Oh dear, that's no way for a lady to speak, is it? And what with a child present. Little Addison shouldn't be exposed to such vile language now, should she?'

Ciara paled at the mention of her daughter's name, but she stayed put. She didn't stand a chance against these thugs and she knew it, but come hell or high water, she was going to protect her daughter.

'How did you find us?'

'I don't think you're really in a position to be asking the questions, do you? Now, be a good girl and get your daughter and your passports, and we can all be on our way. You've got a flight to catch after all,' Davis drawled.

Price took a heavy step forward. Then another. He rolled his shoulders and cracked his neck.

Ciara gulped. 'Leave. Please.'

'It's really quite simple, Mrs Torres. Gather your belongings and come with us, or we'll gather them for you.'

'No.'

Price looked back at Davis, who gave him a single nod. With a shrug, Price moved forward and yanked open one of the kitchen drawers. It flew from its hinges with the force and landed on the floor in a clatter of cutlery. He eyed the contents with a grunt, and then reached out a hand for the next drawer.

'Stop! What are you doing?' Ciara yelped.

'I told you. We are gathering your belongings. Price here is locating your passports. Once that's done we'll take you to the airport.'

A second crash made her jerk back. Kitchen utensils and plywood scattered across the laminate, settling next to the silverware. The green silicone poaching cup rolled towards her foot. She gaped at the mess.

Why was this happening? How had they found her? It didn't make sense. She'd been so careful.

The briefest glint of red caught her eye as Price moved towards a third drawer. She lunged forward and snatched up the letter opener.

Davis' nose scrunched up. He made a tutting sound as he regarded her. 'Now, what are you planning on doing with *that*?'

Price turned. His Neanderthal-like forehead furrowed and his eyes narrowed. He tramped towards her. A serving spoon buckled under his weight when his mammoth foot stomped down on it.

'I told you to get out. So. Get. Out.' Something close to confidence touched her voice. She brandished the blade, giving Price pause. It felt good in her hand. The mottled, black handle felt smooth and sure against her skin, like it'd been made just for her.

Price huffed and closed the distance between them. He drew up to his full height, making her feel tiny and insignificant. At five eight she wasn't short, but Price must have been pushing six two, give or take. She clutched the letter opener tighter.

He lunged at her.

She shrieked and slashed out with her weapon. She felt a slight pressure when it connected with flesh.

Price hissed and pulled his hand back. 'You stupid bitch,' he spat between gritted teeth and inspected his palm. Blood dribbled down his wrist, seeping into the cuff of his jacket. He glared down at her. His face reddened.

White light flashed in Ciara's vision when he struck her across her face. She hit the floor hard and grunted as the contents of the drawers jabbed her in the ribs and thighs. She'd lost the letter opener in the clattering wake of debris and kitchenware.

'I've called the cops,' Addison shouted from her bedroom. 'They're on the way right now.'

Ciara opened her eyes, reeling against the pain in her jaw, and stared up at Price. He rubbed at his hand and gave Davis a questioning look.

'I think you'd better leave.' Another man's voice cut through the silence. 'We've called the police.'

Ciara looked towards the doorway. Dots danced in front of her eyes. Two men stood just outside her flat. Although they were clearly nervous, they stood their ground. The sounds of shuffling and an anxious cough suggested there were more people than she could see.

Thank Christ.

'You heard him. Get out.' Another man echoed the statement.

Davis sucked his teeth and shared a look with Price. He jerked his head at the exit.

'This is not over, Mrs Torres,' Davis said. 'You'd better be prepared to leave the next time we stop by.'

The men pushed their way past the gathered crowd. Ciara let out a breath. Moments later, she was helped to her feet by one of the men.

They peppered her with questions, but the words were just noise, competing with the ringing in her ears and her pounding heart.

How the *hell* had they found her?

Chapter 35

Stephen stood shrouded in the darkness of the near-abandoned car park. Only one vehicle remained, with yellow penalty charge notices stuck liberally across the smashed windscreen. The rest of the car hadn't fared much better. Slashed tyres, keyed paintwork, wing mirrors hanging from wires.

Classy part of town.

An angry hiss escaped his lips when the demon slipped his hand from his pocket and uncurled his fingers, to reveal the single pound coin. The wan glow offered by the far-off street lights offered little in the way of illumination. Yet he could make out every detail, every scratch, every scuff, every minute imperfection.

I *SAID* YOU SHOULD HAVE KILLED HER.

It had taken hours for the demon to become responsive again, but it was making up for lost time with a new run of complaints. To put it bluntly, it was pissed.

She's just a child.

THAT HASN'T STOPPED US BEFORE.

Its words were like a knife to the gut, each one a savage twist of the blade.

THE BLOOD DEBT MUST BE FULFILLED. YOU KNOW THIS.

Boy, did he know it. The pulsing agony in his head hadn't been this intense for years. He'd nearly forgotten how excruciating it could be. The brief release when the demon had become incapacitated had been sheer ecstasy. For a moment he'd even allowed himself to nurture a germ of hope, but when the presence had slowly roused itself, that hope had withered and died, leaving a hollow husk of despair.

And now he'd had to spend the last two hours listening to it bitch.

So, is it just coins you're scared of, or are we talking notes as well?

The demon ignored him. The tension in Stephen's body wound tighter as the presence continued to scowl at the pound in his palm.

It was obvious that it wanted to launch the thing far away. But something prevented it from doing so, like there was a physical block cutting the connection between Stephen's brain and muscles.

Something significant had happened when that little girl had given him the coin, and he was damned if he knew what.

I AM NOT SCARED. The words resonated through his skull.

Wow. Clearly, he'd touched a nerve.

Okay, so what happened?

The demon replayed the memories inherited from its time within the dagger. Most of what it shared with

Stephen was conjecture. Everything it knew about the magic that bound them—that compelled them to follow the call of the sigils—was based solely on the residual whisperings of the dagger's previous occupants.

SHE PAID HER DUES. THE MAGIC REQUIRES THAT A DEBT BE PAID, EITHER WITH A LIFE OR WITH WEALTH.

Well, that information was new.

So, a "your money or your life" situation. Wait, are you trying to tell me you're a highwayman?

A low growl rumbled in his throat. It carried out the ruined shreds of flesh around his mouth. Apparently, the demon was in no mood for jokes.

But it's just a pound.

WHETHER IT'S A SINGLE COIN OR AN INGOT OF GOLD, THE DEBT REQUIRES THAT ALL WEALTH BE SURRENDERED IN RETURN FOR LIFE. THAT COIN WAS ALL SHE HAD AND SHE GAVE IT TO YOU.

Sirens wailed in the distance. The demon returned the coin to Stephen's pocket and glanced over his shoulder.

PERSONALLY, I'D HAVE EATEN YOUR HEART AND TAKEN WHAT LITTLE BELONGED TO YOU. HUMANS MAKE LITTLE SENSE. WHERE I COME FROM ONLY THE STRONG SURVIVE.

Gee, thanks.

Christ. That was all the money she had, and she'd given it away to a homeless man on the street? The sentiment cut deeper than any blade could.

So if she's paid her debt, why are you so angry about it? Wait, you're pissed that you didn't get to kill her. You think you've been cheated. This isn't about the blood debt. This is about you. You like it. You like the slaughter.

OF COURSE I LIKE IT. I AM A PREDATOR. AT LEAST I DON'T LIE TO MYSELF ABOUT IT.

Lie about what?

YOU ENJOY KILLING AS MUCH AS I DO.

That's not true.

Even as he thought the words, he knew it was a lie. The Boswells had ruined his life. Hell, they'd even ruined his death. Hunting them down had given him unbridled satisfaction, but only for moments at a time. When he'd plunged that switchblade into Mickey's chest, again and again, he'd relished every second of it, until all that remained was emptiness in his heart and blood on his hands. When he'd put his foot through Niall's skull, he'd taken a heartless pleasure in the feel of crunching bone.

The Boswells had brought it on themselves. Every last one of them. They shouldn't have gone near his family.

WHAT ABOUT THE TEENAGERS LAST NIGHT?

That was you.

WAS IT? YOU WANTED THEM TO DIE. AS SOON AS YOU SAW WHAT THEY WERE DOING, YOU WANTED TO CHOKE THE LAST BREATH OF LIFE FROM THEIR THROATS. YOU CAN LIE TO YOURSELF, BUT I AM INSIDE YOUR HEAD. I KNOW THE REAL YOU.

You knew, didn't you? You knew that if we followed them there I'd lose control.

THEY WERE CRIMINALS.

They were kids.

THEY WERE BREAKING THE LAW. TRESPASSING. DRINKING UNDERAGE. SMOKING DRUGS. NOT TO MENTION THE PUBLIC INDECENCY.

They were just being teenagers.

THE LAW IS THE LAW.

Don't you dare talk to me about the law! I spent half my life upholding it. You know nothing about right and wrong. About justice.

JUSTICE? YOU DIDN'T KNOW JUSTICE UNTIL YOU MET ME. YOU WERE AS SHACKLED TO THE CONSTRAINTS OF YOUR JUDICIAL SYSTEM AS I AM TO THAT DAGGER. HOW MANY CRIMINALS WENT FREE BECAUSE OF FAILINGS IN THE SYSTEM? BECAUSE OF HUMAN ERROR AND LOOPHOLES? AT LEAST MY ACTIONS HAVE MADE A DIFFERENCE. THINK OF ALL THE MURDERERS, ALL THE RAPISTS, ALL THE VIOLENT THUGS NO LONGER ROAMING THE STREETS BECAUSE OF WHAT WE HAVE ACCOMPLISHED TOGETHER.

The demon had a point, not that he would admit to it.

WE'RE THE SAME, YOU AND I.

I'm nothing like you. You're a monster.

A MONSTER? The demon laughed. I SAVED YOU. I HAVE GIVEN YOU EVERYTHING YOU WANTED. EVERYTHING.

Was the entity *really* trying to make out that Stephen was the villain here?

You think I wanted this? To be trapped for eternity, festering in the cesspit of my own anger, with a demon inside my head? A disfigured outcast with nothing to offer the world but hatred and death? And don't even get me started on this incessant pounding in my head. I swear it's driving me insane. You're one of the worst things that's ever happened to me.

His world came to a stop. Absolutely still, but for the rise and fall of his chest and his soft breath fogging in the biting, night air. The demon's silence was almost as deafening as the rhythmic throb inside his skull. He should have taken it for the warning it was.

I should've let Jonas and Dee finish the binding spell. Been rid of you for good.

The demon broke its silence. YOU UNGRATEFUL CUR. YOU DON'T WANT ME AROUND? FINE. THIS WAS ALL A TEMPORARY INCONVENIENCE ANYWAY. ONCE THE BLOOD DEBT HAS BEEN SATISFIED, I WILL LOCATE A GATEWAY AND RETURN TO MY OWN REALM. YOU'LL BE FREE TO ENJOY YOUR LAST PITIFUL SECONDS ALONE AFTER MY ESSENCE TRANSFERS INTO MY BODY.

The muscles in Stephen's arms quivered, fists balled at his sides.

Your body? Your body will be nothing more than rot and worm food by now. It's been over a century.

YOU KNOW NOTHING. TIME IS FLUID, EACH PLANE CAPTURED IN ITS OWN CURRENT. WHAT

MIGHT PASS AS A CENTURY HERE IS NO MORE
THAN A WEEK WHERE I COME FROM. MY BODY
WILL BE WAITING FOR ME IN THE SACRED
CAVERNS OF MY ANCESTORS.

And there it was.

That's why you were so frustrated after Mickey's death. You thought you'd found a loophole. A way to break the dagger's hold over you with the execution of its master. You were biding your time with me until you could get back to your body. That's why you were so desperate to kill that little girl and her mother. You never wanted to help me. You used my grief as a weapon. Manipulated me like a parasitic con artist.

ALL THIS FROM THE MAN WHO TURNED HIS
BACK ON HIS VALUES. The demon laughed. YOU'RE A
MURDERER. A CRIMINAL. NO BETTER THAN THE
MEN WHO SLAUGHTERED YOUR FAMILY. YOU
PREACH RIGHTEOUS INDIGNATION, BUT YOU'RE
JUST AS BAD AS THEM. WORSE EVEN. YOU TELL
ME, WHO'S REALLY THE MONSTER HERE?

The unsteady click of heels striking concrete cut above the ambient sounds of far-off traffic and city nightlife. The demon turned and honed in on it, inhaling deeply. The reek of alcohol and sickly-sweet vape smoke was mingled with perspiration and cheap perfume.

It wasn't long before he saw the drunken young woman. His heightened night vision exposed details that would have otherwise been lost to the darkness. The corners of her brown eyes were smudged with black.

Residues of shimmering lip gloss clung to her mouth. Her chestnut hair, looking as if it had been straightened at some point in the evening, hung messily around her face. A face that, despite the generous application of makeup, had taken on a greenish hue and was sweating.

She swallowed rapidly. Her eyes widened as she bent forward, and spewed a noxious cocktail of what smelt like doner-kebab meat and white wine across the concrete.

With a groan, she straightened and wiped the back of her hand across her mouth, then down the skirt of her blue chiffon dress. A dress that was so short it was almost indecent. She belched, shook her head and spat on the floor.

GOOD. I WAS STARTING TO FEEL PECKISH.

The demon walked him towards her. She squinted in his direction. A vicious smile touched her lips. 'I told you you'd be back. Couldn't even go twenty minutes without chasing after me, huh? I knew you'd come crawling back.' Her words were slurred. She placed her hands on her hips and quirked them to one side.

She's wrecked.

'What do I care? You're all just fodder,' the demon said for him, each dissonant word edged with steel.

Her face twisted with a cruelty that had no place on someone so young. 'What? What did you say? I'm what?'

As Stephen got closer her confident sneer dropped.

'You're not... who are you? What do you want?' She shrunk back and folded her arms across her body.

The entity cocked its head. 'What do I want? I just want to help you.'

Christ. The words were right, but the tone was predatory, dangerous.

In two lurching strides he was in front of her.

She flinched back more. A gasp hitched in her throat.

The demon lashed out with a fist to her stomach. She doubled over with a wheeze and crumpled. Before she hit the floor, the entity twisted fingers in her hair and yanked her neck back; she had no choice but to gape up at him.

With his free hand, the presence pulled down the scarf covering the lower part of Stephen's face, knowing the sight of his mangled flesh would make her forget the pain in her stomach.

She whimpered and attempted to twist away. The motion only knotted her hair in his fist more.

Tears streaked down her cheeks as the demon lowered Stephen's face to hers. He was close enough to feel the warmth of her ragged breath on his skin, smell the sour tang of bile that lingered on her tongue.

Stop. You're going to get us caught. If you keep leaving a trail of bodies, O.O.T.I.S will find us. You'll be banished back to the dagger, your body left to rot.

The demon's hesitation was so brief Stephen nearly missed it.

He pressed on. *We've killed too many people in too short a time. It's not like it used to be. There are cameras everywhere. I thought we agreed that we'd only kill the people that deserved—*

275

He realised his mistake as soon as he'd thought the words.

THIS IS *NOT* A COLLABORATION. YOU'VE MADE THAT PERFECTLY CLEAR. YOU ARE NOTHING MORE THAN A MOMENTARY AGGRAVATION.

The demon straightened to full height, yanking the woman's head up and back. She had no choice but to rise with him, clutching one arm with both hands, losing one of her heels as her feet scrambled against the concrete.

She dug her fingers into his muscles. Unspoken words formed on her quivering lips, her bitter breath coming out in stilted huffs.

'Please,' she rasped.

The demon wiped a tear from her cheek and made a shushing sound. She cringed at the contact, eyes wide, as it brought the thumb to his ravaged mouth and tasted it.

Stephen was forced to watch her pleas die on her lips. Forced to taste the fear in that single tear. Forced to feel the warmth of her skin as he brushed his lips against her ear.

'Let me help you.' It was nothing more than a whisper, but the words ricocheted around Stephen's mind.

In a heartbeat, the demon jerked her head back and sunk his teeth into her bared throat. Blood flooded into Stephen's mouth, leaked out the gaping fissures in his face and down his jaw, as he tore through cartilage and muscle.

She clawed at his arms. She thrashed uselessly. When she stopped fighting, he let her fall in a limp heap at his feet.

LET ME HELP YOU TO REMEMBER THAT I SAVED YOU. I GAVE YOU THE MEANS TO EXACT YOUR VENGEANCE. I AM THE ONLY THING HOLDING YOUR BODY TOGETHER. YOU ARE NOTHING WITHOUT ME. *NOTHING.*

Warm pulp slid down Stephen's gullet when the demon swallowed. It wiped a hand across his mouth, lifted his face and laughed.

Stephen said nothing.

He felt the weight of the coin in his pocket. The little girl's time was about to run out and there was not a dammed thing he could do to stop it.

Chapter 36

'INTERESTING.' THE TWISTED VOICE inside Stephen faded into the darkness.

The sharp, metallic tang of blood lingered in the air, filling his nostrils. He shifted position, limbs stiff from perching for hours on the damp, grassy knoll outside the flat complex.

Police were already in attendance by the time he'd arrived, frustrating the demon's plans to unshackle itself from the magical bonds tethering it to the Boswells.

Could the presence have forced him to massacre every officer and civilian there in a matter of minutes? Absolutely.

But it had hesitated, taking the opportunity instead to skim through Stephen's memories as a detective, so that it could understand the scenes playing out before it. Any one of them could be an O.O.T.I.S plant, and it wasn't about to get exiled back to the confines of the dagger. Not when the entity was so close to getting everything it wanted. Even so, it had barely restrained itself when the young girl and her mother had been escorted away by a uniformed officer in a marked police car.

Drifting conversation had painted them a clear picture of the events of the evening. He'd even caught the tail end of a discussion between officers about one of the intruders being injured by a weapon. They'd been very excited about it. It wasn't every day that criminals offered up their DNA.

A lot of effort had been made to try and abduct the two women. Chasing anybody half way around the world took some serious cash, which made them invaluable to someone besides the demon. Once the pieces fell into place, a new rage churned inside his chest with such intensity, it quickly became his own. Somebody was trying to take the demon's toys and it wasn't happy.

Stephen's fingers gouged into the sodden earth. The muscles in his arms, like cords of iron, strained. There was no way the demon was about to squander its only chance to satisfy the blood debt. If it lost the pair now, who knew how long before another opportunity arose?

Stephen cast a final glance at the building, where at least one detective still remained inside, and moved to leave. With the girl and her mother giving statements at the local police station, there was little more to learn from hanging around in the soggy grass.

I'VE WAITED THIRTY-FOUR YEARS. I CAN WAIT UNTIL TOMORROW. BUT FIRST I THINK I NEED TO TEACH SOMEONE A VALUABLE LESSON FOR TRYING TO TAKE WHAT DOES NOT BELONG TO THEM.

Twin beams cut through the drizzle of the car park. A metallic, gunmetal grey Audi A4 Avant followed. It pulled into one of the parking bays; its throaty purr cut out and the headlights winked off. The driver, a male in his mid-sixties, removed his driving glasses and stowed them in a little compartment built into the headliner. Something about him seemed familiar.

God, don't they let people retire anymore?

The sound of the car door opening carried across the expanse of concrete, bringing with it the rich aroma of sandalwood and vetiver.

It sparked a memory.

No. It can't be.

He tried to mask the surge of emotion but it was too late.

The demon's focus snapped onto the newcomer.

Onto Charlie.

Seconds felt like hours as his mind fractured under the demon's probing. Memories flickered in the depths of his consciousness. Years of his life presented to the entity in one nauseating burst.

WELL, ISN'T THIS A HAPPY COINCIDENCE.

He was older, a lot older. But beneath the age lines and the grey hair it was undoubtedly Charlie. The way he carried himself, the determined set of his jaw. The familiarity of it was painful for Stephen. For decades he'd longed to see his friend again, hoped that he was alive and well.

But not like this. What he wouldn't give to forget his friend.

But if Charlie was working this case... If Charlie saw the dagger—and Stephen knew it would be there somewhere, because it always was—he'd put two and two together. The pattern between the Boswells was evident, but if anyone could make the connection as to why the girl and her mother had survived and not the rest, it would be Charlie. The man was a machine, and Stephen was sure his friend had only ever been a couple of steps behind their killing sprees.

What was it about that dagger? It was as if it were stalking him, ever since the night Mickey had plunged it into his chest and left him for dead. It always seemed to be at hand whenever they unearthed another Boswell. Not that it had done them any good. The demon had told him the dagger always returned to its master, but its master was dead. He'd seen to that. But, with Charlie here, its recurrent appearance could be a good thing.

Yes, this could work.

SO THIS IS THE GREAT CHARLIE HAYNES? HE LOOKS OLD. FRAIL. I MUST SAY, I'M DISAPPOINTED. THE WAY YOU BUILT HIM UP, I'D ALMOST WISHED THAT HE WERE THE ONE WHO'D BEEN STABBED WITH THE DAGGER INSTEAD OF YOU. BUT THIS HUMAN? REALLY?

Any reply that Stephen might have had was lost in the shock of the moment.

The demon snarled, eased him back into the shadows, and together they watched as Charlie was buzzed into the building. It was definitely time to leave.

LET'S GO KILL SOME CRIMINALS.

Absolutely. Every hour that the demon remained distracted was another hour that the young girl and her mother were safe.

Stephen inhaled and turned towards the trailing scent, left by whichever of the two men had been wounded. The thought of their tortured screams filling the night sent a surge of excitement through their bond.

It wasn't until Stephen took his next breath that he realised, with sickening clarity, that the excitement was his own.

Chapter 37

CHARLIE STEPPED INTO THE flat. He ran a hand over his damp hair and took in the scene.

The place was a shambles.

There was a sizeable dent in the door where it had been kicked in. The remnants of the lock dangled from the chain, no longer attached to the splintered frame.

So, the door was open but still on the chain when they forced entry.

Charlie smiled and nodded to the detective at the door. 'Nick, we really need to stop meeting like this. Henry will start getting the wrong idea about us.'

'Funny.' Nick regarded Charlie through narrowed eyes, but the ghost of a smile touched his lips. 'Henry knows you're not my type.'

'Too handsome?'

Nick started counting on his fingers. 'Too grouchy. Too old. Too—'

'Christ, I get it.' He took in Nick's dishevelled appearance. 'You look terrible, you should go home.'

'Cheers for that.' Nick ran a hand through his auburn hair. 'Stayed on. Long shift.'

'I'd say. You know I was just about to eat, right?' Charlie scanned the room and nodded to a crime scene investigator enshrouded in a white coverall and disposable overshoes. The person returned the nod, clutching a clear evidence bag in one hand.

The scent of fish and chips lingered in the air. Charlie's stomach growled. He'd barely touched his meal before his phone rang. Judging by the plates on the oak dining table, still piled with food that had long since gone cold, he wasn't the only one running on empty this evening.

'Stop complaining, there's something here that you're going to want to see,' Nick said.

'Huh, you don't say? Well, aren't I the lucky boy?'

Nick rolled his eyes, stepped to one side and gestured at the ground. 'Scenes of crime are just wrapping things up, but I wanted you to see this before it gets bagged.'

Charlie arched an eyebrow and followed Nick's finger that was pointing at the detritus covering the floor of the open-plan kitchen. He was about to reply with a sarcastic comment when he saw it. Amongst the splinters of plywood and scattered utensils, next to a carefully placed ruler, was a dagger.

No. *The* dagger.

Just as he remembered it. Its mottled Damascus steel blade was stained with blood.

'It... It's not possible.' He stepped forward and nudged a path with his foot through the mess of kitchenware.

'It matches the description of the knife you mentioned in your case files,' Nick said.

'Dagger.' Charlie corrected. He glanced back at him. 'You read those?'

'Are you kidding? Every rookie DC knows about the Caravan Cannibal, the most prolific serial killer since Jack the Ripper. They still use them during training you know.'

'You haven't been a rookie for a long time, Nick.'

Nick shrugged. 'I may have looked over them again, once or twice, when I learnt they were bringing you in on unsolved crimes. It never hurts to get an insight into the mind of someone you're going to be working with.'

Charlie smirked. 'Fanboy.'

Nick scoffed. Charlie ignored it and turned back to the dagger. In a practiced motion, he pulled his reading glasses from the inside pocket of his slate-grey, wool trench coat and slid them onto his face. When did he get to the stage of life where he needed a pair of glasses for everything? He crouched down to give it a closer look.

'Is it the same?' Nick asked.

Pressure built behind his eyes as the wheels of his mind went into overdrive. 'Looks like it.'

The red gemstone winked at him from the decorative pommel, almost as if recognising him. Every detail matched perfectly with the image that had been seared into his mind, thirty-four years ago. The silver, floral scroll filigree embellishment. The smooth black marble, veined with white and every spectrum of grey.

'How did the knife—'Nick began.

'Dagger. Both edges are sharpened and go down to a point.'

Nick suppressed a sigh. 'How did the *dagger* used to murder DC Anderson get out of evidence in the first place, let alone become a recurring artefact throughout the Caravan Cannibal killings? Replicas?'

Charlie flinched. It had been years since he'd heard anyone say Stephen's name in any form. 'That, Nick, is a very good question. A very good question indeed.' He slowly got to his feet.

'Sorry, Nick, are you guys done in here?' The CS investigator asked.

Nick arched his eyebrow at Charlie.

'Yes. We're done, thank you,' Charlie answered.

With that, the man plucked the dagger from the assortment of utensils, and placed it delicately in the clear plastic evidence bag.

'I hope you got plenty of photos,' Charlie said to Nick. They watched the investigator gather the remainder of his equipment and leave, overshoes crinkling lightly with each step.

'What? Why?'

He gave his friend a level look. 'Because, it won't be in evidence the next time you go to look for it.'

'Hang on. Are you saying that the dagger was never lost, that someone has been removing evidence? You think someone internally is involved with these cases?'

'Not that I've ever been able to prove.' He remembered his last conversation with Jack. There was no way he could voice his suspicions to Nick about Stephen—he'd sound senile. 'All I'm saying is that thing—' he pointed towards the empty hallway where the investigator had disappeared from sight, '—has a mind of its own. And wherever it turns up the bodies usually follow.'

Nick exhaled and rubbed his forehead with his palm. His pale-blue eyes were troubled. 'Charlie, that doesn't make any sense. Ciara Torres and her daughter only arrived in the country yesterday. They said the dagger was already in the flat. Pre-furnished. You think the owner or previous renters are involved?'

Charlie stifled a growl. A knot tightened inside his stomach. He'd had thirty-four years to try and wrap his head around this bullshit, and he still couldn't rationalise any of it. 'All I know is that if that dagger turned up here, then those girls are in trouble. There has to be a connection.'

Nick regarded him silently.

'We're missing something. Ciara and her daughter—where did you say they were from?'

'America. Long Beach, New York.'

'Torres. That her married name?'

'Yes.'

'Maiden name?'

'Delaney,' came the clipped reply from the doorway.

Charlie and Nick turned towards the voice in unison.

Ciara Torres, formerly Delaney, regarded them with a hard look. Charlie recognised that expression; he'd seen it on Debbie often enough.

'Delaney?' Charlie deflated. 'I could have sworn...'

'Sworn what?' Her question was barbed.

He could *see* the resemblance. In the heart shape of her face, the spray of freckles and her deep-brown eyes. He'd seen enough of her dead family to identify the similarities. He flicked his gaze to her left hand, to check for evidence of the scar, but his eyesight was not what it once was.

'Sworn *what?*'

'That you were a Boswell.'

Ciara's eyebrows drew up. She blinked. 'How did you...'

He was right. Another Boswell.

He licked his lips, his mouth suddenly dry from the tension.

A young girl, no more than eight, peered around Ciara, her head just above elbow height. She pulled a hand through her tawny-brown hair and grinned up at them. Her nose crinkled beneath a scattering of freckles that made her look like the poster child for adorable.

'Mrs Torres—' Nick shot Charlie a look, '—we're just wrapping things up. We'll be out of your hair shortly.'

'Fine. We only came back to get our things, then we're leaving.' Ciara ushered her daughter into the flat, gave Charlie a last scowl and disappeared into one of the bedrooms.

It was only after the two of them had entered the property that Charlie saw the uniformed officer who was escorting them. She nodded, waiting by the door.

'Are you a cop?' a small voice asked Charlie.

Charlie looked down in surprise. Ciara's young girl stood in front of him, her eyes wide.

'Police officer? Uh, no. Not anymore. I help them sometimes.'

She considered that for a moment. 'How do you help them?'

'I used to be a detective. So I help them look for clues.'

'Like Sherlock Holmes?'

Nick snorted.

Charlie shot him a glare and then returned his attention to the girl. 'Um. Yes, like Sherlock Holmes.'

'I like Sherlock Holmes. Sometimes my mom lets me watch it. It has Benedict Cumber... Cumber...'

'Cumberbatch?'

'Yeah, Benedict Cumberbatch. He's not American, y'know. You might think he is because of the Doctor Strange movie, but he's not. He's English, like you.'

'Oh. I haven't seen that one yet.'

She took a breath and wrung her hands together. 'Are you going to find the men who broke into the flat and tried to hurt my mom?'

Charlie lowered himself to one knee; his joints groaned in protest. He smiled and looked her in the eyes. 'What's your name?'

'Addison. But you can call me Addy if you like.'

'Addy, my name is Charlie.' He reached inside his trench coat, pulled out a business card and held it out to her. She took it, mouthing the words silently as she read the front. 'You see this man here?' He pointed to Nick, who offcred her a small wave. 'His name is Nick Stacey. He's one of the very best detectives I know. He's going to try his very hardest to catch these men and make sure that they get sent to prison. Okay?'

Addy eyed Nick dubiously, clutching the card in her hand, and gave Charlie a nod.

'How old are you, Addy?'

'Eight and a half.'

'You don't say? That's very grown up. My granddaughter is eight too.'

'Really?' She beamed at him. 'What's her name?'

'Her name is Evelyn. In fact, I have some chocolates in my car that I'd bought for her; she doesn't eat them anymore. If it's okay with your mummy, you can have them if you like.'

Addy wrinkled her nose. 'She doesn't eat chocolates? Why not?'

'She's a vegan now.'

'Oh.' She mulled that over. 'Didn't you know that?'

Charlie rubbed his thumb over his ring finger and turned to Nick. Nick shrugged back at him, a smug look plastered across his face. *Bastard.*

'I uh... No. I didn't. I don't get to see her as often as I'd like. She has school and her mummy is very busy, plus I work too. It's not always easy to find the time. I need to try a bit harder.'

Addison nodded at him with all of her eight-and-a-half years of wisdom.

'Right, Addy let's go.' Ciara's voice could have lowered the temperature in the room. She clutched the handles of two carry-on suitcases, one in each fist, and levelled a flat look at him.

Charlie pushed himself back to his feet. His knees creaked. *I'm getting too old for this.*

'Mom, Charlie said I could have some candy if that's okay?'

'No, honey. It's too late for junk food. Let's just get to the hotel.'

Addison's face dropped.

'Mrs Torres—' Charlie began.

'Look. I know you're just doing your job. But my daughter and I have had a long day. We've travelled half way around the world only to have our new home taken away from us. I've just spent the last couple of hours giving statements. I'm tired. I'm hungry. I just want to be somewhere safe.'

'I understand. I do. Let me give you a hand.' Charlie stepped forward, ignoring the dangerous glint in her eyes, and grabbed the handle of the suitcase on her left.

Her grip tightened, knuckles white against her skin. She jerked her hand and the case away from him, but not before he saw the irregular scarring on the flesh between her thumb and forefinger. Three raised dots in a neat little line.

His reaction gave her a moment's pause. Then her eyes narrowed and her lips pulled back in a snarl. 'I'm not some helpless damsel in distress. I'm more than capable of managing a couple of bags.'

Whether it was because of the stress or the exhaustion, her accent slipped, just on a word or two, regressing back into the familiar Traveller brogue.

He lowered his voice so that only she could hear. 'Ciara, how long have you had those marks on your hand?'

She glowered at him.

'Ciara, you're not safe here. There's a killer who's been targeting your family for years. I've spent the best part of my career trying to find him. He's started killing again and now you're back in England. I don't think it's a coincidence. You need to get away. Take Addison and leave.'

'And where would we go?' She gritted her teeth. 'We've got nothing. No one. If we go back, my husband *will* kill me. Now you think there's some murderer who's been waiting for me to come back to England? So that he can pick up where he left off? After thirty-four years? That's a load of shite.'

'Ciara, please. I'm trying to help you.'

'*Help?* I might've been just a child when we left this country, but I can still remember your lot turning up about a week before and ransacking our site. Shoving us about. Tearing up our homes. I can still remember one of you dragging my grandmother away in handcuffs. So don't you *dare* tell me you've spent your career defending the likes of me. I know how Travellers are seen by you and yours. If you'd given us the same treatment as you give everyone else, maybe you'd have caught them by now. Now get out of my way.'

Exhaling sharply, she pushed past him, leaving him to stare after her. Addison gave him a sad smile, still grasping his business card, then turned to follow her mother.

Boswells. Oh Christ.

'What was that about?' Nick asked, watching as the uniformed officer gave Charlie a curious frown, before escorting the women back out of the flat and out of sight.

'How much do you remember about those case files, Nick?'

'It's been a few years since I read through them. Why?'

'I think it's time you dusted them off. Those girls are in trouble. I can feel it.'

Chapter 38

CHARLIE SAT AT THE breakfast counter in his kitchen, nursing a black coffee. Sleep had been nonexistent. He'd gone to bed on an empty stomach and with a head full of images of that damned dagger.

Googling the thing over the years hadn't turned up anything new. He'd wasted countless hours searching the internet, followed up on anything with even a hint of promise.

Nothing.

It was as if it didn't exist.

He dropped his gaze to the empty barstools beside him and sighed. Had his obsession been worth it?

His kitchen was too big all of a sudden. Too cold. When he'd bought the place, he'd imagined it filled with laughter during visits from Meghan and Evelyn. He'd imagined late-night hot chocolates and too many sweets during weekend sleepovers with his granddaughter.

It hadn't happened like that.

He was lucky if he saw them more than half a dozen times in a year. It wasn't for lack of trying. He and his daughter were two very different people. But he wasn't a fool; he knew what his shortcomings were.

'Buck up, old boy.' His voice resonated in the vacant space. Maybe he should invest in some carpet; it would help to absorb some of that bloody echo.

He took a sip of coffee.

'Bachelor pad' was how his daughter had described it when she'd first seen it. He'd been hurt by her remark.

Charlie placed his mug on the worktop with a clink.

'Right, enough moping. Time to get that son of a bitch once and for all.' He thought back to the crumpled photo of him and Stephen that he'd shown Jack at the station, and winced. Could it really be possible that his friend was still alive?

His late-night session on the laptop had turned up a single lead—if he could call it that. *Ritualistic Sacrifice in Ancient Magical Practices*, available to borrow at his local library.

He'd very nearly missed it. A familiar dagger included in the artwork for the front cover.

Hell, at this point he was just about ready to believe that magic *was* involved. It might explain why the bloody thing never stayed where it was put. And why Jack had reacted the way she did to the photo.

'Right, time to get a move on.' He got up and carried his empty mug to the sink. After washing it out, he placed it just so, on the carved grooves in the marble to drain. Then, with a frown, he dried it with a tea towel, put it back in the cupboard, and wiped the worktop down for good measure.

Sometimes he hated his OCD, but at least it was a well-ordered and systematic hatred.

All libraries smelt the same. That blend of woody smoke and earth, tinged with the slightest hint of something sweet—vanilla maybe? He hadn't stepped foot inside one since Meghan was a child, but the smell transported him back in an instant.

Charlie pushed down a pang of nostalgia and made his way towards the reception desk. He cast a glance at the generously spaced, free-standing, curved, white bookcases as he passed.

'Good morning.' A blonde in her mid-fifties sitting behind the sprawling desk looked up at him over a pair of black-rimmed glasses.

'Good morning. I reserved a book. It should be under the name Charlie Haynes?'

'Well, you're certainly eager. We've only been open a couple of minutes.' She tapped at the keyboard and stared at the screen of her monitor. '*Ritualistic Sacrifice in Ancient Magical Practices*?' She arched an eyebrow at him.

'Uh, yes. That's it.'

God, man. What's wrong with you? It's not as if you wrote the thing.

'Wonderful.' She beamed. 'I'll have to go and get it for you. We keep the older and rarer titles locked away. You wouldn't believe the number of thefts we have. This book is particularly interesting, if you're into that sort of thing.' She winked at him.

Wait, what?

She stood—she didn't look over five feet in height—and disappeared up a flight of stairs. He stared after her.

It wasn't long before the click of heels announced her return. Clutched in her white-gloved hands was the book. Thick, and bound in dark-brown leather with gold lettering and gilded page edges, it was certainly impressive. Despite the aged tatters and scuffs, it was surprisingly well preserved.

'Here we are,' she said, a touch of pride in her voice, as she placed it on the desktop. 'Now, I'm afraid that I can't allow you to remove it from the premises. And due to its age and condition, I'll have to insist that I remain with you while you read it. You'll need to wear these too.' She produced another pair of white gloves from her pocket and held them out to him.

'Oh. Uh, not a problem.' Charlie took the gloves and put them on.

'Is there anything in particular you're looking for?' she asked. 'I have to admit, I'm a bit of an expert when it comes to this topic.'

'An expert on sacrifice or magical practices?'

She let out a peeling laugh and squeezed his arm. 'Yes, that didn't sound too good did it? What I *mean* to say is, I've always had an interest in artefacts and objects, both mythological and of historical significance. I based my dissertation around it, in fact.'

Charlie smiled despite himself. She flicked her hair back over her shoulder and licked her lower lip. If he didn't know any better, he'd have said she was flirting with him. He could be wrong though, it'd been a while.

Okay, it'd been years.

'Oh,' he said, realising that she was expecting him to say more. 'That's impressive. I'm actually interested in this.' He pointed to the faded image of the dagger, careful not to make contact with the cover.

'Ah. Kar'roc's Maw. The Black Blade.'

'So, it has a name.'

'Several. This particular athame is said to have been forged by the archdemon Kar'roc himself, over two thousand years ago. Its name varies, depending on the translation and century.'

Charlie's enthusiasm dropped. 'Oh.' This had been a complete waste of time. It couldn't have been Stephen that Jack had seen in the cemetery...

'Oh?' She rested the fingertips of one gloved hand on the book.

'I was hoping for something a little more... factual.'

'Come, sit with me.' She carried the book over to a round, white table between two padded, bucket chairs, set well away from the large windows.

He followed, removed his trench coat and folded it over the back of the seat opposite her, before sitting down.

'Chloe?' she called out, winking at Charlie. 'Do you mind watching reception while I help this dashing fellow?'

'Sure, Diane. No problem,' said a young woman, who was on the other side of one of the large, curved, white bookcases. She wiggled her eyebrows at Charlie as she passed, a smile turning up the corners of her mouth.

'Right then, Kar'roc's Maw.' Diane opened the book. Her fingers whispered across the pages until she found what she was looking for. With a murmur, she turned the book towards him, and watched as he leant forward to get a better look.

Even without his reading glasses he could make out the dagger with ease. The text was another matter altogether. Sections had faded with age or suffered significant foxing and were barely legible, while others looked as if they had been redacted with black permanent marker. There was something about the book that set his teeth on edge. A niggle fretted at the edge of his order-obsessed mind.

There. A couple of the pages were misaligned out by just a millimetre or two. But now he'd noticed it, it was all he could focus on.

He tore his gaze away and drummed on the table. *Tap, tap, tap.* Pause. *Tap, tap, tap.* Pause.

He took a breath and met her amber eyes. 'Why have these bits been crossed out?'

She wore a curious expression, one that made him feel as if he was being evaluated.

'We've had a problem—' she slanted forward and touched a gloved finger to the marred page, '—with people vandalising our books. It's one of the reasons we have to chaperone the older ones.'

Uh huh. In his experience, vandals usually favoured expletives or something a little more phallic in nature. Not crossing out lines of text.

'I didn't realise that libraries were such hotbeds for crime.'

Her smile returned. 'You have no idea.' She eased back into the chair; her foot brushed his calf as she crossed her legs. 'You seem disappointed with the book so far. I take it that you're not a fan of mythology?'

'Hardly, I'm afraid.' Her touch distracted him enough to take the edge off his suspicions. 'I prefer facts and tangible evidence.'

'Then I must confess, I'm a little confused about why you'd be interested in this book at all. The content is mostly mythical speculation.'

'I've seen this dagger before. This exact one.' He pressed a finger gently on the drawing, to emphasise his point. 'Several times over the course of my career and again yesterday.'

She straightened. 'Yesterday?'

'Yes. I need to know everything about it. Why it keeps resurfacing at crime scenes. I need something real, something I can work with.'

Odd. He hadn't meant to tell her that.

'Crime scenes? You're a... detective?'

Charlie clenched his jaw; discomfort bloomed in his skull. This was all way out of his comfort zone. But if he didn't get something, *anything* that could help him soon, those girls were going to die. 'I was. I work in unsolved crimes now and this... Kar'roc's Maw is somehow connected to a case I worked over thirty years ago.'

'You're telling me that it's real? The Black Blade? Kar'roc's Maw? That seems... unlikely. And if it *is* real, then it's certainly a very disturbing prospect.'

'Disturbing?'

'Well—' Diane pointed to a block of text that he couldn't read without his glasses. 'If this account is to be believed, Kar'roc bestowed the athame upon the mortal world in exchange for entry into our domain.'

'Of course. Makes sense,' Charlie said in a flat voice.

Diane waved a gloved hand at him dismissively. 'The bearer is supposedly able to rend the fabric of reality, unleashing Kar'roc upon the world, in exchange for untold power.'

'Uh huh. Except that they haven't.'

'No.' She agreed. 'Maybe if you give me a little more background about how you first encountered the athame, I could come up with some theories?'

'Sorry, I can't get into the specifics.' He'd already said more than he'd meant to. 'Anyway, I was really hoping that I'd turn up something concrete, not... fairy tales and works of fantasy.'

She'd referred to the dagger as an "athame" for heaven's sake. It was bad enough that there was a psychotic serial killer on the loose. Christ, at least he hoped it was *just* a serial killer. Now he was supposed to believe that demons and witches were involved too?

Sod that for a lark.

'Charlie, I wouldn't be so quick to dismiss this if what you're telling me is accurate. The truth retold is legend in the making.' She regarded his sceptical expression and sighed. 'Consider this then, maybe there is someone out there who has accessed similar material and *does* believe what they've read. Someone who may want to enact such rituals, in an attempt to bring forth a demon.'

'Rituals?' His body stiffened. 'What kind of rituals?'

'Here.' She pointed to another passage. 'This says that in order to realise the athame's full potential it needs to be replenished.'

'Replenished how?'

But he had a gut feeling he already knew what the answer would be.

Chapter 39

'HUMAN SACRIFICE,' DIANE SAID.

There it is.

A chill fingered its way down Charlie's neck and spine. 'Does it include any details of how the sacrifices are performed?'

She pointed to the section of the page, stained with black marker.

Of course.

'Is there anything else? Maybe something on the next page?' He reached for the book. She slid it back, out of his grasp.

A strange expression flickered across her face. 'I still think it would be useful if you could give me a little more information about your cases?'

'Diane, I'm sorry but—'

Her foot brushed his leg again, this time lingering for a second too long to be accidental. His cheeks flushed and derailed his train of thought. She tempted him with a smile.

She smelt good. Like rich spices and fruit.

Christ, what was wrong with him? He shook the thought from his head. A slight pressure built just behind his eyes.

He needed answers. What harm was there in giving her a few details?

He opened his mouth to speak, then closed it again. Unease tickled his mind. She leant across the table and placed her hands on his wrists. Where her skin was uncovered felt soft and warm against his, the gentle pressure immediately soothing—at odds with the pounding in his head.

His apprehension dissolved in the intimacy of her touch; the sensation of it surged through him like a pulse of electricity. He focused on her amber eyes—they drew him in, made him feel at ease, safe even. Why had he been so suspicious? She only wanted to help.

'I found my friend on a Traveller site with that exact dagger in his chest, left to die alone. Of course, they'd all cleared out by the time we got there. Then weeks later the killings started. Mainly Travellers, most of them with a connection to a particular family who'd been living on the site where his body was found.

'I spent most of my career trying to track them down. Even requesting cases that I thought were related. But every time I got close to finding someone who might have a connection with those I *knew* were responsible, they'd turn up dead.' He paused, surprised by how freely his words flowed. Nobody who knew him would ever describe him as verbose, but the words wouldn't stop.

'And the athame?' Diane urged, her focus on him absolute.

She pressed his wrists harder. Calm radiated through him due to her touch, only to be ruined by more pressure building in his head. He winced at the warring sensations.

'Sometimes the dagger reappeared, was catalogued and put in evidence, only to disappear again. Every time it resurfaced it was usually with a string of corpses. If not, they'd follow soon after.

'All the murders were extremely violent, horrific even. Some were more gruesome than others. The eyes had been taken from some of the bodies. We never found them. When the media got hold of the information, they sensationalised it. Made out that the killer was eating them, even dubbed him the "Caravan Cannibal". They probably weren't all that far off, to be honest.'

Diane nodded. 'I remember hearing about that on the news.'

She was absorbed by the conversation. When was the last time anyone had been so focused on him?

'We found strange scarring on some of the victims... here.' He slipped his right hand from under hers and pointed to the fleshy part between thumb and finger on his left. The pain in his skull began to recede. 'It took us a while to realise that the ones with the scars were all biologically related. They were usually the ones that had had their eyes removed. Really threw the pathologist. He said the marks must have been made at birth. Like some cult ritual.'

Why had he just told her that?

'But you don't believe that to be the case?' Diane gave his hand a squeeze; the gentle pressure radiated pleasant and reassuring warmth through him.

His brow knitted together as he tried to order his thoughts. The ache in his head returned and veered towards a migraine.

Charlie shook his head. 'That particular family was notorious for run-ins with the police, and the scars had never been noted before. Not even when the bodies showed up. No, I'm confident that those scars were somehow related to the murders. Don't get me wrong, there were definite cult-like links to some of the killings. One in particular—' he winced at the memory of Aisling Boswell '—was especially grisly. The body strung up. Throat slashed. A message written in the victim's blood. "We will paint the walls of hell red with your blood". Never did work out if the message was for us or the victim's family.'

'And now Kar'roc's Maw has returned, you think the murders will start again?'

'I'm sure of it. I need to find a lead, anything that might direct me to the killer, before they find that little girl and her mother.'

'What makes you think they're the next targets?'

'Their flat was attacked by would-be abductors. Ciara, the mother, managed to fend off one of the men. Want to hazard a guess what she used to do it?'

Diane's amber eyes widened and she shuddered.

Charlie nodded. 'I noticed the same pattern of scarring on her hand as on the other victims'. It must mean something. Is there anything in the book that mentions something similar?'

'I'm afraid not. But—'

'Diane?' Chloe's voice cut across the library. 'There's a call for you.'

'Ah, excuse me. I'll be two minutes.' She stood, slipped the gloves from her hands and placed them on the table.

Charlie watched her walk away, the ache in his head easing the farther away she got.

He blinked and shifted his focus back to the book.

Strange, he'd forgotten that Chloe was even there. In fact, without Diane there, the fog in his mind was lifting.

He thumbed his ring finger and glanced at the reception desk. Diane was bent forward, phone to ear, writing something on a pad.

He fished out his reading glasses from his pocket. He glimpsed at the desk again, slipped them on and flicked through the pages of the book.

Let's find out what's really going on here.

It wasn't so much of an educated guess—he didn't have the faintest clue what he was looking for—as a gut feeling when he stopped on the pages that were askew. He tapped on the surface of the table as he scanned illustrations of what appeared to be ritualistic circles, each one a slight variation of the last. Strange symbols, complete with hand written annotations, covered the margins. And there, right in the centre of it all was the dagger. Its detail was clear, unlike on the other pages. Crucially, none of the text around it had been defaced.

Charlie pressed his lips into a thin line as he read. *Interesting.*

He inhaled, risked another quick look at Diane, and in one swift motion, tore the pages out. The soft whisper of the paper tearing made his heart skip a beat. A knot twisted in his gut at the shame, but he sensed Diane was hiding something. He needed to do everything in his power to help those girls.

He slipped the pages, along with his glasses, back into his pocket and positioned the book on the table in the exact spot where Diane had left it. He hoped that she wouldn't notice until after he was gone.

He exhaled.

'I think she likes you.' Chloe's soft voice caught him off guard.

He stopped himself from jumping out of his skin. How had she managed to sneak up on him so quietly?

'Sorry?' He smoothed his features as she stepped around the table, to stand in front of him.

She rocked on her heels. 'Diane. I think she likes you.'

'Oh?'

'Don't say I said anything, but she's single. Widow. Not that that matters, I mean it wasn't recent or anything. Like, twenty something years ago. So plenty of time to get over it. Not that you really get over it, I guess. But, you know what I mean. Her husband was murdered. Not by her. Oh my God, can you imagine? By some guy with mental health problems sleeping rough, or something.' She looked down at the floor. 'Oh God, sorry I'm rambling. I do that sometimes.'

Charlie blinked. *Wow.*

Chloe smoothed her black hair and waggled her eyebrows at him again. 'So?'

'So?' Charlie repeated, his brain still trying to catch up. 'So, I—'

The click of Diane's heels interrupted her. She mouthed the word *single* at him before she broke into a grin and slipped back towards reception.

Diane slid back into the chair opposite him. 'I'm sorry about that, Charlie. Where were we?'

'Uh...'

'Ah, yes. You wanted to know if there was any mention of physical markings. Not in this book; it's more an overview of various artefacts and practices. However, there is a book on demonology that goes into considerable detail on Kar'roc and the Black Blade.'

Demonology. He resisted rolling his eyes. But, he *had* exhausted every other avenue. As much as his ordered mind reeled against the prospect of demons and magic, his gut told him he was on the right track.

'We don't hold the copy here, but I could pull a few strings and get it sent over before we close tonight? If that's something you'd be interested in?'

'That would be great, thank you.' It wasn't as if he had any other leads to follow up on.

Diane smiled. 'Brilliant. If you come back at five thirty, we can grab a coffee and look over it together.'

'Erm, okay. Lovely.'

She offered him a smile and handed him a folded scrap of paper. 'I'm afraid that I have to set up for a toddler story time event now. See you at five thirty?'

'Sure,' Charlie murmured. He tensed when she slid the gloves back on and picked up the book with the missing pages. It wasn't until she closed it with a gentle thud that he allowed a breath.

With a wink, Diane turned and sauntered away, leaving him alone with the slip of paper.

With her gone, he shook off the feeling of bewilderment easier, and unfolded it. Written on it was a mobile number and a note that read: *Looking forward to it. Dee x*

Why did he feel like he was in over his head, and that it had nothing to do with the dagger?

Chapter 40

AS THE SUN SANK below the horizon and the murky glow of artificial light turned on, it plunged the world outside Ciara's window in deep pools of shadow. She shuddered, sick of feeling scared. Tired of having her "paranoia" rule her.

Can't I just have a normal life?

The hotel room was basic, with just one double bed. It was all that had been available with the short notice given. At least it looked clean and she couldn't see any creepy-crawlies on the sheets. What more could she have asked for?

Yes, it was set back along the banks of a river that reeked of rotten seaweed. And yes, there was a constant stream of traffic and people spilling from the neighbouring cinema, budget restaurants and bingo hall. But at least it was safe. Or so she'd been told.

The flat was supposed to have been safe.

She felt her eyes prick and blinked the tears away before they could surface. She wasn't about to start crying, not with Addy around.

Even though they'd only been there for less than twenty-four hours, she missed the small open-plan flat.

It was stupid really, but that flat had symbolised the start of their new life. And now it was gone.

She took a deep breath, pulled the purple curtains closed, fixed her smile in place and turned towards her daughter. 'Addy, honey, are you still playing with that phone?'

'I'm just adding a new contact.'

Her smile wavered. 'Contact? Who?' Had Dean somehow managed to get in touch with her?

'Charlie.'

'Charlie?'

'Charlie.' Addy nodded and rolled her eyes in a way that hinted at the teenage years to come. 'The man we met last night. He said he used to be a detective, like Sherlock Holmes.'

'Oh.' Ciara exhaled, her heart slowing down. 'Why would you want his number in your phone?'

Addy looked at her as if the answer was obvious. 'Because he gave me his card. And he used to be a detective.'

'Of course, silly me.'

The knock at the door made them both jump.

'Mrs Torres? It's PC Willis.'

Ciara sucked air through her teeth. Call it prejudice, probably stemming from her childhood, but she couldn't stand the police. Didn't trust them as far as she could throw them.

She yanked the door open and glared at the blond officer in his mid-thirties standing in front of her.

'What?'

If her open hostility bothered him, he didn't show it.

'Sorry for the intrusion. DC Stacey requested a welfare check.'

She gave the man a level look. 'Am I supposed to know who that is?'

'He's one of the best detectives there is, Mom,' Addy piped up. 'Charlie said so.'

Ciara let out a sigh as she appeared beside her and stared up at the officer with round eyes.

'Your friend Charlie is right.' Officer Willis smiled down at her. His black stab vest—bulging with pockets, pouches, clips and zips—rustled as he adjusted his position.

Addison openly gaped at the man. Her gaze flicked from the radio, clipped on the vest just below his right shoulder, to the assortment of equipment secured on the thick, black belt at his waist.

'Are they your cuffs? Where's your gun? What's that?'

He chuckled and pointed to metal poking out of the pouch that had been buttoned shut. 'Yes, these are my cuffs.' His hand moved to an elongated leather pouch secured with yet another buttoned strap. 'This is my ASP; it extends if you flick it really hard. And I don't have a gun. You have to be a special type of police officer to get a gun.'

'Oh.' Addy pointed. 'What's that number?'

'Addy,' Ciara warned.

Addison glanced from the officer to her mother and back. Her shoulders sagged.

'It's okay, honestly,' PC Willis said to Ciara, clearly amused.

There was something quite approachable about this officer. He had an easy smile and took Addy's interrogation in his stride.

Probably has kids of his own.

'This—' he tapped the five-digit strip of fabric attached to his vest just beneath the "POLICE" lettering, '—is my force number. Every police officer gets one. It's another way of identifying us.'

Addy nodded and mouthed the numbers.

Ciara folded her arms. 'As you can see, we're fine.'

'Well, I won't take up anymore of your time. Someone else might come to check up on you either later tonight or tomorrow. You clearly have friends in high places.' There was a touch of curiosity in his tone.

Ciara said nothing.

Smiling, he gave both her and Addy a quick nod. 'If you need us, you know the number.'

'Nine, nine, nine.' Addy grinned.

'That's the one.' Willis winked at her. She beamed up at him. 'Have a good evening, Mrs Torres, Addy.'

Ciara closed the door. 'So apparently I need babysitting now.'

Addison looked up at her, tsked and rolled her eyes. 'He was just being friendly, Mom. The cops are the good guys. A cop wouldn't hurt us.'

Ciara pressed her lips into a thin line and remained silent.

Chapter 41

PERFECT. THAT WILL WORK NICELY.

From across the road outside the hotel's car park, the demon watched as the uniformed officer exchanged a few quick pleasantries with the receptionist behind the desk.

The storm inside Stephen's head raged. He struggled to pull his thoughts together into something intelligible. The effort alone was gruelling.

DON'T SULK. YOU SHOULD BE HAPPY. BECAUSE OF US THERE ARE TWO LESS CRIMINALS ROAMING THE STREETS, COMMITTING WANTON ACTS OF VIOLENCE. SOON WE'LL NO LONGER BE AT THE MERCY OF THE DAGGER. YOU SHOULD THANK ME.

Stephen bristled. *Thank you?*

YOU'RE WELCOME.

He wanted to scream. *If it wasn't for the fact that the men were a threat to your plans, they would have been of no interest to you whatsoever.*

THREAT? HARDLY. THE ONE CALLED "PRICE" SQUEALED LIKE A SWINE TO SLAUGHTER IN THE END.

That much was true. He'd never heard noises like that coming from a fully grown man before. The memories weren't going to leave him anytime soon.

At first they'd taken their time working over the two thugs. Slow. Deliberate. Meticulous. Everything conducted with expert precision, inflicting as much pain as the human body could endure while remaining conscious. It might not have been pleasant, but it was a distraction that would buy the two remaining Boswells a little more time.

In their desperation, the thugs dropped information like it was going out of fashion. Names, places, reasons, more names. Anything to make it stop.

It didn't.

Of course, the demon hadn't cared. The names had meant nothing. That wasn't what it had been interested in. These men had tried to take something from it and they'd paid the price.

Christ, had they paid the price.

At some point Stephen had lost himself to the bloodlust, coming back to the moment, dripping with gore and an assortment of bodily fluids. All that had been left of the men was bone and pulp, their bodies riddled with holes made by the demon.

So, what exactly is the plan here? Slaughter a police officer in front of all these people and hope that nobody notices?

The demon flicked Stephen's hand in a dismissive gesture and limped across the road towards the car park.

Just as he got there, the officer pushed open the glass lobby door and exited.

The demon inhaled the scent of the man. Above the sweat and aftershave, Stephen detected their aroma. Not that he needed more confirmation that the women were inside the building; his skull was already threatening to explode. There was a whisper of something else there too. Burnt matches. Brimstone.

THE OFFICER'S A WITCH. A MEMBER OF THE ORDER.

Stephen's body stiffened in response to the demon's consideration to turn back. The demon forced his muscles to relax.

NO. I HAVE WAITED TOO LONG TO RISK LOSING IT ALL NOW.

The presence marched him across the car park towards the uniformed man. The scarf hiding his lower jaw started to slip.

The officer glanced up. His eyes narrowed as Stephen approached.

When the distance between them closed, the demon veered off, but not before it flashed the officer a glimpse of shredded cheeks. Then the presence forced Stephen into a stilted run towards the back of the hotel.

Beneath the shadows, the entity shrugged out of his coat and pulled off his scarf, then tossed them into a commercial wheelie bin. The sound of footsteps echoed behind him.

What are you doing?

DO NOT DISTRACT ME. IF THIS BODY WASN'T SO DEFECTIVE, I WOULDN'T HAVE TO RUSH.

For the first time in an age, the flesh around his mouth knitted back together. It had been so long, he'd forgotten what it felt like for his mouth not to be dry and cold from the constant air exposure.

The relief was short-lived however, when the demon dug his fingers into his eyes, clawing and ripping, until Stephen's vision blurred with his own blood. He staggered. Every breath caused a white-hot explosion of agony across his face.

Jesus! Why?

'My eyes!' Stephen's voice was a hoarse scream. He clutched at his face. 'I can't see. Help me. Help me, please. I can't see. He attacked me. My eyes... God my eyes.'

The officer hesitated only a moment before reaching him. 'Oh Christ. Stay calm, I'll help you.'

The demon turned towards the voice. Warm blood leaked between his fingers. The entity let out a whimper and stumbled Stephen to one side.

Little much, don't you think?

A surge of amusement was the only response.

Firm hands gripped his shoulders, steadying him. 'I'm here. Sit down.' A mix of emotions warred on the officer's face as he helped Stephen to the ground. He knelt in front of him and squinted down the back of the hotel. Probably looking for the attacker.

Apparently confident that Stephen wasn't about to collapse, he released him and grabbed his radio.

The demon moved in a blur. He snatched at the officer's wrist and twisted it, with a sharp crack. The man yelped and yanked his body back. His face paled.

The bleeding in Stephen's eyes stopped. The demon cocked its head to the side, regarding the man with a vicious smirk. The entity sprang to its feet. It blinked away the blood, revealing Stephen's true eye colour.

'It's you.' The officer clutched his injured hand and stood to his full height. 'We'll catch you.'

'No. You won't. In fact, you're going to help me.' As the demon spoke, the flesh around Stephen's eyes continued to repair itself.

The officer took a step backwards. His lips moved in near-silence as he murmured under his breath, repeating the same hushed syllables over and over. The air around him shimmered, like a haze on a hot summer's day, radiating a low-thrumming energy that made the hairs on Stephen's arms stand on end. 'Over my dead body,' the man said.

A giggle scraped up Stephen's throat. The sound that tore from his lips was a full-blown cackle. 'I'm glad you agree.'

The demon lunged at the man, whipped both hands out. One closed around the base of the man's skull, the other grasped his chin as leverage. It drove the momentum from his torso and twisted the officer's head.

His neck snapped. His body dropped.

What was that?

CERVICAL VERTEBRAE.

You know what I mean. Why did it suddenly get hotter?

HUMANS ARE POOR CONDUITS FOR MAGIC. THE ENERGY TRANSFER IS INEFFICIENT, SQUANDERED AS HEAT AND OTHER BYPRODUCTS. THAT *STENCH* IS ONE OF THEM.

My blood is all over him. They'll track you down. And by they, I sure as hell don't mean the local constabulary.

THAT'S WHY WE'RE GOING ON A LITTLE EXCURSION BEFORE WE SAY HELLO TO THE REMAINING BOSWELLS. IT'S NOT LIKE ANYONE'S GOING TO PULL OVER A POLICE CAR NOW, IS IT?

The demon hunkered down next to the fallen corpse, unzipped the stab vest, and started to whistle an eerie rendition of *The Laughing Policeman*. It paused, then thrust a hand into one pocket and retrieved the coin.

The demon studied it with a sneer. A hiss escaped Stephen's lips. It attempted to hurl the coin away. Something shivered through Stephen and the muscles in his arms went taught. The magic that bound the entity to the dagger had cut short its efforts. With a growl, the demon thrust the coin into the dead officer's trouser pocket.

Aren't you going to take his life force? Stephen's own eagerness for the rush of vitality that came from killing sickened him. *We could find out how much he knew. Learn more about O.O.T.I.S.*

The demon considered the still warm body with a conflicted mix of hunger and revulsion. HE IS A WITCH. CONSUMING HIS ESSENCE WOULD BE

EVEN MORE REPULSIVE THAN WHAT YOU EAT FROM THE BURGER VAN.

The thought was dismissed and the demon forced him to undress the dead officer.

It had been a long time since he'd worn the uniform.

Chapter 42

GETTING RID OF THE body had taken much longer than expected. Not that Stephen's experience as a detective had ever involved corpse disposal. Given the part of town he was in, he should have just attached a bike lock to it—it would have been gone within the hour.

GIVES YOU A WHOLE NEW RESPECT FOR THE INNER WORKINGS OF ORGANISED CRIMINAL ACTIVITY, DOESN'T IT?

Stephen let his disgust radiate towards the demon; not that it noticed, as it regarded his neat reflection in the glass entrance door to the hotel.

I THINK WE SCRUB UP NICELY. ESPECIALLY NOW ALL THE BLOOD IS GONE.

Seeing himself kitted out in full uniform again hit him with nostalgia. Admittedly, he didn't look the same as when he'd been a PC, way back when. The white shirt, epaulets, clip-on tie and tunic were gone, replaced with a lightweight, zip-up, black top; but he looked like an officer again.

The fit was surprisingly good, considering the clothes weren't his—prised from the PC's cold, dead body.

THAT'S NOT ENTIRELY TRUE. HE WAS STILL WARM.

The demon gave Stephen one last appraising glance, pulled open the door and strolled into the reception area.

'Okay to go up?'

The receptionist's head bobbed up from behind the monitor, set against a backdrop of purple. Her eyebrows rose. She gave him a measured look, hesitated, then smiled and nodded.

The entity hobbled him up the stairs to the third floor. It wasn't long before he knew, without a doubt, that he was outside the right door. Even if their scent hadn't drawn him, the intense pulsing inside his head did. Although focusing on it now, there was something off about the heaviness, like it was being dampened.

I thought you said their debt was paid? What's the sense in killing them?

I SAID *A* DEBT HAS BEEN PAID. THERE IS STILL ONE DEBT OUTSTANDING. AND I ENJOY KILLING. IT MAKES ME HAPPY.

I won't let you do this.

YOU COULDN'T STOP ME IF YOU TRIED.

The demon chuckled and rapped on the door. It adjusted the utility belt at his waist and cleared his throat. 'Sorry to disturb you, it's PC Anderson for your wellness check.'

Really?

WHAT? IT'S YOUR NAME ISN'T IT? NAMES HOLD POWER. YOU WOULD HAVE DONE WELL TO LEARN MINE.

What was that supposed to mean? Why would he want to know the demon's name? It's not like they'd been destined to become bosom buddies.

Footsteps approached, muffled behind the door. Stephen also heard the sound of running water. There was only one heartbeat now. It pulsed to the rhythm inside his head. Compelled him to hunt. To kill. Despite knowing what was about to transpire and the repulsion that he *should* feel, Stephen couldn't deny the quiver of excitement. After all these years, he might finally be free of the ceaseless pounding.

'Uh... Who did you say it was?' A young girl; Stephen recognised her reedy voice immediately.

'PC Anderson, with the police. May I come in?'

You sick son of a bitch. She's just a kid.

Stephen grappled to restrain the presence with all his strength. If he could buy a few seconds, just long enough to warn her, maybe the pair would have a chance.

Hollow laughter rang in his mind as the demon shrugged off his attempts. A psychological backhand sent his consciousness deeper into the darkness.

NOW, NOW. NO NEED TO BE RUDE.

The door opened to reveal a young, freckled, tawny-haired girl. She looked him up and down, then broke into a gap-toothed grin. 'Do *you* have a gun?'

The demon smiled. 'No. I don't need a gun.' It kept his voice low, loud enough so that the girl could hear him over the sound of the shower in the adjoining room.

Her face dropped for a second, then she shrugged and stepped back, so that he could enter. 'PC Willis didn't have a gun either.'

'No, it wouldn't have protected him. Is your mother in?'

The demon's gaze wandered over the small white-and-plum double room. A modest travel suitcase lay open on the bed, garments strewn across the deep-purple bed cover, a small shoulder handbag beside it. The remnants of a Hawaiian pizza lay in a box on the desk, underneath a wall-mounted television.

FRUIT ON PIZZA? AND YOU SAY I'M THE MONSTER.

'She's in the shower. Do you want me to tell her you're here?'

Shower. Well, that would explain why the demon hadn't already ripped the place apart. There was something about water, something that seemed to reduce the influence of the sigils.

'Sure. I can wait.' The demon limped over to the desk and perched on its edge. It gave the pizza box a final look of disgust and then watched the small girl knock on the door to the bathroom.

Is this all for my benefit?

The demon scoffed.

The presence tracked her every movement. Stephen's fingers dug involuntarily into the edges of the desk, puncturing the MDF with a series of strained cracks. His muscles quivered beneath the uniform, the presence itching to rip the girl to shreds. Not because of the blood debt—the child was free of that now—but because the demon revelled in carnage. Revelled in the pitiful screams of those soon to be dead. And this little girl had cheated it. Cheated it out of a death it deserved.

When the girl turned in puzzlement at the sound, the demon forced a smile and relaxed Stephen's grip. Drawing this out was a thrill. Decades of hunting, killing and anticipation had all led to this moment.

But restraint was something that didn't come naturally to the demon.

'Mom?'

'What's the matter, Addy?' Her voice was muffled by the sound of running water.

'PC Anderson is here for our check.'

'Just tell him we're fine. Don't open the door.'

'Uh... I let him in already.' Addy turned towards Stephen and gave him an awkward shrug.

The shower turned off with a series of splutters and low curses. 'Okay, I'll be two minutes.'

Addy rushed back and stood directly in front of Stephen. She bobbed up and down on her heels. 'Do you know PC Willis?' She stared at each of the items attached to his utility belt and vest.

'We've met,' he said with a touch of breathlessness.

Now that the shower had been shut off, the pain inside his head reached its crescendo. The scent of Boswell blood filled his nose, played on his palate. His mouth filled with saliva. The entity pressed his fingers into the desk again. With a swallow, it eased up the pressure, before Stephen gouged holes in it.

Her gaze worked its way up his torso and stopped on his force number. She blanched and stepped backwards.

Oh God. She'd made him. Things were about to go south and there would be nothing he could do to stop it.

The demon looked down, regarded the number on his chest with interest. A grin spread across his face as the realisation set in. It looked up.

The girl gawked at Stephen's hands, looking like she might vomit. Finally, her eyes met his and she gasped.

'Ah.' The demon held up one hand, inspected the dried blood underneath the fingernails and chuckled. 'Always the hardest part to clean.'

The entity pushed off the desk and took a step towards her.

She whimpered.

The bathroom door clicked open, releasing a swell of humidity. The girl's mother stepped into the room, rubbing at her left hand with a frown. Her clothes were damp in patches, like she'd dressed in a hurry. Her wet hair was wrapped roughly in a towel, twisted on top of her head.

Her scent flooded his nostrils. The demon's rage and revulsion broke over Stephen in waves. Each breath she took was an insult to it; an "up yours" to the decades it had been forced to fester inside this human meat suit.

Meat suit?

The demon lost all control. It lunged across the room towards her. Spittle flew from his mouth as it let out an inhuman snarl.

Shock flickered across her face for a split second, before she surged towards her daughter. 'Addy!'

The girl staggered back and flung her arms up over her face. She let out an ear-piercing scream.

Stephen ploughed into a wall of invisible energy. It sent his body hurtling back across the room. He smashed into the desk; the cheap wood splintered. Stephen groaned. Searing pain caused every muscle to convulse.

'Ouch.' Stephen blinked, regaining control. He pushed into a sitting position amongst the wreckage, as he shuddered out a breath. Just feet from where he'd landed he saw it, gleaming amongst the fractured wood, and casting pale-red shards across the deep-purple carpet.

The dagger.

The two females gaped at him in silence.

The demon's presence had been... immobilised. For now.

'You need to get out of here before it takes me over again,' he said urgently.

'Find Charlie. Charlie Haynes. He'll work out a way to help you.' He pointed at the dagger. Blood trickled down his hand. 'Take that with you. It's important.'

The seconds passed at an excruciating pace. Addy's mother gawked at the dagger, covered in splinters from the remains of the ruined desk.

'I know you,' Addy's voice wavered. 'You were outside the phone shop. You're not a cop at all.'

There wasn't time for this. If they didn't leave now, the demon would rip them to shreds when it regained control.

Addy stared at him, frozen.

Shit. Why aren't they leaving?

'Yes,' he said. 'You gave me money.'

Ciara blinked and shook her head, as if coming out of a trance, and pushed Addy behind her and towards the door. Her eyes locked with his, and widened in recognition. She darted forward and snatched her handbag from the bed, then fumbled through the ruined wood for the dagger; she refused to let him out of her sight.

Stephen sat still. The last thing he needed was to do anything that would bring the demon back to the fore. If he could just give them enough time to get away, to get to Charlie, then maybe they'd stand a chance.

He watched as she backed out of the hotel room, her movements precise as if she were backing away from a predator, which, in truth, she was. It wasn't until she'd disappeared out of sight that he heard them break into a run.

Right. It was time to move. In minutes the police, or worse, *O.O.T.I.S* could be crawling over the hotel. The last thing he needed was for the demon to awaken in a police cell.

'Maybe if I stay, the *worse* will get here first and put an end to all this.'

Still, could he take that chance? It was a risky gamble, with the lives of the hotel staff and guests at stake.

No. He needed to move.

It's up to you now, Charlie.

Chapter 43

CHARLIE SIPPED HIS CAPPUCCINO in the coffee house and watched Diane over the rim of his mug. She turned a page in the delightfully titled: *Identifying Daemon Archetype in the Demise of Humanity.*

How *did* they come up with the names of these things?

Compared to *Ritualistic Sacrifice in Ancient Magical Practices*, the book looked like new. The deep-red, leather-bound cover was intact, the pages not yet yellowed and—if he'd needed any more confirmation as to its age—Diane handled it without gloves.

She chewed her lower lip as she scanned the text. 'I know it's here somewhere.'

He caught himself looking at her mouth, placed his drink back on the table and let his eyes wander around the coffeehouse instead.

It was a cosy mix of exposed brick and warm orange lighting, fixed to the walls with industrial cable. Reclaimed solid-wood tables were spaced out between a mix of rustic, oak chairs and well-worn brown, leather sofas. And the caffeine smell... Was there anything better than the aroma of freshly brewed coffee? It had an intimate feel about it. Chatter melded into the sounds of coffee being prepared, so that each conversation remained more or less private.

Small mercies. God only knows what anyone listening in on this conversation would think.

'Ah, here we go.' Diane turned the book around and pushed it towards him. 'I knew I'd seen it in here somewhere.'

Charlie stared down at the illustrations on the page. 'These are the same markings on their hands.' He kept his voice low.

'Sigils.' Diane nodded, her amber eyes intense. She touched one of the sigils comprised of three dots. 'Hunted.' Her finger slid to another, three vertical dots to the left of a convex line. 'Hunter.'

'And this one?' Charlie pointed to a straight, black line with three evenly spaced horizontal curves running through it.

'Ah.' Diane smiled. 'The closest translation we have for this sigil is "released".'

'Released?'

'As far as we can tell, it means that the individual is no longer being hunted.'

Charlie frowned. 'There's one missing.'

Diane arched a golden eyebrow at him.

'One of the Caravan Cannibal's victims had a combination of these two. Hunter and hunted.'

'That's not possible. You can't be simultaneously hunter and hunted, it makes no sense. Unless...' She spun the book back to her and flicked through the pages.

'As I told you earlier,' she said, finding the page she was searching for and skimming the text, 'Kar'roc's Maw is supposedly able to rip through the fabric separating our world from that of demons and a whole host of unimaginable creatures. However, it needs to be done in a certain place. There are gateways of a sort, locations where the boundaries are naturally weaker.'

She glanced up. He nodded for her to continue.

'The athame houses a particular species of demon, one with extremely heightened senses. Senses that would enable it to unearth such gateways.'

'Right.' Charlie tempered his disbelief. 'You're telling me that the dagger has a demon in it?'

'Yes. Well, no.' She paused as she considered her words. 'Not an actual demon. Its essence, or soul, might be a more accurate description. But the soul of a very specific type of demon.'

'And this demon has spent the last three decades wandering around, murdering Travellers? But not just any Travellers. Those that share the same bloodline?'

'Yes,' Diane squeaked. Her excitement elicited a few curious glances from the neighbouring tables.

Charlie drew in a breath. It was at times like these he *really* missed smoking to settle his nerves.

'It would appear that someone found a loophole. Rather than using the athame as Kar'roc originally intended, it's been exploited. If this account is to be believed—' she locked eyes with him and waved her hand over the page, '—the demon is being used to fulfil blood debts. And has been for centuries. Better than the alternative, I suppose.'

'Blood debts? For who?'

'I couldn't even begin to guess. But it's clear from this text that when the blood debt is invoked, the demon has a master. The "hunter".'

'I'll bite.' Charlie kept the cynicism from his voice. 'How does someone become the master of an ancient, dagger-dwelling demon?'

'Incantation.' Her lips twitched in a smirk, as if it were the most obvious answer in the world.

'A spell then.' He let out a huff. 'Mumbo jumbo.'

'Words have power, Charlie.' Her amber eyes bore into him. 'Words can give wind to the wings of a fledgling dream or clip them before it takes flight. Words can inspire nations or fan the flames of unrest. The right words can even save a life.'

He said nothing.

She considered him for a few seconds, then tapped the book with the tip of her French-manicured nail. 'Words can also summon demons, binding them into servitude of human masters or, as was the original intention of the Maw, using them to call forth an arch demon and set off the apocalypse.'

His bark of laughter took him by surprise. It cut through the little coffeehouse like a gunshot.

He gave Diane a wide-eyed look. 'I'm sorry.'

She weighed his reaction; he wilted under her scrutiny.

'Really, Charlie, I thought detectives were supposed to be open-minded. Adaptable.'

'I'm not a detective anymore. Anyway, I follow facts.' Facts made sense, people didn't. While Stephen had focused on the why, he'd been more interested in the how.

Diane gave him a flat look and pushed the book back towards him. 'And what are the facts telling you now?'

The dagger stared up at him from the page.

Charlie shifted in his chair. 'There's an inscription there, by the gem in the dagger's hilt?'

'Ah.' Her expression brightened, the lines in her brow melting away. 'Now this is really interesting. The gem is a recent addition. And when I say recent, I'm still talking hundreds of years. It's said to contain part of one of the stones from King Solomon's ring itself.'

'Right,' he said, his expression blank.

She tsked, but there was no real admonishment behind it. 'Solomon was said to have been gifted a ring from God in order to command demons. It may give some explanation as to how Kar'roc's Maw has been exploited for all these centuries. All conjecture, of course.'

'Of course.'

When she eyed him suspiciously, he couldn't help but smile.

She continued. 'Blood is fed into the gem, acting as a sort of conduit to the demon, giving it instruction. The demon is then given a host—'

'Host?'

'That's where the human sacrifice comes in. The demon can't physically manifest in our world; it needs a body. It's transposed into the host through the athame, at which point it's compelled to hunt anyone associated with that bloodline, until the debt is repaid.'

'With blood.'

'Not necessarily.' Diane nudged her black-rimmed glasses up her nose. 'Blood is just the collateral. Kar'roc's Maw would have belonged to some very powerful people throughout the centuries. People with enemies, competitors. What better way to secure your position than to have such people indebted to you, literally on pain of death? If they can't pay the demon kills them, and you take everything that belonged to them. And not just them. Their entire bloodline. Power. Money. Fear.'

'That's some incentive to honour a loan.'

'Isn't it just?' Diane took a sip of her latte and shuffled in her chair. 'The sigils serve as testimony to the arrangement. A constant physical reminder of a debt owed. My theory is that they also act as a beacon for the demon, telling it who to obey, who to hunt and who to leave unmolested, once the debt is paid.

'If what you're saying about a third sigil is true, it's possible that whoever invoked the ritual inadvertently used their own blood to summon the demon, making them both the hunter and the hunted.'

Charlie's mouth went dry. He opened it and closed it again as he digested the information. *No. No, it couldn't be.* If he'd needed confirmation of his suspicions then this was it. Sweat pricked at his palms. He sucked in a breath and tried to slow his heart before it exploded out of his chest.

'Charlie, are you alright? You've gone pale.'

'So it *is* Stephen. He's the one that murdered all those people. He's the one that's going to try and murder that girl and her mother. No wonder Jack reacted like that when I showed her the photo.'

'Photo?'

Charlie took his wallet from his pocket and handed over the picture, as he tried to make sense of his thoughts. This couldn't really be happening, could it? This was the sort of thing that took place in fantasy novels, not real life. Maybe it had finally happened. Maybe a lifetime of stress had caught up with him and his mind had snapped.

'Oh God, Charlie...' Diane's hand flew to her mouth. It caught the edge of her mug and sent a flood of coffee across the table. She hissed and scooped up the book.

It couldn't be true. It didn't make sense. But then, the nature of the killings, the brutal single-mindedness, the link to a particular family spread across the country—it all supported what the book said.

But demons don't exist.

Then why was his gut screaming at him to trust the evidence?

Because you follow the facts. Always. And the facts are telling you that demons do exist. That Stephen is alive and that he's about to murder a girl and her mother... unless I can stop him.

A young man in a black apron rushed over to the table and started to mop up the spilt coffee with a cloth.

Diane, still clutching the book smiled back at the barista. 'I'm sorry, my fault. Butterfingers.'

Charlie tapped his index finger in a steady rhythm on the table, as he focused on his breathing. *Tap, tap, tap.* Pause. *Tap, tap, tap.* Pause.

His phone chirruped once from his coat pocket and snapped him back to the present. If it hadn't, he would have missed Diane's look of disquiet.

Her radiant smile slipped back into place in a heartbeat.

Charlie rummaged in his coat draped on the back of the chair.

As if demons weren't enough to deal with.

'Somebody missing you?' Diane said.

'Hardly.' He snorted and checked the screen. 'I don't recognise the number. I...' He trailed off as he read the text message.

Charlie stood so abruptly, his chair rattled. He grabbed his coat and turned to leave. 'Sorry. I have to go.'

'Charlie, wait. What's wrong?'

Diane snatched up her jacket, juggled with the book, and raced after him. She grabbed his arm, stopping him in place.

'You're not leaving me here? Charlie, you drove. I don't have my car.'

Pressure began to build behind his eyes. He blinked at her. Maybe he should stay, or take her with him?

No, what are you thinking, man? That's ridiculous, unprofessional, and not to mention extremely dangerous. He took a breath, ignored the enquiring looks, and focused his thoughts against the mounting discomfort in his head. *I really don't have time for this.*

'I'm sorry, Diane. It's too dangerous for you to come with me. I can't put you in harm's way. Call a cab. I'll give you the money for it another time. I need to leave now.'

She tightened her grip on his arm, staggering slightly when Charlie went to walk away. 'I'm coming with you. You can catch me up on the way.'

His skull throbbed. He grimaced and shook his head, in a futile effort to relieve some of the tension. His cheeks flushed, sweat beading on his brow.

'Charlie, I'm coming with you,' she repeated.

The lights in the coffee shop flickered. Or was that the migraine messing with his vision?

Maybe she *should* go with him. She knew more about the dagger than he did, and if it turned out that Stephen really was back from the dead, possessed by a demon and murdering people, that information could be an asset.

'Fine.'

She released him and gave him a firm nod. Some of the discomfort behind his eyes slipped away.

He yanked the door open and held it for her. A sharp breeze buffeted him. He winced. At least it helped clear the residual fuzz from his brain.

Diane exited and together they made a dash towards his car. He fumbled with his keys along the way.

'Right.' She panted as she buckled herself in. 'Are you going to tell me what's going on?'

'That text message, it was from Addison. The little girl I told you about.' He closed the driver's door, clicked his seatbelt into place, and put on his glasses.

'The one you think is the next target?'

'Exactly.' Charlie pressed his foot on the clutch and jabbed the keyless start button with his finger. The engine gave a throaty purr of approval. 'She said that someone dressed as a police officer just attacked them in their hotel room.'

'You think it's your old friend... Stephen?'

Charlie winced and drove off. 'I think we need to get to them as quickly as possible.' He didn't want to think about Diane's question. He knew he wouldn't like the answer.

'I can't think of a better way to phrase this, but if it was... the demon, why would it not have finished the job when it had the chance?'

He'd been thinking the same thing. 'That's an excellent question. I guess we're going to find out. It's possible that it's just another of her father's hired goons.'

'Goons?'

He caught her confused expression as he shifted up a gear. 'By all accounts her father is not a nice man, and wants them back in the US. He's already tried kidnapping them once. From what I've been told, he has ties to one of the largest criminal organisations across the pond.'

She nodded in understanding. 'Well, if it was the demon, that explains why it would risk attacking them in such a highly populated area.'

'What do you mean? Why would that matter? Not that I know anything about demons, but I wouldn't have thought that "stage fright" would've been an issue.'

'There are other things out there besides demons, Charlie. The human race can barely keep the peace within its own species. Could you imagine the chaos if people were to suddenly realise that all the monsters from their childhood nightmares were real? Not only that, but living among them, knocking them off the top of the food chain? It stands to reason that there are other parties responsible for preserving a level of ignorance amongst the general populace. Parties qualified to manage such threats with more skill and discretion than your everyday boys in blue. Parties that would give even a demon pause.

'No. If what we've theorised is correct, it has no master, no means of travel. If its quarry were to leave the country, the demon would remain in a state of endless purgatory, slowly losing its mind to the compulsion of the blood debt. It must be desperate.'

Charlie kept his eyes on the road, so that she couldn't see his expression. He wanted to scream.

Instead he asked, 'Couldn't it just stow away on a ship, or get a hooky passport and board a plane?'

'I think you're giving it too much credit. Catching a plane would require funds for a ticket and the patience

341

to collaborate with anyone long enough to acquire counterfeit documentation.' She sniffed, as if angry.

It was the first time Charlie had detected anything other than impartial, albeit enthusiastic, academic interest in her tone. He let it go—there was enough on his plate.

'As for the boat,' she said, 'an open body of water would disrupt the magical construct between the demon and the athame. It's hold over its host would be abolished, driving its essence back into the Maw.'

Charlie made a hard left. 'I don't follow.'

'Water is a restorative force. Pure. Life-giving. It acts as a natural insulator against dark magic and demonic energies. Without a master to transport the host body and re-establish the symbiosis, there's no telling how long the demon would remain imprisoned within the athame.'

'The one night it's not raining,' Charlie mused. 'So why doesn't it just take the dagger if it needs to maintain that link? It's appeared at several crime scenes. There's been no lack of opportunity.'

Diane made a soft huffing sound. 'You yourself said that Kar'roc's Maw disappeared from evidence every time it was catalogued. It always returns to its master.'

'But Mickey Boswell is dead. There is no master.' This was turning his brain to mush. Once this was all over it might be a good idea to finally use some of his annual leave.

'You're assuming it was Mickey who invoked the blood debt.' Diane's forehead crinkled as Charlie swung the

Audi round a roundabout and then over a speed bump with a jolt.

'He had the combined sigil on his hand.'

She paused and tapped the book on her lap. 'Just like the blood debt, the athame is tied to lineage. There's no point practicing the dark arts for the acquisition of wealth and power if you're not going to be at least a little proprietary about your magical artefacts. Keep it in the family, as they say.'

Charlie made a sound of acknowledgement and parked the car in one of the spaces outside McDonalds. The agreed meeting place.

Addy and her mother were sat at one of the tables by the windows, under a wash of intense artificial light—one of the few not currently occupied by teenagers or young couples. Ciara was staring at nothing. Her wet hair hung down her back, creating dank patches on her top. One hand gripped her coffee so tightly, the cup had buckled. The other clutched something protruding from her pocket that he couldn't make out.

He waved a hand at Addy, who grinned back. She pointed and said something to Ciara. Some of the tension seemed to ease out of the pair as they stood and made a hurried exit, leaving their drinks on the table.

'Clever.' Diane watched them with interest. 'Brightly lit. Crowded. Close to the river. It's unlikely that the demon would be brazen enough to mount an attack here, desperate or not.'

Charlie gave the book in Diane's hands a cautious glimpse and removed his phone from his pocket.

It might be time to call in the cavalry. His fingers worked the screen.

He unlocked the doors. The pair climbed in the back. He locked them again and put his mobile away.

'Charlie,' Addison squealed, as she buckled her seat belt. 'You came. I told Mom you would.'

'Of course.' He gave her a wink.

Ciara regarded him silently, chewing on the inside of her cheek. She looked as if she wanted to say something. Instead, she glanced across the road at the hotel then down at her pocket, frowned, and put her seatbelt on.

He reversed the Audi out of the space and headed towards the M2.

Diane twisted round to look at the pair. 'Is that the dagger in your pocket?'

Christ.

Chapter 44

CIARA GLARED AT THE back of Diane's headrest. Jesus this woman was relentless. If she had wanted to be interrogated, she'd have just called the police.

No, that wasn't true. She'd had to scream bloody murder to stop Charlie from taking them to the police station. Eventually, he'd agreed to take them to his place until they could come up with a plan. Not that she'd been particularly happy about that either, but what other choice was there?

How long was this journey going to take?

If I hadn't put that stupid phone on charge, I wouldn't have left it in the fucking hotel room. I'd have been able to call Fiona, instead of having to put up with this shite.

'It's remarkable,' Diane said. *Again.*

She'd been fondling that dagger from the moment she got her perfectly manicured hands on it. You'd have thought the thing was made of solid gold the way she was going on. She was welcome to it.

'And you say it was in the desk of the hotel room?'

Ciara sucked in a breath and counted to ten, then released it. 'Like I said, he smashed through the desk. The dagger came flying out. It landed on the floor.'

'Remarkable.'

Jesus.

How many times was she going to have to relive those memories? Just the thought of it turned her stomach. Worst of all had been when they'd watched the man lurch out of the hotel, stare at the exact spot where they'd been standing—hiding inside the McDonald's on the other side of the road—and skulk into the night. She'd almost vomited. It was the only place she could think to take her daughter to that was brightly lit and busy. It wasn't until she was sure he'd gone that she'd felt secure enough to find a table.

'Charlie?' A grinning Addison stared at him wide-eyed. 'Are we nearly at your house yet?'

Ciara couldn't help but smile. The resilience of that girl was amazing. Sometimes she wondered who drew strength from whom.

'Nearly.' Charlie glanced at them in the rear-view mirror. His tired, hazel eyes crinkled around the edge when he smiled.

She could tell by the sidelong glance he gave the dagger every so often that it worried him. They were fucked and he knew it. He knew it, and yet he was *still* helping them. It made her feel bad for the way she'd spoken to him at the flat.

Addison's voice dropped to a whisper. 'Are you sure he won't be able to hurt us?' She wrung at her seatbelt, her fists squeezed so tight, the skin around her knuckles had turned white.

'I will do my very best to keep you safe. I texted Nick, he and some of the other police officers are going to meet us—'

Ciara's next words cut across the car. 'You did what? That psycho who attacked us *was* a police officer. We can't trust any of them. This was a mistake. I knew we shouldn't have contacted you.'

Charlie flinched. It wasn't until Ciara felt the bite of the seatbelt that she realised she was straining forward.

Addy gaped at her, with the same terrified expression she'd had on those evenings when Dean had let his temper get the better of him.

Shite.

'I'm sorry, Addy, I didn't mean to scare you. I'm sorry, I shouldn't have shouted.'

Addy nodded and stared at her shoes.

'I trust Nick with my life. He's a good man.' Charlie's tone was hard, unyielding. Not soft like the way he spoke to Addy.

In that moment, she saw him for what he was: not an old man who should have retired years ago, but someone with authority. Someone who had the experience to control a situation. Someone who could be the difference between life and death for her and her daughter.

'Sorry,' Ciara said after a few seconds. She smoothed Addy's hair in a soothing gesture. 'I just don't know who I can trust. He recommended you by name, you know.'

Charlie flicked his eyes to the rear-view mirror. 'Excuse me?'

'The man who attacked us. He changed. Like someone flicked a switch. He seemed almost normal, scared even. He told us to call you, that you would work out a way to help us, and then told us to take that thing with us.' She inclined her head towards Diane, who was still scrutinising the dagger, her focus on Charlie's eyes in the mirror.

Charlie's eyes widened and narrowed as he digested her words. He shook his head once, then sat up straighter in his seat.

'Stephen,' he said. It was so quiet she nearly missed it.

Diane lowered the dagger and squeezed his arm.

Whatever was going on between the two of them she couldn't work it out. There was chemistry there, but it was stiff, awkward.

Then it came to her. 'Wait,' she said, 'were you two on a first date or something?'

Charlie spluttered. 'Uh, well. I, erm—'

'Yes we were.' Diane brought an end to his floundering.

Ciara's interrogation was cut short when he pulled into a generous grey, block-paved driveway laid out before a 1930's detached, white-rendered house.

White. Not dingy grey or mould and algae-mottled, with flaking paint or cracks. White. Sharp. Clean. White, curved bay windows were separated on either storey by charcoal-coloured tiles—a stark contrast to the rest of the house, painted to match the grey front door.

It was pretty, but lacked character. Still, it was nice. Nothing like the modest bungalow or flat complex she'd pictured him living in. Maybe with a cat or one of those tiny, yapping dogs.

Addy murmured in approval as the car came to a stop, her face inches from the window. Her eyes widened as she examined his immaculate, front garden. Bushes and evergreen shrubs had been meticulously shaped and pruned within mostly bare flower beds that, no doubt, were a picture of colour in the warmer months. Addy loved playing outside.

'Right, let's get everyone inside,' Charlie said. He unbuckled his seatbelt and got out.

They all followed suit.

Ciara followed a step behind with Addy. Charlie unlocked the front door. He held it open and gestured for them to enter. Diane was a pace behind them. Ciara ushered Addy inside and entered after her. Diane was last. Charlie flipped on the lights and locked the door.

Diane surveyed the inside of the house with obvious interest, as she attempted to negotiate the huge book tucked under her arm and the dagger still grasped in her hand. *Ridiculous*. It's not as if the thing would disappear if she put it down. Daggers didn't just up and disappear.

'Wow, Charlie, your house is really clean. Do you have a maid?' Addy didn't wait for him to answer as she skipped through the hallway, past the glass panels that bordered the staircase. She stopped in front of an immense fish tank, full of swaying anemones and darting flashes of colour.

This is a man with too much spare time on his hands.

The inside of the house mirrored the compulsive neatness she'd seen outside. The thought of Addy being scolded for leaving fingerprints on the glass surfaces made her heart beat a little faster.

'Thank you.' Charlie cleared his throat. 'No, I like to keep things clean myself. That way, I can remember where everything is. Right, how about we all go and get something to drink? Maybe some food, if you're hungry.'

'I could eat.' Addy tore her eyes away from the fish and treated him to a grin.

He let out a soft chuckle. 'I'll see what I can rustle up.'

Ciara rolled her eyes and gave her daughter a nudge, as they followed Charlie into the kitchen. She peered into the fish tank as she passed. *Definitely too much spare time.*

Hopefully he had alcohol. She could do with something stronger, to steady her nerves.

The kitchen was masculine and modern. Exposed brickwork spread out above the gas hob, in a nice contrast to the matte-black wall-mounted cabinets. Marble worktops matched the tiled flooring. There was even a breakfast bar island with oversized, smoky, domed lights hanging down over it.

But what really caught her attention was the collection of Lagavulin bottles, neatly arranged in a row next to three garishly coloured storage canisters—a little more feminine than she would have expected, but each to their own.

She pointed for Addy to take a seat on one of the barstools, walked across the room to the selection of bottles, found a glass and poured herself a generous measure of whisky. A smirk tugged at the corner of her lips. *Of course he has whisky; can't be a detective and not drink whisky.* She downed the drink, letting out a hiss when it hit the back of her throat, and poured another finger.

If Charlie minded her helping herself to his booze, he didn't say it. In fact, he looked like he could do with a drink himself. She arched an eyebrow and waved the bottle at him in question. He considered it for a second, then shook his head, instead going over to the fridge.

Suit yourself.

Diane had taken the seat next to Addy. She placed the book on the counter. Her attention was still entirely on the dagger.

Ciara shuddered. That thing creeped her out. She knocked back the second shot. It was like it had been stalking her ever since she set foot on this tiny island.

'What's so special about that thing anyway?' she asked Diane.

For a second, it seemed like Diane hadn't heard the question. But when Charlie placed an assortment of food down on the counter in front of Addy, she met Ciara's eyes.

'You can't recall ever having seen it before?' Diane asked.

'No. Like I said, it was in our flat, and then somehow it followed us to the hotel room.' She screwed the lid back on the bottle and went to put the empty glass in the sink. She thought better of it and placed it just behind her, on the counter. The way this conversation was going, she'd probably need another.

'Interesting.' Diane tapped a finger to her lower lip. Her gaze flicked from the dagger to Ciara. 'It would appear that the dagger's manifestation may be influenced by the proximity of the demon. That might explain why you never encountered it outside of England.'

'I'm sorry, what? Did you say demon?' Yeah. Definitely a good idea to keep that glass handy.

'The demon possessing the body of the man who attacked you.'

Ciara opened her mouth to argue, but there were no words. These people were insane.

Addy watched the three of them, jaw dropped, an apple halfway to her mouth. 'Demon?'

Charlie frowned at Diane, nodding at Addy. Diane gave him a shrug in return.

'Demon,' she continued, speaking directly to Ciara and ignoring Charlie, 'liberated from the confinements of *this* dagger by one of your relatives, albeit inadvertently.' She sighed at Ciara's confused expression, placed the dagger on top of the book, and pointed at the fleshy area between thumb and forefinger. 'You have a marking on your left hand here, correct?'

Ciara's eyebrows knitted together and she exchanged a look with Addy. She closed her fist in a poor attempt to hide the scar. How the *hell* did she know about that?

Charlie had known about it too. *Does everyone bleedin' well know?*

'It appeared when you were a child, yes?' Ciara nodded. 'But Addy has had the exact same one, in the exact same place, from birth?'

Addy glanced up at her, uncertain. She lowered the apple and rubbed at her left hand.

Ciara unclenched her fist and reminded herself to breathe. It'd been a long couple of days. She gave her daughter what she hoped was a reassuring smile, then nodded at Diane again.

The woman opened her mouth, another question already forming on her lips, when Addy gasped.

'Addy, honey, what's wrong?'

'My scar. It's different.' She lifted her hand, peering at it through narrowed eyes.

Ciara crossed the kitchen and took her daughter's hand in hers, turning it gently. She knew her marking intimately.

What the hell? The three dots on Addy's hand, identical to her own, were gone, replaced by a raised, white line, with three short, sweeping curves running through it. It almost looked like she'd been given stitches.

Ciara trailed her finger over the markings. 'Does it hurt?'

'No. I didn't notice until just now, only because Diane was talking about it.'

Ciara blinked. How was she supposed to reassure her daughter when she didn't have a clue what was going on? She lifted Addy's hand to her lips and kissed the scar lightly, before tousling her hair and taking a step back.

Charlie watched them both with an unreadable expression. Diane, on the other hand, was bent forward, staring at Addy's scar with the same fixated look she'd given the dagger all evening.

'Ciara, did your mother have a marking too?' Diane pressed.

Ciara took a breath. Didn't this woman know when to give it a rest? 'No. She didn't—'

'Ah. Probably on your father's side then. It's my theory that one of your relatives used the dagger to invoke a blood debt that targeted your bloodline specifically. I can only assume that it was unintentional. You'd have to have some serious issues to wish for your entire family to be eradicated.'

She shook her head. This was insane. 'Blood debt?'

'Yes.' Diane's eyes flicked to the blade then back up again. 'Someone in your family got their blood on the gem of this dagger and awakened a demon. By doing so, they likely claimed informal proprietorship over the dagger itself—at least for the purpose of fulfilling the blood debt. When that individual—' she pursed her lips and gave Addison a thoughtful look before she chose her next words, '—passed on, ownership of the dagger was transferred to the next closest descendant, and so on. Albeit still in an informal capacity.

'However, the fact that you were unaware of its existence until you arrived here suggests that in order for the dagger to present itself, it needs to be within a certain radius of the demon. Either that or the large body of water separating you from the demon disrupted the energies of the rite.'

Ciara stood in silence. She glanced over at Charlie to see if his reaction married her stunned disbelief. His face was set in a grim expression of acceptance.

Yes, her mother had gone on about how they could never go back home, but she'd just put that down to a bad dose of paranoia. Had there *really* been more to it?

'Ciara—' Diane's tone warmed into something a little more human, '—you must remember something about all this, about why you left England in the first place?'

Heat bloomed in Ciara's cheeks. She took a step forward. Who was this woman, with all her relentless questions? In the space of two evenings, she and her daughter had been attacked. Twice. And now she was supposed to believe in demons? Dredge up memories of her childhood just to enable some nutter's twisted fantasy?

She opened her mouth, ready to release the pent up frustration, anxiety and fear she'd been so desperately trying to contain in front of Addy. The words refused to come, because Diane was right. She did remember something, something she'd dismissed as childhood make-believe.

She leant back against the breakfast bar. Her shoulders slumped. The bluster had all but gone, leaving her with the weight of sheer exhaustion.

'When I was a child I lived on a caravan site, with my family.' She looked up, expecting to find judgement etched across their faces, like she'd seen so many times before. It surprised her when all she found was quiet speculation and rapt interest.

'One evening there was a ruckus. Someone got shot and another stabbed the man who'd been doing the shooting. Everyone lost their minds. Started screaming about how we all had to leave. How we'd been marked by the devil—' she glanced down at her hand, '—and that he'd be coming to collect his due. The entire site packed up and left that night.'

Charlie propped himself up against the wall. His face was pale.

'You've heard this before?' Ciara asked.

'I attended the scene of the murder. The man who got stabbed was another detective, a friend.'

'He was a murderer.' Ciara screwed up her face. Fire rose in her belly once more, only to be doused by an abrupt thought. 'It's him, isn't it?'

Charlie nodded. 'That's the current theory.'

'And we're just waiting here?' She regretted the question as soon as it left her mouth. Addy stiffened where she sat, her eyes wide. Ciara gave her a weak smile.

'Charlie will keep us safe, Mom.'

'I know he will, honey.'

Charlie glanced at Diane, walked over to one of the cabinets, and produced a box of chocolates. He tore off the cellophane, placed the box in front of Addy, and winked. 'Help yourself.'

'Thanks, Charlie.' Addy took one and popped it in her mouth. 'Are these the ones you got for Evelyn? It's a shame she doesn't eat chocolate, but I'm glad she didn't want these. They're really good.'

'Evelyn?' Was she missing something? The segue between this conversation and the last had thrown her completely.

'My granddaughter,' Charlie explained. 'She's Addy's age.'

For some reason Ciara hadn't pictured him with kids. It made sense though, the way he talked to Addy.

A loud knock on the door killed the conversation.

'Nick?' Diane arched an eyebrow at Charlie. She placed a protective hand on the book. 'They got here quickly.'

'Yes. They did.' The lines in Charlie's forehead deepened. 'Ciara, take Addison upstairs. Diane, go with them, please. The bathroom has a lock on the door. If you don't hear from me, don't come down. Call the police and don't unlock the door.'

Ciara felt her heart lurch. She forced a smile. 'How about we go have a look upstairs, Addy?'

'Sure.' Addy chewed on her lower lip as she studied each of them in turn. She slid off the barstool and edged towards Ciara, took her hand and gave it an uncertain squeeze.

Ciara smiled and squeezed back, then ruffled her hair as they made their way out of the kitchen.

Blue lights pulsed through the frosted strip of glass to the side of the front door. The glass was too opaque to make out who was on the other side, but the way Charlie held himself made it clear that he wasn't going to risk opening it until she and Addy had gone. Ciara shared a look with Diane. They walked upstairs in silence, Addy in front, Diane heading up the rear.

The sound of Ciara's heart hammered in her ears. A dull warmth spread from the scar on her hand, just like at the hotel room.

Probably psychological. They'd just been talking about it after all. At least she hoped it was psychological.

Oh Jesus. She'd just placed her life—Addy's life—in the hands of strangers, and now fate was knocking at the door. Literally.

What have I done?

Chapter 45

CHARLIE WATCHED THE THREE of them disappear from view at the top of the stairs. It wasn't until he heard the click of the lock on the bathroom door that he exhaled.

Nick was punctual, but not *that* punctual. There was no way he'd have made it here that soon, even with his foot to the floor. Still, it might be one of the other officers. If not, that would mean the four of them had been followed. He'd been so focused on thoughts of Stephen and the dagger, it hadn't occurred to him he could have picked up a tail.

He turned to regard the door as the knocking came again. No more or less urgent than before. That could be a good sign, right? *Sure.*

'I'll just be a minute.'

He clenched his fists and dashed back into the kitchen.

Tucked back against the exposed brickwork, next to the black cabinets that held his assortment of glassware, were a set of three storage canisters that Meghan had bought him that Father's day to 'brighten the place up a bit'. She'd yet to see them on display.

If all goes well, I'll still be here to see her face when she does.

He removed the lid from the hot-pink one, with humming birds in an assortment of colours, and turned it over. Taped to the inside was the key to his shotgun cabinet. He ripped it free, replaced the lid, and hurried back into the hallway and his aquarium.

His knees cracked in objection when he squatted. He turned the key in the lock of the cabinet's false bottom that he'd had custom-built by Red Sea MAX. He pressed on the front of the panel. There was a soft clunk when it sprang forward and slid open, to reveal his Krieghoff K-80 shotgun. Everything had been perfectly designed, right down to the small, electronic safe, in its own carefully crafted space.

He punched in the code to open the door, and grabbed a handful of cartridges, pressing all bar two of them into his pocket. He removed the K-80 and loaded it.

Charlie pushed the cabinet's false bottom closed and stood. He walked towards the door with the butt of the K-80 nestled against his forearm, but the barrel open.

Would not closing the chamber be a mistake if there was a body-snatching demon at his door, and not Nick? Of course. But he couldn't put his friend in danger.

The knocking came again.

'I'm coming,' he said.

He was only a few feet from the door when it burst inwards. The impact knocked him onto his back. His head struck the tiles. Spots danced across his vision.

What remained of the door landed on top of him. And it weighed a tonne.

Shit.

Charlie sucked in a breath. He shoved the door off and rolled to one side. It hit the tiles with a loud clunk. His lower lip throbbed. He sucked on it, tasting blood.

A man wearing a police officer's uniform stood in the doorway. It took a fraction of a second for Charlie's eyes to focus and for his brain to catch up.

'Steve?'

It didn't matter that he'd prepared himself for this moment. Seeing Stephen again, looking just the way he had before they'd buried him, crushed him. Emotions clawed through him, pressed down on his chest, made it hard to breathe. Each one fought for dominance, pushing him closer towards breaking point.

'Cha-r-lie.' It was Stephen's voice, but different. Higher. Coarser. The way he elongated his name, mocking him, sent a shiver down his spine. But it was enough to snap him out of his stupor.

'You're not Stephen.' He reached for his shotgun only to find it gone, knocked back from the impact. 'Stephen is dead. I was at his funeral. I watched his coffin get buried.'

'Not deep enough, clearly.'

Familiar blue eyes regarded Charlie as he pushed himself up into a sitting position. They'd never looked so cold as they did right now.

'Why are you here?' If he could stall for long enough, maybe Nick could get here in time to save the girls.

Stephen limped over the threshold into Charlie's home. No, not Stephen. Diane was right. A demon wearing his skin like a suit.

It inhaled, its gaze locked on the top of the stairs.

'I think you know. You were always good at putting the pieces together. Or so I'm led to believe.' The demon tapped a finger against one temple, its focus snapping back to Charlie. 'I'd expected more from you, if I'm honest. Age disagrees with you it would seem.'

'It happens to the best of us.' Charlie pressed a hand to the back of his head and checked for blood. It came away clean. That was something at least.

Using the motion as a distraction, he shuffled backwards.

The demon sneered with an expression Charlie had never seen on Stephen's face. It made him look cruel, malicious, even. So different to the man he'd known.

'I honestly can't see what he saw in you. These memories,' the demon said, taking slow, deliberate forward steps, 'have put you on quite the pedestal. The great Charlie Haynes. Defender of the innocent. Methodical. Meticulous. But that's not the whole picture is it? Charlie Haynes. Socially awkward. Compulsive. Naive. Blind. Broken.'

The crushing of wood beneath feet accompanied each step as the demon drew closer. Charlie shuffled farther back. He twisted round and lunged for the shotgun.

The demon was quicker. Impossibly so.

Charlie yelped when it kicked his hand and the gun. The K-80 skittered across the tiles.

Stephen's hand wrapped around his throat and he pulled Charlie to his feet with inhuman strength. *No. Not Stephen.* Charlie wheezed and gripped its wrists, in an attempt to transfer some of his weight to the demon and take the pressure off his neck, before he passed out.

The demon sulked. 'That was rude. I thought we were friends. Friends don't shoot each other, Charlie.'

'You're *not* Stephen.' The words came out as a cough and a gasp, but the venom behind them was unmistakable.

It snorted out a laugh, and pulled Charlie in closer, so that he could feel the demon's breath on his face. The smell reminded him of a butcher's shop: raw, humid, meaty.

'You've already said that. You really *are* old, aren't you?'

Charlie tightened his grip, as his feet struggled to find the floor.

'I'm only sixty-six,' Charlie croaked. 'Compared to you, I'm a whippersnapper.'

That gave the demon pause. It frowned at him then rolled its eyes. Its lips twisted into a sneer.

'I see you've been talking to someone about me. I'm flattered.'

This was good. Keep it distracted.

The demon leant its face in closer, until their noses were just inches apart and Charlie had no choice but to stare into those remote, blue eyes. 'You're alone, Charlie. You always have been. You always will be.'

The demon was getting personal. Trying to hurt him. It didn't like him knowing anything about it. That was good. That was something he could use.

'Alone? Alone is being trapped in a dagger. Trapped in the human realm without a body of your own. Forced to submit to the will of your master, or live the remainder of your pitiful existence in purgatory.'

The demon's face contorted and its grip tightened around Charlie's neck. 'You've done your homework.'

Just as Charlie's vision started to tunnel, the demon relaxed its hold. Charlie took a shuddering breath.

'You seem to know a lot about me. But I know everything about you, Charlie. Everything *he* knew *I* know.' It looked around his hallway, eyeing the pictures on the walls. 'I don't see Debbie in any of those.'

Charlie flinched. Old wounds always cut the deepest.

It observed his reaction and chuckled. 'Your daughter and... granddaughter? Close, are you?'

'Don't you *dare* mention them,' Charlie spat. Fire ignited in his chest.

'Touch a nerve?' The demon trailed a finger down Charlie's split lip and examined the smear of fresh, red blood on it. A slow smile spread across its face. It lifted the finger to its mouth and sucked it clean.

The demon's eyebrows rose. 'Ah. I see. And I thought you were a detective?'

Charlie glanced away, only for a fraction of a second, but the tell was clear.

'You knew?' the demon scoffed. 'You knew that she wasn't yours? That your wife was a harlot? *He* saw her, you know, the day he died. She was defiling your marital bed with another man. Yet you still have her offspring's pictures on your wall? Still keep up the pretence of being her father?'

Charlie gritted his teeth and said nothing.

'Answer me, or I will make you watch as I go upstairs and tear that girl and her mother to shreds. I will flay the flesh from their bones and—'

'Yes. I knew. I knew about the affairs. Of course I did.' *Keep it distracted.* 'I suspected she might not be mine. But being a father is more than just having a child. It's about being there, being part of their lives. Doing all you can—'

'How?' the demon interrupted. 'How did you know she wasn't yours?' Its eyes danced, as if it could sense how much pain dredging up his past would cause. If the demon was able to exploit Stephen's memories of him, then it would know without a doubt that Charlie was emotionally impaired. But Stephen's memories were out of date.

Thirty-four years was a long time. He'd grown a bit since then.

'How?' Its voice rose. The demon shook him.

'After Debbie—' he gasped a few strangled breaths between words '—I had a relationship with someone else. She wanted children. It didn't happen. Doctors said that I was the problem. That I always had been. I'd never

365

have children. Our relationship ended not long after that.'

'Pathetic. Debbie made a fool out of you. You raised someone else's offspring. You should have slain the spawn as soon as you discovered the truth. You are weak. Your kind is weak. You deserve to be wiped out, like the primordial spume you are.'

'We're not the only ones who'll be wiped out. Kar'roc's ritual will kill you too.'

The demon laughed—a discordant cackle without humour or warmth. The sound turned Charlie's bowels to water.

'I have no intention of returning to that dagger or fulfilling Kar'roc's will.' The demon snarled, pulling the torn flesh up into a savage grin. 'I just have to satisfy the blood debt and then I will be free to find a gatekeeper and return home.' It trailed off, speaking more to itself than to him.

Charlie recoiled as much as the demon's grip would allow.

Strands of skin, connected like threads between the gaping holes in Stephen's cheeks, quivered with every breath he took. His tongue rolled in the dank shadows of his mouth as he swallowed. Saliva trickled in slick rivulets down his chin.

The demon said, 'I've wasted enough time.'

With a huff, Charlie hit the floor. The demon headed towards the stairs. Charlie sucked air into his lungs, relieved at being able to breathe again. But his hip spiked with a sharp pain after landing badly.

Charlie crawled across the hallway. Every inch of his body screamed in agony. He reached his weapon. He looked up, tracking the demon as it shambled up the stairs one at a time.

He kept the target in sight as he mounted the K-80. The stock brushed his cheek when he drew the butt in tight against his shoulder pocket.

He sucked in a breath.

The demon launched itself over the handrail before Charlie could take the shot. Steel buckled in its grip. The entity landed on the floor before him.

Charlie squeezed the trigger.

An explosion of sound detonated through the hallway.

The shot, aimed for its head, shredded the demon's chest. The impact sent it hurtling backwards, through the panels lining the stairs, in an eruption of glass. Something small and metallic skittered from Stephen's pocket.

A shaking Charlie barely heard his rattling breath above the ringing in his ears. His injuries throbbed as he eyed a prone Stephen warily.

Fragments of glass fell from the ruined panels, bounced off Stephen's still body and skittered across the tiles. Everything had happened so fast. Charlie struggled to process the situation. It didn't make sense. If the demon could move that quickly, why didn't it just get out of the way of his shot?

And what had just rolled behind the fish tank?

With narrowed eyes, Charlie reached out a foot and nudged Stephen's boot. Other than a slight wobble there was no reaction. The muscles in his stomach unclenched. He exhaled.

Thirty-four years and it was finally over. The girls were safe and, other than a few bruises, he was fine.

Then he heard a sharp inhale. The demon sat up. Its eyes blazed with fury. Beneath the torn and tattered remains of the stab vest, the wound in its chest was knitting back together, fibre by fibre. It was hypnotic and utterly terrifying.

The demon sprang to its feet, let out a howl, and launched itself at Charlie. The K-80 was knocked out of his hands before he could squeeze off the second round.

Charlie's eyes widened. Fresh terror clawed its way up his throat in a desperate gasp.

He was hoisted off the ground in an instant. The demon gouged its fingers into his upper arms, pinning them against his sides.

Charlie sucked a frantic breath through his teeth. His heart leapt into his throat.

Droplets of saliva struck him in the face as the demon rasped through its mutilated mouth. Charlie could feel its muscles quivering while holding him.

Its eyes narrowed.

'Shut up,' it muttered. 'I said shut up!' This time the words came out as a roar. A strange expression flickered across its face, and for a second, the rage ebbed from its eyes.

In that brief moment Charlie recognised the humanity. '*Stephen?*'

Its grip faltered.

Charlie wrenched himself free.

'The demon's going to kill them, Charlie.' Stephen's words were hurried, desperate. 'They're the only thing standing in the way of it getting back to its body. Back home. I can't stop it. It's too strong. The things the demon made me do. Charlie... the things I've done...' His voice hitched and he shuddered. 'I'm a monster. You need to stop it, Charlie. You need to stop *me*.'

Then it was over. His friend was gone.

Charlie shifted his weight and threw a punch. There was a sickening crunch sound when his fist connected and fractured Stephen's jaw.

And then the demon laughed. Again. Each giggle was accompanied by the grinding sound of the jaw resetting.

'Well, well. I didn't think you had it in you,' it said. 'Good for you, going out on a high.'

Charlie didn't have time to flinch before the demon launched him across the room. His head struck something hard. Agony like he'd never known exploded through his skull.

His world went black.

Chapter 46

'GET INTO THE SHOWER,' Diane ordered Ciara and Addison. She locked the bathroom door behind them.

'What?' The woman had clearly lost it.

'Get into the shower. The water should disrupt the energies around your sigil.' She placed the book on the pristine, white sink unit and frowned, as if putting it down pained her. 'It might buy us a little time.'

'Sigil? What are you talking about?' Ciara didn't even attempt to mask her frustration. It'd been a long night and she'd had enough of this bullshit.

Diane turned to regard her, dagger still in hand, a thoughtful look on her face. 'Your scar. It's how the demon has been tracking you. Like a magical homing beacon.'

Ciara stood her ground. 'We're not getting in the shower.'

'We don't have time for this, please. Just trust me.'

'Trust you? I don't know you from Adam. This was a mistake. Come on Addy, we're leaving.'

Addison chewed on her lower lip. She looked from her mother to Diane and back again. 'Mom, I think—'

'I *said* we're leaving.' Ciara took a step forward and grasped Addy's shoulder. No way was she spending a second longer than she had to with this head case.

Diane blocked her path and pointed to the shower. 'No,' she said in a level voice, 'I'm sorry, but you're not.'

Diane flicked the fingers on her outstretched hand. A blast of air whipped across Ciara's cheek. The shower spluttered into life and stole the words from her mouth.

Ciara's jaw snapped shut.

Addy gasped.

What the hell?

'Please, Ciara. Get in the shower. It's the only thing giving us a fighting chance.'

She sighed at Ciara's startled expression, closed her hand, and snapped her arm back. A jet of water shot from the shower across the room. It stopped just inches from Diane's face, twisting and coiling like a living creature. Then, with a flick of her wrist, the spiral of water exploded in a spray of mist that hung in place, before dropping to the floor.

'Sure,' Ciara whispered, eying Diane as her heart lurched in her chest, 'we'll get in the shower.' Why not? It's not as if things could get any stranger.

She nudged her goggling daughter towards the shower. 'Come on, Addy.'

At least it was clean. The large glass panes that enclosed it, set against marbled-grey tiles, were spotless. How *does* he keep this place so tidy?

Giving herself something else to focus on was the only thing holding her mind together. Warm water drenched her, plastering her hair and clothes to her skin. What the hell had they just witnessed?

Diane nodded as the room started to fill with a fine vapour.

'So what? We just wait here?' Ciara shifted under the spray, still eyeing Diane.

'I know it seems ludicrous, but it might give us an edge if—'

A loud blast from downstairs rattled the glass panes around them. Ciara shot Diane a look and pulled Addy in close against her.

She strained to hear anything above the sound of the running shower. She took a breath and blinked the water from her eyes, grateful that it hid the tears she no longer had the strength to fight.

Minutes of fragile silence passed in what felt like an eternity. Maybe she'd just imagined the noise?

The bathroom door exploded inwards, in a burst of chipped paint and wood fragments.

Ciara recoiled and almost slipped. She caught herself with a gasp. The scar on her hand was burning. She ignored the pain and folded her arms around Addy. Whimpers cut through the spattering water sound. It surprised her when she realised that it wasn't Addy making them. It was her.

Keep it together.

The officer from the hotel stood just outside the bathroom, his face a grotesque display of mutilated skin and muscle. His uniform was a mess, covered in glass fragments and dust. She could see his blood-smeared chest through a gaping hole in his stab vest, pitted with what looked like pellets of shot, but there was no matching wound. How could there be no wound?

Shite. It really is a demon.

It was like something out of a nightmare, and she'd had her fair share, but she wasn't prepared for this. Nothing could have prepared her for this.

The thing muttered to itself, some unhinged, one-sided conversation. Then its head snapped up and it stared directly at them. Its bright-blue eyes were cold and calculating. The eyes of a predator. The eyes of a monster.

She saw Diane stiffen as it took a few slow, hobbled steps into the bathroom. *Oh Jesus. Oh Jesus.*

'You,' it snarled at Diane, jabbing a finger at her.

Diane took a brave step forward. The humidity dampened her blonde hair so much that it clung to her cheeks.

'Me,' she said with confidence.

What the hell? They knew each other? What was happening?

'Brilliant. I get to kill the witch who tried to murder me *and* end my imprisonment. Two birds, as they say.' Its blue eyes locked onto the dagger in Diane's hand. It hissed. 'Clever girl.'

'We were trying to help you,' said Diane.

'Liar! You were trying to help *him*. And when you realised that you couldn't, you tried to kill us both. You think I want to be here, trapped in this realm? You think I wanted to be captive for nearly a century with only the memories of my long-dead brethren for companionship? And then to be forced into the body of a crippled, meat bag on the verge of death? But enough about us, I'm here for little Cici.' The demon smirked and gave Ciara a hungry look.

Ciara felt her chest tighten. 'How do you know that name?' Nobody had called her Cici in years.

It tapped a finger against its skull. 'Your father told me. Well, *told* might not be the right word...'

'My father died in a prison riot. I barely knew him.'

'Prison riot?' The demon snorted. 'Is that what they told you? It's because of Niall Boswell that I'm here, you know. If he hadn't pawned that dagger, hadn't got caught stealing it back... Well, none of this would be happening right now. Anyway, you'll have to excuse me, I've got places to go, people to eat.'

Ciara stepped backwards, pulling Addy with her. Her back pressed against the tiles. They should have just run. She'd been a fool to put her trust in these strangers and now they were going to die.

The demon's body tensed. A manic grin spread across its face. It sprang forward.

Diane raised her arms up, palms outwards, dropping the dagger—it clattered to the floor.

Ciara screamed. She twisted round, putting her body between the demon and Addy. She squeezed her eyes shut, swallowed and waited for the fatal blow.

The air crackled. Pressure built until her ears popped. A sharp clapping sound filled the room. It vibrated through her like a shockwave. Glass shattered.

She cringed. Waiting.

'Mom, what's happening?'

Ciara opened her eyes, looked down at Addy and held her tight. 'I don't know... It's okay. We'll be okay.' She hoped the words didn't sound as hollow as they felt.

She looked over her shoulder. The panes enclosing the shower had been obliterated. Glass and twisted metal was spread across the floor. She was glad they'd kept their shoes on.

Diane stood panting, her hands still raised in front of her. She took a few steps forward. Her body was rigid, muscles coiled, ready to pounce. Were there curls of steam rising off her body? No, that couldn't be right.

The demon writhed on the ground. A shard of glass the size of Ciara's hand protruded from its thigh. Its exposed skin was a mess of gashes and nicks. Blood trickled freely where the flesh had either peeled back or was missing completely.

It let out a snarl, yanked the glass from its leg, and tossed it to the floor, like it was nothing more than a minor inconvenience.

'I remember that smell.' It sat up. Its wounds wove themselves back together as it spoke. 'Brimstone. Your magic has the exact same stench as your husband's. Did you know that?'

Smell? Brimstone? Ciara's forehead creased as she digested what it had said. So when it had called Diane a 'witch', it wasn't just being colourful. She was literally a witch. *Jesus*. That would explain what they'd seen earlier... magic. Actual magic.

'Shut your mouth,' Diane hissed. The mist coiling up from her body dissipated, replaced then by a visible layer of shimmering heat. The ends of her hair curled as it dried in the undulating warmth. She lifted her arms up high; her muscles quivered, as if she were holding a great weight.

The demon hissed as Diane appeared to lift its body off the floor, suspending it in mid-air.

Ciara blinked up at the floating demon. Her jaw hung open.

'Ciara,' Diane panted, 'get me the dagger. Hurry.'

She refocused when she heard Diane call her name a second time. She snatched up the dagger and rushed to Diane's side.

Addy let out a gasp when she turned away from the wall.

Ciara held the dagger out to Diane, flinching when the demon turned its gaze on her. It thrashed against invisible bonds, making guttural noises that caused the hairs on her arms to stand on end.

Beads of sweat ran down Diane's temples as she staggered in place to hold the demon. Her chest heaved. She managed to fumble the dagger from Ciara's hand without releasing the demon. Her lips moved silently. The colour drained from her face. She swayed.

Ciara wrapped an arm around Diane's waist, to help steady her.

Diane nodded, her mouth still moving in a soundless chant, while her body shook with the effort. She lowered her chin to her chest.

'You're a coward, just like your husband,' taunted the demon. 'Do you remember how he screamed when I tore out his insides, putting him down like a cur in the street?'

The demon's laughter sent a chill down Ciara's spine. *Jesus, that thing murdered Diane's husband?* She gagged.

Diane's head whipped up. She stopped chanting. Her mouth was set in a snarl, revealing something almost feral underneath the prior calm. She brought her arms together, fingers splayed on one hand—tendons standing out—the dagger clutched in the other. In Ciara's arms, her body was trembling.

The demon grunted. Its discordant laugh was abruptly cut off when invisible bonds began to crush it, contorting its limbs the tighter they got.

Diane's body went limp. Ciara went down with her, breaking her fall as best as she could. Glass punctured her palms.

The demon dropped to the floor just feet away from her.

The pain from the glass was nothing compared to the fist of ice clenching her gut.

She wrestled her arm free from under Diane's unconscious body. Tears stung her eyes as she hooked her hands under Diane's arms and kicked backwards, pulling the woman with her.

The demon pushed itself back to its feet and cackled, eyes wild. Whatever magic had been crushing the thing mid-air apparently hadn't caused any lasting injury. With a snort, it moved towards Ciara and raised its hand.

'No!' Addy screamed, and threw herself in front of the demon, before it could strike.

'Addy!' Ciara scrambled forward. She grasped frantically for her daughter.

But the demon was fast. Impossibly fast. Whatever rationality it might have had was gone. Spit foamed out of the gashes in its face when it let out a growl so low, she felt it shudder through her chest. It drove its fist down towards her little girl, hard enough to crush her skull to pulp.

Ciara screamed. A scream of raw fear and anguish. A scream of gut-wrenching helplessness. A scream of sheer desperation.

The demon ricocheted off an invisible barrier, flying backwards with such force, that it took out half the doorframe and adjoining wall with it. Dust and debris scattered out into the hallway where the demon lay unmoving, save for the rise and fall of its chest.

Addy stood, feet planted firmly, one slightly in front of the other, her arms crossed over her face.

Ciara clambered forward, all but tripping over Diane in her haste, and scooped her daughter up in her arms. She squeezed her tightly as new sobs burst from her.

'Quick. We need to go.' Ciara released her grip and checked Addy over for injuries.

'What about Diane? We can't leave her.'

Ciara hesitated. She considered the unconscious woman. Finally, she nodded at her daughter. 'You go downstairs, I'll get Diane.'

'But—'

'Go. Now. Find Charlie. Take the dagger.'

Addy's lower lip trembled. Her red-rimmed eyes flicked from her mother to the demon. She lifted her chin, took a breath and nodded. She snatched up the weapon and dashed out of the bathroom. Within seconds she had disappeared down the stairs.

Ciara crouched down next to Diane. She had to get them both downstairs before that thing woke up.

She hooked her arms under the unconscious woman's armpits and started to drag.

The sound of glass scraping against tiles made Ciara wince with each pull. The noise of the water running in the shower masked most of it. She glanced at the demon through the hole in the wall with every frantic haul.

Diane was surprisingly heavy. Her biceps were on fire with the effort. *Just a bit farther.*

She kept pulling her back. Her foot crunched on glass and slipped. Her ankle twisted. She lost her grip on Diane and landed heavily. It knocked the air from her lungs.

Blind panic shot through her when something moved in her peripheral vision.

Chapter 47

'IT'S OKAY. IT'S ME.' Charlie clutched his arm to his body. He sucked in a breath through his teeth and met Ciara's eyes. 'Get downstairs. I'll take care of Diane.'

'But your arm, you won't be able—'

'It's fine. Really. Just go. Addy is waiting for you.'

She wiped her eyes and nodded. He watched her leave, her shoes tracking brick dust down his clean stairs carpet.

Charlie shuffled forward. Each step sent spears of pain through his head, through his arm, through his whole damned body. If it wasn't for the adrenaline, he was confident he would have passed out by now.

He'd regained consciousness to find Addy leaning over him, her face screwed up and her huffing out anxious sobs. He'd told her everything was fine. He'd just bumped his head.

His head swam—a concussion for sure—and his arm was definitely broken. Possibly a few of his ribs too. There was also a nasty gash on his leg that would need stitches.

He breathed through the pain and surveyed the chaos before him.

Diane lay motionless next to the mess. Her body was sprawled among glass fragments.

Stephen...

No, stop thinking of it as Stephen.

The *demon* stirred, covered in a thick layer of dust and rubble.

He limped towards it. He clenched his jaw so tightly, it ached. He thought back to the pages he'd stolen from *Ritualistic Sacrifice in Ancient Magical Practices*. Just yesterday, hell just that afternoon, he'd have laughed at anyone who'd even suggested he'd be going toe-to-toe with a living, breathing demon.

He made a slow, wide circle around the demon, dragging his foot behind him, adding stains of blood to the already devastated carpet. Coming full circle, he stuck his hand in his pocket. Scowling down at the possession inside his friend, he took a step forward.

For years, all I wanted to do was see you again, my friend. But not like this.

As if sensing his thoughts, the demon's bright-blue eyes flickered open and locked on his.

'Charlie.' It frowned up at him and propped itself up on its elbows. 'It's Stephen. Please, there isn't much time.'

Charlie kept his face neutral, despite the spasms in his pained heart.

'You have to end this. I should've died that night. With them. Please end it. Please.' Stephen winced; his eyes momentarily lost focus. He shook his head and blinked. Fragments of dust fell from his hair. 'The dagger, you have it? You need—'

The change in expression was instant. The demon sprang to its feet and hoisted Charlie off the floor by his shoulders. Chunks of brick scattered with the movement.

A wave of nausea rode through him and he yelped in pain. The demon grinned; its ruined cheeks split further with a wet, fleshy tear.

'Charlie,' it drawled. Its fingers gouged into his flesh. 'I think it's time you and I said goodbye. It's been fun, really. But I've seen all your toys now and I'm bored.'

He spluttered a reply, 'I still have a few things you haven't seen yet.'

He knew the demon had tracked his every movement since coming upstairs. Seen him rummage in his trouser pocket.

It smirked. 'Oh, Charlie. I'm not that kind of boy.'

Charlie worked his hand free. He clutched the dull coin he'd found behind his fish tank. He'd intended to wave it in the demon's face, make a grand show of it, but with it gripping his shoulders like a vice, he could do no more than jiggle it stiffly by his side.

'What's this?' Its eyebrows lifted. The demon released one of Charlie's shoulders, then thrust its hand into its own pocket, searching. It hissed.

Suspended by his broken arm turned him from a poker-faced, world-weary cynic into a bawling child. Charlie roared. His vision dimmed. He tried to remember how to breathe.

Time to play a hunch.

With only seconds of lucidity remaining, he pressed the coin into the demon's palm. Just like Addy had told him she'd done, in the car ride from the hotel to here. The demon howled and released its grip on him. Charlie stumbled, twisting his ankle on the fragments of brick. He kicked them away with a curse and steadied himself. He stuck his hand into his pocket, where the coin had been.

The howl changed into a rasp of laughter.

'A little information is a dangerous thing, Charlie.' The demon placed the coin into its pocket and wiped a tear from its eye. 'Disappointing. Entertaining, but disappointing. You thought that would work? The child paid off her debt; the coin was all she had to her name. You have property, savings, investments. And *even* if you had relinquished it all to me, it would make no difference. You don't have a sigil. You're not part of their bloodline. You *really* thought that would work?'

'No. I thought it would make a good distraction.'

The demon's forehead crinkled in surprise as it followed the trail of blood and brick dust that Charlie had dragged through the carpet, to make a crude circle around them.

'A circle?' It shook its head and tsked in mock disappointment. 'Oh, Charlie, didn't you know? You're supposed to be on the other side. Otherwise you'll be trapped inside. With me.'

It lunged at him, in a blur of motion that made Charlie's eyes water.

Charlie twisted and drove his knee into the demon's right thigh. Its eyes widened, and the demon shifted its weight to Stephen's lame leg. Then it pitched forward. Right into the dagger Charlie had in his hand.

A wall of energy snapped up around them, with a sound of a sighing blade. It encased them in a circle that distorted the world outside it.

'With Solomon's Seal I bind thee. With Solomon's Seal thou art bound. With Solomon's Seal I compel thee. Reveal thy name and speak not falsehood.' Charlie's words reverberated around the circle like a clap of thunder. His embarrassment was mitigated by the impotent rage he saw in the demon's eyes, as it stood immobile. Blood seeped down the dagger and guard, and over the hilt in Charlie's grip.

'Reveal thy name and speak not falsehood.' Charlie shuddered out a breath. Sweat dripped from his forehead and into his eyes. He blinked it away. How much strength was from sheer will and how much was from fear he couldn't say. He felt the demon's breath on his face. If this went sideways he was fucked. Pure and simple.

'Reveal thy name and speak not falsehood,' he repeated. A sense of dread closed over him. Why wasn't it telling him its name? Had he done something wrong with the incantation? He'd followed the instructions on the stolen pages to the letter. The circle. Check. The blood—he'd had plenty of that readily available. Check. The words. Check.

Muffled shouts reached him through the translucent wall. They punctuated a series of dampened thuds, as though someone was banging on the barrier. Charlie chanced a glance. He could make out Diane's blurred form.

The demon snarled. Its lips curled back to show its teeth, compressing the maimed flesh around its mouth into puckered, red lines. 'I am Chekonost.'

'Chekonost, I claim dominion over thee. Thou art my servant until the end of days. I command thee return unto thy vessel until my will be done.'

The roar was deafening—a shockwave felt as much as heard. Charlie did all he could to keep his hand on the dagger and not cover his ears.

The screaming stopped.

Charlie opened his eyes. He couldn't remember closing them.

The wall of energy around them shattered. Stephen slumped forward against him. Exhausted and broken, Charlie fell backwards.

They hit the ground together.

Diane was there in an instant. A strange look flickered across her face as she pulled Stephen's body off Charlie and helped him to sit up.

Stephen was truly dead. He'd seen enough bodies to know when the light had gone out. For the second time in his life he'd seen his friend's corpse with that damned dagger sticking out of it.

'Holy shit,' Nick squeaked. Charlie turned in his direction. A handful of officers stood just behind him, their expressions ranging from open disbelief to quiet contemplation.

'What time do you call this?' Charlie said, with a weak smile. His voice cracked as he spoke. He looked away when tears streamed down his cheeks.

'I... uh... Jesus. What just happened?' said Nick.

'Caravan Cannibal.' He didn't have the energy to elaborate.

'But he looks like he's in his late thirties.'

Charlie gave Nick an imploring look.

The detective considered him, and dropped his questions for the time being. Nick stared at the corpse for a few seconds more, then he looked at Charlie, as if seeing his injuries properly for the first time.

'Charlie, Jesus.' Nick turned to one of the uniformed officers behind him. 'Call an ambulance. Now.' He squatted down next to him and began assessing the extent of his injuries. 'And someone turn that shower off, would you?'

'I'm fine.' Charlie made a feeble attempt to wave Nick off. The action sent lances of pain through his upper body.

'Like hell you are.' Nick's darting eyes took in the blood that had saturated Charlie's clothes. He winced.

'Are the girls okay?' Charlie asked. 'Addy and her mother?'

'Yes. They're fine. A bit shaken up, understandably, but other than that they're okay. Bennett's downstairs with them. He still hasn't forgiven you for the little stunt you pulled with the clementine, by the way.' A wry smile touched Nick's lips, easing some of the tension in his face. 'Can you stand?'

Charlie grunted. 'I may need a hand.'

'Want me to get you a walking stick?'

'Watch it, Nick, or I'll tell Henry what you really think of his cooking.'

'Henry knows what I think of his cooking. Why do you think we're on a first-name basis with the owner of our local Chinese?'

With Nick and Diane's help, Charlie managed to get back on his feet. His entire body was on fire, as they shambled towards the stairs, a raging agony that made him suck breath through his teeth with every other step.

'Seriously, Charlie,' Nick lowered his voice. 'What happened back there? It looked like you were standing behind a wall of water or something... then it just disappeared.'

Charlie paused where he stood and took a laboured breath. Nick stared at him in confusion, Diane in quiet scrutiny.

'Can we go over it later?' Charlie said.

Nick frowned, but nodded.

Charlie didn't want to talk, to answer any questions. He just wanted to pass out. Everything hurt. Especially his brain. It had been well and truly scrambled. And now his hand itched. Of all the damned things affecting him right now that was the most distracting.

He manoeuvred his left arm awkwardly around Nick's shoulders and squinted at his left hand. Diane's grip loosened and she let out a gasp.

Oh. Well that's just brilliant.

Chapter 48

HUSHED VOICES STIRRED CHARLIE from his sleep. He listened to them for a while, his eyes shut and his breathing steady. He knew exactly where he was from the smell of disinfectant and the beeping of medical equipment.

'He's going to be fine you know. He's a tough old son of a bitch.' Jasmin's tone was light. If he hadn't known her so well, he might have missed the hitch of concern in her words.

'He shouldn't even have been involved. He should be retired.' *Meghan.*

The shock of hearing his daughter's voice nearly made Charlie sit bolt upright in his bed. He kept up the illusion of sleep. Not that he was spying on them. He wanted to let them finish their conversation. In any case, he was in no condition to be exerting himself after his surgery. The doctors had told him as much before they'd put him under.

'You've met your dad, right?' Jasmin continued. 'Retirement would drive him insane. Anyway, he's still one of the best.'

Meghan huffed. 'According to him, they only call him in because they feel sorry for him. To make him think he's still relevant.'

'Is that what he said?' Jasmin's voice held a touch of amusement. 'Megs, you *do* know that's bullshit, don't you? They bring him in because when they do, cases get solved. The man's a legend. The way his mind works... he sees things that would get missed otherwise. I seriously don't know how he figures it out.'

'Really?' Meghan stifled a sob. 'When did we get so out of touch? He's my dad, Jas. Why don't I know these things about him? And now look, he's hurt. What if he'd been killed? What if I never got to see him again?'

Ouch. That yanked on the old heartstrings. Charlie felt a twist in his gut. Maybe it was time for him to "wake up".

'Hey, hey, it's okay. He's going to be fine.' There was a rustle as Jasmin shifted positions. Meghan's sobs became muffled. 'I mean sure, he's going to be sore as hell and even grumpier than usual, but he'll be fine.'

'Thank you, Jas. I mean it. Thank you for being there for me. For all of us.'

'You should tell him, you know.'

Silence followed.

Jasmin persisted. 'Megs, you should tell him. I mean, he probably already knows.'

Charlie squirmed a little. This was feeling more awkward by the second. Definitely time to wake up.

Charlie inhaled loudly and blinked open his eyes.

There, perfectly convincing.

'Dad.' Meghan stood up from the chair at his bedside. She leant down, as if to hug him, then grimaced and straightened again. Her gaze was on his bruises and bandages, as if it were the first time she was seeing them. She nervously tucked a loose strand of her chestnut-brown hair behind her ear and smothered a sob with her other hand.

Jasmin remained where she was stood. There was a playful arch to her eyebrow and a pull at the corner of her mouth that told him what she thought of his poor acting skills.

Meghan looked thinner than the last time he'd seen her, her cheekbones stark against her porcelain skin. Next to Jasmin she looked delicate and small. He wanted to scoop her up in his arms and hold her tight, just like he used to when she was a girl.

'Hi, Meggy. I thought you'd gone on holiday?'

Meghan sucked on her lower lip, the way she used to when she'd been caught in a lie. Charlie smiled.

'I'm sorry about that, Dad. I should've told you we'd gone away. It just completely slipped my mind.'

'Don't worry about that sweetheart, it doesn't matter.'

Jasmin cleared her throat. 'I have to make a move. Charlie, I'm glad you're okay. I do think all this is a little excessive though. You could've just told me you didn't want to spar with me again.'

Charlie barked a laugh, and regretted it instantly when his broken bones complained about the sudden movement. They started towards him. He took a deep breath and waved off their help.

'I'm fine. I'm fine,' he assured them. He sighed when they exchanged unsure glances. 'Really. Jasmin, thanks for letting Meghan know I was here.'

'Oh. Uh, that wasn't me. In fact I didn't even know you were here until Megs called me. I'll come back and visit you tomorrow.' She smiled, then turned to leave. Her gaze, filled with concern, lingered on Meghan for a few seconds. Then, she pushed past the privacy curtain, leaving the two of them alone.

'If Jasmin didn't call you, how did you know I was here? Nick?'

'Nick Stacey? No, I mean, he did call me, but I got a text before that. From *your* phone actually.' She sat back down on the visitor's chair, scooped up her handbag from the floor and rummaged around in it until she found her mobile.

'My phone?'

'Someone called Addison texted me from your phone. She said that you'd been hurt saving her and her "mom" and were being taken to the hospital.' Her thumbs worked the screen. She handed him the mobile.

Charlie used his left hand to take it—his right was going to be useless until the cast came off—and squinted. He moved it closer and farther away from his face. 'I, uh, I can't see this without my reading glasses.' He handed it back.

'Oh. Sorry, I didn't think.' She blushed and took the phone back. 'She said that I should come see you, because family is important, and that I was really lucky to have you as a dad...' She trailed off and blinked rapidly at the ceiling.

'Addy's a sweet kid. I'm glad she messaged you. I miss you and Evie.' The silence hung between them. He rubbed his ring finger. What did it say about him that he could square off against a demon, get beaten to within an inch of his life, but couldn't tell his daughter that he needed her? That he loved her and his granddaughter more than anything else in the world?

The scarring on his left hand itched. He ignored it; he didn't want to think right now about what it meant for him.

One thing at a time.

'We miss you too, Dad. We do.' Meghan broke eye contact and slipped the mobile back into her bag, then tucked the bag under the chair. 'Did you catch him?' she asked, changing the subject. 'The Caravan Cannibal?'

Charlie paused. It was still difficult to process everything that had happened. For thirty-four years he'd followed that dagger, always one step behind it. Impotent while he'd watched the tally of bodies mount up over the course of his career, with nothing to show for it other than borderline alcoholism and a fractured home life. Then to come face-to-face with the very man he'd spent his life trying to find justice for?

Except it hadn't really been Stephen. It had been a monster wearing his skin, using his likeness to commit the most heinous murders. Then Charlie had been forced to watch what remained of his friend die all over again.

ELIZABETH J. BROWN

'Yes,' he answered, when Meghan looked alarmed by his silence. 'We got him. He won't be able to hurt anyone ever again.'

She took his good hand in hers and squeezed it gently. Her eyes glistened with tears. 'That's great, Dad. I know how important this case was to you. Look, I have to collect Evie. She's at a friend's house. We'll both come back later today if that's okay?'

Charlie beamed. 'Of course that's okay. I look forward to it.'

Meghan let go and got her bag. She stood and kissed him on the forehead. 'I love you, Dad. I'll see you later.'

Charlie felt his heart swell. Just as she reached to pull back the curtain, Charlie said, 'You make a lovely couple by the way.'

She turned, her green eyes wide. 'How... how did you know?'

He chuckled softly. 'I used to be a detective, you know. Quite a good one.'

'So I hear.' She fidgeted with the strap of her bag, then met his gaze. 'Don't tell Mum. Please. I can't deal with her turning it into some massive drama. She'll just make it about her somehow.'

'I promise.' He drew a cross over his heart. 'Jasmin is a wonderful young woman. I can see that she makes you happy.'

Meghan exhaled and relaxed her shoulders; the tension eased from her face. It was good to see her happy.

'Meggy?'

'Yes?'

'I love you too.'

'Thanks, Dad,' she whispered with a smile. She wiggled her fingers in a wave and drew the curtain closed behind her as she left.

Charlie watched the space where she'd been for a while before his eyes drifted shut. It didn't matter what anyone said. She was his little girl and she always would be. Family was more than just blood. Now, thanks to Addy, he'd been given a second chance to prove it.

Chapter 49

BEING DISCHARGED FROM HOSPITAL was a drawn out process of waiting around for hours for a consultant to sign off on his medication, while Meghan fussed over him like he was a child. It didn't help that Jasmin and Evie had found his squirming hilarious and had shared more than a few jokes at his expense.

'Yeah, well, Jasmin still eats meat,' was the best he could come up with.

Evie had just giggled, rolled her pale-green eyes, and called him a 'grass', at which point he'd grumped about her veganism and said she'd 'know all about grass'. They'd laughed even harder.

By the time he'd finally got home he was exhausted. So when the doorbell rang, he considered ignoring it completely or telling the caller where to go.

'I'm coming,' he growled after the third ring. He shuffled towards the door. His upper body ached with the movement.

He pulled the door open to see Diane stood on the other side. The scowl slipped from his face. Aside from a few superficial grazes on her cheek, she looked no worse for wear after the skirmish with the demon.

In fact, she looked amazing.

Loose, golden-blonde curls settled on the neckline of her camel-coloured coat. He followed the lines of that coat down to the thick belt that cinched at her waist—in a way he definitely approved of—past the knee-length hem to a pair of black, ankle boots with dangerous looking heels, and back again.

'Diane... uh, Dee...'

She smiled at him and flushed; her amber eyes crinkled at the edges, beneath her black-rimmed glasses. 'Charlie, aren't you going to invite me in?'

'Uh, of course.' He took a step back and she sashayed past him, then closed the door behind her.

'Can I take your coat?' he asked.

'No, no, don't worry about me. It's fine, honestly.'

So, a fleeting visit then. His disappointment took him by surprise. 'To what do I owe the pleasure?'

'I just wanted to check in on you. Find out how you were doing.' She didn't comment on the missing glass panels or buckled steel handrails of his staircase. Although her gaze flickered over them.

Nick, bless him, had gone out of his way to clear up as much of the damage as he could. Everything else would take time.

'Oh. I'm fine.' He gestured towards the living room.

She pursed her lips.

'Okay, a few broken bones and sleepless nights,' he admitted.

She nodded, then walked into the living room.

'Are you really staying here, with the mess?' She took a seat on his navy corner sofa and crossed her legs.

'Oh, no. I'm just getting a few things sorted before my daughter, Meghan, comes and gets me. I'll be staying with her until things are straightened out here.'

'That's good.' She met his eyes and patted the cushion next to her. 'I won't bite.' She smirked, clearly enjoying the effect she was having on him.

He shook his head in defeat and sat next to her at an angle, trying not to jostle his broken arm in the process.

'Charlie?' He liked the way she said his name. 'How are you *really*?'

'It's not as bad as it looks.' He sighed in response to her frown. 'The doctor said that the fractures are already healing. In fact, she seemed quite shocked by how fast. Thought maybe the breaks weren't quite as severe as they'd appeared in the X-rays.'

'I see.' A flicker of apprehension touched Diane's face. She squeezed his knee and beamed. 'It's brilliant that you're on the mend. I was worried about you.'

His heart skipped a beat. She was worried. About *him*. The corners of his mouth turned up. Her hand felt warm on his leg. The gentle pressure from her fingers radiated out through his skin. The only thing ruining the moment was the growing discomfort in his left hand; it vied for his attention. The pulsing irritation there was becoming harder to ignore.

His cheeks flushed with a sudden warmth. It was getting difficult to think. 'I... I don't suppose you'd like to take me up on that offer of coffee? We were interrupted the last time.'

Her eyes widened. She released his knee and smoothed the nonexistent wrinkles from her coat, not meeting his gaze.

I'm an idiot. Say something, Charlie. Say anything, damnit.

Silence.

'Well, considering what you did to my book at the library, I should probably decline,' Diane said.

Ah. So she'd noticed that.

'But—' her tone softened, '—I'd like that. Yes.'

The relief he felt was palpable. His shoulders relaxed and, to his embarrassment, he actually exhaled.

'I don't know why I felt so nervous about that,' he admitted. 'You'd think banishing a demonic entity inhabiting the body of my closest friend into an ancient, ritualistic dagger would've given me a bit more backbone.'

He'd meant it as a joke, but there was that look again. A definite unease. He drew back from her. She was hiding something.

'Dee? What is it? We did defeat it, didn't we? The demon is back in that dagger where it belongs, like the book said?'

Her smile fell back into place and she leant in. 'Charlie, asking me out shouldn't scare you. You're the bravest person I know. The way you saved that little girl and her mother from that lunatic.'

Wait, what?

'Lunatic? You mean demon. Dee, what's going on?'

She touched his hand and let out a soft laugh that made him feel thirty years younger. Her skin was warm against his. He became abruptly aware of how close she was. The rich, sultry scent of her perfume was all around him. It made his head swim.

She met his eyes, her hand still resting on his. 'You know how absurd that all sounds, don't you? Doesn't it seem more rational that the killer was just someone suffering from a mental disorder, culminating in dangerous and violent behaviour both towards himself and others?'

Charlie frowned. That *did* make a lot more sense. He'd worked on similar cases in the past. But something else tugged at the back of his mind. 'I, uh...'

The pressure of her touch increased. The intimacy of it pulsed through him, spread up his arm and through his body like electricity, giving him reassurance and certainty.

'Someone in the throes of psychosis? An episode of delusion?' She leant in even closer. Her breathing deepened. 'We both know that demons don't exist. What we all experienced was a stress-induced fear response to a grave situation, nothing more. Isn't that what you think?'

God, but she was intoxicating. He watched her lips as she spoke. Lost himself in them completely. Everything she said sounded right. Demons didn't exist.

He slipped his hand out from under hers and brushed it down her cheek. She closed her eyes and shuddered beneath his caress. When she opened her eyes again, the ambers were little more than thin halos around pools of black.

Charlie hesitated, just for a second, then pressed his mouth to hers. She melted into him, moaning softly.

A sharp pain stabbed through the skin between his thumb and forefinger. He drew back sharply, all but yelping. 'What the—'

'Charlie?'

As the fog of lust evaporated, he studied the scarring on his hand. The pain that had been radiating out from the three dots and curved line was now a dull throb. His mind clarified the farther away from her touch he got. He sat back from her and arched an eyebrow.

'I think I know exactly what I saw.' The steel in his tone made her flinch. 'I think demons *do* exist. I think that because of whatever reason you're trying to cover this up. And I *think* you had better explain to me what just happened, what you just did to me, or get the hell out of my house.'

Diane straightened. Her gaze locked onto his hand. Seconds passed in silence as she chewed on her lower lip.

He waited.

Finally, she met his eyes and said, 'Perhaps, it's time I introduced you to my employer.'

Epilogue

CHEKONOST'S SCREAMS RANG THROUGH the darkness of the void. The echoes of his frustration died away, until only the chattering whispers remained.

He'd been so close to gaining freedom. Now it was too late. Even with the elixirs and ointments preserving his original body within the sacred caverns, the rot would soon take hold, long before he could take residence in another meat bag. His one chance had been stolen from him, plucked from his grasp by that ageing detective.

Everything was lost. He was trapped once again. Trapped until his essence faded and became another undertone in the dagger's discordant melody, or until it was torn asunder by Kar'roc's impending breech into the mortal plane.

He hated humans. Hated their bovine stupidity. Their unwarranted arrogance. Still, it wouldn't be long. Humanity's reign was coming to an end. They had no idea. Absolutely none.

There was a change in the air. How could they not sense it? Feel it? Hear it? Oblivion was singing its brimstone chorus, heralding their fate and they were deaf to the ballad of their own demise.

Yes, mankind was on borrowed time.

Thank You

Readers are the most powerful and effective tool when it comes to independent authors such as myself. So firstly, I would like to thank you for taking the time to read my book. Secondly, if you enjoyed it, I would be very grateful if you could leave a review (just a few words would do) on whichever platform you prefer.

Don't forget!
If you haven't already, you can get your **FREE** Brimstone Chorus starter story at elizabethjbrown.com

Acknowledgements

My heartfelt thanks:

To my husband and son, for your continued belief and support—without which none of this would have been possible.

To the friends and family (even the ones who still refer to me as 'unemployed') whose eyes are sore from reading all the early and unedited drafts.

To my amazing cover artist Ben Baldwin and my eagle-eyed editor Kate Gallagher, whose talents have made this book the best possible version of itself.

Thank you all for encouraging me.

Author Note

Please note that I am a British author and use UK English spelling and grammar throughout my books.

About the Author

Elizabeth was born in Kent, England. This probably explains her obsession with tea and cake. She currently writes the Brimstone Chorus series, dark fantasy featuring demons, witches and a whole host of things that go bump in the night.

For more information about Elizabeth J. Brown and her books, please visit elizabethjbrown.com

Readers' group:
www.facebook.com/groups/1361685394266696
Facebook: @ElizabethJBrownAuthor
Twitter: @EJBrownAuthor
Instagram: @elizabethjbrownauthor

Books by Elizabeth J. Brown

THE BRIMSTONE CHORUS SERIES

The Foundling - FREE download
(elizabethjbrown.com)
The Laughing Policeman
The Fractured Few

Printed in Great Britain
by Amazon